The ROSWELL

PROTOCOLS

a novel

by

Allan Burd

The Roswell Protocols © 2009 by Allan Burd

This book is a work of fiction. All of the characters, organizations, and events portrayed in this story are either products of the author's imagination or are used fictitiously. Any resemblance to actual persons, living or dead, events, or locales is entirely coincidental.

For more information on author:

www.allanburd.com

ISBN: 0-9705588-4-8

ISBN-13: 9780970558848

eBook ISBN: 978-1-61550-151-9

Box Nine Books

www.boxninebooks.com

For Bert, Roberta, Michele, Dylan, and Tyler
My beginning, middle, and end…

"I've loved the stars too fondly to be fearful of the night."

Galileo Galilei

"Government is not reason; it is not eloquent; it is force."

George Washington

PROLOGUE

November 9th, 2009
Colorado

Airman Charlie Faber gently applied pressure to the brake of his Ford Explorer, slowing his approach to the heavily guarded gates of the U.S. Space Command's Space Surveillance Center. He glanced at the clock on the center of the dashboard—1:30 a.m.—the same time he had always arrived. He sighed. Another dull evening doing the usual: park the car by 1:35 a.m., get to the coffee pot for a quick pick-me-up—cream with a teaspoon of sugar—by 1:45 a.m., then be stationed at his post in Box Nine from 2:00 a.m. to 10:00 a.m. for eight boring hours of observation. It was unsettling how easily he had become accustomed to this position he had been assigned to six months ago.

He rolled down the car window and showed the MP his badge. "Good morning, Marty."

"Morning, Chuck. Like clockwork," the MP replied, pressing the button that lifted the gate.

"Yeah, every night—same bat time, same bat channel. Maybe I'll get lucky and within the next six months they'll transfer me to a real post—or at least first or second shift."

"You and me both," the MP responded.

Charlie nodded good-bye and drove his car into the nearby parking lot. Two minutes later he and twenty others on night shift detail boarded the military shuttle bus that would take them inside Cheyenne Mountain, or as the locals referred to it, Crystal Palace, because at certain times of the year, particularly in the winter, the snowcapped mountain reflected the sun, making it appear like a giant crystal.

The bus rumbled along the two-way road, slowing momentarily at the large, gray, thick metal blast-doors that guarded the entrance. Charlie anxiously watched the doors sluggishly open then close menacingly behind the bus as it made its way inside. He always felt as if he were being sealed into a tomb he couldn't escape from for the next eight hours—and he was.

The bus left Charlie at a bank of elevators. He took one to the third floor, wondering to himself about the contradictory nature of the Space Surveillance Center. The facility, though brightly lit, always appeared dull. Climate control kept the temperature high, but somehow it always felt cold. Even the mood, which hung thick in the air, smacked of apathy though the entire facility was founded on an ever-present sense of paranoia.

All in all, Charlie thought, it was not the most pleasant place to work. At least he hadn't acquired that pasty, sallow complexion that most of the first shifters had. He couldn't imagine being locked inside from 10:00 to 6:00 every day, hardly seeing sunlight. Perhaps third shift wasn't that bad after all.

After a cup of coffee, he quickly made his way to his station in Box Nine, where the government closely monitored orbital traffic. The room was a lot smaller than one would expect. Six orbital analysts, known as knob turners, and a commander were stationed there. Except for Commander Stromfeld, Charlie, at thirty-one, was the oldest of the seven officers on duty.

Charlie took control of the console while exchanging a few pleasantries with his second shift counterpart. His computer console showed various locations across the globe, and the blips on those maps showed any air or space traffic above those locations. The buttons and dials on the console allowed him full access to SPADATS, the Space Detection and Tracking System, so he could isolate specific locations if it became necessary. If there was any activity in space, Charlie would know about it.

He briefly scanned the status report from the previous shift. It read—*No unusual air activity*. He glanced at his friend, Airman Mark Jones, who sat at the console next to his, and raised his eyebrows and shrugged, silently indicating he was ready for another eight boring hours of observation. Mark rolled his eyes in agreement.

For the first one hour and thirty-five minutes of the shift nothing unusual had happened. All the "blips" flew in their recognizable flight or orbital patterns and were easily identified. Then, unexpectedly, a new flashing red light flickered onto Charlie's display. He quickly flipped through his manifest, making sure he hadn't missed anything that could've corresponded to the blip. Nothing did.

"What the?" Charlie muttered. An unidentified bogey wasn't all that uncommon. It could have been an enemy satellite changing course for a new spying route, or a dead satellite with a decaying orbit about to reenter the atmosphere. More likely though, it was a meteoroid. Astronomical reports forecasted a meteor shower tonight. But still… this didn't resemble a meteoroid. "Commander, I got a new bogey that just tripped the fence over the Mid-Atlantic. Apogee reading at eighty miles and heading down."

Commander Stromfeld glared at Charlie. "Flight Pattern?"

"Coming straight down at free fall velocity, sir," Charlie replied, his gaze glued to his monitor.

"Check the inventory log for any dead satellites or other known objects that might be orbiting in that sector."

"Nothing on the list, sir."

"What's your estimate on size?" Stromfeld asked.

"Judging from the blip... approximately fifty yards in diameter. Should we bother NORAD with this, sir?"

"Not yet. Jones, get the TIP team online. One hundred fifty feet is downright big. I'm not sure whatever it is will burn off in the atmosphere. If it does make it through, I want to know where and when it's going to hit."

"Yes sir, Commander," Airman Jones answered.

Charlie, with Stromfeld now over his shoulder, hoped it was just a meteor that would die in the atmosphere and nothing more sinister. As much as he hated the boredom, excitement had the potential to be far worse. Two minutes passed as they watched the object continue to fall.

"Jones, what's the TIP team's analysis?" Stromfeld asked.

Airman Jones ripped the hard copy from the printer and read it. "If it survives atmospheric entry they estimate six minutes to impact in the Mid-Atlantic. It's impossible to give an exact estimate due to the fluctuating density of the atmosphere, but it should land in the water. No danger to civilians, sir."

Stromfeld grabbed the printout to see for himself. "Let's hope we have no nuclear subs in that vicinity." He turned back to Charlie. "Status?"

"Bogey is now at fifty miles heading into the mesosphere and still descending along its current trajectory—no loss of size noted." Charlie knew that ablation, the process where the friction a meteor generated by speeding through the atmosphere burned off its outer layers, reducing its size or turning it to dust, should have affected it by now.

"Damn." Stromfeld raced back to his desk and reached for the gold phone. "This is Commander Ray Stromfeld at the Space Surveillance Center. Flash alert for CINC-NORAD. We mark an unidentified bogey, approximately 150 feet in diameter, descending fast into the Atlantic Ocean. ETI six minutes, point of impact longitude 74 degrees, latitude 48 degrees, radius of error three miles."

The blip was at forty miles altitude when Charlie, stunned, said, "Holy... object just changed course, sir."

Charlie appreciated that Stromfeld didn't question his observation skills. About five months ago, Charlie had successfully identified an ELINT—an Electronic Intelligence Satellite—that was confusing everyone else on post. Since then, the Commander developed a respect for his abilities. Still, this direction change Stromfeld had to see for himself. Charlie waved him over.

"Huh, hold on." Stromfeld put the phone on his desk and walked over to Charlie's console. "New flight pattern?"

"It's still descending, only at a different angle and much slower. It now appears to be in an orbital spiral over the northern hemisphere," Charlie reported.

"Any ideas?"

"It's definitely not a meteor."

"Unknown satellite?" Stromfeld suggested.

"The speed's not right. Plus, I've never seen a satellite execute a maneuver like that. That course change was almost ninety degrees."

"Jones." Stromfeld snarled.

Jones ripped the new Trajectory Impact Projection estimate from the printout and handed it to Commander Stromfeld.

"Damn." Stromfeld raced back to the phone. "Modify previous Flash Alert. Bogey changed course. New point of impact, Ellesmere Island, Northern Canada, longitude 85 degrees 30 minutes, latitude 75 degrees 45 minutes. Radius of error one mile. ETI in twelve minutes . . . that's 3:51 a.m. our time. Requesting Priority One Action message to Commander in Chief of North American Aerospace Defense Command for full use of all available networks of the SPADATS. Also requesting Priority One use on the computer-linked telescopic system along bogey's current trajectory. We need a picture of this thing, and we need it fast."

The computer-linked telescopic system based in Malabar, Florida would take about four minutes to receive the coordinates, process them, align itself with the bogey, and transmit a real-time picture back to the Space Surveillance Center. On an ordinary day, this feat of computer technology would seem extraordinary.

Today, it wasn't fast enough.

The room began to fill with more men, most with a command rank on their uniform. The tension grew. Most analysts, not used to being around so many high ranks at once, stayed silent fearing that saying the wrong thing would make them look stupid in the eyes of their superiors. A senior commander asked Charlie for the status.

"Bogey is still on current descent trajectory. Speed also remains constant, sir."

Time moved in slow motion. No one knew what it was, but speculation filled the room, every hypothesis shortly cut down by some inconsistency which soon led to a new hypothesis. The cycle continued, but everyone knew the chatter was meaningless until they received the real-time pictures from Malabar.

"Commander, two bogeys are approaching on an intercept course," Charlie said. "Probably Canadian RAF."

"How much longer until those pictures come in?" Jones whispered.

"About a minute for pictures, one more for impact," Charlie answered.

"It's going to be a long minute," Jones mumbled.

Thirty more seconds passed when, suddenly, the blip disappeared. The occupants of Box Nine stared with disbelief.

"God dammit!" shouted Stromfeld.

"I don't understand it, sir. The bogey's gone." Charlie fooled with some knobs and dials, but the blip did not reappear.

One senior commander, seemingly unfazed, took control. "No need to panic yet, gentlemen. We'll be receiving visuals in about ten seconds."

All eyes focused on the screen in front of them. The first picture finally flashed on and there was—*nothing*. If the object had exploded, they would have at least seen debris, but there was nothing there. All the billions of dollars in high-tech equipment had resulted in nothing.

Stromfeld again reached for the gold phone and ordered a Priority One Teal-Amber search of the northern sky. The telescope would survey the night sky at an exact counter rate to the earth's rotation. This would, in effect, freeze the stars in place and highlight any unusual object in the sky.

That search lasted for five hours and also ultimately found nothing. All members present in Box Nine were fully debriefed at the end of their shift and instructed to make no mention of the incident to anyone, not even to the other analysts on first and second shift.

At 10:00 a.m. Charlie's replacement arrived. He was only twenty-two but had already developed that sallow complexion from being deprived of sunlight for most of the day. He exchanged the usual pleasantries with Charlie as he took control of the console. He put down his cup of coffee and read Charlie's report: *No unusual air activity. Airman Charlie Faber, Nov. 9th, 2009.*

IT
BEGINS

1

November 9th, 2:50 a.m. (Pacific Standard Time)
Prince Rupert, British Columbia, Canada

Stacy Michaels gazed out over the wooden railing of her deck. A cold breeze brought with it the changing season. The moon shone down like a beacon of silver light, highlighting the cascading mountains in the distance. Thousands of stars illuminated an otherwise dark sky. Occasionally, a sliver of orange light from the Aurora Borealis cascaded over the horizon. Without any city lights to interfere, Stacy admired all the beauty of the heavens.

At least she did until a storm system from the west picked up speed and splashed cloud formations across the awesome celestial backdrop—as if Mother Nature herself had experienced a mood swing. But even as the night brooded, Stacy remained out on her deck. She couldn't sleep and much preferred the open outdoors to the confines of home, even in the cold and even though her home was spacious enough. She poured herself a glass of wine, wrapped herself in a down blanket, and lowered herself into a lounge.

Taking a sip of White Zinfandel, she began to think of an idea for her next children's book. "Okay Princess," she said to herself as she grabbed a pencil and pad from the nearby table. "What perils will your kingdom face for your eighth adventure?" Unconsciously, she tapped her pencil on the pad as she gazed through the sliding glass doors into her own kingdom, an old country-style chalet filled with all the modern appliances this century had to offer.

A white tiger rug, with fangs ferociously displayed, covered the stained wooden floor—its yellow-green eyes staring down the arched fireplace. To the left was a semi-circular, two-piece leather sofa, jammed together so there was plenty of room to lie down and stare up through the skylight above. Perfect for sleepless nights when the weather didn't permit her out on her deck. A glass-topped end table, splattered with glamour magazines, adjoined the couch. On the adjacent wall, a white oak entertainment center supported a digital music player with mounted speakers, a large screen HDTV, and a DVD player. Over to the left, the pass-through showed a glimpse of the kitchen.

It was a very romantic setting, she thought. Unfortunately, a man wasn't included in the picture.

She started sketching the Princess, beginning with the long silky black hair that framed her face. Then she added her trademark big brown eyes that mesmerized all those handsome knights. The pencil moved downward as she sketched her slim and shapely, well-proportioned body. The princess was quite beautiful. Stacy caught her reflection in the glass door and chuckled, wondering how many of her readers knew that Princess Zinthia was her mirror image, only modified to give her an animated cartoon look that children adored.

"So why is your castle so empty?" she mused. Her pencil tapped rapidly on the pad now as she mulled over the answer. "It's because you're a strong modern woman who chose to keep her individual freedom to pursue her own career." Then she sighed because she knew that was a lie.

A quick sip of wine brought the truth to the forefront. Every time she managed to get close to someone, her constant nightmares, chronic insomnia, and irrational fears always scared them off. Sudden panic attacks for no apparent reason would leave her deathly afraid and frantic during daylight. A "total freak-out" her last boyfriend called it. While sleeping, they would force her awake screaming and sweating, but with very little recollection of her nightmare. But since she had moved here five years ago—with the help of her therapist Dr. Miller—they became increasing less frequent and had almost completely subsided.

Yes, soon she would be fine. "Okay, Princess Zinthia… perhaps it's time for you to finally meet your knight in shining armor, Sir Right." That brought a sly smile to her face. She scribbled some notes on the pad then reached out for another sip of wine to warm her.

A thunderous clap abruptly shattered the calm. It was as if the night itself cried out in a pain-filled gasp and its scream, echoed and amplified by the mountains, ripped loudly through the cold moist air. The wooden deck beneath her feet shuddered. Her metal lounge chair vibrated and shifted under her weight. Her wine glass shook, and White Zinfandel splashed over the rim onto her blanket. Then the rumbling air moved menacingly through her. For a few seconds it jarred her soul, then it passed, and the night grew silent once again—but eerily so. It was an experience she had never had before, yet somehow it was familiar. Her hands trembled as she gave in to the sudden urge to race indoors, tearing the blanket away from her and tossing it aside. She shivered as she fiercely pulled open the sliding doors, her entire body tingling with fear, and within a time span as short as ten seconds, her last five years of therapy came completely undone.

2

November 9th, 2:52 a.m. (Pacific Standard Time)
Palo Alto, California

She screamed continuously.

At first with slow, short moans, but as the sensations heightened, her screams quickened, growing lengthier and more poignant. With a final exultation, she arched her back and let out an uncontrolled wail of ecstasy.

Then he screamed as well and both Logan Grey and Lisa Morgan collapsed their muscular supple bodies together and relaxed in each other's arms, a long moment passing before either one was able to resist the urge to lie blissfully in silence.

"You are incredible," Lisa cooed. "I had a feeling those body language skills of yours would pay off in bed."

Logan blushed, smiling back at her. He was having a great day. No, even better than that—a perfect day. Only twelve hours earlier he had finalized the deal to sell Ms. Morgan's brand name cosmetic line to a Japanese firm for forty-seven million dollars—a deal which made Lisa a multimillionaire and netted him a cool ten percent of the take. And he had earned every penny, he thought. The negotiations had gone on for a month and been on the verge of falling apart before Lisa gave in and hired him as a consultant. He even managed to get thirteen million dollars more than the original final offer. A feat which served to remind him that he was the best.

There were plenty of other negotiating sharks for hire out there. Like them, Logan had the gift of gab, knew many different cultures intimately, and spoke seven languages, including American Sign. But that wasn't what made him the best. What set him apart, above all the rest, was his obsession with kinesics, the science of body movement.

Each culture had different forms of expression through body language. What meant yes in one language might mean no in another. But even more than that, everyone had "tells"—subconscious movements that uncovered their inner motives or feelings that they would not willingly reveal. If you observed and knew what to look for, almost anyone could be read. In this negotiation, the difference between 34 million and 47 million dollars came from Logan noticing that each time Mr. Kiru, CEO of Shadeio Cosmetics, was willing to go higher in price he would pause a few seconds longer than usual and slowly bring the tips of his index fingers to his chin. Logan knew that since Americans as a culture conversed faster than the Japanese, Kiru's additional pause between sentences were designed to unnerve Lisa at the times Mr. Kiru himself was the most nervous. He used that strategy to try to keep the asking price low. Once Kiru's strategy was known, it became child's play for Logan to push him to his limit.

"Oooo . . . Are you getting shy on me now?" Lisa teased with a purr as she rolled over to face him. "I'm surprised. So commanding and aggressive in business, dynamite in bed, and now you're getting shy."

Logan tilted his head, adjusting his pillow underneath him so he could stare at her while still lying comfortably. "Not shy . . . I was just thinking. Actually, I'm the one who's surprised. In all that time we worked together, you never showed any interest in me. I mean personally interested." Logan knew that was a white lie. Over that time, he had picked up plenty of unconscious clues that alerted him to the fact that Lisa was attracted to him. Picking up those "tells" was what he was best at. He was just too polite and professional to point them out. Besides, Lisa was the one who hired him. She wasn't the one he was supposed to be reading.

"Bull," said Lisa playfully. "I know you must've picked up on my signals right away." Logan was slightly taken aback by her candor. "Hey, after working with you for a month, I know how good you are. The fact that you didn't hit on me when you knew you could have just made me appreciate you all the more," she added, as she leaned over and gave him a long passionate kiss.

A kiss which he eagerly returned. "And here everyone told me you were business before pleasure," Logan said.

"I am," she replied. "But now, thanks to you, my business is done. Are you ready for more pleasure?" She rolled on top of him.

After a long enjoyable moment, Logan gently pushed her away. "I'd love to," he said, "but in about five hours I've got a meeting with the prestigious Ms. Harrison of Micro Circuits Technology."

"Leaving me behind for another woman already, huh?" she joked.

"She's seventy, but yeah... I have a real fetish for the older babes," he kidded back.

"Well, she's just going to have to wait. I'm not quite done with you yet." Her hand worked its way to a more convincing position, as she kissed him again. "What was it you called this again?"

"Win-win negotiating," Logan answered. "Everyone gets what they want. Everyone wins." He kissed her again, ready to make love to her for the second time tonight.

3

Ottawa, Canada

"Damn."

The soft vibrating sensation in his left leg alerted Major David Gaines of the Canadian Royal Air Force that the pager he had reluctantly taken with him on his five-mile morning jog was ringing. He reached into his pocket, slowing his gait, and quickly scanned the number scrolling across the digital readout. It was an emergency beacon from his immediate supervisor, Commander Smythe.

"Damn," he muttered again.

I knew I should've left this at home, he thought, his morning routine interrupted but it was his duty, and Gaines always put his country first. However, he was two miles into his run and thus a good distance from his home.

He turned down the next main throughway, detouring from his usual route, to Kendales, the only store he knew would be open at this hour of the morning that still had a working public phone. He crossed another street and ran into the deli, past the hanging salamis on the wall, and into the phone booth in the corner. As his breath fogged the glass, he caught the sweat beading at the fringes of his short-cropped jet-black hair in the reflection. Paying no heed to his muddled appearance, he rapidly dialed headquarters. "Gaines here."

The voice on the other end relayed a message. Gaines hung up, a stern expression on his face. His wiry muscles tensed. He stretched briefly then sprinted homeward.

A meteor? That's what the message said. *Emergency. Meteor Warning. Destination Southern Section of Ellesmere.*

His mind raced faster than his feet. *Who knew what damage a meteorite could do to that island? Were there any top-secret military systems there? What was the danger to the surrounding communities?* Of all things, a meteor . . . it was so *improbable.*

He reached home in less than fifteen minutes, grabbed his keys, and went straight to the garage for his Volvo. Within half an hour, he pulled up to the headquarters of Canadian Intelligence, flashed his badge to the guard at the gate, and drove inside. He parked his car and walked to another guard booth where security required him to show his badge again.

Once through, a soldier escorted him to briefing room L304 on the lower level. Along the way there was more activity than usual indicating there was more to this event than met the eye.

The briefing room was small, containing only a narrow conference table in the front, and behind it, a large LCD monitor built into the wall. In the middle of the table, a holographic projector displayed a non-rotating image of the earth that literally hovered inches above the surface. Standing to the left of the table was Commander Bruce Smythe. On the other side was the man in charge of Canada's Defense Department, Admiral Walter Brock. Two other officers were seated: Commander Weston from foreign intelligence and Commander Britton from the air force. Gaines was the last to arrive.

"Be seated, Major," the Admiral said. He was a short, portly, elderly man completely bald except for a few gray hairs that adorned his temples. However, despite his meager presence, he commanded a great deal of respect.

"Er . . . Yes, sir, I—," Gaines stammered as he took his seat.

"Commander, bring the men up to speed," the Admiral ordered sternly.

Commander Smythe stood up. "Around twenty minutes ago SPADATS detected an unidentified object that entered the earth's atmosphere," he said, referring to the Space Detection and Tracking System jointly operated by the United States and Canada. He placed a flash memory drive into the projector port as he spoke and what appeared on the radar screens earlier this morning was now being replayed in fast motion on the holographic globe. He approached the three-dimensional hovering image and used his index finger to point out the highlights. "The object first appeared here and followed this path— slowing down along the way. We expected impact here, at precisely 5:51 Eastern Standard Time."

Expected? Gaines' interest piqued even further.

Smythe continued. "Our first thought was a meteor, but we now know this was not the case. I apologize for any misinformation relayed to you on your call-in, Major. The deception was not intentional. At the time, we truly believed it was a meteor."

After Gaines nodded his acceptance, Smythe continued.

"As it approached on its final path, we sent two F-18 Hornets to intercept. Their orders were to destroy, if necessary, as long as there was no danger of misdirecting it and endangering lives. They were scheduled to intercept it here over the ocean." The holographic display now showed the flight path of the two fighter planes. When the blips representing the fighters were moving closer to the object, Commander Smythe pushed a button returning the holographic replay to real time speed. "I'm now going to playback the recording between the pilots immediately prior to intercept. I think it's better if the three of you experience this for yourselves—so listen up."

The tape began to play. Radio static followed by... "Hound, we're within range. Do you have the target on radar?"

"Copy that, Lynx. Fox is on the scope and about to be downed."

"Don't fire until you have visual verification, Hound. Do you see anything yet?"

"Not yet—sun's too low on the horizon, blocking my view. Wait . . . did you catch that?" The surprise in his voice could be heard over the slightly static transmission.

"I think so."

"Whatever that thing is, it ain't a meteor, eh. The sun is glinting off metal."

"Lock on and fire, Hound. Whatever it is, we can't let it touch down."

"Acquiring lock, Lynx." The beep beep beep beeeeeep of the radar finding its target came in loud and clear. "Locked and ready. This hunt's over buddy. What the f— that's impossible—the target just vanished. What are you reading, Lynx?"

As Hound said that, the blip representing the object on the hologram also disappeared, meaning that ground tracking had lost the target as well.

"Same thing, Hound. No radar, no visual—nothing. Let's use search pattern Alpha to scout the area."

Commander Smythe hit the stop button. The blips on the holographic globe froze in place. The pilot's recording went silent. "Needless to say, they didn't find anything. Any theories?"

"What about NORAD?" Britton asked. He leaned his overweight body inward as he spoke.

"Our friends at NORAD say their telescopes haven't revealed anything yet. Also, we contacted our NATO allies, and they've also offered no answers," Smythe said.

"What about the gun cameras?" Gaines asked, referring to the cameras lodged in the bellies of the aircraft.

"Revealed nothing at this time," Smythe answered.

"How about a new experimental space craft created by the Russians?" Britton asked. "Or the Americans for that matter."

"Doubtful," Weston replied. "This object didn't burn up in the atmosphere, which indicates it had some kind of heat shielding. I know of only two countries with the capabilities to develop the kind of shielding technology that would allow an entry like that; Japan and the US—but neither one's quite there yet."

Britton cleared his throat. "Maybe they are and we just don't know it. The potential advantage to returning space vehicles and satellite salvage teams is significant enough where they might have pushed their progress forward a year or two."

"If they had it, trust me, I would know," Weston said. "Besides, the object vanished into thin air. Unless, of course, the Japanese got some type of alien cloaking device, I would rule them out."

"Perhaps that's not so far off base, gentlemen," Gaines said. All heads turned his way the odd glare of so many higher ranks causing him to pause.

"Come again?!" Weston said.

"Don't be shy, Major. I'd be interested in hearing all theories," Smythe interceded.

"Well, what about an extraterrestrial spacecraft?" Gaines said, seriously. He paused again waiting for their reactions.

Commander Britton rocked back in his chair; his hand pressed against his forehead. "Extraterrestrial space craft. Oh, c'mon."

"For years there have been documented cases of aircraft reported on radar speeding through Canadian air space and maneuvering like no known man-made vehicle," Gaines said. "We ourselves have had over 750 sightings and events on record, before we transferred the records to the National Research Council."

Britton erupted. "Nonsense. Next thing you know, you'll be telling us this is a time-traveling machine from the future."

"Well, actually sir, that is also a conceivable, though farther-fetched, possibility," Gaines said.

"Any other ideas?" Admiral Brock asked. There was a moment of silence. "Nothing. Okay. Weston, continue to check all your sources. If anything turns up, I want to know about it immediately. Britton, have those pilots interviewed again and send all transcripts to Major Gaines. I want this done within the hour. That will be all."

Commander Britton and Weston acknowledged their orders and left the room. Gaines rose slowly, preparing to follow them out.

"Major Gaines, one moment please. Commander Smythe and I decided we want you to handle the investigation."

Gaines glanced at Smythe who gave his nod of approval. "Why me, sir?"

"Well, to speak frankly, I think you're the best man for the job."

"What about Britton and Weston?" Gaines asked.

"Britton's main concern is our military. Since this doesn't appear to be an immediate threat, I don't think he'll give it any real thought. Weston's a good man, but he also has more immediate concerns. I want you because you'll give this investigation the proper attention it deserves, and Bruce tells me you've got a good open mind. Frankly, I don't know of anything else either, besides some friggin' alien or time traveler that can do what this thing did. In this envelope are the transcripts, film, and tape. As more information comes in, I'll forward it to you. Look it over and let us know what you think. I'll see you Major, in one hour."

"Yes, sir," Gaines said, saluting the Admiral.

"One more thing, Major," Smythe said with a rare grin. "Take a shower. You stink."

"Yes, sir." Gaines smirked and went to work.

4

Marine Corps Base Camp Pendleton, California

General Henry Chesterfield rolled over and reached through the darkness for his bedside phone, wondering what could be so important that someone had the temerity to call him at this ungodly hour of the night. His strong stubby hands gripped the receiver and placed it against his ear as he sat up in bed. Clearing his throat with the low unappealing growl of an elderly man just awakening, he answered. "Chesterfield here. What's up?"

The voice on the other end filled him in on this evening's events. Chesterfield rubbed his eyes, becoming more awake with each detail he heard. By the time he received his orders he had moved all the way over and was now sitting at the edge of his bed. Checking the clock—3:38 a.m.—he bent down and put on his slippers. "Yes, sir. I have the perfect man for the job. I'll put him on it right away." He pushed the button labeled "program one" which simultaneously disconnected his call and connected him with Colonel John Chase. The phone rang twice before it was answered.

"Colonel Chase. Good morning, General."

He figured Chase must have known who was calling by the caller ID display on his phone. "Not any more it isn't. Initiate the Roswell Protocols. Then meet me in my office and I'll fill you in on the details."

"The Roswell Protocols, General?" Chase asked, as if making sure he had heard that right.

"Yeah," Chesterfield stood up. "How 'bout that?"

5

Prince Rupert, Canada

So alone… so vulnerable.
Stacy's thoughts spiraled out of her control.
Why did she choose to live here? The nearest house was two acres away. Town was a ten-minute drive. Even this living room was too large.

She stared at the expansive room, watching wearily as the moonlight shone through the skylight and windows, casting shadows that eerily crept along the walls. Curling into a fetal position on the couch, she pulled the blanket up to her chin, desperately trying to fend off her paranoia.

The house creaked.

Stacy jumped up, rapidly scanning in all directions. Her heartbeat hastened and she involuntarily gulped down her next breath. She cursed herself for not completely closing the blinds of the sliding glass door leading to her deck.

The house creaked again.

No, not the house—the skylight directly above.

Quickly looking upward, she saw nothing but a hazy night sky through the thick glass. Backing away, she felt a sharp jab in the back of her leg, whirling around only to see the end table she had just bumped into wobble back to its original position.

She gasped, placing her hand on her chest until her breathing became more controlled. A menacingly shaped shadow flickered across the couch. She raced to the sliding doors, double checked the locks, confirmed the wooden doorstop was firmly in position, and then sharply yanked the cords sealing the blinds shut. She noticed the window across the room and raced there to do the same.

A few nervous moments later, Stacy finally sat back down. She fidgeted then impatiently jumped back up and went to the kitchen for more wine. She took a sip, feeling the sweet dizzying warmth on her tongue before uncharacteristically slugging down the remainder then wiped her lips, and poured herself another glass.

The house groaned again—a short grunt followed by the short rap of wind bouncing off glass.

Stacy held still so as not to make a sound. When she heard no further noises, she slowly made her way to the countertop and grabbed a twelve-inch-long Ginzu knife, holding it in a white-knuckled grip.

Ever so slowly, she stepped out of the kitchen and back into the living room. The shadows crept faster along the walls as the quickening winds repeatedly tapped on the windows until the house went deafeningly silent. She whirled toward the kitchen, further tightening her grip on the knife, waiting for whatever it was that she was sure was coming to get her. And even though in the back of her mind, she knew her intense irrational fears had returned, she was completely unable to calm herself. The only one thing she knew for certain was this would be a very long night.

6

Palo Alto, California

Ring… ringggg...

"Who the hell is calling at this hour?" Logan Grey mumbled as he awoke. A glance at the digital clock told him he had gotten less than an hour of sleep.

"Ooh, Shut it off," Lisa moaned.

Ring… ringggg…

Logan fumbled about, grabbing the phone in the dark. "Yeah."

"Is Wolf there?" the deep voice asked.

"Wolf?"

"Is Wolf there?" repeated the voice.

"Wolf! Holy shit… uh, yeah… Wolf here." Logan sat up stumbling to find the lamp. As he clicked the switch illuminating the room, Lisa sat up and shielded her eyes.

"Party time, Wolf. Be there at seven. We'll bring the six-pack," the voice said.

"I'll meet you at, um… Sam's," Logan replied, barely remembering the proper countersign.

The person on the other end hung up.

Logan couldn't believe he got *the call*.

About two years ago, at a business conference where Logan gave a seminar on international business relations, a man from the National Security Agency had approached him about his expertise on the social differences of various cultures and in kinesics, the study of body language.

Logan had consulted for the government in the past, but the man from the NSA came with a slightly different angle. He asked Logan if he thought he could communicate with an otherworldly being. Could he successfully interpret the movements and facial expressions of an unknown entity to understand what it was communicating? The man insisted he wasn't joking.

Even though Logan wasn't sure, he confidently responded yes. As a result, he was offered a monthly stipend for being "on call", briefed on procedure, and given the code name Wolf. He couldn't believe the government was paying him such a sizable fee in case E.T. ever showed up. If only the taxpayers knew, he laughed to himself at the time.

As the unearned paychecks piled up, Logan got curious. He began buying books and reading articles on the subject. While in Chicago on business, he visited the J. Allen Hynek Center, the only private organization respected by the government still studying the phenomena. He also attended some MUFON meetings in various cities and managed to make friends with some credible people who claimed to have seen UFO's. He even asked former President Jimmy Carter about his experience when he met him at a symposium in Atlanta. The more Logan learned, the more he believed it could be true. Heck, he thought, if the NSA was interested, it had to be true. Still, he never expected to receive the call—especially now.

He tried to control his panic and think things through. Party time meant they needed him immediately. One six-pack meant one hour. Six-pack meant pack for six days. *Shit! There goes the Harrison account. And more.*

He was beginning to realize his situation. The National Security Agency finally needed him—in one hour—and he was half hung over with a beautiful naked woman in his bed. He took a deep breath and tried to control himself.

"Who was that?" Lisa asked.

"Oh, shit! You need to go," Logan said.

"What?"

"Sorry. That call was important." Logan got out of bed, held the sheets across his waist and reached towards the floor with his free hand, and began to hand Lisa her clothes.

"That's funny. Most men like me to stay," she replied, coyly.

Logan stared into her deep green eyes, a wave of sadness overcoming him as he settled down. "I'm sorry. I really am. Top secret government stuff... and I shouldn't have even told you that much." Logan's expression said more than his words. "I'm not permitted to explain."

Lisa grinned. "I understand. Don't worry, I usually don't stick around for long anyway," she added with a wink as she got dressed. "Hey, no hard feelings. I had a wonderful time."

She kissed him passionately, but with a definite sense of finality. Then she headed for the door before turning to him one last time. "By the way, thanks for making me a millionaire." Then she left, gently closing the door behind her.

"Great, just great," Logan mumbled. He liked her, but this was no time for regrets.

Still naked, he went into the kitchen and put up a pot of coffee. He then went into the cabinet for aspirin and downed two with a large glass of water. While the coffee brewed, he made his way into the bathroom for a quick shave and shower. He emerged feeling much better.

He got dressed and made his way back to the kitchen for the coffee, relaxing for a few minutes before returning to his bedroom to pack. *Damn, how can I pack when I don't even know where I'm going? "They should have made up some damn code for where I'm going." he thought.* He threw in some business suits along with the usual attire, essential clean underwear, and toiletries.

He still had some time left before anyone arrived. He reached for the telephone and left a message for his secretary to cancel all his appointments for the week. When he hung up, the magnitude of his possible responsibilities really hit him. The United States government was calling on him to communicate with an alien. *Was he really about to meet a totally new life form not of this world? What would it be like? Would it be friendly? If it was an alien life form, how did the government contact it? Did they come to visit and ask to be taken to our leader? Did the government shoot down a UFO and capture the alien pilot? Or maybe the government was simply calling in his marker for an international trade negotiation? But...*

On a whim he called a student he knew at Berkeley who was just crazy enough to be up at this hour. The phone rang four times before someone picked up.

"Seismic studies, this is Larry. What can I do for ya?" The voice was slightly muffled, and Logan imagined the Twinkie that Larry was probably snacking on.

"Hi, Larry, this is Logan—Logan Grey."

After a gulping sound, Larry responded. "Hey man, what are you doing up this early?"

"Well, I was sleeping, but then I thought I felt a tremor. I was wondering if you had anything on your seismographs."

"Here? Sorry bud, nothing shaking now in Northern Cal."

"How about anything over the last few days? Anything on the charts—and not just here, all over the world?"

The smacking of Larry's lips together stopped. "All over the world? I don't think you'd be able to feel quakes from across the globe. What do you really need Logan? Is this related to that research you were doing a few months back?"

When Logan began to get more involved in his extraterrestrial research, he had read that scientists believed strange glowing unexplained lights were phenomena related to earthquakes. Something about tectonic shifts creating pressures so great that they discharged energy in the form of geoluminescence. He didn't really understand it, but he did speculate that if a UFO ever crashed the impact would register on a seismograph. He found one incident where a minor tremor correlated with a reported crash, but that could have been coincidence.

"Okay, you got me," Logan fessed up. "So have you got anything?"

"Hold on, let me check." A moment of silence passed. "Nothing major on the charts."

"How about minor? Anything low on the scale?"

"Anything low . . . c'mon, we get readings of hundreds of minor tremors every day. Last year alone California had over 18,000 quakes."

"Give me anything that strikes you as odd—any readings that are slightly higher or more frequent than normal."

"Hold on…" After three minutes of "hmmms" Larry replied. "Yeah, what do you know . . . got three unusual tremors. One, two days ago in the South Pacific. That's common, but it was a little stronger than normal. Got a three-point-three yesterday afternoon in LA. Got another one a little over an hour ago, in the Northern Canadian Coast Mountains… by the border. Does that help?"

"I'm not sure. I'll let you know. Thanks."

"No problem."

Logan hung up. They weren't here yet, so he made one more call to his colleague Pierre Le Buc, a linguistics professor at Miguel University in Montreal with similar skills who also consulted for major corporations and the Canadian government. About a year ago, they had dinner at a restaurant just outside Montreal. After a few beers, Pierre began to ask unusual questions about communicating with otherworldly life forms. Would it be as simple as reading people or as difficult as communicating with dolphins? As their conversation continued, Logan came to the conclusion that Pierre might have been called on by his government same as he was, though Pierre was far more open to discussion on the subject.

"Hello, you have reached the home of Pierre Le Buc. Please leave a message at the beep and I'll return your call as soon—"

Someone knocked loudly on Logan's door. Logan hung up before the message ended. It was time to go.

7

Tokyo, Japan

The sun had set over two hours ago on the Pacific Rim, but darkness had not yet claimed the super-metropolis called Tokyo. That wouldn't happen until a little after midnight when the trains made their last stops, dropping off their final passengers before heading back to the yard. At this hour, thousands of neon lights radiated colorfully throughout the Ginza District beckoning pedestrians to shop. Pachinko parlors chimed noisily, exciting the risk-taking patrons within. In the Kabuto-cho district, businessmen needing to release the pressures of their long hectic day filled the karaoke bars. In the Shimbashi and Shinjuku districts the dance clubs were welcoming the young and adventurous.

Even in the Kasumigaseki district, just southwest of the Imperial Palace grounds, within the building that houses the Diet, Japan's parliament, things were happening. It was just forty minutes ago, when the officers working under the unusual pyramidal roof learned of the unknown object that appeared on their radar scopes. Like the other countries who witnessed the phenomenon, their sky watchers quickly deduced the object wasn't a meteor.

As was standard operating procedure, they tracked the object and calculated the point of impact. New programming instructions and coordinates were relayed to the closest satellite in the area, the Sonysat 4W. It was their most sophisticated weather tracking satellite, which also doubled as a spy satellite. Via computer relay, the camera's F-stops were opened to maximum, and the lenses were repositioned to take photographs of the descending object from four different angles as it passed. Soon thereafter, the image was captured and transferred to a mainframe at military headquarters, copies of which were quickly circulated among the attending generals in the room. The results were extraordinary.

Unfortunately, impact predictions indicated the object would touch down in Canada. There was no way they could retrieve it. Then they learned the object disappeared off their radar tracking surveillance system. The generals were thankful that others would not be receiving this unexpected gift from the stars, but equally disappointed that they would never know what it was.

All, that is, except General Sato Yamakazi. His esteemed colleagues were small-minded, he thought. Instead of despair and relief, the object's mysterious disappearance filled Sato with hope. He alone believed it still must have crash landed, only not where anyone expected it to be. To him, this unexpected turn of events was an opportunity that allowed a chance at recovery, but he was the only one who saw it that way. The other generals respectfully disagreed and slowly the room emptied—the moment forgotten and the extraordinary photos left to be filed away into obscurity. General Yamakazi returned to his office.

He sat behind his desk, his hands folded together in his lap, while he pondered how to accomplish the seemingly impossible feat of locating and retrieving this object on his own. He gazed at the sword his predecessor had bestowed upon him for his years of faithful service. The general was proud of the gift, a short sword used to kill the enemy in combat during WWII that he displayed directly below the portrait of the man who wielded it. He rubbed a hand across his receding brow, leaning back in his high-backed black leather chair while he formulated a plan. As it came together, he stood and paced across the rug.

Yes, it could work, he thought but he would have to act quickly. Having the SonySat 4W already in position, he believed he could succeed. It was a bold plan. One surely his colleagues would disapprove of. If they knew. So he'd run the operation clandestinely. The risk to his career was great, but the rewards were even greater. If he succeeded, newfound power would be his and Japan would once again become a military force to be reckoned with.

He reached for the phone and summoned his most loyal subordinate. Within a minute, Officer Yoshiguro Musamato knocked on the door.

"Come in," Yamakazi ordered.

The young officer entered the imposing office. He stared briefly at the large portrait of the recently retired General Sakiguso which hung on the wall, as if under scrutiny by a second superior officer. He then closed the door behind him, bowed, and stood at attention.

Sato furrowed his brow and spoke with a strong booming tone. "Tomorrow is the second phase of our field test for the Ninjas." The Ninjas were the two new state-of-the-art stealth helicopter prototypes developed by the Tobison Corporation. They were currently stationed on the *Tsunami*, an aircraft carrier patrolling the Pacific. Fortunately, their field test fell solely under Yamakazi's jurisdiction. "Cancel it. I am issuing new field test orders, security classification level six, eyes only. You will personally see to it that these new orders are promptly received, and you will make sure they are kept in the strictest confidence. Send the Tsunami northeast..." He continued, revealing his plan to the junior officer.

A bead of sweat dropped from Musamato's brow. "Hai," he responded with a curt bow.

Once absorbed, Yamakazi continued. "I want a high delta search pattern program downloaded into the SonySat 4W, radius 200 miles around the initial scan. When they locate the intended target, I am to be immediately notified, and those results will be kept with equal confidence." Sato paused for a moment to add a new element to his plan. "Also, I want the Masuka clan quietly notified to be on the lookout for any unusual information. Remind them they will be compensated handsomely, as usual, if they manage to procure anything of value." His eyes bore down on the young soldier who appeared hesitant. "Any questions?"

"No sir," he answered.

"Hai, I'll be expecting to hear about your progress shortly."

Musamato bowed quickly then left the office.

Yamakazi smiled as he viewed the portrait of Sakiguso. He would be pleased, Sato thought, as he imagined his predecessor gazing down upon him with a look of approval. The plan in motion, he strode back to his chair and sat down. He would wait patiently for events to unfold, savoring every minute of his walk on the path to greatness. His hunt for the ultimate prize had begun. It would soon be his.

8

Moscow, Russia

The bitter afternoon wind bit at Nikolai Rasputin's face as he rushed across Red Square, the ceremonial center of Moscow. Despite his quickened pace, he still paused a moment to appreciate his surroundings. To his south he admired the Cathedral of St. Basil the Blessed, better known as Pokrovskiy Cathedral, each of its ten domes a different design and color. It was built by Barma and Posnik Yakolev from 1554 to 1560 to commemorate the defeat of the Mongols by Ivan IV the Terrible. Nikolai knew its history well, as he did each building within eyesight. He turned to face GUM, the state department store built in the Old Russian style. He turned to the north towards the State Historical Museum built from 1875 to 1883. Then, he turned left to the most impressive historical landmark, the Kremlin, his destination.

It wasn't his favorite view—he much preferred to see it from across the Moshva River at night when the floodlights brightened it, revealing all its full glory—but it still impressed him. No matter how many times he came here, he never failed to appreciate its magnificence.

He strode onward towards the east wall, passing the bulky Lenin Mausoleum beneath it, and quickly made his way past the Nikolskaya Tower. Eventually, he came to the Spasskaya Gate Tower, whose clock chimes are radio broadcast throughout Russia every day and walked through the gates. His solemn brown eyes studied the crenellated red brick walls, the many palaces and cathedrals, each different in their brilliance, wondering why he was being called here today. *What assignment did General Vaskev have for him this time? What new national crisis would separate him from his family again, so he could serve the greater cause?*

With his mind preoccupied, Nikolai's six-foot four, solidly muscular physique strode on as if on autopilot. He pondered his own history wondering what brought him to this place the first time all those years ago. The answer was the idealism of socialism. He believed with all his heart his nation could be, and should be, the greatest in the world—millions of people working in unison to serve the state, each person contributing to make the whole greater than the sum of its parts. It was a goal he spent his whole life in the military fighting for.

Unfortunately, he was losing faith. There should have been no hunger or poverty. Each person should have been respecting and helping his fellow man. But that was not the case. Communism had failed, and the cause, Nikolai thought, was the greed and corruption of the leaders who inhabited this very building he held so dear.

Nikolai saw many of them come and go. Most were the same. Once they achieved power, no matter how well-intentioned, they eventually used it to further their selfish desires instead of the needs of the community. To achieve their goals they had to cooperate, which led to compromises, which in turn became indebtedness to the undesirable. Each man eventually did whatever was necessary to hold onto their positions and status, like an addict holding onto drugs. It was a contagious disease, he thought, infecting everyone it touched until it became an epidemic that brought down a country... his country. Absolute power indeed corrupted absolutely.

However, Nikolai had never craved a position of power, so he was free from its trappings. He only sought to serve his country as best he could. General Vaskev was also an exception, Nikolai had known him for years, always admiring and respecting his unwavering devotion and honesty. If there were only more people like Vaskev, he thought, who believed as strongly as he did.

He looked ahead and saw the door to General Vaskev's office, not even remembering the path he had taken to get here. He turned the brass doorknob and entered without knocking.

The office was overpowering in its emptiness. The walls were adorned with paintings of the Iconoclasts and shelving units housing Vaskev's personal medals. The only furniture was Vaskev's desk, a few chairs, and an area containing an antique table and a tea station. The rest was vast open space.

"Good afternoon, Comrade Nikolai," Vaskev said from across the room. The slender General stood up and walked over to the tea station.

Nikolai closed the door behind him. "Afternoon, comrade." They had known each other long enough to be informal. Nikolai removed his coat and hat and hung them on the solid brass coat rack next to the door.

"Would you like some tea?" Vaskev asked, as he poured himself a cup. "It's a Latvian brand, quite good."

"Spaseeba," Nikolai said. "I assume you didn't invite me here for some tea."

"Ah yes, always right to the point." Vaskev filled a second cup with hot water. He drained the tea leaves through a small round silver strainer then placed the sterling silver pot back on the burner. "About an hour ago our radar systems picked up a very mysterious object heading into NATO air space. We were not able to record its final descent, as our radar does not reach that far over the horizon, but our agent in the Pentagon relayed some unbelievable information. He claims this mysterious object just disappeared. No explosion—it just vanished."

Nikolai walked towards him and took the cup. "You retrieved this information in only one hour."

"Yes. Apparently, our agent thought it so significant, he bypassed the usual channels and called his handler directly from a cellular phone."

Nikolai took a sip, the hot liquid warming his body. "A rash and foolish move. For an agent to take such a risk with so little information does not make much sense, nyet?"

"Well, it did not... until we received these photos from our spy satellites. Look at these," Vaskev said, as he lifted an envelope from his desk and handed it to Nikolai.

Nikolai placed his tea on a coaster and opened the flap. He turned the envelope over and the photos slid into his hands. He quickly rifled through them, studying a couple of shots from different angles. "And you think this spacecraft has touched down?"

Vaskev nodded.

"Where is it?" Nikolai asked.

Vaskev smiled, a gleam in his eye. "We do not know. But we will soon." He glared directly into Nikolai's eyes, "and then I am sending you to retrieve it."

9

Ottawa, Canada

Major Gaines glanced up sharply as his secretary's voice spoke through the intercom. "Admiral Brock and Commander Smythe to see you, sir."

"Thank you," Gaines replied. He disconnected then stood up to await their arrival.

The two men entered his small, modestly decorated office. Brock glanced at the room's most notable adornment; a stuffed moose head mounted on the left wall.

"Looking much better, David," Smythe said.

Before he examined all the data, Gaines had taken the Admiral's advice and showered. He now wore the full-dress uniform befitting an officer of his rank.

"What have you discovered so far?" Brock asked.

"Quite a lot, sir. For starters, the object is definitely a spacecraft of unearthly origins." He looked straight at his commanding officers expecting some form of disapproval or at least astonishment. However, if they were surprised in the least bit, neither one showed it.

Gaines grabbed a pile of photographs off his messy desk and walked to where Smythe and Brock stood. "I listened to the recording again then went over the pilots' personnel files. I even called them. Both pilots are highly competent. I fully believe they saw what they saw. Then I replayed the videotape from the gun cameras. It looks exactly as the pilots described—a metallic object reflecting the sun. I brought the tape down to the lab for further analysis. They froze the frames and zoomed in close enough to get me these." He spread the pile of enlarged images on his desk in front of his superiors, clearing away some papers as he did so. They showed the silhouette of a metallic disc-shaped craft stark against the sun's light. "Because of the brightness of the sun it wasn't possible to get better detail, but I think these pictures are clear enough."

Admiral Brock picked up the photos, studying them a moment through squinted eyes before passing them to Smythe.

"Nice... very nice," Smythe said.

"I called all the bases in the country and asked them to notify me if they spot anything unusual. I got a call back from the boys in BC. They tell me they're getting calls from the Prince Rupert police department concerning complaints about a sonic boom. They apologized to the police but tell me they didn't have any flights overhead at that time. The funny thing is these complaints came in only seconds after the object disappeared from the radar. I don't think that's a coincidence," Gaines said.

Brock observed the maps plastered on the wall, particularly focusing in on the one of Canada. He raised a finger and traced a line between Ellesmere and Prince Rupert. "How does a ship disappear on radar over Eastern Canada and suddenly create a sonic boom a few seconds later on the other side of the country?"

"I'm not sure," Gaines said.

"For all we know there could be a second spaceship," Smythe said.

"I don't think so," Gaines said. "I believe the sonic boom heard was the spaceship dropping below Mach 1. I have no proof, but I believe they landed somewhere in the mountains. When I spoke to the pilots, I arranged for them to fly in and do crisscross patterns over the area. I figure these men deserve to see this one through. Besides, they already know about the craft and the fewer people who know about this, the better off we are. I also placed a call to Professor Le Buc. I believe he'll be able to assist us. When he arrives, we're leaving with a team of twenty men. Rebecca will be with us, too. We'll rendezvous in Port Simpson. When we get a definite location, we'll fly into the mountains by helicopter and have a look. Just one thing. I'll need someone here to arrange the extraction."

"That's already in the works," Smythe said.

"Good," Admiral Brock replied. He scrutinized the moose head again then looked back to Smythe with raised eyebrows before turning his focus back to Gaines. "Keep us posted on your progress."

"Will do sir," Gaines said. Both men exited the room. Gaines restacked the photos. Before placing them in a box he became transfixed on the image. With a little luck he'd get to see the real thing up close before the day was done.

10

Pacific Ocean

The radar screen showed nothing.

The man stationed at the console adjusted the knobs, increasing and decreasing frequencies, but still nothing appeared on any of the screens. The officer next to him watched the monitors linked to satellite surveillance. Nothing appeared there either. The Senior Watch Officer stood over them trying to assist their efforts. Their targets were out there somewhere within range of their ship's radar. They just couldn't find them.

Takashi Tanaku, Captain of the aircraft carrier named Tsunami, paced the bridge, watching their frenzied movements from a few feet away, a wry grin on his face. He was a powerful man. The massive ship he commanded measured more than 1000 feet in length and displaced more than 95,000 tons of water as it plowed through the North Pacific Ocean. He oversaw the seventy-three aircraft on board, as well the ship's powerful built-in armaments. Also under his control was a tracking and detection system so technologically advanced it contained the newest phased array radar detecting equipment plus linkups with various satellites so it could see the enemy coming under any weather conditions. However, despite all that, the Ninjas had avoided detection. Their initial field test was proving to be a success.

"Locate them!" Tanaku barked in an angry tone. "The enemy is out there, and he is making you look like incompetent fools." He didn't expect them to succeed. He just wanted to push them harder the way an enemy's captain would push his men if the Ninjas were ever used in real combat.

The SWO grabbed the radio from his belt and spoke to the spotter on the upper mast. "Do you see them?" he asked. It was 1:00 a.m. The sky was near pitch black, the spotty cloud cover blotting out most of the starlight.

A curt "no" crackled through the radio.

"Keep searching," the SWO snarled again.

Captain Tanaku approached the radar operator and peered over his shoulder. They all knew it merely a test, but it was important they acted as if the threat was real. "You are an embarrassment," he screamed. Gaijin are hovering all around us and you detect nothing. You are useless. We will be destroyed in moments because you fail."

The panicked radar operator moved faster than before. The other two officers quickened their pace as well. The radar officer realigned the angle of the rotating antenna, hoping to achieve a solid bounce. Still unsuccessful, the SWO leaned over and altered the frequency to extremely low frequency radio waves hoping to bounce a signal off the water that would reflect back and give away the Ninjas' position. Nonetheless, the thin line continued to sweep around the display in silence.

Captain Tanaku turned his attention to the officer monitoring satellite transmissions. For purposes of this test, General Yamakazi had authorized a satellite containing a synthetic aperture radar system and infrared camera to detect heat emissions from missiles, aircraft, and vehicles, to hold a synchronous orbit over their position. The reflected radar waves were then quickly analyzed by the satellite's onboard equipment and relayed directly to the monitors on the console. The same held true for the images taken by the infrared camera.

"Officer?"

The officer remained calm and professional. "Negative, Captain. The radar I can understand, but the infrared scanners should be detecting something against the cold backdrop of the ocean."

"Hai," Tanaku acknowledged, the pleasure more apparent on his face despite the fact his crew was failing. The Ninjas were functioning to perfection. His ship housed the most advanced tracking systems available, and the Ninjas were evading them all.

"There. We got one, Captain!" the SWO yelled excitedly, pointing to the blip on the radar screen that just appeared. A second later, loud beeps pierced their ears, indicating the Ninja successfully locked its weapon systems on them. The test was over. The Ninjas had won. An instant later the satellite's radar relayed the Ninja's position to the other screen.

Captain Tanaku peered over to the overzealous SWO who bowed his head in defeat, and Tanaku settled. "Excellent. It went completely undetected until the moment it chose to strike."

"It was also able to hit us before the satellite even detected its presence," the officer said.

Another blip appeared on the radar screen indicating the second Ninja was on the opposite side of the ship. An instant later a second series of loud penetrating beeps echoed through the metal-walled bridge adding insult to injury. Both Ninjas had successfully completed their missions. The radar operator removed his headphones and slammed them down.

Tanaku briskly walked over to him. "Be silent! Childish outbursts will not be tolerated on my bridge."

The officer quickly bowed his head and apologized profusely.

Tanaku calmed. "I see you don't like to lose. Good. The test is over. Call the pilots in. I will personally congratulate them upon their arrival."

"Hai," the SWO said.

Captain Tanaku left the bridge and stepped down the stairs that led to the main deck, pondering what the Ninjas would mean to the Japanese military. Not much, he thought. The Ninjas will probably mean more to our economy. Our government will probably decide to mass produce them and sell them to our allies at a tidy profit. That was a good thing. Though he truly enjoyed emerging victorious in combat, war was not something he desired.

Tanaku reached the seven-inch steel door that led to the deck and opened it. The cold shrieking night wind bit him as he reached over to the hook on the wall and grabbed a coat. He put it on and trudged out onto the damp metal deck, making his way towards the helipad, holding his cap on so the wind wouldn't steal it, and watched as Shadow—the first Ninja prototype—quietly descended, its black, sleek design blending in with the dark.

First Officer Namato came running toward him, his green coat flapping in the wind. With one hand, he too held his cap. In the other, he cradled an envelope close to his chest. "Captain," he shouted above the roar of the ocean, "emergency action message."

Captain Tanaku took the envelope from his hand. He ripped open the flap and handed Namato back the sealed authentication code. He then reached inside his shirt pocket and pulled out a sheet of paper with many codes written on it, reading the correct one from the list. Namato unsealed his code and read it back to the captain. They matched. Captain Tanaku then double-checked Namato's authentication code verifying the orders were valid.

Tanaku silently read the orders. He did not understand why, but his mission's parameters had just drastically changed. Instead of simply field testing the Ninjas, these new orders instructed him to move his carrier into the North Pacific near Canadian waters and requested he prepare them for a real sortie into Canadian air space.

Whisper, the second stealth helicopter prototype, appeared out of nowhere above their heads. They watched it descend almost noiselessly onto the slippery deck. As it touched down next to Shadow, Tanaku wondered what mission he would be preparing them for, search and rescue or a sneak attack.

They were incredible machines. Their outer hulls were painted black for maximum camouflage at night. They were slanted in shape to deflect radar and built with a synthetic material embedded into the metal to absorb the radar waves they couldn't deflect. The material was also insulated to prevent the heat of the engines from radiating. This had the dual purpose of hiding it from heat seeking missiles and infrared scanners. The rotors were muffled to keep sound to a minimum. Its onboard weaponry consisted of short-range missiles and one front-mounted, fully mobile machine gun. During a nighttime sortie, they would be practically invisible, silent, undetectable, and extremely deadly.

Either way Tanaku wasn't pleased. Based on their coordinates, his new orders amounted to no less than readying his crew to invade Canada. He watched the pilots and gunners as they climbed out of the Ninjas. "They will have their work cut out for them," he said to Namato.

"I do not understand, sir."

Tanaku handed the orders to Namato. "This will explain everything. Prepare these men for level four battle drills. Meet me in my quarters in five minutes and we will discuss the rest."

11

The Kremlin

General Vaskev nodded as Vasha, his petite elderly secretary, stepped lightly into the room and handed him a one-page report from a field agent indicating the Canadian's best guess as to the location of the downed extraterrestrial spacecraft.

She left as quickly as she came. Like a mouse stealing cheese, Nikolai thought.

Vaskev fumbled for his reading glasses and placed them loosely in front of his eyes. He scanned the report. When he finished, he handed it to Nikolai, who read it with interest.

"That's it?" Nikolai said. "It is not enough information."

"Nyet. We must be patient. It will do us no good to run around like wild geese," Vaskev replied, placing his glasses back in his pocket. "Our sources are reliable. They will provide us everything we need, in time."

"We must have this space vessel. We must be able to study it—determine where it came from and how it got here. Think what we could do with that kind of technology," Nikolai said.

"Think of what our enemies could do with the technology if we don't get it," Vaskev said. "We must possess it or destroy it. It can be no other way."

"We must know exactly where it is," Nikolai insisted.

"Yes, we need to be ready to act swiftly once our agent discovers its exact location."

Nikolai paced, his patience waning. Time was of the essence and they still didn't have the information they craved. "We should not be forced to rely on our spies for something like this. What if they fail? Our military satellites should be searching the globe as we speak."

"Be patient, friend Nikolai." Vaskev walked over to the tea station and poured two more cups of hot water. In them he placed a sterling silver tea ball each containing one bag of tea. The leaves dissolved and oozed out of the pores turning the clear liquid dark. He handed Nikolai the cup, which stopped his pacing. "The answers we seek will come soon enough."

12

Palo Alto, California

Two sinewy men, both attired in dull neutral-colored suits, greeted Logan at his doorway. Based on their size, demeanor, and short haircuts, Logan immediately sized them up as military. As one man bent down to pick up Logan's suitcase, his jacket creased, revealing a shoulder-holstered revolver.

"This way, Mr. Grey," the man instructed, firmly but politely.

"Er... sure," Logan said.

One man tossed his suitcase into the trunk, the other opened the door for Logan. He slid inside the limo onto a comfortable leather seat. Inside were two more men; the driver and another similarly dressed man. A soundproof glass panel separated them. The initial two men joined Logan in the rear portion of the vehicle, and they sped off.

"Where are we going?" Logan asked.

"You'll know when we get there," replied the driver.

Logan leaned back in the cushioned seat and sighed. There was nothing he could do but go along for the ride.

A few minutes later, the driver peered into the rear-view mirror and nodded to one of the men. That man signaled the third man. The third man revealed a key then unlocked a compartment built into the side panel of the door and pulled out a briefcase.

"This is for your eyes only, Mr. Grey. Read it now. When you arrive, they'll expect you to be fully briefed on the scenario." He handed Logan the briefcase.

Logan placed it on his lap and opened it. Inside were a sealed envelope, a pen, and maps of the world and Canada. He read the report, bringing himself up to date on last night's events. At 2:37 a.m. Pacific Standard Time, an unidentified spacecraft entered Earth's atmosphere. Drawn on the map were the object's flight path, expected point of impact at Ellesmere, and where the object disappeared. It was the last line that interested and concerned him the most. Two words: "Whereabouts unknown".

Whereabouts unknown? Then what the hell do they need me for? I'm supposed to talk to them, not find them.

Logan grabbed the map and reread the report. He then drew a line between Ellesmere and the Coast Mountains. Almost two thousand miles apart but... Logan grabbed his cell phone.

The third man stopped him. "Sorry, sir. No outside contact. Our orders are to bring you straight to base."

"I need to verify some information that may directly relate to what's in this briefcase. I won't reveal anything."

The third man handed Logan a secure cellular phone. Logan took it and dialed.

"Seismic Stu—"

"Larry, it's me, Logan. One more question. That tremor that occurred last night, the one along the U.S. / Canadian border, what's the exact time that it occurred?"

"Hold on." After a brief pause, "2:50 a.m. Why?"

"Just curious... no real reason. Thanks again, bye." Logan disconnected the call. He grabbed the pen and, on the map, drew a huge circle around the Canadian Coast Mountains along the border. "Gotcha!"

13

Marine Corps Base Camp Pendleton, California

The conference room was small with concrete gray walls and a cement ceiling painted dull white. Bright lighting shone down on a brown oak conference table. Sprawled across the table, were three markers—red, blue, and green—and a polar map of the world with blue X's marking the important locations of the morning's extraordinary event. Of particular importance were the large X on Ellesmere Island and a second X over the Coast Mountains around Prince Rupert. Around the X, a red circle approximating a 100-mile radius was drawn with a question mark next to it.

Dr. Jeff Blaze stood at the end of the table. Having earned his doctorate in astrophysics from MIT—top of his class—he had landed at NASA, then moved over to the Jet Propulsion Laboratory in Pasadena before the government lured him to their top-secret military base at Groom Lake and ultimately here to Camp Pendleton, California on special assignment. He was addressing his two commanding officers, General Henry Chesterfield and Colonel John Chase.

"Okay, this is what we know." Blaze grabbed the green marker. "The vehicle originally descended at gravitational velocity. It changed course, slowed down, and was expected to impact here, when it disappeared." Blaze pointed to the first X. "Exactly 4.6 seconds later a sonic boom was reported here." Blaze pointed to the second X. "Assuming these two events are directly related—and I'm sure we all agree that they are—this puts the average velocity of the vehicle at..." Blaze did the calculations on his Texas Instruments TI-66 while holding the marker between his fingers like a cigarette. "450 miles per second—that's 162,000 miles per hour. Very nice. I'd also say—given that they dropped down below Mach 1—they achieved an even higher velocity during those few seconds."

Blaze peered up to ensure that he had not lost his audience. "Now, accounting for the decelerated velocity the craft should have landed along this line." Blaze drew a curved line between the X's then continued the line a little further to the west. "Depending on the altitude of the craft at the time of the boom, it should be somewhere along this line. The higher the altitude, the further away from the boom the craft is likely to be."

Colonel Chase jumped in. "According to the radar, the craft disappeared at about twenty thousand feet. Could you close in on the location with that information?"

"Unfortunately, no. We still have a couple of variables that we could never be sure about. The first is the angle of descent when the craft slowed to the speed of sound. Was it in a steep nosedive, therefore landing here—" Blaze pointed to a location along the line close to the X, "—or was it fairly level, therefore landing here?" Blaze pointed to a location along the line further away from the X. "Also, up until this point we've assumed the vehicle flew straight. That is highly unlikely. It's more likely the vehicle flew in a curved pattern." Blaze drew an arc between the

X's. "This increases the possible area of impact sites." He scribbled a zigzag line over the circle.

"What's the bottom-line gentlemen?" Chesterfield asked, in a gruff voice. "I'm not committing six men and millions of dollars in military assets for nothing. What if this thing didn't crash at all?"

"That's doubtful, sir," Chase replied.

Blaze backed him up. "Yes, it wouldn't make sense for a vehicle accelerating away from earth to suddenly slow down, announce its presence with a boom, and then speed away again."

Chesterfield glared doubtfully at Chase.

"Listen, Jeff. What's your best estimate on where this ship landed?" Chase asked.

"You're the pilot. You tell me," Blaze responded, not to irritate Chase, but to lead him into thinking like a pilot.

"If I piloted this craft..." Chase paused. "The initial descent into our atmosphere showed the pilot lost control of the craft. A ship with these capabilities should have incredible mobility, so obviously something went wrong. Either pilot error or a system malfunction. Where the ship slowed down and changed course, I'd say they started to regain control, slowing their fall using an orbital swing to buy themselves time to correct whatever malfunction occurred. But they fail. The pilot knows he's about to impact, so he takes a chance and throttles it, trying to head back out into space as fast as possible to avoid a crash."

Chesterfield interrupted. "That's probably why the ship disappeared off the radar screens. It was moving too fast for us to track it."

"Yes, but they crashed anyway. Just not where they or we expected them to," Chase said.

"If you were piloting that craft, what kind of escape route would you have executed?" Chesterfield asked.

Chase pondered it. "A sudden jerk upward might be too much for the ship or the crew to handle—although I don't see how they can withstand the G force to begin with—so he'd accelerate slightly downward and then curve upward, rising at a fairly level angle towards outer space." Chase used his finger to trace the path on the map. "Unfortunately, they lose all velocity and they're forced into a crash landing. But we heard a sonic boom. That means they had enough control to slow the ship down before the crash."

"Or the ship's safety protocols kicked in," Blaze said. "Sorry to interrupt."

Chase nodded and continued. "Otherwise, we would have only heard the impact when it hit and that hit would have been catastrophic. When the craft decelerated below Mach 1, they were here..." his finger crossed the X, "which means they must've landed in the mountains below, right around here." Chase firmly pressed his finger onto the map.

The mood changed, along with their prospective search area. What seemed as unlikely as locating a needle in a haystack had just become possible.

Blaze drew a circle where Chase's finger had been. He smiled. "Now we know where to begin."

"Good," Chesterfield said, abruptly breaking the mood. "Place a call to the men in Alaska. Arrange a meeting place near the Pearse Canal. Tell them I've given authorization for three Seals, security clearance five or higher. Program the satellites for a sweep of the area. Call the car and have them reroute that kinesics guy to meet us at the airfield. The three of you will fly together and you

can brief him on the way. Arrange for anything you need
to find this thing. I'll make sure a pilot is ready and waiting
for you."

"Yes sir." Chase said. He called the number connecting
him to the car en route.

14

The man next to Logan removed the phone from his jacket, flipped down the receiver with a flick of his wrist, and answered. "Yes, sir."

"This is Colonel John Chase, authorization code Alpha Bravo Tango. Reroute the passenger to airbase Gamma. We'll meet with him there."

Overhearing a Colonel was on the line, Logan frantically signaled the man to pass him the phone, mouthing the word important.

The man nodded. "Sir, Mr. Grey would like to speak with you. He insists it's important." The man handed Logan the phone.

"Colonel—" Logan started.

"Mr. Grey. I'll be straight with you," Chase interrupted. You're looped in on this against my judgment. I'm not a fan of including civilians in on top secret operations. This had better be important."

"Understood," Logan replied. "With that risk in mind, I think I know where the alien ship landed."

There was an uneasy pause on the line.

"I'm waiting, Mr. Grey. Counting the seconds," Chase replied.

"Er... sorry sir. I believe the spaceship landed in the Coast Mountains. Somewhere around the U.S. Canadian border." Logan quickly ran his fingers across the circle he drew on the map. "Between 54- and 56-degrees longitude and 130 degrees latitude."

Another pause followed.

"I'm putting you on speakerphone," Chase said. "General Chesterfield and Physicist Jeff Blaze are with me in my office. Could you please repeat that?".

"Sure. Um... I think the alien spaceship crashed somewhere in the Canadian Coast Mountains. Somewhere near the border between longitude 54 and 56 and latitude 130." Logan stumbled like a rookie ball player trying to maintain his dignity among a crowd of seasoned veterans.

"How did you come to that conclusion?" Chase asked.

"I have a friend who works seismology down at Berkeley. When you called me, I called him. Don't worry, I didn't reveal why. Anyway, he told me the times and locations of all the unusual seismic activity in the last two days which I just matched up against the time the spaceship disappeared from radar, or at least the time you indicated in this report."

Chesterfield's voice came faintly over the speaker. "For the past two hours we've used approximately two billion taxpayer dollars' worth of the best surveillance, tracking, and recon equipment available, including a combined 126 man-hours with the most highly trained men money can buy, and this guy gets the same results with a phone call. No wonder we've got a Democrat in the White House."

"We'll keep that theory in mind, Mr. Grey," Chase said then hung up abruptly, without definitively letting Logan know if he was right or wrong.

15

"Daddy, make my blankie into a magic carpet. Pleeeease," the cute young girl begged in the sweetest voice she could muster. Her brown eyes widened and blinked at her father as she quickly sat up. "Pleeeease," she begged again while curling her bottom lip just so, creating the most irresistible pout she could.

Her father never stood a chance. The rugged handsome man smiled back, his face beaming with pride at his beautiful little daughter. "All right, sweetheart, but only once. Then it's time for bed... lights out," he insisted.

"Okay, okay," she said excitedly, scooting beneath the covers.

Her father grabbed the ruffled end of the thick wool blanket and deftly flicked his wrists, lifting it into the air, until the blanket took on the shape of a parachute and gently glided down upon her.

"Wheeeee hee hee," she giggled.

"Goodnight sweetheart," he whispered as he kissed her gently on the forehead.

"Wait, wait... Don't forget Mr. Cuddles and Rufus," she said, referring to her two favorite stuffed animals.

Mr. Cuddles was a soft white polar bear that she loved to hug. He got it from the wooden toy box with clowns pasted all over it. Rufus was a huge, fluffy Irish Setter, easily as big as the child. He grabbed him off the rocking chair it shared with Raggedy Ann and Barbie. He gave her

Mr. Cuddles and placed Rufus at the edge of her bed to keep her safe—just the way she liked it.

"Goodnight, Daddy," she said, smiling broadly.

He smiled back then left the room, turning out the lights and closing the door behind him. The only illumination remaining was from a Daisy Duck night light plugged into an outlet on the side of her bed.

"Shh," she whispered, raising a finger to her mouth, motioning for Mr. Cuddles to stay quiet. She waited until her father's footsteps faded down the hallway then reached into her night table's top drawer and pulled out a flashlight. Crawling out of bed, she tiptoed over to her doll house and brought back three plates, three cups, and a tea kettle. All miniaturized and made from plastic, the toys were painted bright pink, her favorite color. She tented her blanket and brought everything under the covers, placing Mr. Cuddles and Rufus opposite from her.

"It's time for our nightly tea party. A plate for you Mr. Cuddles... you too Rufus, and a plate for me. A cup for you, and for you, and one for me. Now, who would like to have some tea? You look thirsty, Rufus." She held the toy kettle and poured Rufus a pretend cup of tea.

The flashlight went out.

She pulled the covers off and tried to turn it on again. It didn't work. She shook it, listening to the batteries rattle back and forth. Again and again, she flicked the switch, but it stubbornly wouldn't turn back on.

A fearful chill crept up her spine. The room was darker than usual, darker now than it had ever been before.

"Daddy," she whispered, hoping her father would hear her, without accidentally waking up Mommy. "Daddy," she cried, a little louder this time, but still, she received no answer. She shook, no longer caring if she woke everyone up. "Mommy," she yelled.

But no one answered.

The house shook, slowly at first then the vibrations increased in intensity and volume. The little girl realized the reason her room was so dark was because her Daisy Duck light was out. She had never been in the dark without Daisy before and that terrified her.

"Daddy... Daddy," she shouted. Still, no one answered. She ripped off her blanket, jumped out of bed, and ran for the bedroom door as an eerie violet light penetrated the room. In the afterglow, the door seemed much further away. She tried running faster, but her body wouldn't obey her wishes and the bedroom door drifted further away. She turned around, searching desperately for Rufus. Surely, he would protect her. But the bed and all the things on it had vanished, replaced by three hideous silhouettes that walked menacingly towards her. She couldn't see them clearly, yet she knew without doubt they were monsters.

She screamed at the top of her lungs as the monsters closed in. Somehow, she reached the door, grabbed the knob, and pulled it hard. It wouldn't open, no matter how hard she pulled. The monster's eerie presence loomed behind her. Their slimy hands grabbed her leg and pulled her towards them. Clawed, long, clammy fingers menacingly caressed her cheeks.

She closed her eyes tight, wishing them away, only to feel the warmth of their rancid breath waft across her nostrils, the nauseating smell sickening her. She instinctively pawed at the cold, wiry arms that held her, desperate to escape their horrific grasp, failing as the creatures overpowered her. She opened her eyes, finding herself staring directly into soulless, vacant eyes. Her next scream rubbed her throat raw.

She awoke gasping for air. Stacy Michaels sat up, her body dripping with sweat, her chest in uncontrollable heaves, her heart pounding like a bass drum. This was the most intensely terrifying nightmare she'd had in years.

In the morning, she would call Dr. Miller.

16

Coast Mountains

The grizzly lumbered forward, his heavy paws trampling the early morning dew. His weight shifted from side to side as his massive steps caused the leaves to rumble in his wake.

It was late last evening when the crashing extraterrestrial spacecraft rocked his territory in these woods. The thundering sonic boom jolted the giant beast awake and the successive sounds of trees snapping as easily as twigs, followed by an impact that shook the ground with vibrations of intensity and frequency the bear had never felt before, brought him swiftly to his feet. Then, when the nauseating stench of charred earth and burning air trickled across his wet snout, his survival instinct kicked in and the grizzly fled his territory for higher ground.

Now it was morning, and after a fitful, restless sleep on new uncomfortable ground, all the grizzly desired was to return home. As he neared his territory, he grew disturbed by the unfamiliar scents that brought back the fleeting, unpleasant memories of the night before. He stirred violently, becoming more agitated as he heard movement in the trees above him. Something he had never seen before dropped down from the branches about fifty yards in front of him.

Sensing the threat, he hoisted his 500-pound, furry, brown frame onto his hind legs and let out a roar. His incredibly muscular shoulders arched, and he extended his long-curved claws prepared to attack. But this did not deter the unknown creature as it did with so many of the lesser animals that lived here. Instead, to the bear's unpleasant surprise, the thing moved slowly, curiously toward him. The grizzly propelled his heavy body toward it at thirty miles per hour. This unknown intruder invaded his territory and needed to die.

His attacks were mighty and swift, but the agile opponent evaded each one. A dark, webbed hand slapped down hard across his nose, stunning him. The grizzly refused to back down. This was his home. He had marked it, and he would defend it. The grizzly attacked again, swiping with his strong front legs. The thing leapt over the bear and slashed his back with a metal blade, before landing gracefully behind him.

The grizzly rose on his hind legs, rotated around, and roared with fiery anger and maddening pain. The thing didn't move. It just stared at the grizzly, gazing upon him with dark, soulless eyes.

Wounded and fighting a losing battle, the bear's instincts told him to flee. But he found the thing's scent so disagreeable, so unpalatable, so threatening, he could not and would not tolerate its presence in his territory. Growling loudly, he lunged forward at it. Then a beam of blue light ripped through the grizzly with such destructive force that it instantly halted his charge. A strange, final sensation, beyond pain, gripped the bear as its entrails exited wildly from its body, splattering the forest behind and with a sickening splash his massive lifeless body collapsed to the ground.

17

Skies Above the Coast Mountains

"How are you holding up, Hound?" Lynx asked through the radio microphone strapped to his chin.

"It's not the same, buddy. We've got to get ourselves back into the Hornets soon," Hound replied.

The two pilots were referring to the jet fighters they normally flew. Today, however, they were flying Blackhawk helicopters. They didn't have the speed or power to match the F-18's, but this was a search and locate mission. The Hornets were great in combat, but to find a stationary object hidden in the dense greenery of the mountains below them, a helicopter was far more practical, and both Lynx and Hound had previously logged some hours in them. Plus, the copters were also equipped with defensive measures in the unlikely event they might prove necessary.

Lynx scouted the forest below through the thick curved front glass windshield. Everything in the mountain range appeared normal—unending rows of green, sprinkled with wood and snow. "To see what we're going to see, I'd be happy flying a washing machine with wings on it. Anything yet?" Lynx asked.

Hound was two miles west. "Not yet. You're the lynx-eyed one. How about you?"

Claude Devereaux had earned the codename Lynx because, like the big cat, he was known for his sharp vision.

"Nothing. I'm going to make a high pass over the southeast region. I'll contact you again in ten minutes. Lynx out."

Lynx turned the metal bird and increased his altitude by 500 feet. Ever since this morning when he first glimpsed the UFO, he wished to know exactly what it looked like. He also wished he would get a chance to fly it. For now, though, he would settle for one out of two. He took a moment to view the landscape. The scenery was spectacular. The mountain tops, hidden in snow, rose into the clouds. The ground was covered with bright green trees as far as the eyes could see; only now turning brown with the season. Claude always laughed at that because it reminded him of his niece, who, when she saw them, always said they looked like little broccoli florets. However, there was one notable flaw. Just over the third ridge to the north, a "scar" marred the tree line. "Hound, do you copy?"

"Yeah, Lynx. You got something?"

"Sure, do pal. Just over the third ridge. I'm going in to take a closer look. Meet me here as soon as you can."

Lynx flew closer, noting at the higher end of the line, toward the east, the tops of the trees were sheared off, and to the west the trees became shorter, creating a wooden slide into a valley. It was clear the UFO came from the east and crash landed there. He flew high, hovering over the west end of the line to get a bird's eye view of the craft. A large group of trees were collapsed inwards making it difficult to see what was underneath.

"Hound. How far away are you?" Lynx asked.

"At least another minute. Any problems?"

"Well, I located the object. The landing path's easy enough to see, but it's thick down there. I can't get a good enough view. There's no place to land either. The closest clearing I can spot is at least a half mile away."

"Can you see the ship?" Hound asked.

"Not really. The trees are blocking most of it. I'm going to drop lower... see if I can get a better look." Lynx eased the helicopter down.

"Be there in a minute. Just—," bzzzzzzt "—careful—" squaaark squarrk squeeee.

The intense radio static wasn't Lynx's only problem. His dashboard lights flickered on and off and he had to tighten his grip just to keep control of the copter.

"Lynx? Getting some interference here buddy. What's going on? Lynx. LY... squeee... Damn. Hold tight, buddy. I'm com—"

"No rush. I'm fine," Lynx said. "That was intense. All my systems suddenly went whack. I had to increase my altitude. Whatever's down there must be emitting some kind of E-M field."

"Let's play it safe and get back to base. Our mission's accomplished. I'm sure they'd love to hear what we found."

"Copy that, Hound," Lynx said. He pulled back on the throttle, lifting the Blackhawk further in the air, and turned in the direction of the base. He disappointedly scanned the crash site and whispered to himself, "I'll see you another time, my friend. Another time."

18

The refitted C-11 transport plane shook under the constant battering of turbulent cross winds on its way to Alaska. Inside its metal hull, two of the three passengers, Dr. Jeff Blaze and Logan Grey, sat in uncomfortable plastic seats that faced each other across a wide aisle. The third passenger, Colonel John Chase, stood up front leaning against the bulkhead, doing his best to ignore the rough ride.

Blaze studied both his companions. No two men could be more opposite, he thought. Blaze knew the many nicknames Chase acquired over his career, most of them unflattering, but the one that stood out in his mind right now was "Nails." Chase was certainly tough, as the cliché goes. In his mid-forties, Chase was in better shape than most men half his age. His square head, covered by a short blond spiky crewcut, sat sturdily atop his thick neck. His nose was crooked. Clearly, it had been broken at least once. Two scars marked his face, one above his left eye, the other on his chiseled chin. When he stood at attention, his lean hard body rigid, he looked like a nail. Blaze knew he could be as stubborn and narrow-minded as one as well.

Logan was a different animal. He had the polished look of a successful yuppie. He was a handsome young man— early thirties, Blaze guessed. He was also in good shape, but unlike Chase who was whipped into shape by the army, Blaze was sure Logan belonged to one of those thousand dollar a year health clubs with the fancy weight machines, treadmill, and saunas. Just the kind of man that Chase liked to chew up and spit out, and it was obvious he disliked Logan already.

"What's the plan? Or did you gentlemen decide to keep me in suspense?" Logan asked.

Blaze glanced at Chase and got a nod of approval. "We're on our way to Alaska to meet up with a SEAL team. From there we're going to head into the mountains and see what we find."

"So, I was right?" Logan said, edging up in his seat.

"Huh?" Blaze said.

"You know, about where it crashed," Logan said.

Blaze chuckled. He unbuckled his seat belt, walked across the plane and sat down next to Logan. "Yeah... really pissed off the general too. That was quick thinking."

"Yes, yes it was," Chase said.

Blaze raised an eyebrow. It was a rare admission on Chase's part, indicating that at least for the moment he was willing to cut Logan some slack.

"Thank you, Colonel..." Logan stumbled, not knowing the man's name.

"Colonel John Chase." He extended his hand and Logan shook it firmly. "This is Dr. Jeff Blaze, our resident physics expert. Welcome aboard Mr. Grey."

"Logan's fine, sir." He exchanged a handshake with Blaze as well. "So, this is the real deal, huh... real aliens, real spaceships?"

"Only one, spaceship that is," Blaze answered, raising one finger. "Who knows how many aliens?"

"Hmmm," Logan murmured.

"Now that we know the general proximity, our spy satellites should be able to pinpoint its exact location,"

Blaze said. "They should have an answer for us by the time we arrive."

"What if it's on Canadian soil?" Logan asked.

"We'll let our diplomats and politicians handle the fallout," Chase said. "We find it, examine it, and if possible—," he stared directly at Blaze, "—extract it."

"What if there are alien survivors?" Logan asked

"That's what you're here for," Chase replied. "I'm going up front—see if the spy guys came up with anything yet." Chase glanced at Blaze with an "I told you so" expression of disapproval then walked to the back of the plane.

Blaze stared at Logan. "You almost had his acceptance."

"Next time I'll keep my dumb questions to myself. I've read up a lot on these things, mostly the scientific stuff, some of the psychobabble. What's your take?"

Blaze grinned ear to ear. He loved talking about science but rarely had an interested audience. "I gather you're familiar with Drake's equation?"

Logan shrugged. "Somewhat."

"Well, it's a framework for how someone might estimate how many space-faring civilizations might be out there. Drake figured logically that the answer to that question depended on how you view the variables. The variables being how many stars are out there? How many of these stars have planets? How many planets do these stars have? How many of these planets are capable of supporting life? What percentage of that life will be intelligent enough to reach the stars? And what's the life span of these species?"

It took Logan a few seconds to digest all that information.

Blaze saw the confusion in his eyes and slowed down. "The first three I believe are fairly simple. In our galaxy we have about a trillion stars. I'd say probably a billion have planets. On average, five planets apiece give us five billion planets. I'd estimate at least twenty percent are capable of supporting life. That's one billion planets that might have life just in our galaxy."

"That's quite an abundance. If that's true, how come we haven't found any yet?" Logan asked.

Jeff smiled coyly, reminding Logan of the mission he was currently on. "You see, the hard part of the equation is the final variables. Just because a planet can support life, doesn't mean life will exist or that intelligent life will evolve. And even when it does, it still might be incapable of reaching the stars. For example, take dolphins. They're clearly intelligent, but they'll never travel through space. Then there's the big question. How long can a technologically advanced civilization survive? How long can a civilization with the power to control the vast energies needed to travel through space, survive without managing to blow itself up? Perhaps it takes five billion years to evolve a species that's smart enough, but only a hundred years to completely self-destruct. Look at us. We live on the brink of nuclear holocaust every day."

"That's a scary thought," Logan said. "So how do you answer those final variables?"

"We can't. So, we guess. In order for a civilization to reach the technologically advanced stage where they're capable of interstellar travel, they need resources, particularly metals. Assuming their technology is founded on electricity and magnetism, their planet would need metals to build advanced machines."

"Like a spaceship," Logan said.

"Or a computer, or a light bulb, or any other simple gadget we take for granted in the twenty-first century. So, we search for stars that are rich with metal elements."

Logan nodded, acknowledging he understood.

Blaze continued. He enjoyed having a student who was both interested and a quick learner. "Now, let's take a step back. Our galaxy, the Milky Way, was born around fifteen billion years ago. Back then it was just an immense cloud of hydrogen and helium gases. These gases formed the first generation of stars which contained only hydrogen and helium. During the life of these stars, the hydrogen burns up through a process called fusion. When the star gets to a certain temperature, the hydrogen combines with the helium, burning off energy and creating heavier elements like carbon and oxygen. Then the star uses these elements as fuel, creating even heavier elements and releasing more energy. Stars are like giant ovens in the sky cooking up the ingredients of life.

"When these stars finally cooked up the element iron, they began to die because iron absorbs energy instead of releasing it, so these stars eventually ran out of fuel to burn. Some of them exploded into a supernova, which created even heavier elements, the metals, and spread these elements outward across space. These elements eventually formed into new stars. These are what we call second generation stars. They underwent the same process as first-generation stars, but because of their more complex makeup, they created even heavier elements. And when these stars went supernova, they spread even more complex elements across space. That's where we come in. Our sun is a third-generation star giving our solar system the elements we have in our periodic table, which includes plenty of metals.

Consequently, everything on our planet, including ourselves, is made up of these elements. Are you following me so far?"

"Yeah, the further we go away from the center of the galaxy, the more likely we'll find planets that contain metals," Logan said.

"Correct. Now, the stars at the galactic core couldn't possibly produce life because they were just hydrogen and helium. Besides, our studies show there's probably a huge black hole consuming the core of our galaxy, so life wouldn't survive there anyway. The second-generation stars could have supported life, but as intelligent as that life may have been, I doubt they would have had the materials necessary for interstellar travel. Remember, these star systems would not have contained all the elements, particularly the metals that we have on earth. Perhaps, they would have been able to build primitive tools, but not the more sophisticated machines like we have now."

"But it's still possible? I mean these second-generation life forms would be so much older than us that they might have advanced beyond needing metals," Logan countered.

"Yes, perhaps their technology was founded on bio-organic materials, but it's much less likely. Which leaves us to search the third-generation stars. These stars have all the necessary elements for life to flourish and reach out to other stars. So, our best bet for finding life in our galaxy is to look in our own neighborhood, because all the stars as distant as we are from the center of the galaxy are third generation stars. This makes our search a little easier.

"The final thing a civilization needs is time... time to evolve to the point where they are intellectually capable of utilizing these resources. It took us five billion years to get where we are. So, it stands to reason that the older a star system is, the higher the probability it will contain intelligent life. We look for stars in our neighborhood that are around five billion years old."

"Assuming, of course, that other life evolved approximately at the same rate as our own," Logan said.

"Yes,"

"So, we need to search neighboring stars that are around five billion years old that probably have planets capable of supporting life," Logan summarized.

"You got it. Let's take the closest stars and see which ones fit the criteria."

"Alpha Centauri, that's the closest. Only four point three light years away, right?" Logan said.

"That's the second closest. Proxima Centauri's closer, but that star's doubtful. It's too cool, and it's a flare star. I doubt any planets there would have proper living conditions, what us scientists call a habitable zone. Now Alpha Centauri's a different story. Alpha Centauri's a binary star. That means the system is made up of two different stars. One of them, Alpha Centauri A, is just like our sun—several billion years old with a large habitable zone for planets to support life. I'd say that's a pretty strong possibility."

"You think these aliens come from Alpha Centauri?" Logan asked.

Blaze raised his hand, telling Logan he was getting too far ahead of himself. "A strong possibility, however, they're not our only close neighbors. About six light years away is Barnard's Star. It's much cooler than our sun, so its habitable zone is much smaller. To support life, it must have a planet very close to it."

"Like Mercury," Logan said.

"Exactly. But while we've found over 300 extrasolar planets in our galaxy, we're still not sure if Barnard's Star has any."

"Any others?"

"Lalande 21185. That one's like Barnard's Star, and we've found two Jupiter-sized planets there, so far. I'd call it a possibility too."

"How many possibilities are there?"

"Other than those three, I'd say Epsilon Eridani and Tau Ceti round out the top five, but there are plenty of others," Blaze said.

"So how do they get here? Even flying at the speed of light it would take them at least four years."

Blaze smiled again. Logan just brought up another one of his favorite topics. "That's what I hope to find out. I do have some theories though. You sure you want to hear them?"

The plane continued to jostle them. "Do we have anything better to do?" Logan asked.

Blaze didn't hesitate. "Magnetic propulsion. Somehow their ships can ride along the electromagnetic radiation in space to take them close to the speed of light. Perhaps they create a low frequency electromagnetic wave that pulls the ship behind it like a carrier wave. I'm not sure, but they found a way to tap into the electromagnetic forces surrounding us all. When this spaceship disappeared off our radar screens, it did so without a sound. Not even a peep. It was just gone."

"So?" Logan shrugged.

"Well, air is a medium. Just like fish live in a sea of water, we live in a sea of air. We may not see it, but it's there. When an object moves through the air, the air molecules get pushed aside to make room for the object. Just like fish and water can't occupy the same space at the same time. When an object accelerates past the speed of sound, it expands the air around it. But the air can only disperse at its natural rate, which is the speed of sound, so it builds up into a wall, called a shock front, which creates a sonic boom. I've studied the UFO phenomena for years, and I've never heard of any of these spaceships making a sonic boom.

"The only way I can think of to avoid the sonic boom, is to part the air before you accelerate through it. A magnetic field surrounding the ship will do just that, parting the air an instant before the ship contacts it. The ship will then be able to ease through the air without creating a sonic boom. It's the difference between a fat guy executing a cannonball off a ten-foot diving board into a pool and an Olympic diver. The fat guy makes a huge tidal wave in all directions landing with a splat. The Olympic diver slips into the water with barely a splash or a sound."

"But you said this ship did make a sonic boom," Logan said.

"Only before it crashed, which indicates its magnetic field failed, which is probably why it crashed." Blaze explained.

"Well, whatever propulsion system they use, that's still four or more years traveling in space."

"To us and the Alpha Centaurians—if there are any— yes. Remember Einstein's famous formula $E = mc$ squared. Energy equals mass times the speed of light squared. This can be translated another way to calculate how much energy it would take to accelerate a mass to the speed of light. Basically, the closer you get to the speed of light, the amount of energy required expands exponentially. So only something without mass can reach the speed of light. Hence, according to Einstein, the speed of light is nature's speed limit. Nothing can surpass it. It would appear that the vast interstellar distances would preclude space travel, because even at the speed of light it would still take years to arrive at a destination, if time was absolute.

"But Einstein taught us that time is not absolute. He proved the closer one travels to the speed of light the more time slows down. So, to the space travelers only a few weeks might pass, whereas four years passed on Earth. If you got in a spaceship and flew to Alpha Centauri and back at the speed of light, you might age only two years while Earth and all your friends would be eight years older. One of my theories is that these space travelers spend their entire lives exploring the cosmos and signal back their findings to their home world. They're probably some sort of subculture within their species because they age at a much slower rate than the rest of their people."

"That's just one theory?" Logan chuckled.

"Yeah. My next one's a little more complex. Einstein also taught us that space is curved. The gravitational attraction of a star is so great that it curves the space around it. The light we see from distant stars is also affected by the pull of gravity and also curves. What we perceive to be flat actually isn't. Did you ever fly to Europe?"

"Lots of times."

"Did you ever pay attention to your flight pattern?"

"Not really," Logan said, shaking his head.

"If you look at a flat map and plot the shortest distance between, say New York and Paris, you would think that the fastest way to travel would be straight across the Atlantic Ocean. But in fact, the plane flies north along the Eastern coast of Canada and flies in south over Ireland. This is because the shortest distance between two points on a globe is a curve. To see this, just put a string on a globe between any two points and pull it. That will give you the shortest distance, called a geodesic."

"Okay."

"Now let's say we built a new transportation system to take us through the earth. The geodesic would no longer be the shortest distance between the two points. The shortest distance would once again be a straight line. I believe the aliens discovered some way to cut through space. We know nothing can travel faster than light, but if they found a faster route to reach Earth, perhaps they could get here quicker. Perhaps it takes light years to travel the route created by gravitational forces, but maybe they can get here in months by creating a shortcut through the fabric of space."

"That's a little farfetched, isn't it? I mean, how can you cut through space? It's not even tangible. It's just... well, it's just space."

"Over 500 years ago, everyone thought the earth was flat. It seemed flat, but it's round. We thought the universe was stable, but in fact it's expanding every day. We thought time was absolute. Now we know time varies. With each discovery, our perceptions of the universe change. What science knows today would seem like magic to our ancestors. What science will learn tomorrow surely would seem like science fiction to us today.

"We know for a fact that space is curved. It's measurable, and it's been proven. Shouldn't something be on the other side? The black holes that exist in space, stars that collapse in on themselves creating a mass so dense, a gravitational field so strong, that nothing, not even light, can escape from. Where does all that light go? How could so much matter be contained in a point in space? Maybe, just maybe, these black holes are literally holes in space. One-way holes because you can never come out the way you get in, but holes nonetheless. On the other side of the hole might be a region where time doesn't exist due to the powerful gravitational field. Perhaps, these aliens use these regions to travel vast distances in little time. Hopefully, we'll have some of the answers after this expedition."

"Yeah. Hopefully."

Chase emerged from the rear compartment and interrupted their conversation. "Good news, bad news. Our satellites located an anomaly in the Coast Mountains. That's our ship. Unfortunately, they also picked up Canadian military action in the area. We must move quickly or we won't be the first ones there. We'll be rendezvousing with the Alpha Contact Team shortly. From there we move in." Chase walked back to the cockpit.

"It's kind of hard for you to believe this is really happening, huh?" Blaze said to Logan.

"What's hard to believe? I'm on a mission to contact aliens with Captain Kirk. You must be Spock. Me... I must be the unknown ensign who gets beamed down to the planet, destined to die before the next commercial break."

"It's even better than that," Blaze said. "You're really Lt. Uhura."

19

Despite the turbulence and the small size of the airplane, Professor Pierre Le Buc was more comfortable than if he had been on a commercial jet. The soft leather seats were spacious with an abundance of leg room. All the creature comforts of first class, and supersonic speed to boot, he thought. It was good to see how the Canadian brass spared no expense when it came to traveling in luxury. Glancing out the window, hardly able to see the ground thirty thousand feet below him, he wondered what strings Gaines must've pulled to get this aircraft.

He observed the other passengers. Twenty soldiers, two pilots, a stewardess, an unknown woman, and Major Gaines were on board. The stewardess supplied everyone with beverages, except for alcohol, and was very pleasant in manner and form. Enough so to keep the soldiers' thoughts occupied with something other than their upcoming mission, most likely the reason for her assignment.

He studied the soldiers. Overall, they were an impressive group with none of the usual signs of nervousness. No lip biting. Only one nail biter. No quick foot tapping. Three men had I-pods and appeared very relaxed, although one of them twiddled his thumbs in such a way it indicated to Le Buc he was tenser than he was willing to let on. Another group towards the front of the aircraft were huddled together talking about something. The noise level of the supersonic transport prohibited him from overhearing their conversation, but he noticed from their mannerisms, and the way their posture and verbosity changed around the presence of the stewardess, that they were busy discussing the more machismo topics of the day. A few rows closer to him a soldier was immersed in a copy of an X-Men comic book and was about to be rudely interrupted by the soldier in the seat in front of him. This conversation he was able to overhear.

"You readin' bout that chump, Wolverine. Man... he's nothin'. Gambit's where it's at," the soldier Prestone said, as he snatched the comic book out of Dupres' hands.

Dupres stood up quickly. "Nothing? He's a born and bred Canadian. He'd slice and dice Gambit's pretty boy butt anytime."

"No way, homme. Gambit's too slick, too fast. No way that hairy little runt can lay a claw on him. Besides, Gambit's got style and the moves—gets all the chicks."

"Gimme that." He grabbed back his magazine. "What you grinnin' at?" Dupres asked a third soldier next to him.

"You two don't know what you're talking about. We all know Cyclops is the man." The third soldier, Carter, said it like it was fact.

"Cyclops? Cyke sucks," Prestone said.

"Yeah," Dupres said. "Shooting beams out of your eyes is lame, man."

Carter stood up next to them. "That may be true, but every night he comes back to the mansion and gets to bang the White Queen. Awooooh!" His howl attracted some of the other soldiers' attention. "There ain't no better superpower than that." The three men broke out in laughter and exchanged numerous high fives and low twos.

Le Buc got up and made his way to Major Gaines, who had been staring quietly out the window until the three soldiers' antics caught his attention.

"Don't worry. They'll do their jobs," Gaines said.

Le Buc sat down next to him. "Au contraire, mon ami. To tell the truth, I'm impressed. Seems to me like your team is prepared, cohesive, and experienced. But the lack of conversation pertaining to our immediate mission... they don't know all the intriguing details, do they, David?"

Gaines grinned. "For now, it's a standard rescue and recovery mission of a highly sensitive nature. I figured I'd wait until we heard from the advance team before I filled them in on the more interesting aspects. If Lynx and Hound find nothing, it's better these men don't know."

"What's her role in all this?" Le Buc motioned towards the attractive woman who was heading in their direction.

Gaines slapped Le Buc's knee softly. "That, my good friend, is Rebecca, my top intelligence officer and protégé."

"Ahh." Le Buc had spoken with her on the phone numerous times before when he communicated with the Major, but at 30,000 feet he did not make the connection. "It's nice to finally put a face to the voice."

"I thought you of all people would have put that one together," Gaines said.

"She's not what I expected."

"Older?"

"No. A brunette—somehow I was expecting a brunette." Rebecca was blonde. "She knows."

"What makes you say that?" Gaines asked.

"She exudes confidence—solid poise, perfect posture, very professional. Around so many, excuse the phrase, crude gentlemen, most women would appear less at ease."

"She's much more capable than most women," Gaines said.

"Yes, but it's more than that. Every once in a while she lets slip a slight smile. Not the usual friendly-type smile, but a slight rise on the left side of her lip. Enough to cause a dimple to show for a split second. It's like she knows a secret that no one else can be let in on."

"You don't miss much, do you?" Gaines said. "Yeah, she knows. She's our lifeline. She'll communicate our status to Smythe. If anything goes wrong, we tell her, and she'll call for backup."

"Wouldn't satellite transmission be more efficient?"

"Yeah, it would."

"Ahh... pest control needed again, Major. Who's eavesdropping this time? The Americans... the French... our friends from above, perhaps," Le Buc said, with a rise in his left eyebrow. Pierre enjoyed poking fun at the trivialities of the spy game.

Gaines shook his head. "No. Sorry to disappoint you. Nothing that interesting—just the Russians. A problem we haven't solved yet."

Rebecca approached. She seemed a little rough around the edges but there was a captivating vibrancy in her bright blue eyes, Le Buc thought.

"Professor, I would like to introduce you to Rebecca."

"Pierre, to you my dear."

"A pleasure to finally meet you. David talks about you all the time," Rebecca said.

"Oh, he does now, does he? Well, unfortunately for me, he's been keeping you quite the secret," Le Buc replied.

Rebecca smiled. "You are just as charming in person as you are on the phone." Then her demeanor changed from pleasure to business. "This just downloaded through the fax. It's from the Admiral. The hunt is over. Lynx and Hound found the ship."

20

The Kremlin

Vaskev grabbed the thin strand attached to the silvery ball that released the tea leaves and gently pulled it twice, adding more flavor to his fourth cup of tea. "So, Nikolai, you never did tell me the full story of Kabul Four."

Vaskev was not referring to the city in Afghanistan, but rather a military outpost stationed a hundred miles north and a mission from during the Russian-Afghanistan war. It was rumored then the rebels obtained drums of Tabun, a deadly biochemical weapon, and stored it there. Almost odorless, Tabun was notoriously difficult to detect until it made lethal contact with the skin. Intelligence reported the rebels were planning to release the gas across an undisclosed Russian city, taking as many lives as possible.

KGB Intelligence also reported the rebels wouldn't hesitate to use it throughout Kabul if they had nothing left to lose. Of course, this made the Russian generals extremely hesitant. What good would it be to conquer Afghanistan if it would be destroyed in the process? They chose Nikolai to neutralize this situation. It was his first mission.

Nikolai impatiently paced the room, his large footprints wearing on the General's antique Persian rug, stopping only momentarily to sip his tea. He lowered the cup from his pursed lips to answer. "Ah, comrade, I thought you knew everything."

"Da. The popularized version is well known. War hero destroys Afghanistan chemical weapons depot. Saves thousands of Russian lives. Shows the people why we must take Afghanistan to protect the mother country." Vaskev leaned forward in his chair, furrowed his brow, his piercing eyes locking with Nikolai's. "So, Nikolai, tell me what really happened at Kabul Four."

The expression of frustration left Nikolai's face. He gazed back at Vaskev as if his battle-weary eyes could see right through him. "That was a very long time ago," Nikolai answered. His face took on a somber tone as he recalled the grievous loss he suffered that day. "Kabul Four stood vulnerable in the middle of their desert. A conceit because they knew we would not risk an air strike for fear of accidentally releasing the toxic agent, and its position made it extremely secure against a ground attack. The only way in was across 500 yards of open ground protected by a small army of Afghan rebels, six guard towers with mounted machine guns, and an electrical fence. Plus, a secondary force manned the roof of the compound, armed with anti-air rocket launchers. And, of course, the possibility that if cornered they would just release the gas and kill us all."

"But you did succeed," Vaskev replied.

"Da. The simulations showed we had three minutes from the time they'd see us coming until they would release the Tabun. We had to hit them hard and fast, without using the firepower needed for such a surgical strike. Our only choice was deception, execution, and luck. My squad—Ground Team One—would charge across the desert from the mountains in the northeast. Air Team One would provide our diversion, firing their missiles fifty yards south at nothing but sand. I doubted the deception and the cover of night would get us close enough, so I arranged a second air team to eliminate all the guard towers without hitting the base. No easy feat. Air Team Two, using helicopters, would fly in beneath their radar and carry out that task."

Nikolai gazed over at Vaskev to see if the old man was paying attention. After all he was sure Vaskev knew all the details. "We struck at precisely 3:00 a.m. I had twelve good men behind me. When Air Team One's first missile exploded to the south, we used the distraction and charged in from the north. We counted on the blinding lights of the explosions to ruin their night vision. It worked long enough for us to make it about halfway. Then all of hell broke loose.

"Air Team Two was late. I found out later their lead pilot was afraid to admit he was not in the proper position when I radioed for readiness. Thousands of lives were at stake and this idiot was more afraid of losing his job than the consequences if we failed. There we were, without proper cover, weighed down in bulky containment suits and gas masks in a gun battle against rebels who had no such restrictions and were eager and willing to die for their cause.

"My men fought well. We took down most of the rebels and the fence. One of my men even managed to take down a tower with a grenade launcher before he was struck down. Then a rebel in another tower began shooting at everyone in sight. Our soldiers, their soldiers—it did not matter, like fish in a barrel. One bullet grazed my arm, ripping open my containment suit. Seven of my men were killed.

"Then Air Team Two finally arrived. They landed two missiles at the east edge of the depot, destroying half of the building, and sprayed the area with machine gun fire. They must've taken down at least thirty rebels along with the perimeter fences and four of the towers before a man on the roof shot him down. The shock wave gave the remaining tower guard pause. When he stuck his head up to survey the damage, I had a clean shot and picked him off.

"Though I was sure our mission was a complete failure. I was sure the destructive force of the missiles had released the deadly chemicals, and even if they hadn't, we only had a minute left to make sure the rebels didn't. I removed my mask—at this point it did not matter—and charged the base. Two others followed me in. Mikhail blew the door open with plastique. He was the first one in and met by a machete wielding maniac that nearly took his arm clean off. Boris and I shot the man down immediately, but we couldn't spare the time to make so much as a tourniquet for Mikhail. We knew if we didn't find the Tabun immediately, it would not matter. We worked our way down through their base to where intelligence told us the drums were stored. Fire and smoke were everywhere. Bullets flew down every corridor.

"When the shooting stopped, I was the only man left. Boris lay beside me in a pool of his own blood. I checked my watch. Three minutes had already passed. I charged forward towards their storeroom, but the lack of time made me too impatient. I found myself staring down the rifle barrel of a wounded Afghan rebel. I'll never forget the anger in his eyes. Now I would be the one to face his wrath. But better to die quickly from a bullet in battle than to be eaten from within by poison gas.

"The soldier was about to pull the trigger when his head exploded. Mikhail, who we left for dead, had followed us.

He shot down the soldier, pulling the trigger with his left hand. Saved my life. The two of us made a dash for the Tabun. You know what we found there, don't you, General?"

"Da." Vaskev nodded.

"It was all a bluff. The rebels couldn't obtain the real thing, so they faked it. For almost a year we fought tentatively, the fear of chemical destruction gnawing in the back of our minds, while they were aggressive, fighting with everything they had. Our parliament could not even let the people know of our humiliation—"

They were interrupted by a knock on the door.

"Come in, Vasha," Vaskev shouted.

Vasha entered the room. "This envelope just arrived for you. I believe it's what you've been waiting for." She handed him a sealed manila envelope.

"Spaseeba."

After Vasha left the room, Vaskev opened the envelope and read the message. Then he passed it over to Nikolai. "Our agent has done well."

Nikolai read the note and smiled. The waiting was over. His mission was about to begin. "I always wanted to visit the Coast Mountains of Canada." Nikolai said. "I hear they are quite beautiful this time of year."

"Da," replied General Vaskev. They lifted their cups, clinked them together, and took their last sips of tea.

21

Prince Rupert, Canada

Stacy Michaels stood tentatively at the door to the office of her psychiatrist. Perhaps she had overreacted. It was only one bad night. Her hand shook nervously as she raised it to knock, her mind spiraling between doubts and denial.

The door flung open, startling her. A gasp of air burst from her lungs. She couldn't deny it. Even the sudden unexpected movement of the door had caused her panic.

"Good morning, Stacy. Come on in," Dr. Brad Miller said. He was pushing fifty and looked every bit of it. His salt and pepper hair topped his aging face. Large bags drooped under his blue eyes. A sloppy beard hid his plump chin. His rawhide belt held up his tan slacks and flabby paunch.

She rushed in and he closed the office door behind her. "I wish I could say it was good to see you again. They're back," she blurted out. "It's happening to me all over again and I don't know why." Her eyes watered as she sat on his comfortable old couch. Soon she tasted her salty tears on her lips.

"Why don't you tell me what happened. Take a deep breath and start from the beginning."

"Last night... last night I was relaxing on my deck—I still have a little trouble sleeping so I relax outside with a glass of wine. I was staring at the sky thinking about the plot to my next book when 'boom'—everything was shattered."

"What do you mean... boom?" Dr. Miller asked, as he sat in the chair across from her.

"That was it. I was staring into space and suddenly the sky exploded. But it wasn't thunder. The sky just went boom. After that, everything started again. I was so scared I ran inside and locked all the doors—including the one to my bedroom. When I finally fell asleep, hours later, my nightmares began all over again—more intense than they've been in years."

"Ah, yes. The sonic boom... I didn't hear it myself, but it did make the news this morning. You weren't alone. It spooked a lot of people. The news said it was a military aircraft from a local base—nothing to be concerned about."

"Military jet..." Stacy felt foolish. It took a long moment for her mind to wrap itself around that simple explanation. She sighed, relieved yet still shaken she had fallen back so easily. "The monsters came back?"

"The same monsters or new ones?" Miller asked.

"The same. The shark men with gray skin and black eyes. I was a child again, playing with my stuffed animals when they came for me."

As they talked for a while, Stacy rumbled through all the possible explanations they had bounced through for the last five years: Post-Traumatic Stress Disorder from a repressed memory or possible child abuse, or even the movie "Jaws", yet none of those rung true. But something had clearly traumatized her.

"Does knowing it was just a jet make you feel better?" Miller asked.

Stacy thought for a moment. "Yes, but..."

"I'll tell you what. I could just write you another prescription for more Xanax, but we've done that many times already and we still haven't gotten anywhere. If we're going to make these irrational fears go away, we need to get to the root cause, and that's where your case has me stumped. The only thing left I can think of to do is regressive hypnosis therapy. This means we'll hypnotize you into reliving your past. It's not guaranteed, but I'm out of other ideas and I'm not a big fan of continually prescribing drugs. Are you up for this?"

"Will it make my nightmares go away?" she asked, hesitantly.

"It's a possibility, but better than nothing."

"Sure, why not. What have I got to lose?" Stacy's tears subsided with the illusion of a possible cure.

"Good. My morning's relatively free. If you're up for it, I'm pretty sure I can set something up for 11:00. Let's meet back here in two hours and maybe we can avoid another harrowing night."

22

Russia

Nikolai strode up the steel steps and boarded the Cogskovsky, a supersonic aircraft capable of reaching speeds up to Mach 3. He felt invigorated, his muscles relaxed, his limbs spry. This was a good assignment. He would be able to serve his country and get to glimpse extraterrestrial technology that man had only dreamt of, but some other life form made a reality.

With luck, there would be no bloodshed. His plan to snatch it out of Canadian hands revolved around trickery and stealth. Spy craft the old-fashioned way. That would be good, he thought. The wasteful killing became tiresome and aged a man well past his years.

His only regret was that, once again, he left behind his son, Mikhail, whom he named after the man who saved his life, and his beautiful wife, Katrina. He would miss them. He wondered if they would miss him as well. One day he would have to keep that promise he made to his wife years ago and retire.

He took his seat and strapped himself into the contoured chair. Moments later the plane jostled about as it taxied on the runway. Then, like a silver streak, it sped off, lifting forcibly into the skies. He leaned his head to the side to catch some shut eye, knowing that he'd best rest while he had the chance. In Alaska, there was plenty to prepare, many paths he could take, each dependent on how the situation was playing out when he got there. Improvisation would be the word of the day. He would finalize the details in his mind when he arrived, and to do that, he needed a well-rested mind and body. The one thing that was certain to him was that he would succeed. He always had. And with that thought, he fell asleep.

23

Russia

Nikolai's wife Katrina stared out the foggy apartment window. She would not miss the view of the brick wall of the tenement next door. Nor the uncomfortable couch. Nor the aging kitchen. Nor the old-style decor, the neighbors, or the neighborhood. She had had enough. It was time to go. Everything she needed—false documents, a few changes of clothes, toothbrush, a few cosmetics, and copies of top-secret documents—were packed in a carryall she slung effortlessly over her shoulder.

As for her son, Mikhail, other arrangements were made for his departure. Where she was going, it was best that he was not along for the ride. For now, he was safe, and if she survived, she would be able to get him later.

As she walked towards the door, she scanned the walls focusing on a spot where the wallpaper separated and curled; glad she would never see it again, yet nostalgically remembering how happy she was when she first moved in. Unfortunately, that was a long time ago. *Why Nikolai? Why?* But this was the way it had to be.

Her mind drifted back. She fondly recalled falling in love with Nikolai the first time she saw his handsome face proudly displayed on the front page of *Pravda*. The victorious hero who stood for everything good and noble about Russia. A strong leader who fought not for glory, but for the love of his countrymen. He was her dream come true. She remembered the article, written just one week after his return from his mission to Kabul Four, and had it stored safely away between the plastic pages of a scrapbook she took with her.

The memories flooded to the surface. How several nights later she had met him in person at a victory party hosted by distinguished members of the Politburo. How her well-connected brother managed an invitation and how she continuously begged until he agreed to take her along. How upon arrival, she quickly made her way towards Nikolai, as she was determined to do, and made the most of the opportunity. It was as if they had known each other forever, becoming close almost immediately. They shared the same beliefs and stood up for the same causes. Within a year they were man and wife.

But that was many years ago. For years she stood by him as he served the state then felt bitterly betrayed when the state no longer served them. They fought more and more. She would argue it was time to take care of themselves. He was adamant that his country must come first. She would say it's time to face the present. Nikolai was caught up in the ideals of the past. He was strong and stubborn. It was the reason she fell in love with him, and it was the reason she now felt very alone.

Her mind was made up. She could no longer remain Nikolai's wife under these conditions. It was time to take her life into her own hands, for better or for worse.

Wrapping a scarf over her face, she exited the small apartment for the final time. Closing the door behind her, she jogged down the rickety stairs and out of the building. On the next block, she ran down cracked concrete steps, deciding to take the subway. She could have taken the car, but she wanted to be inconspicuous, and traveling by the most used public transportation system in the world—eight million riders daily—was the best way to go.

She got off at the station after Gorky Park, nudging her way through the crowd, and eventually made her way up into the street. She hesitated, scanning the surrounding buildings to regain her bearings. Then she walked three blocks south, where she knew she would find a man named Piotr Kelstov. A man who, one way or another, would get her in to see Volikoff.

She had never met "Dapper" Pete before, but his reputation was well known in the neighborhood. This was where and when he was known to hang out. All she had to do now was stake out the area and wait for the first person who fit his description—handsome young man, stocky build, hair slicked back, always impeccably dressed in a suit that cost more than the typical Russian earned in a month. More importantly though, she looked for the attitude—the one that showed no fear, the one so smug because his association with Volikoff allowed him free reign over the neighborhood.

She didn't wait long. A man fitting that profile stood across the street, leaning against a vehicle she was sure wasn't his. She approached him slowly and stared him straight in the eye. "I need to speak with Volikoff," she said bluntly.

Dapper Pete sized her up. Clearly, he didn't see her as threat. "Mr. Volikoff is not available. Perhaps I can be of service. Name's Piotr." The arrogance oozed off him like toxic sludge.

"I doubt that. I seek a man. Not a frightened little cub who stands tall only by terrorizing his own brethren too frightened to fight back because of the cub's protector."

Pete reached out and grabbed her by the throat. "Perhaps, I'll show you what kind of man I am," he said, angrily, his perfectly white teeth gritted.

In a swift, almost invisible motion, she grabbed his wrist with her left hand and twisted it inward and upward, nearly breaking the bone. A split second later, she lifted her right knee hard into his testicles. With a sharp moan, his eyes glazed, and he doubled over onto the sidewalk, curled up like a baby. She reached into his jacket and removed his small .22 caliber pistol. Then she removed his hands from his groin and replaced them with the barrel of the gun.

"Dapper Pete, huh," she said, this man becoming the focal point for all her pent-up rage. She pulled his head up by the hair and stared directly into his tearing eyes. "Unless you would like to be known as Dickless Pete, please, tell me where I can find Volikoff."

He tilted his head toward an apartment building down the street. Two men, probably armed, stood on the porch. Her actions had drawn their attention.

"You may be of service after all." She grabbed Pete by his hair, pulling him up off the concrete. Standing behind him, she forced his head back with a tight grip on his oily hair and placed the gun at the back of his neck. "I think you can be my bodyguard. One misstep though and you're fired."

They plodded forward, Pete as her shield. The two men on the porch drew their weapons—Makarov PM's—and steadied them in her direction. Their "all-business" demeanor never changed as she closed in.

"I wish to see Volikoff," Katrina said. "I have information for him that will prove extremely profitable. May we dispense with the unpleasantries and get down to business?"

The man on the left nodded and lowered his gun. "If business unwanted we will kill you afterward."

Katrina dropped Pete in the street and holstered her gun. The men holstered theirs and brought her inside and led her to an apartment on the third floor.

From the outside it was nothing special—just an ordinary apartment in an ordinary building. On the inside, it was quite the opposite. The walls separating it from the neighboring apartments were taken down giving Volikoff one huge apartment that took up half the floor. It was five times the size of what Katrina called home.

The apartment had a twelve-foot marble dining room table atop an elegantly designed, old-world Persian rug. Above that was a dazzling crystal chandelier. To the sides were two brass stands with 18th century busts resting comfortably atop them. Artwork adorned the walls. Katrina noticed the Monet's and the Picasso and one she thought was a Da Vinci and quickly estimated their value at over 200 million.

They led her to the den, where the decor unexpectedly traveled two centuries ahead. Volikoff was relaxing on a leather sofa watching ESPN on a 62" High-Definition Sony TV. Beneath it was an SVD player—the successor to the DVD—and six small multi-phase VII speakers. One bodyguard sat with him, the other watched from across the room. Katrina felt as if she had just passed through a time portal.

He gave Katrina a quick glance and then went back to watching his program, dismissing her as if she were insignificant. It was a gesture intended to show disrespect to any outsider. Then he glanced again. "Forgive me. This is a surprise. To what do I owe the unexpected pleasure of your company, Mrs. Rasputin?"

"You know her?" one of the two men who led her up asked.

"And you don't? No. Why should you? Please forgive my employees, Madam. This new generation has little use for our history," Volikoff said. He stood up to face her.

"I wish to speak with you alone," Katrina said.

Volikoff gave his silent approval.

"I wouldn't recommend that, sir. She's dangerous... took down Piotr right on the street."

Volikoff became angry. "Do you have such little respect for me that you believe I cannot handle myself alone with a lady? Go, now, before I mistake your concern for an insult," he commanded with a stern voice. They left and closed the door behind them. "Now, what can I do for you?"

"I understand you have contacts within the Japanese government to whom you broker classified information."

"I would sell nothing to them. They are an enemy to our people," Volikoff said, dismissing the accusation with a wave of his hand. "I granted you an audience because of my respect for your husband's accomplishments. Do not insult me by calling me a traitor."

"Spare me the patriot routine. It's unbecoming of you. My husband is not the only one who has friends in the Politburo. They are as corrupt as they are greedy—and they led me to you. The Japanese pay a great deal of money for good information. Money you would take in an instant to feed your comfortable way of life."

Volikoff's features softened. "Your friends, I would imagine, are probably well paid to look the other way," he said. "Provided, of course, that the information can cause no real harm to our country."

"Of course," she replied.

"Suppose I did know of some people who knew some other people who were less patriotic than I. Why would that interest one such as you?"

"Because I have information which will prove very valuable to them, and I wish to sell it to you."

"Forgive me, but I find that hard to believe. Surely a woman of your stature would have contacts of her own."

"That's true, but you can obtain a much higher price," Katrina said. The chatter from the TV was annoying her. She nonchalantly reached for the remote and turned it off.

"I see. Why should I believe this is not an elaborate scheme to set me up?" he asked, taking the remote from her hand.

"I'm sorry, perhaps you misunderstood me. I'm not interested in selling the information directly to the Japanese. I'm selling it to you. You can choose to make whatever arrangements you deem necessary without me."

"How much?"

"650-million-yen wire transferred directly into this bank account." She handed him a piece of paper supplying the name of the Swiss bank and the account information.

"That's too much."

"They'll pay you three times that—maybe more. This information is only useful for a short time. You pay me now. I'll give you the information coded. When I'm certain that my money is safe, I'll phone you the decoding sequence."

"How do I know this information is as good as you claim?"

"I am the wife of Nikolai Rasputin. There is not one thing my husband does that I am not aware of. You will have to trust my word."

Volikoff weighed his options. "I could lose approximately seven million American dollars."

"You could gain thrice that."

He stared hard at her. "You have a deal," he said.

He lifted the phone and arranged the monetary transfer from one of his many bank accounts to her bank in Switzerland. When he hung up, she handed him the coded information. It contained sets of coordinates, mapping an area within a thirty-mile radius located in the Coast Mountains, and a message revealing what could be found there. It was copied from her husband's mission file when he briefly stopped at home to pack and say good-bye.

"It appears that we are not so different after all. Da Svedanya."

***

The note of disdain on her face as she left told Volikoff that he had indeed made the correct decision. Twenty minutes later the transfer was verified and Volikoff received the decoding sequence. It did not mean anything to him, but he knew his Japanese associates would understand, and that was all that mattered. He didn't need to know the information to understand its worth. He arranged for an immediate meeting and within the hour he was twenty million American dollars wealthier than he had been this morning.

***

An hour after that, the information made its way via the Masuka clan into the anxious hands of General Sato

Yamakazi, ending his hours of frustration searching in all the wrong places. Sato would make sure when all was said and done, the "right" corporations would receive the "appropriate" contracts. But that was tomorrow's work.

Sato quickly ordered the new coordinates to be programmed into the spy satellite. He studied the map at his desk and smiled brightly at his unbelievable luck. The spaceship's location in the Coast Mountains was ideal for him to plan a strike. Close to the Pacific Ocean, he could order the Ninjas in and out with a minimal amount of risk.

He immediately called Musamato in and issued new orders. When Musamato left, he slumped back into his chair. His momentary uncharacteristic weakness in posture alerted him to how tired he was. It was getting late. He decided he would go home, get some rest, and return later when the operation was ready to proceed. He picked up his phone and called for his car. Making his way to the door, he eyed the portrait of General Sakiguso that hung on his wall, smiled mischievously then turned out the lights. Tomorrow would be a glorious day.

24

Major Gaines anxiously scanned the report. Both the existence and location of the spacecraft had been confirmed. It was time to alert his troops to the true nature of the mission. He walked to the front of the plane, his gait and demeanor enough to capture everyone's attention. When the aircraft grew silent, he made his speech.

"Men, due to the intelligence report I have just received, I can now reveal to you the full purpose of our mission. I apologize in advance for keeping these facts from you prior to your assignment, but the necessity of confidentiality prevented me from revealing them to you sooner. Once you hear my briefing, I'm sure you'll all understand." He proceeded to fill them in on the incredible details. When the stunned comments silenced, he continued.

"Our goal is to secure all evidence intact for research purposes. This includes all biological, chemical, and technological findings. We'll be landing shortly and splitting up into four teams. Two helicopters will then transport us to the nearest clear areas which surround the crash site. From there we proceed on foot. As an additional precaution, we will all be wearing class three containment suits. The extraterrestrials may have unintentionally brought with them biological agents which are dangerous to mankind. We don't believe this to be the case, but contaminants are a possibility, so for now we'll err on the side of caution.

"We have no idea what type of craft we will find. We don't know if any beings survived the crash, or if so, what their condition or intentions might be. Extreme caution must be exercised at all times. If it becomes necessary, we must be prepared to defend ourselves, but do not—I repeat—do not fire upon anything unless you are positive it is life threatening. We are about to explore the unknown and that can be a fearsome thing. Do not let that fear rule you. I chose you for this mission for a number of reasons. In particular, the fact that all your psychological profiles indicated you were open to the possibility that alien life exists and they are most likely not interested in taking over this planet."

That comment drew a slight chuckle from the men, exactly the response Gaines sought. "Today, you will each have the privilege to be part of a larger team that will experience what and who these aliens are. What we learn today will benefit the future of all Canadians. We must make the most of this opportunity."

The remainder of the briefing was short, with only a few questions. Gaines was satisfied that the men understood the full significance of what they were about to face. He wanted them prepared, yet at ease, and that seemed to be the case.

Moments later the plane landed on a remote plateau high in the mountains, approximately ten miles from the crash site. Major Gaines, Rebecca, Professor Pierre Le Buc, and the crew of soldiers disembarked, off-loading with them boxes of equipment and weapons. On the far side of the plateau were two helicopters. The plane they came in on sped down a makeshift runway and flew off. Within a few minutes they would board the helicopters, fly into the mountains, and begin their final pursuit.

25

Chief Petty Officer Namato ran to Captain Tanaku's side, bowed slightly, and handed him new orders. After confirming their authenticity, Namato bowed again before leaving Tanaku alone in his quarters.

Tanaku read them slowly then reread every word just to make sure he fully understood. It was one thing to be informed his ship was going into conflict. But to be told they would be going to battle over a crashed extraterrestrial space craft... that, to say the least, was unsettling. He sat on his bed and absorbed these new orders.

His mission was to recover a downed extraterrestrial spaceship. He was to retrieve what he could and destroy what he could not—even if the Americans and the Canadians got in his way. He set aside the extraordinary aspects. As phenomenal as they were, it was still secondary to invading Canada. He grew uneasy, though his face still displayed a facade of calm. He knew this mission could not be accomplished without conflict and loss of lives on both sides. Though returning home successfully with such a valuable prize would gain him that much more respect and honor, it wasn't worth the price that would be paid in human lives.

He left his quarters and walked out onto the upper deck of his aircraft carrier, further pondering his mission while admiring the view. He wondered what the politicians thought. *Did they even care about the consequences of their actions? Were they tiring again of not having enough land and depending upon others for resources? Hadn't they learned from previous wars?* No, he decided. The orders had probably been issued for both economic and political reasons. A new technology in their control would bring vast profits and power to Japan. They had that to gain and nothing to lose. If their mission failed and the lives of gaijin were lost, an apology would be issued and that would be that. There would be no bad press because it was in every country's best interest to keep this quiet. The only losses, if any, would be sustained by him and his men. Nevertheless, despite his personal objections, he would begin to prepare his crew once daylight broke.

At nightfall they would strike.

CONTACT

26

All in all, they were an intimidating sight, Gaines thought. Twenty armed men each equipped with semi-automatic weapons, each uniformed neck to toe in a bulky blue environmental containment suit that made their appearance even scarier. Their square shaped heads remained uncovered, reminding Gaines of his college football team before they donned their helmets to take the field. He scanned their faces, noting each one displayed a veneer of raw strength and professional toughness. Their eyes were steeled with pure determination. If they had any fear of the unknown, it was well displaced by discipline and courage. He was proud to lead them.

The first eleven men charged forward, boarding the nearer of the two waiting helicopters. He shouted some last-minute instructions to team leaders three and four as the pilot lifted the chopper into the air, on its way to the two drop zones that were NNE and NNW of the spacecraft. The remaining nine soldiers followed suit, their booted feet shifting from soft ground to pounding steel as they climbed aboard the second helicopter like a finely oiled machine. Professor Le Buc and Major Gaines took up the rear.

"Are you ready, Professor?" Gaines asked.

"I wish you would stop calling me that. Makes me feel antiquated," Le Buc said.

"Where's your firearm?" Gaines asked, after eyeing Le Buc up and down.

"Oh, come now. Surely you've realized I would never carry one."

"I want you armed. It could get dangerous."

"Nonsense. You know my opinion on this too."

"Look, we both believe the same thing," Gaines said, "but if we're wrong, I'd prefer to err on the side of caution."

"If we do find intelligent alien life in these woods, I can guarantee you they'll most certainly be more civilized than we are."

"Then carry one to protect yourself from the unintelligent earthly wildlife that exist in these woods. Bears can be very unpredictable."

"You'll have to do better than that."

"How about doing it to make me happy? We have a timetable to keep and I'm not going to let you on that chopper without a side-arm."

"For you..." Le Buc sighed. "Very well."

Gaines handed him a firearm and showed him the safety and the switch between single round and automatic. "Fine. Now get on." He placed one hand on Le Buc's shoulder, the other on his back, and helped his old friend aboard.

The pilot started the engine, and the whirl of the rotor kicked up the dirt and snow surrounding them. Before boarding, Gaines jogged to Rebecca.

"The advance team reported radio transmission trouble in the region. I'll confirm contact with you when we're in go position. If you don't hear from me on time, you know what to do."

"I know the drill," Rebecca replied.

"You're our lifeline."

"You can count on me."

"I know," Gaines said, with a quick smile. He ran back beneath the rotors, took a deep whiff of diesel exhaust—a ritual that psychologically prepared him for combat—and boarded the helicopter. He glanced at Rebecca as she signaled the pilot to go. One day, he thought, I'm going to have to do something about her. Years ago, when Gaines asked her why she chose the hectic life of the military over settling down, she confided in him she was infertile, and since she could never have the family she wanted, she chose to make the most of her career. At first, this fact made Gaines shy away. He always thought one day he would want children, so why become romantically involved if it couldn't last, especially with a co-worker. But the more he got to know her, the more it didn't matter.

The helicopter lifted with a shudder, on its way to the first of its two drop points. Gaines would lead Team One from the SSE. Rodgers, the tall bulky man seated across from him, would lead Team Two from the SSW. Gaines gazed over the rest of the men. Most everyone stared straight ahead as the whirl of the blades carried them over the tree line. A few minutes of thoughtful silence followed.

"Phoenix," Carter blurted out unexpectedly, making his voice heard above the background noise. "She's the best."

"Huh?" screamed Prestone.

"Ya know, Phoenix of the X-Men. Beautiful redhead. Knockout bod. Cool head in a tough situation. That's the kind of woman for me," Carter yelled.

"She's not bad but give me Storm any day of the week. Better bod and she's a leader. I like my women to take charge."

"Damn," another soldier called out. "Don't you guys ever fantasize about real chicks?"

Major Gaines had to chuckle. "Enough comic book talk, gentlemen. This is it. We're at the first drop zone."

They placed their blue helmets over their heads, sealed them tight, and double checked their weapons. Major Gaines, Prof. Le Buc, and four other soldiers got up. Rodgers slid the door back for them, holding it fast in the buffeting winds, and Team One jumped out, landed on the ground three feet below, and fanned out smoothly away from the helicopter and into formation. The copter door slid closed, and it took off.

Gaines grabbed his radio. "Rebecca, can you read me?"

"Affirmative," Rebecca replied.

"We are in position, ready to go."

27

As the helicopter regained flight altitude, Rodgers, leader of Team Two, eyed his unit. They had no idea what they were walking into and that thought scared them. However, as they all looked toward each other, they all knew they could count on each other one hundred percent. Whatever they would face, they would face it together, the whole unit being greater than the sum of their individual parts. Soon, they leapt from the metal bird fully confident they would succeed.

On the ground, Rodgers un-holstered his radio. "Rodgers to Gaines. Do you read me?"

"Gaines here. No problems with the transmission. Reading you loud and clear, over."

"Team Two in position. Ready for go," Rodgers reported.

"Team Three, do you copy?" Gaines asked.

"Barely, Major. Lots of static. Team Three in position. Ready for go," Rankem, leader of Team Three, said.

Rodgers heard him perfectly over his two-way but apparently Major Gaines did not.

"Come again, Team Three," Gaines said.

"Team Three in position. We're good for go," Rankem repeated.

Rodgers got back online. "Team One, this is Team Two. I can read both of you fine but we're having trouble cutting across the zone. Relaying, Team Three is in position. Good for go. Looks like we'll have to relay our messages through adjacent squads as whatever's in the middle is interfering."

Simply put, Team One could only reach Team Two and Team Four and his team could only communicate with One and Three.

"Team Four, is a go," Gaines said. "Begin approach."

Rodgers, relayed the message to Team Three then signaled his unit—Carter, Dupres, Prestone, and Vangrell—to move in.

The five men spread out sideways to cover maximum ground and headed towards the ship, on full alert with every step they took. Prestone was the point man in the middle. He sprinted ten yards ahead and crouched behind a boulder. Their uphill route made them more susceptible to an attack, so they were extra cautious, just the way Rodgers wanted them to be.

Prestone peered up above the stone, scanning the forest ahead for any signs. Wind kicked the snow on the ground into swirls. A few birds, slow to head south in the cold weather, chirped from above. Prestone flashed a hand sign to Rodgers. Rodgers checked his Geiger counter. The radiation in the area was at normal levels. Rodgers flashed a thumbs-up then pointed his finger, indicating to move on.

Each man took cover approximately twenty yards ahead, scanning all angles as they charged forward. Once halted, Prestone and Rodgers repeated their routine. When the all-clear sign was given, they quickly made their way to another cover point.

Dupres flashed five fingers, then three, indicating to Rodgers they reached a radius of 800 meters, their designated check in distance.

"Team One in position. All clear," Major Gaines' voice exclaimed through the radio.

Rodgers spoke. "Team Two in position. All clear."

"Team Three in position. All clear," radioed Rankem.

Rodgers heard the message and passed it on then only heard the garbled static of Team Four's reply. The interference was getting worse.

"Team One to Anchor. Do you still read?" Gaines's voice asked.

"Still—" bzzt bzzzzzt skkt "—ust bare—," bzzzt. Rodgers barely heard the reply, but enough so he knew that all four teams were good.

"Go," Gaines gave the order.

"Go." Rodgers repeated the reply for Team Three then signaled his team to move on.

Prestone continued as point man, remaining about thirty yards ahead of his group. Team Two continued their stop-and-go routine until Dupres signaled five. They were halfway there.

Dupres looked spooked. Something was amiss. He motioned and Rodgers went to his position. "Ya hear that?" Dupres asked.

Rodgers listened carefully for a moment. "Birds. So?"

"Loud birds. Lots of movement," Dupres said, nervously.

"A nest?" Rodgers guessed.

"Nah, activity like that. I think they're feedin' on the dead," Dupres said.

"The birds are alive. That means no deadly contagion or radiation. So, let's not get too ahead of ourselves, huh?" Rodgers placed a reassuring hand on Dupres' shoulder.

"Team One—" skt "—sition. All clear." Gaines' voice shot through the radio far less clear than before.

"Team Two in position," Rodgers replied. He glanced at Dupres before continuing. Dupres shrugged. "All clear," Rodgers added, deciding not to burden Gaines with speculation.

"Team Three in pos—" skt "—clear."

Rodgers heard nothing but static from Team Four.

"Team One to Anchor." skt skt... heard Rodgers, not completely understanding the reply.

"Team One out—" skt "—ten-minute intervals. Go," commanded Gaines.

"Team Three—ten-minute intervals. Go," relayed Rodgers.

He knew from this point on they would be too far into the interference zone so for the next ten minutes, each team was on its own. Rodgers signaled his team onward.

They slipped through the dense, snow-covered forest a cohesive unit heading cautiously toward the birds. The chirps grew in volume. Every sound identified itself as he drew closer—leaves rustling, wings frantically flapping, birds cawing at one another.

Something was happening. Dupres signaled Rodgers. He wanted the team to stay a few steps back. He would take point.

28

Dupres crouched behind a tree hoping to get visual confirmation. A blackbird swooped above the tree line, but the spot of the forest it flew from was filled with trees that obscured his view.

He stepped to his right. *Movement.* He crouched behind another tree and aimed his weapon toward the swaying leaf-covered branch. His finger tensed on the trigger. His left eye focused through the magni-scope waiting for the target to reveal itself.

Suddenly, the leaves burst apart, a small gray blur zipping through them. The squirrel leapt off the branch, landed softly on the ground below, and scurried about.

"Damn," Dupres whispered, with a sigh of relief.

Then he looked again, noticing something odd about the squirrel's shape. He zoomed the rifle's scope onto it. Something was hanging out of its mouth. He magnified the image, feeling his last meal begin to regurgitate when he finally realized what it was. The little rodent was nibbling on an eye. He signaled to the others to form a tighter formation then hurried forward to discover what he already suspected was true. At least a dozen ravens and rodents were scavenging the remains of a carcass which was hideously scattered across the landscape.

"Sacre Bleu," Dupres whispered to himself.

Rodgers and the others approached from different angles, all forced to step over various dead animal parts along the way. Their expressions varied from disgust to fear. The fact that the enviro-suits spared them from the stench of death was of little consolation.

Rodgers bent down to examine the corpse. "This is… was a grizzly."

"Man, what the fuck can do that to a grizzly?" Prestone asked, tapping his right foot nervously.

"Poor sonuva bitch was blown away," Dupres said. "We ain't got nothin' that could do this."

"Fuckin' Predator, man. We're up against a fuckin' Predator," Prestone mumbled. His mask fogged under his heavy breathing as he looked around in paranoia, holding his weapon shoulder high.

"Team Two to Team One. Code Delta," Rodgers said into the radio.

His radio crackled. "—aines here." bzzzzt skttt "—status?"

"Dead grizzly," Rodgers responded. "Never seen anything quite like this. Guts scattered everywhere. Whatever killed this bear, Major, it wasn't human. And it wasn't friendly either."

Dupres nodded. "Got that right, boss."

A few feet from them, Prestone approached Carter and reiterated his assessment. "A fuckin' Predator. Like in the movies. That's what this thing is man, a fuckin' Predator." Prestone's voice quickened. "Ya know, I saw a grizzly up close… when I went campin' as a kid. Walked straight into it. It stood on its hind legs, let out a roar. I pissed myself. Never seen anything more terrifying my whole damned life. Thought it was all over. Then it just walked away—left me standing right there."

"What's your point?" Carter asked, surveying the terrain.

"Grizzlies don't attack unless they're threatened," Prestone said. "Whatever did this, man, must've been one nasty sonuva bitch. A fuckin' Predator, man."

"We can handle it pal, just like the X-Men," Dupres said. "We're all in this together and we'll come out fine. Just gotta stay cool... like Gambit."

"In this together. Alright. Alright." Prestone calmed. He placed his fist on top of Dupres'. "Just like X-Men."

bzzz skt "—status change to Omega alert. I repeat—" skt skt "—ange to Omega—" sktt "All copy." They all heard Gaines in the radio.

A blur of charcoal gray flashed between two trees about fifty yards away.

"Did you see that?" Prestone asked. "Something moved between those trees over there." Prestone's paranoia level just jumped three notches.

Dupres signaled the others to be alert. The heightened alert did nothing to help calm their nerves.

29

Through his magni-scope, Prestone saw something gray dart between the branches ahead. He zoomed in on his scope. Staring back at him from a distant tree were two large menacing jet-black eyes surrounded by a smooth, gray, nearly featureless face. Strands of stringy black hair covered the sides of its head and where its nose should have been, only a small crease could be seen. Its mouth was small, and its chin was rounded and smaller than a human's.

"Jesus H. Christ," Prestone whispered to himself. Its mouth moved. Prestone instinctively pressed his index finger on the trigger. "I'm not going down, motherfucker!" he shouted, as he pumped fifty rounds of ammunition out of the barrel of his gun.

Without even seeing the target, Carter immediately followed, peppering the trees Prestone was firing at with more gunfire. Vangrell and Dupres turned, scanning the perimeter with their guns cocked, watching for a target to present itself. Rodgers crouched behind a boulder and reiterated the Omega alert to the other teams.

An inhuman high-pitched scream, like a thousand fingernails scraping a blackboard, echoed above the noise of the weapons. Prestone and Carter halted their fire and glanced at one another. Carter shook his head and Prestone, though still filled with fear, knew he had made a mistake. He had just done exactly what he wasn't supposed to do.

"When this is over, you and I are going to have a serious talk," Rodgers snapped at him.

"What kind of creature makes that noise?" Vangrell asked.

"One we weren't supposed to kill," Rodgers snarled.

A bolt of blue light streaked across the timberland and ripped Carter in half. His upper body collapsed forward, his legs blew back, his innards splattered.

The sudden brightness caused Prestone to close his eyes. When he reopened them, Carter's flesh and blood smeared the outside of his clear facemask.

The team responded as one. Vangrell, Prestone, Rodgers, and Dupres fired indiscriminately toward the origin of the blue beam then all but Prestone ducked for cover. Frozen, Prestone stood his ground with his finger on the trigger. A second bolt of blue shot down from the trees and tore through his body. Whatever punishment he had coming to him for his amateurish misstep no longer mattered as the force beam violently ended his life.

30

Dupres, always the professional, kept his cool and pinpointed the exact location of the beam's source. He instantly concentrated his barrage on that position and then in a line along the entity's most likely escape route. A second high pitched shriek marked his success.

"HOLD FIRE! HOLD FIRE!" Rodgers ordered.

He hand-signed to Vangrell to go right and for Dupres to arc left while he approached head-on, thus flanking the alien. As a unit, they surrounded where it should have fallen.

"Nothing," Dupres said. "Damn!"

"No, you got a piece of him. Look at this." Rodgers pointed to a trail of red liquid on the ground.

"Look at that," Vangrell said. "Sucker's got red blood just like us."

"This went too far," Rodgers said. "Let's track it. If possibly, let's take it alive so we all go home."

They cautiously followed the trickles of blood which led under a thick brush of trees.

Dupres used his gun to lift the branch which hid the trail. "This way."

"I'll take point," Rodgers said, moving to the forefront. "My gut says its close."

Rodgers suddenly motioned halt. He pointed to several blood stains which led behind a grouping of trees. The perfect place for a surprise last-ditch attack. He once again signaled Dupres and Vangrell to surround it before peering around the trees. "Nothing but forest and dirty snow," he reported.

An alien jumped down from a limb and thrust a sharp metal blade into Vangrell's back. Vangrell's lifeless body slumped face-first to the ground. A bloody gray alien stood over him. Rodgers spun his weapon toward the alien but never got off a single round of ammunition as the alien reacted lightning fast and fired a blue beam of pure force which punched through Rodger's chest.

Dupres stared directly into its hollow eyes. It looked like it was dying, angry, and desperate. Dupres ran forward, firing wildly at the alien. The first volley hit it in the arm, causing it to drop its weapon. The second, third, and fourth ripped across its muscular upper torso, dropping it to the ground.

Then a bolt of blue energy blasted the ground in front of him, the fringe of the blast skimming Dupres' helmet, slamming down. It was a glancing blow fired from high, one that immobilized him and knocked the weapon from his hand. His vision hazy, Dupres scanned for the enemy.

A group of aliens dropped from the trees. The alien he killed didn't come alone.

31

Pearse Canal, Alaska

Exactly twenty minutes after Chase, Blaze, and Logan landed at the rendezvous point, they still had no knowledge of the whereabouts of their support team. Blaze and Logan sat at a table, bored by the inactivity. Chase paced wildly, clearly losing patience.

Upon their arrival, the post commander informed Chase that they had spotted the Canadian military scouting the area and soon after informed him of chopper activity over the region. It was not the news Chase wanted to hear. It was imperative that they got to the ship first, but now he knew the Canadians had beaten them there and only because the Alpha Contact Team was late. Worse, he still had no answers to their whereabouts. It was an intolerable situation.

"Radio dispatch again," Chase ordered, pounding his fist. "Tell them no more bureaucratic bullshit. I need answers and I need them now."

"Yes, sir," a soldier replied.

"You know what. I'll fucking tell them myself." Chase hurried off to the command center.

***

"He looks pissed," Logan said.

"Did you need your kinesics skills to figure that out?" Blaze replied, sarcastically.

"Very funny."

"Hey, whether you've realized it yet or not, this mission is of the utmost importance," Blaze said. "Think about the technological secrets that ship holds. Unlocking them would mean significant advances for our country."

"What marvelous weapons we could build," Logan said, with a sigh.

"If we don't get to it first, think of the marvelous weapons our enemies will build."

"It's the Canadians for crying out loud, not the Russians or some Middle East terrorists."

"Who's to say what anyone's going to do with it? This ship could irrevocably tip the balance of global power. Whoever has it—whoever controls it—becomes the leader of the free world overnight. Even if it's 'only the Canadians', how do we know they won't sell it? How do we know it won't end up in the wrong hands? Personally, I'm not willing to take that chance. That ship has to be ours."

"You believe if we have it, it'll be more secure," Logan said. "Some greedy bureaucrats will probably decide to sell it, and before you know it, everyone will have it. Take the Gulf War. We sold them planes and missiles, then we had to send good men over there to stop them from using 'em."

"Here he comes," Blaze said, referring to Chase who was stomping in their direction with a scowl on his face. "What happened?" Blaze asked him.

"Big time SNAFU. Some shit for brains assfuck in Anchorage with more clout than brains decided this mission's so top secret he didn't want anyone informed until we got here. So, nobody told air traffic control or the pilot or the men of our priority status. When a storm front came in, they saw no reason not to delay the flight until it passed. By the time someone figured out what was going on, it was too late. They won't be here for hours, if at all. To make matters worse, the CO told me he's got reports of Canadian military activity in the area. A couple of choppers were spotted ten minutes ago, heading right towards the ship."

"Jesus," Blaze muttered. He removed his glasses and rubbed his eyes as if he'd just got a headache.

"What does that mean? We turn around and go home?" Logan asked.

"You wish," Chase snapped. "It's just the three of us. We're going in alone."

32

To his surprise, Dupres was still alive, watching helplessly from the ground as the group of aliens approached him. Through hazy vision, he counted five. One gray, like the one he killed, but with stringy hair, a bulkier build, and smaller, though still unrevealing, dark eyes. Another was jet black, bald, a slightly visible nose, and a thicker jaw. Two others were dark blue, one surprisingly short with blank white eyes. The fifth one had a reddish hue that seemed to melt away to grayer skin tones as he neared.

The black alien reached down and grabbed Dupres' weapon. Another bent over his body, removed his helmet, and placed its slippery webbed fingers upon his face. Dupres cringed as its long digits examined his wound. As the alien tilted his head to one side, Dupres couldn't help but notice his own blood staining the snow-covered ground.

The taller blue alien removed the radio from his hip pouch. It stood upright and stepped away from him. Removing a small tool from a camouflaged pouch attached to its chest, the alien took the radio apart and examined its components. It turned to the others and spoke something that brought a reaction to their faces. The useless radio was dropped, an alien kicked him in the head, and the aliens departed.

Dupres was thankful to be alive. Except now he was helpless, on the verge of unconsciousness, and with his radio in pieces he had no way to warn the others that there was a small army of aliens with powerful weaponry heading their way. With that distressing thought filling his head, he blacked out.

33

"Major Gaines—" skkkt "—eam Four—" skkt "—respond."

Lieutenant Boudreaux, leader of Team Four, barely heard Gaines' voice call out through the bursts of static from his radio. He had heard a staccato of gunfire, but Gaines' initial orders were to remain in position unless new orders said otherwise.

"Team Four here, Major," Boudreaux replied, hoping his response got through. If not, soon he'd have to call an audible.

skttt "—ega, Team—" skkkttt "—gone," skkt "—tatus—" skt "—ree—". Major Gaines' voice became inaudible over the radio.

"What's up, Lieutenant?" Steele, the point man for Team Four, asked Boudreaux.

"From bad to worse. Best I can tell is we're in Omega status." Boudreaux pressed the button on the radio again. "Please repeat, Major." Static was his only reply. "At least we're still getting static. That's means they're still there." He pressed the radio button again. "Team Four to Team Three. Can you copy?"

"—here," a voice replied.

"Omega, I repeat, Code Omega," Boudreaux said to Team Three.

"—ger. Tea—" skttttt "—sponse." skkkktt "—peat, Team Two no re—," Team Three reported back.

Boudreaux stared at Steele in disbelief. "Did he just say Team Two was unresponsive?"

"Doesn't mean they're dead," Steele said.

"Maybe," Boudreaux replied. His mind rolled over the Omega alert with this new news. With fire in his eyes and determination in his voice, he gave the command. "No more check ins. Gloves off. We go straight for the ship."

34

Lt. Rankem, leader of Team Three, ordered his men to split up. He knew Major Gaines wouldn't approve, but he didn't care. He was more than willing to face whatever consequences later. For now, he knew Team Two was in trouble, and he was going to help them any way he could even if that meant splintering his unit so only a smaller number of them stayed on mission.

"Jackson, Avery, Vox, you go on ahead. Vox, you're in charge," Rankem ordered, handing Vox his radio. "We're in Omega status, so secure the ship and destroy anything that gets in your way. Don't hesitate. Whatever's between us and that ship is deadly. Hesitation could cost you your life. Lowell, you're with me. We're going to find Team Two." Rankem nodded affirmatively at his men, and they separated according to his instructions.

Three of his men gone, Rankem and Lowell slanted down the snowy mountainside toward Team Two's last known position. Rankem took the lead running to a point of cover. Lowell followed behind. At each stop they peered out, scoping the landscape for activity.

"There," Rankem said. Tapping Lowell on the shoulder he pointed to the body lying on the floor. "Damn, that's Vangrell. Can't tell if he's dead or alive while he's in that damned enviro—" Rankem stopped in mid-sentence as he noticed the two massacred bodies lying close by. "Get down," Rankem said.

His warning came too late. In a flash of blue, Lowell's head exploded. The gray matter of Lowell's brain washed Rankem's suit and Lowell's limp body collapsed to the ground. On instinct, Rankem rolled behind a nearby boulder, narrowly avoiding another blue beam aimed his way.

He needed a second to catch his breath and assess his limited options. Crouched down with his broad back pressed firmly against a creviced rock, he held out his semi-automatic weapon ready and returned fire.

The leaves rustled above his position. A lithe blue inhuman creature dove down from above. Its large jet-black eyes focused squarely upon him. The creature had one arm cocked, ready to thrust a sharp metal blade through his heart.

Without hesitation, Rankem pressed the trigger and unloaded twelve rounds into the alien's body before it landed on top of him. Now there were more organic remains and fluids on his suit but at least these weren't one of his.

"That's for Lowell, you ugly son of a bitch," he shouted. "And that's only the beginning," he whispered. Another beam of blue struck the ground near the boulder, this one missing him.

Rankem sprung up and fired high into the trees. A high-pitched shriek roared out and an alien plunged from the tree and scrambled away on all fours. Cautiously, he approached his target. Then a blue bolt struck him down from behind and exploded out of his chest.

35

Vox heard gunfire in the distance. Worse was the silence that followed. Vox didn't know whether their friends were alive and victorious, or dead. He only knew that whatever had happened was over. But orders were orders, and they had their own task to complete.

Vox raised his binoculars and caught a glimpse of what had to be the spaceship. The sun reflected off a metal hull that made it difficult to see. Nevertheless, he signaled Avery and Jackson forward. They would see it in full soon enough.

"Any life signs?" Avery asked him.

"Not yet. But I see the ship. I'll go up another ten. Watch my back." Vox cautiously moved forward. Seeing nothing, he waved the others up. Vox lay prone and studied the terrain through his binoculars. Then he fixed in on the ship. "Gotcha," he said.

"What have you got?" Jackson asked.

"The ship." Vox pointed. "It seems mostly intact—big, but not huge. Fifty, sixty meters across—round, but not perfectly round. Brownish coppery metal... can't make the rest out from here but it's what we've been looking for."

Vox advanced, taking cover behind an oak. This time he had a good view without the binoculars. Although partially covered in ground and snow, there were no visible portholes or windows, and he was amazed that the craft appeared to be in good condition considering it had crashed. There were areas of black indicating friction burns, but he didn't see any dents. There was, however, a gaping hole in the side of the ship.

Without looking back, he signaled Jackson and Avery to come to his position. When he turned his head to talk to them, instead he saw two aliens, dressed in black skintight cloth. Each held a circular metallic object pointed directly at him, as if he were being held at gunpoint. Behind the aliens were Jackson and Avery, their bodies slumped on the ground.

Don't hesitate, Vox thought. That was what Rankem told him. Hesitation could cost him his life. But he was frozen.

One alien, greenish gray with smooth skin, hollow blue eyes, a short mouth with a sharp-toothed grin, reached forward and grabbed the radio from his hip holster. His weapon was still in his hand, but there was no way he could fire in time.

Don't hesitate, he thought.

He stared as one alien put its circular metallic object into a device strapped to its forearm and pulled out a small tool, swiftly dismantling his radio. The alien studied the components briefly then threw the useless pieces to the ground. It turned to the other and screeched.

Don't hesitate, Vox thought.

And this time he didn't. Thinking the aliens were momentarily distracted, he raised his weapon. An instant later a blue flash was the final thing he saw.

36

Steele nodded to Team Four leader Boudreaux. Thirty feet ahead, high up in a tree, crawled something with gray skin, four to five feet tall, long limbs, a lithe muscular build, and wore attire resembling a navy Lycra body suit. Twenty feet to their left, a second one moved swiftly and silently towards their position, this one a violet-blue swirl of motion. Boudreaux flashed the hand sign indicating the gray one's position and signaling to the remainder of his team, Parker, Paneur, and Buck, to take it out.

The three soldiers simultaneously sprang from their hidden positions and fired at the gray. it never stood a chance, falling under a hail of gunfire. Its short piercing death cry was one Steele would not soon forget. But now it was his turn to act.

As the violet alien aimed something at his men, Steele leapt out and shot it down from the tree before it could fire. Steele bent down to examine the alien's fallen body.

"Looks dead," Steele said.

"Then leave it," Boudreaux said. "We'll have plenty of time to examine them later. Right now, let's secure its ship."

Steele nodded and continued. About two hundred yards ahead, through the gaps of the trees, he saw the spaceship, a copper-hued marvel of engineering.

Boudreaux gave the command to approach as a unit, each man in a line guarding the others flank, each man's head swiveling constantly to make sure nothing snuck up on them from behind. Within a hundred meters, Boudreaux flashed the halt sign.

"You see that?" Boudreaux asked.

"The ship?" Steele said.

"No, not the ship. There." Boudreaux pointed to a moving tree limb some twenty yards ahead. "There are more of them, and they know we're coming."

"Spot any?" Parker asked.

"Not yet," Boudreaux said. "Only signs of movement."

Paneur spotted one and pointed. "Dark one. Approaching low and fast."

Steele turned in that direction and glimpsed two other aliens ducking for cover. Through hand signs, he let Boudreaux know and the team leader ran forward, firing his weapon at them all the way to his next chosen cover-point behind a tree. The others followed, all five soldiers laying down continual cover fire as they charged from point to point. The silence indicated none of their bullets hit a target.

Flashes of blue light erupted around them from all angles. The forest exploded in an insane symphony of color, sound, and death. Paneur took a hit square in the chest and dropped.

Parker fired back. Branches fell from trees but no aliens. Two beams hit him simultaneously from opposite sides, separating his body in two different directions.

An alien appeared in the open. Buck shot it in its chest. Spurts of dark blue goo oozed onto its shadowy attire. As it dropped to the ground, Buck shot it twice more, confirming the kill, before he was violently blown away by a blue blast.

Things were happening too quickly. Steele blanketed the forest high and low with cover fire and darted, a flash of blue light striking the ground where he stood just a moment before. Steele redirected his fire accordingly. His bullets ricocheted off the trees, shredding their weather-beaten bark as he made his way to Boudreaux.

The forest quieted. Boudreaux and Steele, the last two soldiers in Team Four crouched down behind a giant oak and peered out.

"It's just us left," Steele said.

"I know. How many did you get?" Boudreaux asked.

"Not sure. How many are them are left?" Steele asked.

"Don't know." Boudreaux answered. "We're only about twenty meters from the ship. I say we go for it."

Steele nodded. "After we kill them sonuvabitches, you and I are gonna have ourselves a drink." Steele tapped an extra flask he had on his hip. "I always fill it with vodka. Gives me something to look forward to."

"Absolut?" Boudreaux asked, referring to the brand.

"Absolutely," Steele answered.

Boudreaux smiled. "Ready?"

Steele reloaded and locked his gun in reply.

They never got started. The oak they hid behind exploded as the aliens focused their beams at the tree. The force of the blast blew them ten yards away as wooden shards splintered their suits and their bodies. Lt. Boudreaux died quickly. Steele was not as lucky. He laid on his back, his face bloodied, his body wracked with pain. A two-foot piece of oak stuck out of his right leg.

Pain is good, Steele thought. *Focus on the pain and stay awake.* Which wasn't too difficult because everything hurt.

A mist of snow kicked up by the blast floated slowly to the ground, providing him with a moment of cover. To his left was his gun. Reaching out with his left arm, he grabbed an embedded rock and dragged himself closer to his weapon. He pushed off with his good leg and clawed the cold hard dirt until he was within reach. Grasping the weapon firmly with both hands, he leaned against the nearest tree and waited, forcing himself not to black out before he got his shot.

As two aliens walked through the settling mist, Steele fired wildly. He had caught them completely by surprise. A navy-blue alien with white eyes was hit in the neck and head and fell. The second, a gray, was hit in the arm, causing it to drop its weapon as four more bullets strafed across its upper torso. It let out a high-pitched wail that echoed strangely and loudly throughout the woods.

Steele dropped his gun and covered his ears. He was sure that any living creature within earshot was doing the same. The pain was excruciating. His head felt like it was going to explode. Until finally, the alien succumbed, taking its death cry along with it.

Steele uncovered his ringing ears. His environmental suit was ripped to shreds and soaked in blood. His right leg not only had a piece of tree stuck in it, but he also thought he saw a protruding bone. He didn't even try to get up. He stared at the bodies of the dead extraterrestrials. His friends were avenged. He had won. Now he could allow himself to rest.

37

The alien's earsplitting shrill had stopped, but its echo still rang in Gaines' ears. Everything had gone wrong.

"I assume you don't need my linguistic services to interpret that," Professor Le Buc said.

Gaines didn't answer. "Luc, I need you to backtrack out of the interference zone. Get a message to Rebecca concerning our situation."

"That won't be necessary, sir," Luc said. "A few seconds after that noise, the interference ceased. Here, listen." Luc held his two-way radio out and held the com button. There was no static at all. "That's the good news. The bad news is, I tried calling the other teams. No one's responding."

Gaines grabbed his own two-way. "Team Two, do you copy?" No answer. "Team Four... come in. C'mon, damn it—answer me." Gaines tried again and again but each time silence followed. "Team One to Anchor. Do you copy?"

"Anchor here," Rebecca answered. "What's going on?"

"Murphy's Law hit us like a ton of bricks," Gaines said. "Status Code Omega. Teams Two, Three, and Four are unresponsive so we assume the worst. Relay our op-stat to the Admiral. We're going to proceed but have him send in the second wave."

"Where are you now, Major?" Rebecca asked.

"Approximately 200 meters from our target. We don't know why, but the interference is gone. It might mean the ET's cut their power—"

Blue light flashed out of nowhere and pulverized Luc. Team One responded simultaneously in full measure unleashing their weapons toward the origin of the beam.

Major Gaines rolled behind a boulder—accidentally losing his radio—and readied his automatic weapon with the practiced ease of a man with a lifetime of battle experience. He also fired in the direction of the flash, only broader than Bell, Trask, and Rivera, to cover a wider area.

Le Buc was not as graceful. Covering his head with one hand, he ran as fast as his old legs would take him behind the nearest tree. Rebecca's screaming voice, barely audible over the sounds of rapid gunfire, came from Gaines' radio. Le Buc crawled along the open ground for it, a beam sailing just over his back.

"Leave it," Gaines yelled at him.

Le Buc didn't listen. He scooped up the radio then rolled behind a tree close to Gaines.

Gaines shook his head. "That was foolish."

"Le Buc here. We've been attacked," Le Buc said into the radio.

An extraterrestrial landed near Le Buc. It was about four meters tall and had a lean, wiry build. Large hollow eyes melted into its pitch-black face, right above a slight bump of a nose and a small mouth. White stringy hair draped over its narrow strong shoulders and skin-tight black garment which resembled a neoprene wet suit. A sharp metal blade extended from a band around its forearm.

"Holy shit," Le Buc said.

The alien raised its arm, prepared to strike.

***

Le Buc's message was all Rebecca needed to hear. She ran over to two pilots who were keeping warm over a pot of coffee. "You, radio Admiral Brock, Code Omega, request immediate backup, designate second wave." The pilot put down his cup and broke for the secure satellite radio. Rebecca turned to the second pilot. "How many suits do we have left?"

"None, Ma'am. We only brought enough for the soldiers," he answered.

"Weapons?"

"I got a few automatics left in the back of my chopper."

"That'll have to do. You're with me, flyboy. We're going in."

***

Le Buc froze. Whether it was from fear, curiosity, disbelief, or dulled reflexes didn't matter. He was going to die.

Gaines fired a hail of bullets that ripped into the alien with a ghastly finality. It fell dead and dark blue liquid oozed from its wounds.

"You should've at least tried to communicate with it," Gaines said, as he ran to Le Buc's position and took back his radio. He took a second weapon from a zippered pocket in the suit and handed it to Le Buc. "What did you do with the other one," Gaines asked.

"I left it in the helicopter," Le Buc confessed. "This is not the form of communication I wanted to engage in."

"I'm not sure whether to admire your principles or scold your naivety."

Le Buc stared at the dead alien's bloody body. "Perhaps if your contentious colleagues learned a language other than barbarism, you wouldn't be so confused."

"You're assuming this was us. Stay against this tree. I'll do what I can to see that I get you out of here alive."

Gaines shot out from behind the tree only to see Bell blown to pieces. Whatever started this conflict didn't matter. He was responsible for his men, and if he couldn't keep them alive, he would avenge their deaths. Firing a full magazine from his automatic rifle, he shredded the dark haired, gray alien who had just killed Bell.

38

The forest quieted, which only made Riviera more nervous. Somehow, in all the chaos and carnage, him and Trask got separated from the others. He signaled Trask. Two fingers pointed up then one pointed high, then two in a circle, informing him he had spotted two of the enemy—one high in the tree and one circling around behind him. He gave Trask the responsibility of taking out the enemy circling behind.

Rivera, meanwhile, hid behind a huge misshapen boulder and focused his scope on the alien high in the tree. It was an ugly sucker and would be a difficult kill but one he was well capable of making.

"Stay still and you're mine. Stay still and you're mine," he repeated to himself. His index finger tensed on the trigger. But the alien didn't cooperate. It disappeared behind a limb, denying Rivera a clean shot. He would have to be a little more patient.

***

Trask held his weapon steady as he moved to cover Rivera's back. Even though he hadn't spotted the enemy yet, he knew if Rivera said the enemy was circling around then the enemy would be here. He just had to find it before it found him.

There!

Trask spotted the dark blue alien a moment before it saw him. Without hesitation, he fired. A piercing shriek followed the short burst of rapid gunfire as the alien stumbled back, dropping a metal object from its hand. Still alive, the alien quickly dove away behind a large rock and was gone.

"Damn you, Trask. Damn you," he whispered to himself. He had the advantage and lost it. "Okay, keep calm, you still got a piece of him."

Trask moved in cautiously and saw the dropped object. Slightly buried in the soft snow was a coppery, metallic, circular object about the size of a hockey puck. Trask picked it up, feeling its warmth even through his gloves.

He noticed an oddly shaped indent on the top, going from its side into the middle, surrounded by a perfectly symmetrical seam. In front of that was something similar to a liquid crystal display. A blue light covered three quarters of the display. The remaining quarter was black. On the curve was an opening about an inch wide and half an inch tall allowed, that allowed the energy to discharge. Overall, the weapon resembled a metal donut.

The alien leapt at Trask from the side, so quickly he didn't have time to react. A cold wet foot knocked the gun from his grasp. In a blur of motion, the alien pirouetted around as a blade sprang from its metallic wristband and thrust into Trask's arm.

Trask screamed, releasing the alien weapon. If he hadn't moved at the last second, the strike would have pierced his heart. The alien dove for its weapon. Trask kicked its greenish-gray head, sending it sprawling backwards then grabbed the alien's weapon with his good arm, pointed it at the alien, and placed his finger in the indent.

Nothing happened. The alien smirked and dove towards him. Trask pushed the indentation again. Nothing. Then the alien thrust his blade through Trask's neck, releasing a spurt of red. How the weapon worked was a mystery Trask would take to his grave. His last thoughts were of his friend Rivera, who he knew he failed.

***

Rivera kept his scope on the alien as it made its way through the trees. He was losing patience waiting for an unobstructed shot and his body heat began fogging the edges of his clear face mask. With one hand he undid the left latch to his helmet, then the right one, then slowly lifted his helmet off and placed it on the ground beside him. He knew the Major would be furious, but he needed to breathe better to make the shot.

Head free, he took a deep breath, peered back through the scope and reacquired his target. "Almost, almost," he muttered, as the alien was about to reach a gap in the branches.

A twig snapped behind him. He peeked down at his helmet and in the clear face mask caught the reflection of another alien sneaking up on him from behind. The alien had dark fluid covering one arm and a blade covered in crimson protruding from the other.

Instinctively, he knew Trask was dead. Had he not removed his helmet, he would've been too. He patiently watched the creature through the reflection and when it was only a few feet away, he turned and fired.

His bullets found their mark but instead of watching his kill, Rivera rotated back to his original target. He now had an unobstructed view of a blue-skinned alien with yellow eyes. Unfortunately, its weapon was pointed at him. Before he could pull the trigger, a narrow blue beam shot directly through his magni-scope, piercing his eye, and exploding his skull.

39

Major Gaines spotted the deadly blue flash ahead. Immediately, he charged towards the source, keeping low to the ground. Since he hadn't heard any return fire, he assumed his men were dead and at least one deadly E.T. was still out there.

Crouching behind a tree, he scouted the area through his scope, moving it back and forth to view the trees. He stopped when he spotted movement. A lighter skinned alien was squatting amongst the branches peering in his general direction.

Does he see me? What was it thinking?

It was tough to tell by observing its dead eyes. But this one was just sitting there in the middle of a heated battle, which didn't make sense to him.

Gaines increased the magnification on his scope to zoom in on its head. This one looked exactly like the gray aliens of legend—bald, narrow features, large black vacant eyes. Didn't matter. He lined it up in the cross hairs to kill it then compensated for the wind and gravity by adjusting his aim two inches to the left.

As he tensed his index finger on the trigger, he noticed it. Not quite a smile, but the right side of the alien's lipless mouth slightly curled. A grin. The same grin that any of his poker pals might have made at him when they knew they held the winning hand.

He cursed himself for a fool. This alien was playing decoy, and he took the bait hook, line, and sinker. He dove sideways as a force beam came from another direction and blasted the tree behind him. Recovering quickly, he rolled onto his back and fired at the shadow descending upon him. However, while his battle instincts had served him well, he was unlucky enough to be in the path of the falling tree.

"Shit!" Gaines muttered, unable to avoid the tree's full reach. He winced under his helmet as a thick branch landed on his left leg and pinned him to the ground. Luckily, the protruding branches struck the ground first, lessening the full impact but he lost his grip on his weapon when he knew he would need it most.

He pushed the tree with his free right leg hoping to move it enough so he could pull free. It wouldn't budge. A wave of urgency overtook him as he sensed the aliens closing in. He kicked again and again, striking the tree repeatedly with his boot, each time with more force and urgency than before, but it was too heavy. His weapon was only slightly out of reach. He got close. So close that his fingertips were only inches away when the alien bent down and picked it up.

40

The alien stared at the dull metal finish of the semi-automatic machine gun it held awkwardly in its hands. It stroked its long fingers across the barrel, feeling the warmth generated from the recently fired shots. Its skin changed from a dull gray to a gun metal gray as it did so.

With a surprisingly quick motion, it expertly slipped its arm and head through the strap and placed the butt of the rifle against its thin, wiry right shoulder mimicking the way a trained soldier would use it. It held the mount with its left hand, peered through the scope, and aimed the crosshairs at Gaines' head. It reached around with its right hand, menacingly cracked its stunted knuckles, and placed a finger on the trigger.

Gaines jerked back in panic. The loud pop of three single shots echoed in his eardrums. The alien convulsed in a violent jerky motion and fell lifelessly to the ground, its skull cracking against the fallen oak with a sickening thud, its skin fluctuating through shades of green and brown before fading back to light gray.

Le Buc stood there, shaking uncontrollably, holding his weapon out as if it were an extension of his arms. He dropped it, quickly peeled off his protective helmet, and vomited onto the dirt.

Gaines breathed a sigh of relief. "Professor, help get this tree off me."

Le Buc wiped his mouth and ran over. "Sorry, first... first time I ever killed anything."

"Only you would apologize for saving my life," Gaines said. "Grab a branch. See if you can get enough leverage so I can get loose."

"Certain—" A gasp of air escaped his mouth. His eyes widened in shock. A soiled metal blade protruded from his chest.

The blade retracted and it was the Professor's turn to slump lifelessly to the earth. An alien stood behind him.

Gaines' eyes dilated with grief and rage, but there was nothing he could do. He was still pinned beneath the tree and his weapon was strapped around a dead alien's body.

The other alien with the blood-covered blade looked familiar. It was the same alien he had set in his sight only moments ago, though now its skin was darker with a greenish brown flow that altered with every step.

The alien reached out and removed the radio from Gaines' holster. It retracted its blade, unfolded a seamless pouch from its chest, and pulled out two small metallic tools.

While it was seemingly distracted, Gaines saw his possible salvation. Sticking out from beneath Le Buc's body was the grip of his gun. Le Buc had fired only three shots, which meant there was plenty of ammunition left in the magazine. Gaines stealthily reached for the gun. The alien was quickly and expertly disassembling the two-way and Gaines hoped it wouldn't notice what he was doing until it was too late.

The alien placed the tools back into its pocket and withdrew a small metallic box from its wristband. Gaines kept one eye on it and one eye on the gun. He was now inches away. A few more seconds and he would have it.

The alien stepped on Gaines' outstretched arm. It grabbed the pistol and tossed it aside, stared directly at

Gaines for a moment, then returned to examining the radio. Seconds later, the small metal box emitted a short, high-pitched beep. The alien discharged the radio component from the box and threw it away. It returned the box to its wristband and spoke softly in its high-pitched tongue with a repetitive clicking sound.

With a threatening 'swoosh' the blade popped forth from its wristband. Gaines raised his arms and good leg in a defensive position, prepared to make one last attempt to fight back. If he would die, he wouldn't die helplessly.

The alien retracted the blade. It removed a circular metallic object about five inches in diameter from a compartment. The display indicator on top was fully blue. The alien pointed the weapon at him.

Instinctively, Gaines knew it wasn't opting to show mercy. It was choosing to avoid an unnecessary physical confrontation deciding to simply blast him to pieces from close range. He would die quickly and wondered if DNA testing would be the only way to identify his remains.

41

Multiple shots rang out as an eruption of rapid fire zipped through the air. The alien turned quickly and fired its weapon toward the source instead of Gaines. The blast annihilated an oak with a deafening roar. When the debris of the blast settled, more shots strafed the area. The alien leapt into the nearest tree, climbed quickly, and skittered across the branches to adjacent trees escaping safely back towards its ship.

For the second time in as many minutes Gaines was saved. However, for the third time he had a weapon thrust into his face.

"YOU IDIOT!" Chase shouted. "You two, look around." Chase pointed at Blaze and Logan. "Blaze, if anything else comes back, fire at it to back it off—but do not aim directly at it. You—," Chase turned his barrel on Gaines. "—give me one good reason why I shouldn't blow your fool head off right now."

"If you're going to shoot me, shoot me. If not, get this tree off me now," Gaines shouted back, lifting his torso off the ground. A sharp pain shot through his abdomen, telling him his leg wasn't the only injury he had sustained.

With his boot, Chase pushed him back down. "I don't think you understood me correctly. I'm not bluffing."

"Fine," Gaines said. "The body you're standing over may still be alive. He's a civilian. He needs medical attention."

Chase knelt and placed his fingers on Le Buc's neck. "He's dead—just like you're going to be if you give me a good reason why I just walked through a war zone consisting of human and alien body parts."

Gaines closed his eyes. His friend was dead, the pain in his heart far worse than the pain in his leg and his ribs.

"Answer me!" Chase ordered, nudging him with his gun.

"I'm Major David Gaines, Canadian Intelligence Officer. I'm here for the same reasons you are."

"No, not the same reasons," Chase yelled. "We came here to learn, not to kill. You God damn Canadians made a mess of everything. Do you know what you may be responsible for?"

"Jesus… get this tree the hell off of me," Gaines said, in a low firm tone.

Chase stood tall and backed away. "Leave him be. Let him rot here."

"No," Logan said defiantly.

"Don't," Blaze whispered, placing his hand on Logan's shoulder.

"It's enough," Logan repeated a little louder, as he pushed Blaze's hand away. Logan reached down and turned over the dead body. When he saw it was his colleague, Pierre Le Buc, he jumped back. "I got dragged out here to communicate with these things, not get slaughtered by them, and certainly not to leave other men to die."

"I advise you to stay out of this Mr. Grey. For your own good," Chase replied.

"Not likely," Logan said.

Chase aimed his gun at Logan's chest. "Then let me put it this way. Due to the actions of this man—whom you're so decisively set on saving—your services, most likely, will not be required. Therefore, you're expendable."

Chase's eyes were focused. His arms and hands were steady.

"I'm not going to leave him here in the middle of God knows what because you say so," Logan said.

"You don't realize what's at stake," Chase said.

"It doesn't matter. This man needs help." Logan bent down to lift the fallen tree, stopping when he heard the clicking sound Chase's gun made as it was cocked.

Chase spoke in a low rough tone. "You're a civilian. Nobody knows you're here. Nobody on my end is going to care if you don't come back. Now back away from him and that's an order."

"Sorry, I'm not one of your soldiers," Logan said. Then, as he began to lift the fallen tree to free Gaines' pinned legs, Chase fired.

42

Logan watched smoke drift out of the barrel of Chase's gun. He turned his head to see where the bullet went and noticed a chip and a friction burn on the bark of a tree high up behind him. "Are you through?" Logan asked.

Chase paused. "Aw shit," he mumbled. He quickly scouted the perimeter for any sign of extraterrestrials then lowered his weapon.

"You're one lucky sonuva bitch. You know that, Major," Chase said. He bent down to assist Logan with lifting the fallen tree off Gaines' legs.

With the room they created, Gaines pulled himself free and stood "You're trespassing on Canadian soil," Gaines said, as he wiped the dirt off him.

"Lucky for you. We just saved your pathetic life," Chase replied.

"I'm grateful. That's the only reason I'm not placing the three of you under arrest."

"That's a laugh. You don't have any men left alive to do that," Chase said.

"You heartless bastard. Good men died out here today," Gaines screamed.

"And you almost joined them. There was no need for any of this," Chase screamed back.

"We were just defending ourselves."

"Save it." Chase returned his attention to Blaze and Logan. "Let's go. We still have a job to do. Keep your eyes peeled for the aliens, but do not engage."

"Where the hell do you think you're going?" Gaines asked.

Chase got into Gaines' face. "We're going in to do the job right."

"No, you're not," Gaines said. "Like it or not you're under Canadian jurisdiction and you—"

"Shove your jurisdiction," Chase interrupted. "Besides, how're you going to stop us?"

"With very little difficulty, I assure you," a female voice rang out.

Chase spun and pointed his weapon at the voice.

"Drop your gun before I drop you," Rebecca said, her gun pointed at Chase.

"No dice," Chase replied.

Logan stepped between them, hands raised. "Maybe we can settle this without blowing each other's heads off?"

"That's up to your friend here because I'm not going to back down," Rebecca said.

"Neither of you know what's going on here. There's far more at stake than either one of you realize. We're not just going to walk away," Chase said.

"Explain," Gaines said.

"After she lowers her weapon," Chase replied.

"You first," Rebecca countered.

"If you drop it, I guarantee you she won't fire," Gaines said.

Chase locked eyes with Gaines and Rebecca. He found neither one wanting. He returned his weapon to his holster. "This is the deal," he said. "The five of us go in together. Any technology, weapons or otherwise, we find, gets shared between our countries. Same deal on anything else we learn as well. Agreed?"

"What do we need you for?" Rebecca asked. "The ship's already on Canadian soil."

"Besides the fact that we saved his ass," Chase said. "We know more about them than any of you. We go in on this together, we'll tell you everything. Plus, I have what you need. Dr. Jeff Blaze is our top physicist. He's an expert on aerial phenomena. He'll know what's what once we get on board. And Mr. Logan Grey here is a kinesics expert. He knows everything about body language and can communicate with them. After the way you guys handled the situation, that's going to come in very handy."

"No deal," Rebecca shouted.

"No. It's agreed," Gaines said, overruling her. "How do I know you have the authority to back up your claim?" Gaines said to Chase.

"When—if—we can secure the ship, you can arrange the extraction," Chase said.

"What makes you sure I'll keep my end of the bargain?" Gaines asked.

"Because your government is going to want to know everything we know, and that will only happen with full cooperation," Chase answered.

Gaines nodded his approval.

Rebecca lowered her gun and walked towards him. "Le Buc... Is he—?"

Gaines just nodded his reply.

"I'm so sorry, David," she said. "I know what he meant to you."

Gaines walked back to Le Buc, who laid face up, his bloodied body wrapped in the biohazard suit, his eyes obscenely vacant. All the knowledge, all the warmth that made Le Buc the man he was, was gone. Gaines placed his fingers gently on Pierre's eyelids and closed them. A proper memorial service would have to wait.

"Let's make it count," Gaines said.

43

As a unit, they approached the ship. Chase took point. Rebecca and Gaines guarded the flanks. Logan and Blaze stayed close to each other and brought up the rear.

Logan felt totally out of place, dragged out of his comfort zone into this surrealistic, military sci-fi nightmare. Within the confines of a conference room, he reigned supreme, able to read the tiniest inflection in someone's voice, the slightest change in body movement or expression, always holding the advantage. However, here in the cold, snow-covered, mountains, fighting aliens and the Canadian military, he felt next to useless. Blaze was the only one he could relate to.

Why couldn't they have called me in later, when they captured one? he thought. Remembering the carnage he just walked through, he realized why. Death had been the result of unsuccessful communication.

"Is he always this intense?" Logan asked Blaze.

"Only when the situation's this serious. How did you know he wouldn't kill you?" Blaze asked.

"His eyes. When they were solely focused on me, I couldn't tell. But he took a brief glance your way... kind of an assurance to you that he wouldn't do it." Logan paused. "There's more going on here then you're letting on."

"What do you mean?" Blaze asked.

"Come on," Logan said. "I understand why we had to come in quickly without waiting for the ACT team. We had to beat the Canadians to the ship and get whatever information we could before they got to it. That's what you need me for—to translate and communicate with any alien survivors. Then we get here and there's carnage. Obviously, the Canadians beat us here, but there was a war... like we were being invaded or something. However, upon first contact, Chase spares the alien and treats the Canadians like they're the enemy."

"He has his reasons," Blaze said.

"Well, don't you find it strange how he didn't show any surprise when he first saw the alien? He never even asked Gaines about them, like he already knew the answers. And how come they're wearing protective suits and we're not?" Logan asked. "You know more than you're letting on."

"Later," Blaze said.

***

Gaines' injuries were minor enough not to deter him. He had removed his torn, now useless, protective gear and allowed Chase to lead the way since he seemed to know more about the aliens than he did. And if he was the next victim of an alien blaster, so be it.

They had arrived and Chase waved them up to his position. From their vantage point on the landing scar, they had a full view of the craft. It was big... approximately the size of a baseball field. It was coppery in color, except for the areas that were scorched during its untimely descent. It was round, but with noticeable angles as opposed to a perfect circle, with grooves and panels along its hull. To their right, a hole was blown out of the side of the craft, the ragged copper-colored metal bent outward as if something had exploded from the inside.

"Extraordinary," Logan said.

"Extraterrestrial," Blaze said.

"Admire it later," Chase said. "Keep your attention on what's out here. You see that hole to the right? That might be what caused them to crash."

An alien emerged from the opening, studied the terrain, spotted them, and darted into the forest. It wasn't the same alien they had seen before. This one had jet black hair with skin that flowed between varying shades of blue and black, a stockier build, and it carried a pouch on its back.

"I don't think that hole caused the crash," Blaze said. "I think they blasted that hole to give them a way out. Their normal exits are probably buried or blocked by the fallen trees."

"So we'll use it to get in," Chase said.

"There's no way we're getting in there without a fight. They're going to pick us off one by one from the trees with those damn energy weapons they have," Gaines said.

"I'll risk it," Blaze said, fascinated by the ship.

"There," Rebecca called out, spotting a gray about thirty yards to her left moving gracefully and silently in the trees.

"Move," Gaines yelled.

They all dove for cover as a blue beam flew over their heads, destroying a small tree behind them. Despite his injuries, Gaines rolled to a kneeling position and raised his semi-automatic towards the creature.

"NO!" Logan yelled, knocking the gun away before Gaines could fire.

"Are you crazy? That thing will kill all of us," Gaines said.

Logan turned toward Chase and Rebecca, who were also ready to fire. "NO! Don't fire. Don't do anything. Don't even move."

Rebecca glared at him.

"Don't you see? It just gave us our way out. It just communicated with us," Logan said.

"What are you talking about?" Chase asked.

"You had him in your sights before, but you intentionally fired high. You let him live and just chased him away. Now he's returning the favor. You gave him a warning shot, now he's giving us one. He's giving us a way out," Logan said.

"You're saying he's giving us a chance to leave," Gaines said.

"Yes."

"That's not an option," Chase said. "If we walk away, someone else won't and then things will get much worse."

"It hasn't fired again," Logan said.

"It's just staring at us," Rebecca noted.

"That's good," Logan said.

"Maybe it's not alone. They could be surrounding us, and we don't even know it," Rebecca said.

Logan took a deep breath. "Or not." He stood and made himself vulnerable.

Gaines pulled him back down. "That'll get you killed."

"Don't you see?" Logan asked. "There's only a few of them left. This one didn't attack us back when we were saving your butt. We were vulnerable then, too, but instead of attacking us, it fled and never came back. It would only have done that if it were equally vulnerable.

The fact that it didn't kill us a moment ago makes me believe even more that it's willing to talk."

"Maybe it doesn't think it could take all five of us," Rebecca said.

"I've seen their weapons in use. If it really wanted to, it could've taken us all out in one shot," Gaines said.

Logan slowly stood, his hands in the air. "Trust me."

44

Logan stepped out into the open. In a moment he'd either be proven correct, or he'd be dead. The alien had moved. He scanned the area, reacquiring it a few feet lower and to the left of its previous position perched on a different branch. Its weapon was pointed directly at him.

Now what? Logan wondered, having not thought this far ahead. Speech might be misunderstood. The same if he made the wrong gesture or expression. He ran through some hand signs that were globally recognized, *but were they universal?* He kept his hands wide open, palms up—showing the alien he was unarmed—and stepped forward.

The alien fired. A blue force beam ripped across the earth in front of him, creating a hole and spraying him with dirt and snow.

Logan didn't move. "Don't take the bait," he said to the others.

"You're going to get yourself killed," Gaines said.

"He's already doing better than you," Blaze said. "Let him do his thing."

Logan ignored them and focused on the alien. It was telling him to go away, which wasn't an option. But he wasn't sure how to reason with a being who had the superior firepower and position after they just killed its friends and wanted to steal its property.

It raised its weapon slightly higher again, pointing it directly at Logan's chest, motioning Logan to back off. He was stuck. Retreat wasn't an option yet if he moved forward, he was dead.

Think, Logan challenged himself. *What do we know about them? Nothing. There were no cultural differences he could work his way around. It was like communicating with an animal. An animal. That's it!*

Logan crouched down in a non-threatening posture, turning his eyes away from the alien while keeping his hands visible, like a gorilla would against a stronger opponent.

The alien screeched and instead turned its weapon on the other four and fired.

"Scatter!" Chase yelled, diving away, taking Blaze with him as the beam came at them. Gaines and Rebecca dove the other way. The blast struck the area where they used to be.

Logan stood up to see if anyone was hurt. It was a thoughtless mistake. By simply standing, he changed his position from a passive one to a threatening one. The alien returned its focus on Logan and aimed its weapon.

Gunfire rang out and the alien slumped forward, falling from the branch before it could fire.

Logan was confused. No one he came with had the chance to fire back. Slowly, a bloodied and battered figure limped from the underbrush, making his way towards them.

"Hey, ya oughta be more careful who you're trying to make friends with," the man said.

The others came over to Logan. Chase approached the alien and cursed.

"Thank God you made it," Gaines said. "Anyone else?"

Lt. Steele shook his head. Gaines closed his eyes and raised his head in dismay.

"Who are these guys?" Steele asked.

"American military," Gaines answered.

"Good. Let's finish this thing," Steele said.

"Did you have to?" Logan asked.

"Yeah, I did. I had the sucker in my sights for a while. When I saw you, I decided to give you a chance. You got balls… big ones. Made me think too. Maybe diplomacy might've worked, but things just went too far. Make no mistake, you were next."

"Let's go," Chase said.

They all stared at the ragged hole. This was it. There was no turning back, nor did anyone want to. It was time to enter the spaceship.

ALIEN
GROUND

45

Chase and Gaines entered first. They stepped over the jagged edge and across scattered metal then reached a dark narrow passageway that was slightly illuminated at the far end.

Blaze followed, sweeping a finger across the smooth copper metal. "Cool and damp. I'd consider it soothing if not for that nauseating smell," Blaze said. "Like a combination of salt water, urine, and locker room."

"The air's thick but breathable," Chase said.

"Warm and wet like a sauna," Gaines said.

They walked towards the dim artificial light, emerging inside a huge circular room illuminated by violet glowing rectangular panels inlaid on silver walls about halfway between the floor and ceiling. Cylinders of varying size and color, all with rounded lids, filled the room. The wall opposite them had an open doorway that led further into the ship.

"All clear," Gaines yelled down the tunnel.

Logan, Rebecca, and Steele arrived shortly thereafter and fanned out into the room.

"Incredible," Steele said.

"You notice anything wrong with this picture?" Blaze asked.

"You mean other than it's dull and anticlimactic," Logan said. "I was expecting something more fantastic... more otherworldly. This is nothing more than a storage facility on LSD."

"Not the décor, the condition," Blaze said.

"It's in pretty shape for a ship that crash-landed. Nothing spilled," Gaines said.

"Exactly. The impact alone should have sent these canisters flying." Blaze walked over to one and tilted it. It wobbled back and forth before returning to its motionless state. "There's nothing holding these down."

"Maybe they cleaned up afterwards," Steele said.

"Meh," Blaze said, with a disagreeing tone.

"Why bother?" Logan asked.

Instead of an answer, Gaines issued a command. "Steele, guard the tunnel entrance. Anything comes in after us or tries to escape—terminate it. Rebecca, guard that door. Same orders." Gaines approached a light green cylinder as his team complied. He opened the latch on the lid. With a whirring sound and a puff of vapor, the lid slowly slid backwards, revealing small colorful spheres within. "Cold," Gaines noted.

"A refrigeration unit," Blaze said. "The light greenish hue is probably krypton gases used for their cooling system." Blaze slipped on gloves, grabbed a violet sphere and, unconcerned, popped it open. Inside were leaf-like greens and a soft, burgundy substance that looked moist and squishy. Blaze closed it and put it back. "Best guess. Meal packs. This is their food."

Gaines popped another unit open. It was empty. Then another, also empty. "Nothing."

"Intergalactic travelers would need more food than this. Grow pods?" Logan guessed.

"Emergency rations?" Blaze said.

"The one with the back pouch probably took what it could carry," Chase said.

Chase approached another container. This one was wider and shorter, with a thicker latch. He undid the latch, and the cover lifted without a puff of vapor. Inside was a cushioned panel with twenty-four slots. Sixteen slots were empty. The remaining eight held donut shaped copper hued objects with an indent and a blue display. He grabbed one and held it in his hand.

"Their weapons locker," Steele said, upon seeing the object.

Chase grabbed one and walked over to Steele. "Step aside. Steele did. Chase aimed it down the tunnel and pressed the indent in the middle. Nothing happened. "I didn't think they'd work for us." Chase yelled across the room. "Hey, Blaze, what do you make of these?" He tossed him the alien weapon.

Blaze caught it in one hand. "A force-emitting laser. From the bluish color, I'm guessing argon based. Obviously more advanced than we have, but the principles should still the same—stimulated emissions of light discharging a burst of photons, probably adjustable. Probably focused through an yttrium aluminum garnet crystal—or some alien equivalent. Incredibly impressive."

"You certainly know a lot," Gaines said.

"I'm a physicist. The biology of different species varies tremendously according to their environment. We have bears, fish, snakes, rodents, all different because they adapt to their environments. They even recently discovered a microbe that lives in volcanic vents called an archaea. It's totally different in DNA structure from man, plant, or animal." He stared at Logan. "That discovery dramatically expands the thermally habitable zone, by the way, meaning there's probably even more life out there than we could imagine. Anyway, despite the differences between life forms, one thing always remains the same. We are all subject to the laws of physics. Biology is regional. Physics is universal. All species obey the laws of time, space, gravity, light, pressure, temperature... these laws aren't going to change. The aliens may possess more knowledge than we have. They may know how to manipulate the forces of nature better and have access to more elements. They may be able to create better alloys, like the copper alloy that makes up this ship, but the principles of physics are the same."

"And you're a physicist," Gaines said. "Got it."

"Want to try the shorter canister next?" Blaze asked with an enthusiastic smile.

Chase and Gaines approached it. This was the easiest to open. Inside it contained tiny spheres with markings on them, each stored in a different compartment. On the other side of the cylinder were half empty containers and odd-shaped vials storing colorful liquids of various viscosities. Another section contained a few small unrecognizable devices and gray materials. Notably some of the compartments were empty or only half-filled.

"Any guesses?" Chase asked.

"Tools. Repair equipment." Gaines said, with a shrug.

Blaze noticed the items. "Medical supplies. Let's not play with those."

"I think this is just a storage room," Logan said.

"Let's move on," Gaines said. "We need to secure the entire ship. We can worry about the details later."

Rebecca nodded from the inner doorway. "This corridor splits up three ways. Right, left, and up a ramp. Let's split up into three teams of two to cover the ship quicker."

"No, I want Steele here to guard our backs and make sure nothing goes in or out," Gaines said. "Rebecca, you go with Logan. I'll be with Colonel Chase and Dr. Blaze. That okay with you?"

Chase shrugged. "Whatever. We're going up."

"Hey, wait a minute," Logan said, not liking the prospect of being the odd man out.

"If you see one, just talk to it until we get back." Chase said.

Don't worry, sport. I'll look out for you," Rebecca said with a smirk, as the other three walked up the ramp.

46

"They'll take the high road, we'll take the low," Rebecca said to Logan. She went back into the room, opened one of the green hued cylinders and filled her knapsack with as many of the different, small, colored, meal spheres as she could carry. She stopped briefly and held a brown one in her hand. "Hey, Steele, you hungry?"

"No thanks," Steele answered, with a chuckle.

She threw the brown one in her pack as well.

"What are you doing?" Logan asked.

She ignored him. "Hold the fort, Steele. We'll be back for you soon."

Steele winked and gave her a thumbs-up.

Logan followed Rebecca as she entered the corridor and went left. The hallways were as bland as the walls in the storage room and made of cold silvery metal. Conspicuously bare, the only notable features were the dimly lit, violet, waist-high, rectangles that poorly illuminated the corridors and underfoot, every twenty feet or so, the floor had seams indicating a hatchway below.

Rebecca, gun gripped tightly in her hands like the trained soldier she was, led the way. Logan, unarmed, walked behind her. The corridor circled inward with a new passageway appearing on their right, leading to the middle of the ship. Rebecca placed a green meal sphere against the intersection of the passageway and continued on the current path. Twenty feet further they came upon two sliding metal doors, one to their left, one to their right.

On the side of each door was a panel with markings on them. Logan reached out to touch the panel.

"No," Rebecca said. "We secure the corridors first. Then we try the doors."

"I think they're rooms," Logan speculated. "See how the markings on the third lines are similar."

"Save the guesses for later. Corridors first, then rooms. Here, hold these." She handed Logan the knapsack with the colored spheres. "Use a brown one to mark this door."

***

Gaines, Chase, and Blaze were well into the ship's second level. The hallways were cold and bare.

"Disappointingly basic," Blaze said. "Structurally brilliant, but without heart. A strict work of functional engineering.

Upon encountering another intersection, Chase chose the inward passageway over the perimeter. At their next 3-way intersection with a ramp, Chase eyed Blaze, who pointed upward.

Chase took point. Almost at the top of the ramp, Chase raised his head and gun above the ridge that was the third level and scanned in all directions. The corridor was clear, with another up ramp nearby. He waved the others up and Blaze nodded his head at the next ramp. After a similar routine, they all stood on the fourth level. Left and right were their two choices, each short hallways that ended with doors. Both doors had a full vertical seam in the middle.

"Your call, Gaines," Chase said.

"Thanks for finally asking," Gaines said, less than sincere. "Left."

"Left it is," Blaze said. He hit the large circle on the panel next to the door. It didn't open.

"Now what?" Gaines asked.

"The ship's dead," Blaze said. "Judging from the bad lighting and these doors, they must've killed the power. These auxiliary lights probably operate on some kind of battery."

Gaines tried to pry the seam open with his fingers to force the doors. "They're not budging."

Chase unsheathed his belt knife and tried to wedge it between the doors. He didn't even chip the metal. "Damn, didn't they plan for a power failure?"

"Can I borrow that?" Blaze asked. He took Chase's knife, jammed the blade between the panel and the wall, and punched the handle causing the panel to pop off. Underneath lay a complex matrix of crystals.

"Pretty fancy wiring," Gaines commented.

"Yet not a wire in sight," Blaze said.

"Can you bypass it?" Chase asked.

"Let me see," Blaze said. "A highly advanced crystalline lattice network, thousands of alien microchips, millions of pathways, any one of which might open the door if we had power. Sure." He reached his hand into the panel and smiled coyly. A second later both the right and left sides of the door slid open slightly leaving a four-inch crack between the doors.

Gaines was surprised and suspicious. "How did you?"

Blaze pointed to the trigger-like lever he just pulled. "It's the only mechanism in here that has nothing to do with a power source. Every powered entrance needs a manual emergency latch."

"Good figuring," Gaines said.

Chase grabbed the left side of the door, his gun drawn at his side. Blaze grabbed the right. "You ready?" Chase asked.

Gaines clicked the selector switch of his weapon to single shot to limit damage to the ship in the event of a firefight and knelt low with his gun pointed straight ahead. If the aliens were inside, they already knew they were coming.

He nodded.

Chase and Blaze pulled the door ajar.

47

Logan scanned the empty corridor. At the next intersection, Rebecca told him to place a green sphere down. "This doesn't feel right," Logan said.

"You mean me with the gun and you with the markers," Rebecca replied, her focus solely on the task.

"Huh. Oh, no, I mean this ship. I can't believe that life this advanced could be this dull. This ship... it's cold, dark, barren... a tomb has more personality."

"Mmmm," she noted, not seeming to care.

"Is this what happens to us? We concentrate so much on the sciences that the arts wither away?"

They came across another intersection. Up ahead, Rebecca saw the first marker she placed down by the storage facility. They had made a complete circle. "Let's veer inward," she said. She turned the next corner, ready for trouble. The way was clear. So far, they hadn't encountered a single alien. "Drop a blue here."

Logan pulled a blue sphere from the sack and placed it down. "There's got to be more. Every culture has beliefs, arts, entertainment... no matter where they're from. There's no way they could be any different."

"Maybe they only brought the bare essentials," Rebecca said.

"Doubt it. Even the most sterile environments I've been in had pictures of friends and family lying around."

"You're talking too much."

"Yeah, I tend to do that when I'm nervous."

"Is your boss always such an asshole?" Rebecca asked.

"Don't know. Just met him today," Logan answered.

Rebecca crouched low, holding her gun straight ahead, and spun quickly around the next corner. Empty, just like the rest. "Drop a green here. So, what about you? He doesn't seem too interested in your well-being."

"I don't think he cares if I live or die. I'm a civilian. In his mind that probably makes me a second-class citizen. He doesn't respect me the same he does other soldiers, and now he thinks I'm useless to him."

"Are you?" Rebecca asked, sharply.

Logan didn't bite. "Only time will tell."

***

Chase and Blaze yanked the doors wide open. Gaines hesitated a moment, waiting for any possible hostile activity. When nothing bolted out of the room, he ran in, swiveling in all directions. The room, silver and metallic like the storage facility, branched out in a circular arc toward them, most likely meaning the other door was for the same room.

Chase entered behind him. Upon seeing the layout, he signaled Gaines to go around to the right, while he went left. Chase weaved around devices of some type and ten seconds later they met on the other side of the circular room, standing at the door on the other side of the hallway.

Above the door was a flat platform which ran above the ceiling of the short corridor. They couldn't see if anything hid on its surface. About eight feet above the platform was the peak of the domed ceiling. Pressing his back against the wall, Chase signaled Gaines to look atop the platform.

Gaines climbed onto one of the devices in the room to bring the surface of the platform into view. "It's clear," he said.

Blaze opened the other door which led to the hallway, and back to the door they had used to enter the room. "The upper level is secure, Colonel."

Chase scanned the room. It was circular, the hallway at its core obscuring one side of the room from the other. Scattered throughout were four freestanding devices somewhat similar in shape to that of an overhead projector. They were made from a copper alloy with a silver-tinted liquid on the flat portion and bulbous stems protruding in various directions. Along the walls were scattered alien writings and what appeared to be instrument panels.

"What do you make of it?" Chase asked.

"Don't know," Blaze answered. "The layout is odd and everything's dead. I need to locate the power source that will turn all these machines on."

"I'll tell you what I think. I think this is the cockpit," Gaines said. "We're on the highest level of the ship and those grooves across the ceiling mean it probably opens, giving the pilot a nice view. I'll even bet he sits up there." Gaines pointed to the platform.

"On what? There's not a speck of furniture in this room," Chase replied.

"Maybe they stand," Blaze said. "I tend to agree with the Major. This is the ideal spot to pilot the craft."

"Any chance you can restore power?" Chase asked.

"Not sure. I need to trace the source," Blaze said, while examining one of the devices.

"Okay. Stay here. Gaines and I will secure the rest of the ship," Chase said.

"No. We all stay together," Gaines said.

"Argue all you want. I'm going. He's staying. You can do whatever you wish," Chase said, as he left the room.

Blaze shrugged his shoulders at Gaines and began studying the alien equipment.

"Shit!" Gaines muttered. "For your sake, I hope there really are no aliens on board, because you're on your own. Personally, though, I think they're around here somewhere," he added, as he departed.

***

A few seconds after they left, Blaze thought he heard a thump behind one of the walls. He turned around in panic, unsettling thoughts filling his head at once. A bead of sweat dripped from his forehead as he removed a Smith & Wesson from his knapsack.

He hadn't planned on using it—*he was averse to killing*—but self-preservation was another matter. He searched the room again, making a complete circle around the hallway. He noticed access hatches in three different places, each one large enough for a human, or an alien, to crawl through. It was possible, even likely, that something hid behind these walls.

He took a long deep breath. His heart pounded so loudly he could hear the palpitations. Calming himself, he placed an ear to a hatch, making sure he didn't hear another sound. He undid the safety on the gun then wedged his fingernails into the seam and pried the hatch open.

48

Steele grew tired and dizzy. His wounds were much worse than he'd let on and his pride was about to get the better of him. When he returned to consciousness from his initial encounter with the aliens, the first thing he did was remove the piece of oak stuck in his leg. It wasn't the first time he had removed shrapnel from his body on the battlefield, but he had forgotten how excruciatingly painful it was.

He was then relieved to see what he initially perceived as his bone protruding through his skin was actually the inner lining of the protective suit. His leg hurt like hell, but nothing was broken, and his other wounds were mostly superficial.

He reached for his hip flask and poured the vodka he was saving for a victory drink onto his leg to sterilize the wound. The overwhelming pain burned his nerve endings. Tormenting impulses traveled to his brain, but he muffled his scream, conscious that the enemy was still about.

Long moments later, he recovered enough strength to tear pieces of the suits lining into strips and used them to bandage his wounds. It was makeshift at best, but good enough to stop the blood loss and good enough to continue the fight.

Now, guarding the only known entrance to this flying saucer, Steele found the blood loss was proving too much. He had pushed himself too hard and was paying the price. He struggled to maintain alertness but with each passing moment the effort increased exponentially. Despite his guts, and his spirited heart which wouldn't even consider letting his men down, he knew in his head he would only last a few minutes more before he passed out.

49

"You think they have automatic defenses in here? Or worse, a self-destruct program? Maybe that explains why there are no aliens around. They don't want to be here when their ship explodes," Logan said to Rebecca.

"I think you talk too much," Rebecca answered.

"Just covering all the angles." Logan turned the corner behind Rebecca. He felt safe with her. She was no-nonsense, always alert—clearly a professional who could handle herself. He pointed up ahead to a marker sphere they had previously placed. "There's a blue one."

"Yeah, I see it. We've covered all the corridors. You ready to try a door?" There was one just a few feet to her right.

"Yes, but not this one," Logan said.

Rebecca eyeballed him.

"It's these symbols—the alien's written language on these panels. I've been watching them as we passed by every door. The first two symbols on the third line are the same on most but the first two lines differ. I'm willing to bet that those symbols mean a bedroom or living quarters of some kind. The aliens have to sleep somewhere, so I figure, like a hotel, there are more bedrooms than any other type of room, and there are more rooms with these symbols than any other room. The first two lines must be the occupants' written names or room numbers. However, this one's different. It only has one line, three symbols."

"I don't care," Rebecca said.

"You might. If we open a bedroom, we're only likely to face one, maybe two aliens. If we open a kitchen or a work area there may be more—a lot more."

Rebecca paused to ponder it. "Doesn't matter. We have to check them all anyway." She placed her hand on the panel and pushed every button. Nothing worked. "Hold this." She handed Logan her weapon. "If you see anything, shoot first, talk to it later."

She placed her fingers in the slight crack between the doors. Leaning to one side she tried to pry it open. It didn't budge. She stared at the panel by the door then pulled at it until the cover fell off. Behind it, crystalline alien circuitry flowed like entwined rainbows.

"Whatever they lacked in arts they sure made up for in the sciences," Logan said. "That layout looks advanced and brilliant."

"Step back," Rebecca said. "There's a lever that doesn't fit in with the rest." She pulled the latch. With a loud array of clicking noises, both sides of the door slid apart, returning to their sheaths within the walls.

Logan's heart rate increased dramatically. He pointed the weapon straight ahead and prayed. The room was about twenty-by-thirty feet in area, all the walls made of the same bland, silver metal he had quickly learned to hate. He breathed a deep sigh of relief that it was empty.

***

Blaze leaned over the access tunnel which ran behind the walls and beneath the flooring. He poked his head down and looked both ways into the five-foot-by-five-foot passage. No life signs—just tons of advanced technology for him to learn from. Thin crystalline strands led along the walls in spidery trails. Blaze smiled. It was a lattice design more advanced than had ever dreamt of and he was the one who got to decipher it. This was the work he was born to do.

He was sure he could figure out how to restore power to this spaceship. Since metal crystals were a great conductor, the crystalline strands had to run electricity or some other power to every part of the ship. It was just a matter of figuring out which strands were connected to which machines and then following those strands back to their power source. From there, he would either discover the power source was dead—and he'd have to learn how to bring it to life—or somewhere along the way the circuit array was disrupted preventing the power from going where it needed to go.

He stood up, trying to decide which device on the "bridge" would be the best starting point. They were all pretty much the same, so he just arbitrarily chose one. There was just one final thing to do before he left this room. He removed a metallic device shaped like a smoke alarm from his backpack and magnetically attached it to the upper wall. He noted the time on his watch, added fifteen seconds to it, and entered it onto the display panel of the device. The only difference was that the device kept time to the nanosecond. When the times synchronized, he pressed the on-button causing the red digital display to change quickly, indicating the passing of time to the nanosecond. A minute later he compared the time on his watch to the clock on the device, ensuring they were perfectly synchronized. Satisfied everything was in working order, he entered the tight passageway and began tracing his chosen circuit back to its source.

***

"One more," Rebecca said.

They had already covered eight rooms, all made of the same smooth silvery alien metal as the rest of the ship. But they weren't completely empty. Various objects and alien clothes were found scattered on the floor. What was odd was the pattern these objects were found in—as if they had been simply dropped instead of thrown about from the impact of the crash.

"You get the feeling the entire ship is abandoned?" Logan asked.

"No. Keep alert," Rebecca answered.

They had approached the final door on the first level. Falling into the routine they had established, Logan knocked the panel off and unlocked the door while Rebecca stood ready to enter. However, this time the door didn't open, not even a crack. They glanced at each other as their alertness levels shot up a hundred percent.

"It's not opening," Logan said. "What's your call?"

Rebecca tried to pry the door open, but it didn't budge. She searched for options. A few yards ahead of the door lay a hatch on the floor. She bent down, lifted the hatch off, and slid it to the side. She got down on her knees, holding her gun out in front of her and poked her head down into the hole. She thought she glimpsed movement, but before she could confirm, Logan grabbed her by the shoulder and pulled her up.

"I'll go first," Logan said.

"Spare me the macho act. I thought I saw something down there, but it was too dark to be sure," Rebecca said.

"I'll go first," Logan repeated.

She stared him directly in the eyes and stood up. "Your funeral."

Logan got on all fours and peeked into the tunnel. It was dark, much darker than the hallways. He was barely able to see anything.

This was even stupider than making himself vulnerable to the alien outside the ship and at least that maneuver had a purpose, he thought. Maybe his ego was bruised by having someone else protect him for the last twenty minutes, or maybe he felt the need to conquer the fear he acquired when the alien pointed its weapon at him. Either way, he was committed.

"Pass me a flashlight," Logan said.

Rebecca got one from her backpack and placed it in Logan's outstretched hand. He turned it on. The tunnel was about five feet high and five feet across. It stretched in two directions, one going directly beneath the door, the other away from it. The floor was flat and brown in color. The walls were engraved with alien symbols and almost half-covered with crystalline strands that weaved in and out. Logan picked his head up, swung his knees beneath him, and jumped in feet first.

Fully in, he had a much better view as the beam from the flashlight shone down the tunnel. Pointing away from the room, the corridor extended before branching off in many directions. Towards the room, it went further than he could see. "It's clear. Come on down."

Rebecca jumped down. She, too, scanned both directions with her gun ready in case Logan missed anything. She walked in the direction that led underneath the door and cautiously proceeded, having to crouch slightly as she walked. Several steps after they crossed over where they thought the locked door was above them, they spotted another hatch in the ceiling. She pushed the hatch, but it didn't budge.

She signaled Logan to try. He placed his palms on the hatch and when she gave him the sign, he thrust upward hard, forcing the hatch from its position. Rebecca sprang to her feet so her head and arms, gun included, stuck through the hatch above floor level.

The first things she saw were two large jet-black eyes inches away from her own.

50

Late Afternoon
Ottawa, Canada

Commander Britton lit up the stogie, took a drag, and leaned back in his soft leather chair. It had been a long day, and it wasn't over yet. First that crazy meeting this morning and now this. An officer had just dropped a report on his desk concerning the odd maneuvering of a Japanese aircraft carrier in the North Pacific. It was in international waters, but still a little too close for his taste. He needed to come to a decision on how to act.

He studied the Cuban cigar as if it held the answer. He always smoked one before making a big decision. Most people thought it was because they calmed his nerves, allowing him to think more clearly. The truth was, every time he lit one up and tasted the first inhalation, it made him feel powerful. To him, the cigar was a symbol of strength, a reward for the successful, especially a hand-rolled Havana. He didn't like those commies, but by God they made a great cigar. Each puff reminded him of the prestige of his position, each exhalation of the power at his disposal. If he chose to give the command, surely the lesser nations of the world would tremble. He reached for the phone.

"Yes, sir," answered Landeau.

"Landeau, we have anything on the Japanese today?" Britton asked.

"Just a moment, sir." Britton heard the ruffle of some papers in the background. "Yes sir. Intelligence reports indicate that they're testing new stealth weaponry today. Helicopters, sir."

"Any indications as to where?"

"Reports indicate the test site base as an aircraft carrier named Tsunami."

Britton rechecked his report. It was the same aircraft carrier that was too close for comfort. "I'll assume that we're watching."

"That's correct. We have one of our ships following it as we speak—plus satellite surveillance."

"Are they aware of our presence?"

"Most likely they are aware of our ship. I can only speculate about their knowledge of our satellites."

"Hmmm. All right, Major, I'm giving you new orders. If that carrier comes any nearer to our borders, I want you to make sure our presence is known. Don't confront them. Just let them know we're ready, and we don't appreciate having them in our neighborhood. Understood?"

"Yes, sir."

"Good, keep me posted." Britton took another puff and hung up.

51

Rebecca nudged the alien's head with the barrel of her gun. "It's dead," she said as she climbed out of the tunnel and surveyed the room. "All clear. Come on up."

Logan braced his hands on the room's floor and pushed himself up. This room was not like the others. It was larger and the lighting in the room brighter. The most notable feature was a huge metallic sphere about twenty-five feet in diameter surrounded by a clear protective shield. Extending from the top of the sphere was a transparent ten-foot cylindrical tube filled with thousands of crystalline strands, matching the strands in the tunnel. The strands divided into groups, and each led to different sections of the room. Each section was marked with alien symbols, except along one wall which was ruptured, destroying a section of the strands.

"This is different," Logan commented.

Rebecca double-checked the alien for any life signs, finding none. Its skin was dark blue, slippery, and cold. She rolled the alien over and found a huge burn wound on its chest. A smattering of blue fluid was smeared and trailed off to a small, coagulated puddle. "He wasn't in here alone. He died over there, and someone dragged his body over this hatch."

Logan swept a finger across the puddle. "It's dry. He must've died hours ago."

"I think another alien was recently in here, locked the room down, and moved its body to this spot, setting it up so it would fall onto the hatch as he used it to escape. Might be what I heard in the tunnels," Rebecca said.

"What do you make of the room?"

Rebecca looked around. "Their control room or engine room—something of vital importance to this ship's operation. That thing over there," she pointed to the large sphere, "has got to be some kind of power source while those crystalline strands must transfer that power all over the ship."

They both heard metal slapping metal in the tunnels. In a split-second Rebecca was on the ground, prone position with her gun aimed directly toward the open hatch. A human hand holding a Smith & Wesson emerged from the opening. A second later, Blaze pulled himself out of the tunnel.

"Jesus," Logan snapped. "You nearly scared us to death."

"I could have accidentally blown your head off," Rebecca said, lowering her weapon. "Where are the others?"

Blaze had no reaction to their anger, intently studying the room in its entirety, the beam from his flashlight caressing every wall. "They're searching the rest of the ship. I'd say your assessment is correct. I just traced the filaments from the machines on the upper level, and they led here. In fact, all the filaments seem to lead here one way or another."

"You just crawled through the tunnels of this ship by yourself," Logan said. "Are you nuts? You could have been killed."

"Yes, well I guess my curiosity got the better of me. Don't say it. I know what happened to the cat." Blaze walked over and felt the clear material surrounding the sphere. "This confirms it. It's still slightly warm. Someone just turned this off a little while ago."

"Should we look for an on switch?" Logan asked.

"Now's not the time," Rebecca barked. She walked over to the door and pointed out a sealed latch. "This door was locked from the inside. That's why we couldn't open it. We also know that one of the aliens was just here and I'd guess is still on this ship."

"Maybe that was the one we saw leaving the ship," Logan said.

"I doubt it," Rebecca replied. "I thought I saw something in the tunnel before."

"I thought I heard something, too, but when I crawled through the tunnels, they were empty," Blaze said. "And when I was with our fearless leaders, we went straight to the upper deck without spotting anything. I think the survivors abandoned ship, and maybe we're letting our imaginations get the better of us."

"I'd prefer to make sure," Rebecca said. "I want to make another pass through these tunnels. It would be a great place for them to hide, and I'd prefer to find them before they find us. Doctor, since you know these tunnels better than us, would you care to lead the way?"

"I'd rather stay here and learn. Trust me, the tunnels are empty," Blaze said. Rebecca shot him a glare. "All right, let's go, but I'm telling you, they're empty."

"I hope you're right," Logan said.

Rebecca climbed down the hatch first. She scouted each way making sure it was safe. With his Smith & Wesson still firmly in hand, Blaze joined her. Logan climbed in behind them.

***

Chase and Gaines combed the third level like the professional soldiers they were. One man charged forward to the next cover point while the other guarded his back. The roles continually reversed until all the empty corridors and rooms were completely searched. Like Rebecca and Logan, they only found scattered materials and unknown objects on the floors of each vacant, silvery, bland room. Only two rooms differed and were significantly larger than the others. In them were canisters and cylinders like those found in the "storage" room. They guessed the rooms were probably the mess hall and the infirmary, but there were no other indicators to back that hypothesis up.

"Third level's secure," Chase said.

"What about these floor hatches?" Gaines asked.

"We'll cover the hard parts last. Let's stick to the primary areas for now."

Gaines nodded as they made their way to the second level. Gaines pointed to the first door. Chase popped the panel, pulled the latch, and the door slid open. Gaines rushed in with his weapon in front of him, prepared for anything. Chase quickly followed. The results were the same as before. The room was empty with a few odd items strewn about in no discernible pattern.

"You get the feeling we're being set up?" Chase asked.

"By them or by you?" Gaines sniped.

Chase ignored it. "The ship's too empty, too quiet."

"They might've figured we'd overrun them eventually, gathered what they needed, and split."

"Split where?" Chase asked.

"I don't know."

"And they couldn't have taken everything."

The twosome moved back out into the corridor. "Maybe they travel light," Gaines said.

"The homeless don't travel this light. Look at this place—no tables, no chairs, no beds. It ain't right."

They heard a thump. Gaines put his index finger to his mouth, telling Chase to be quiet. They listened intently. Moments later they heard another thump.

Chase placed his index finger on the trigger and aimed his gun at the floor. He motioned with the barrel of the weapon, indicating the sound was coming from directly beneath their feet.

Chase stepped lightly over to the nearest floor hatch and whispered to Gaines. "Wait for it to pass then pull the hatch."

Once the sound passed beneath their feet, Gaines yanked the hatch off and Chase pointed his gun in the direction of the last noise. To his surprise, something grabbed his wrist from the other direction, twisted it, and yanked him in.

***

Steele faltered. His back rested firmly on the wall. His breathing was labored and his legs wobbled like jelly, yet he resisted the urge to rest thus abandoning his post. Nevertheless, his body quit where his spirit wouldn't. Gradually, he slipped downward, and by the time he slumped onto the cold floor, unconsciousness took over.

He was awakened moments later when a hand gripped his shoulder.

52

Whatever grabbed Chase's wrist, dislodged his weapon and flipped him around so hard and fast that his back slammed the floor. Chase kept his chin tucked into his chest, preventing him from bumping his head, and absorbed the impact with his free arm. Then made a grab for his knife. However, a gun was thrust into his face before he could reach it. He looked into the eyes of his assailant.

Rebecca smirked and withdrew her weapon. "You step too loudly. If I were an enemy, you'd be dead."

Chase rolled to his feet, ducking his head beneath the low ceiling. "You are the enemy," he growled. "Nice move, though," he added.

Gaines stood above the hatch, his gun still drawn, now the only member of their five-man team not in the access tunnel. He lowered his weapon. "I think we'd be better off sticking together. Things are getting too tense. I don't want us shooting at each other."

"Sounds good to me," Blaze said.

"All right," Chase agreed. "What's down here?" He took Blaze's flashlight and studied the tunnels.

"Power conduits," Blaze said. "These are the tunnels they run their wires through—in this case these strands—to transfer power to the rest of the ship."

"Power?" Gaines said.

"We found their energy source," Rebecca said. "We don't know how it works, but it is the focal point for all these crystal strings."

"Was it on?" Chase asked.

"No," Blaze answered. "Still warm though. They must've cut it off just before we got here."

"That would explain why our radios started working again," Gaines said.

"The power source was probably emitting electromagnetic radiation that interfered with all transmissions." Blaze said. Off Gaines' glare he added, "Don't worry, we didn't mess with anything."

"Good. Let's not fool with anything we don't understand," Gaines said.

"We found one dead in the engine room. No aliens anywhere else," Rebecca said. "But there might be one hiding in these tunnels."

A parade of footsteps echoed from down the corridor, rapidly getting louder. Gaines, the only one left on floor level, looked down the hallway. An alien, dressed in black, its skin a kaleidoscope of violet and silver, matching the background with each step, ran toward him as fast as a cheetah.

Before Gaines could raise his weapon, it was upon him. It dove over the hatch and in an instant its slimy webbed hand knocked his gun away and its other hand smothered his face as it barreled him over. As they hit the ground, the creature pinned Gaines down with surprisingly strong limbs.

Chase, seeing the alien leap over the opening, anxiously searched for the gun he had lost when Rebecca took him down, cursing for not retrieving it right away. Luckily, Rebecca still had hers. She leapt up through the hatch and thrust her gun toward the alien. Its leg shot back like lightning and kicked her square in the mouth, sending her tumbling back into the tunnel. The reflexive shot went wide, and the bullet ricocheted harmlessly off the wall.

Chase found his weapon as Rebecca landed on top of him, preventing him from getting a clean shot.

More footsteps echoed about. Dupres among them, still in his bio-suit, sans helmet, a nasty gash on the side of his head, dropped to one knee and carefully fired a warning shot over the alien and his commanding officer. Then a second one into the ceiling guaranteeing the alien would hear it.

The alien shrieked at him, revealing its sharp, tiny teeth. Then it released Gaines and ran. Another soldier fired three consecutive shots, all hitting the fleeing alien. Crimson colored the walls as the alien slumped to the floor.

"Damn," Dupres said, slapping his palm to the steel. He glanced angrily at the other soldier. "You dumb rookie."

Another soldier ran to the alien, confirming the kill.

Dupres walked over to Gaines. He extended his hand to help him off the floor. "You okay, sir?" Dupres pulled Gaines to his feet.

Gaines rubbed the back of his shoulder where it hit the floor. It hurt. "Other than becoming a walking bruise, I'm fine. Good to see you, soldier."

"You too, sir," Dupres answered. "Back up team arrived."

More soldiers came into the corridor. One of them saluted the Major. "Lieutenant Carlson, sir. Leader of extraction team Alpha. We'll have the ship secured and ready for transport ASAP."

"Any other survivors?" Gaines asked.

"Dupres was the only one we found," Carlson answered.

"Where's Steele?" Gaines asked.

"He'll be fine. We've got a medic looking at him," Carlson said.

Rebecca rose through the hatch. After she pulled herself up, she touched her lip. She stared briefly at the blood on her fingers and wiped it off.

Chase came out of the hatch next. He noticed Rebecca's lip, then her angry eyes. "Guess there's no chivalry in outer space."

Logan and Blaze came out next as quickly as they could.

"No chivalry here, either," Rebecca said. Major, any objection to taking these men into custody?"

Gaines paused. "None. Take them outside. Watch them closely. If they try to get away, shoot them."

Chase immediately raised his gun. "You double crossers."

An array of soldiers pointed their guns at Chase.

"Put the gun down, Colonel," Gaines said, calmly. "You're not going to win."

"What about our deal?" Chase yelled.

Gaines walked up to the barrel of Chase's gun. "I think it's time we renegotiated."

"Kill him, I kill you," Rebecca said, with a smile.

Chase lowered his weapon.

Gaines reissued the order. "Take them outside. Hold them. I'll be out in a few minutes." The soldiers quietly disarmed them and took Chase, Logan, and Blaze away.

Once gone, Gaines turned to Dupres. "You were on Team Two. What the hell happened out there?"

Dupres paused.

"I need the truth, soldier. No bullshit," Gaines insisted.

"Prestone..." Dupres shook his head. "Guess it don't matter no more anyhow. Prestone freaked."

"Damn," Gaines muttered. He thought he chose better. Each man was supposed to be able to handle this extraordinary situation. Obviously, he chose wrong, and no matter what anyone else said, he would take it upon himself to bear the responsibility for this tragedy.

"It wasn't just the aliens, sir. It was the bear... I mean the grizzly. We came across a dead grizzly as we approached the ship—but it wasn't an ordinary kill. Its guts were scattered everywhere. I think that's what freaked him out. He must've thought that whatever could do that to a grizzly would do the same to us."

"Who fired first?" Gaines asked.

"Prestone. Next thing we knew, blue bolts of lightning were striking right and left, and we were in the fight of our lives."

Gaines became agitated. Chase was right. His troops made a mess of the whole situation. His chosen man initiated the action which started the killing that left nineteen good men dead as well as an uncounted number of extraterrestrials. And now that one mistake was forcing him to cooperate with the Americans. "Anything else, soldier?"

Dupres' voice was quieter now. "When the fight was over, they had me dead to rights. I was defenseless and surrounded. Thought I was a goner for sure, but they spared me. That's not the act of a hostile enemy, sir."

Major Gaines remembered when he was pinned under the tree, at their mercy. Would they have really killed him? He thought so, but now he would never know. "No, it isn't," he agreed.

"They destroyed my radio too, cutting off my line of communication," Dupres added.

"What now, Major?" Rebecca asked.

"Now it's time for me to have a serious chat with Colonel Chase," Gaines replied.

53

Blaze, and Logan were separated from Chase as all of them were kept under the watchful eye of four soldiers. Chase patiently sat on a stump, while Logan and Blaze simply watched as more Canadian soldiers swarmed the spaceship.

"What now?" Logan asked.

"We wait," Blaze answered. "It's incredible, isn't it? Even better than incredible... it's phenomenal—the design, the intricate circuitry... hundreds of years ahead of us. The places they go, the things they've seen... just phenomenal."

"Yeah, we would be the dominating force on this planet for eternity," Logan said, with more than a hint of sarcasm.

"Forget about that," Blaze said. "It's an unavoidable consequence given today's realities, but ultimately, it's insignificant. Governments are always going to strive to create more efficient, more powerful weapons. It's what they do—and until the world becomes a more civilized place, that's what they're going to continue to do. What's important is that we'll use the technology for more than just war. Think bigger Logan. We're talking about unlocking the secrets of space travel, exploring the cosmos, developing newer, safer, more efficient sources of energy. The possibilities are limitless."

Logan's expression remained skeptical.

"There's no way you can tell me that you're not even the slightest bit curious about what's out there," Blaze said. "Exploration is what we do. Discovery is what we're all about. That's what keeps us going. What makes us alive. What makes us human. If it weren't for curiosity, we would still be hunched over fires, eating dead animals, and living in caves.

"Did you know our government's been trying to build flying saucers for decades? In the 40's, it was the XF5U-1 and Lockheed's Avrocar. In the 60's, it was the Hawker Siddeley Kestrel. In the 80's, the Moller M200X and the Sikorsky Cypher. All saucer shaped aircraft. But they didn't work. Each time they ran into problems. The ship's too unstable at low speeds. What kind of energy source could sustain it? How do our pilots survive the G-force exerted upon them at such high velocities? Sitting right in front of us is the answer to all these questions and more... much more. We can finally show the world what wonders are out there."

"I don't think mankind's ready for all that knowledge," Logan said.

"I find that insulting," Blaze replied. "I'm certainly ready for it. Am I not to be considered part of mankind? Must only the malevolent and simple-minded people be considered mankind? How come the best and brightest among us aren't grouped into that category? Let me tell you something. I will not be held back for the incorrectly perceived benefit of the herd. One way or another, I'm going to learn everything about that ship and I'm going to use that knowledge to bring us right into the 25th century. If the rest of the world doesn't want to come along because they're not ready... fuck 'em." Blaze grinned at Logan and winked. "So, how about you, Logan? Are you going to come along for the ride?"

Logan smiled. "So, you're genuinely in this for the science? Working for the military is only a means to an end for you?"

"My true motive is education," Blaze said.

Logan laughed. "So, beneath all that intellectual exterior, you're a true fuckin' pioneer."

Blaze grinned. "In every sense of the word."

Logan admired Blaze's positively contagious optimism. "All right, Doc. Count me in."

54

"Area is fully secure and firmly under Canadian control, sir," Lt. Carlson reported.

"Reexamine every inch of this ship, Lieutenant," Gaines ordered. "I want every room, every hallway, every access tunnel, searched again. These beings may have places to hide on this vessel we haven't even thought of. Keep it clean, too. I don't want anything touched or moved unless necessary."

"Yes, sir."

Gaines turned to Rebecca. "Take over for me. I'm going to find out what the Americans really know."

Rebecca nodded. Gaines exited the ship. He passed two guards who saluted him. He briefly acknowledged their show of respect then glared at the Americans as he approached.

He liked Logan and was willing to give the physicist Blaze the benefit of the doubt—after all, he was just a scientist—but Colonel John Chase was another matter. Gaines despised him. Nothing would please him more than to send him packing. But he thought it better to stay in control as this mission was too important. It had cost him a close friend and eighteen good soldiers. To forsake them for personal satisfaction would diminish their sacrifice. No matter his personal distaste, he had to get answers.

What were the Americans hoping to accomplish? Was it really for just a piece of the action, or something more?

And if so, then why didn't Chase want to save him? What could he have possibly accomplished alone? They definitely knew more than they let on. Answers were long overdue.

"I think it's time you and I had an honest talk," Gaines said to Chase.

"Care to join me here, Major? Pull up a stump," Chase replied, smarmily.

"Stow the attitude. You've got two choices. Either you level with me now or our deal's off."

"After," Chase responded.

"After what?"

"After the ship's safe at a secure underground base and American personnel are firmly in place."

"That's not the way we're going to work things."

"Then we have no deal," Chase said.

"Fine. I don't even know why I bothered giving you an option at all." Gaines turned to Carlson. "Deposit him and his men back over the border. If they give you a hard time, use whatever force you deem appropriate."

"That would be unwise, Major," Chase said. "You need me. You just don't know it yet. Without me your country's in grave jeopardy."

Gaines didn't buy it. "I hope you enjoy delivering your report to your superiors, 'Sorry, General, but I was too much of a stubborn ass to cooperate.' Yeah, that'll read real nice. I'm sure your commanders will be proud."

Chase chuckled. "Your report's not going to read much different. Ya see, I thought you might react like this. Hell, I would. So, I brought along a little insurance policy. While we were aboard, we planted a bomb on the ship. At the push of a button, all that alien technology goes bye-bye. All those men you lost today died for nothing."

Gaines' eyes narrowed.

"Oh, I know what you're thinking," Chase continued. "I'm lying. You were with me the whole time. I couldn't have. Well, you're right. I didn't. Dr. Blaze did when we left him alone. Feel free to check it out. It's on the upper deck. But don't let your men touch it. It's magnetically adhered to the wall. Any attempt to remove it will set it off. Don't bother trying to disarm it either. That would be messy. I'm the only one who's got the code. Don't try code sequencing either. Three incorrect guesses and it goes off."

Gaines wanted nothing more than to wipe Chase's smug look off his face. "Check it out," Gaines ordered one of the men.

"Top level. You can't miss it," Chase yelled to the soldier.

Gaines paced through the snowy dirt, waiting for his soldier to return. With each step his anger grew. A minute later, when the soldier returned with an affirmative reply, he lost it.

His movement was so swift and unexpected it even took his fellow soldiers by surprise. He hit Chase with a right hook across the jaw hard enough to rattle teeth.

Chase checked his jaw with his fingertips, moving it awkwardly, then spat red on the ground. "Violence is the last refuge of a defeated man," Chase said.

Gaines threw another punch but this time Chase ducked and counter-punched Gaines directly in his ribs. The blow caught him in his previous weak spot and Gaines fell to one knee. An array of weapons lifted. Chase wisely backed off, hands in the air.

Gaines launched himself from one knee, tackling Chase hard. His shoulder thrust firmly into Chase's gut, he took him off his feet and used his weight to knock the wind out of Chase. Then Gaines followed with a short jab to the mouth and an uppercut to his jaw. Chase's blood splattered the snow.

Gaines then turned him over, shoved his head into the dirt, and locked him in an arm bar. He pressed his right knee firmly into Chase's back. Using his free hand, he grabbed the back of Chase's hair and lifted his head up so he could listen and because it inflicted even more pain. "Disarm it," Gaines said in a low threatening tone.

It took Chase about few seconds to catch his breath. "After," he said, laughing.

Gaines shoved Chase's head back into the snow. Everything had gone wrong. He had lost a good friend, good soldiers, and he himself was battered and bruised. First contact had turned into war, an alien survivor escaped, and the ship—the most important find in the history of mankind—was in jeopardy of being blown to bits.

Gaines withdrew his weapon and pushed it directly against Chase's temple. "I'm through playing games with you. You got three seconds to cooperate or you're dead. And dead men can't set off explosives," he said, with an uncharacteristic, unexpected edge in his voice.

"One... two...," Gaines counted.

"Okay," Chase said. "In the interest of international peace, I'll tell you the important details now. The rest of the information, the scientific stuff, will have to wait til later."

Gaines flipped him over so they were face to face. "The bomb?"

"The device has to stay in place until I know you'll keep your end of the bargain," Chase said.

Gaines cocked the gun.

"I'll remove it when the ship is secure at a base," Chase said. "That's the best I can do for you, Major. Shoot me if you must, but I have my orders, and I'll die before I disobey them."

Gaines mulled it over. Chase was everything he disliked about the military all rolled into one—everything Gaines swore he would never be. He should shoot him and be done with it, but he wasn't a murderer.

"Talk!"

Gaines removed the gun and let Chase get to his feet.

"I'm not sure they have the proper security clearance for this," Chase said, referring to the other soldiers within earshot.

"These men are standing in front of an extraterrestrial spacecraft. Talk," Gaines said.

"We've encountered them before, face to face," Chase started.

"Go on."

"1947, Roswell, New Mexico... I'm sure you're familiar with the story. Let's walk. This stuff's even more top secret than this. I'd prefer sharing with as few people as possible."

"Something that dwarfs even this find?" Gaines read Chase's eyes. "Fine, but this better not be another lie."

"No bull. Roswell really happened. It's just that no one knows the real details—the important stuff."

They strolled off into the woods.

"Yeah, a spaceship crashed," Chase continued. "Much smaller than this one. A lot more damaged too, but we were able to salvage some of it. Not enough to reverse engineer, but we gained a lot of insight by studying the design and the materials."

Now Gaines understood why they seemingly knew their way around the ship. The layout must have been the same, albeit on a smaller scale.

Chase went on. "They've got a superconducting form of copper alloy that doesn't need refrigeration. They use it to conduct electricity, creating an electromagnetic field around the ship. Essentially, they use magnetism as a means of propulsion which makes them incredibly maneuverable and fast. We've been trying to duplicate it for years with little success. But we're close. Blaze can give your technicians the details later. However, with this ship, and what we already know, it should cut our development time down to five years. Without our help, it'll take your guys more than four times that long. You need us, Major."

They crossed an area in the woods where a battle had taken place and came across the body of an alien. "What do you know about them?" Gaines asked.

"A lot. We found four beings at Roswell, just like the story says, three dead, one alive."

"Are they the same species?"

"Yeah. I know what you're thinking. When word leaked out about the crash—containment wasn't as good in those days—everybody and their grandmothers started seeing UFO's and aliens. The only way to separate the lies from the truths was by using disinformation. The organization in charge back then, Majestic, leaked stories that altered their descriptions. They decided to make them appear less threatening. The real ET's had hair. We told people they were bald. The real aliens had webbed fingers with claws. We made their hands more human. This way we knew who was telling the truth. These are the same ones. Though this bunch clearly showed a greater diversity of skills than the ones we found. We never knew they had chameleon-like abilities or two vastly different colors of blood"

Gaines bent down to closely examine the alien. He pushed the strands of hair off its blue face. The eyes were only slightly deader than before. He didn't like that. He liked reading people by looking into their eyes. With the aliens, it was like they had sunglasses on all the time, and Gaines never trusted a man who hid his eyes. Out of curiosity, he rubbed the skin. "Skin's not like ours."

"You mean besides the fact that it's blue," Chase said. "It's blubber. They have a thin layer of blubber beneath their skin. Our biologists say they're more like dolphins than humans. See this slit where a nose is supposed to be? They don't breathe through there like we do. It's just for smelling—particularly, it helps their sense of smell underwater. Our top guys think they must've conquered their planet's oceans before heading out into space. Or they originated underwater in the first place. That's why their eyes are like a fish's. That's why their skin and their voices are like a dolphin's. They're equally adaptive in and out of the water. They do breathe and eat through their mouths, like we do, but they also breathe through two blow holes on the back of their neck."

Gaines turned the head sideways and pushed the hair away from the base of the neck. He was surprised to see that Chase wasn't lying. There were two openings within the soft tissue on the nape. He started to place his fingers on the "blow holes" when he realized they were moving.

The alien grabbed Gaines' hand. He tried desperately to free himself, but the grip was too strong. Chase jumped back, stumbling as he did so. Instinctively he reached for his weapon, but it wasn't there. The alien's head turned toward Gaines. He could barely see its pupils, even at this close range. The alien spoke—a high-pitched, incomprehensible shriek, followed by a series of short clicking sounds and a whistle. Then it released Gaines' hand and fell back down.

"Jesus," Gaines muttered. His heartbeat slowly returned to its normal rate. He tilted its head and double-checked the now still blow holes. He checked its mouth and even felt for a pulse, which was unproductive since the skin around its wrist was too thick to feel one. No movement at all. It was dead.

Gaines stood up, regaining his composure. "I want their biological profiles sent to me immediately. Autopsy reports, too. I want to know exactly what we're up against."

"No problem. You ready to hear the more unbelievable stuff... the important stuff?"

They continued walking to put some distance between them and the extraterrestrial body. Gaines knew that within the hour Lt. Carlson's evacuation and recovery squad would retrieve the remains, as well as every other piece of physical and biological evidence. All would be inventoried and categorized, and a detailed report would be prepared for him to review later. His priority now was to figure out what to do next and for that he needed to concentrate on what Chase had to tell him. "Go on."

"Just keep in mind it was the 1940's. We weren't as sophisticated back then. Majestic performed autopsies on the dead and held the one that was still alive in an isolated chamber. The idea was to keep it alive so we could learn as much as possible, but it wasn't working. Every effort at communication failed, and the alien's condition was deteriorating. It had trouble digesting our food. Our medicine was insufficient. So not knowing what else to do, Majestic called in a team of top brains—marine biologists, astrophysicists, archeologists. They even called in a friggin' psychologist.

"The scientists did a good job too. One guy theorized that our environment had to be more deadly to them than they would be to us. He said that man had thousands of years of evolution to develop immunities to most of the viruses on this planet. The aliens had no such defense, so he risked going into the chamber totally unprotected. No plastic suit, no gun, nothing. Just walked in there and talked to it. They didn't understand each other, but that seemed to be the turning point. The psychologist said it gave the alien hope. Who the hell knows?"

"Is that why you weren't wearing any biohazard suits?"

"Yeah. The possibility is still there that an alien virus could affect us, but the odds of it surviving our atmosphere are slim. Besides, we know they've been back many times since then and they haven't infected anyone yet."

Gaines showed surprise upon hearing that.

"Not wearing suits was a risk," Chase said. "But a minor one. I decided to take it to meet with them face to face, just like that scientist did."

"Telepathic?" Gaines asked.

"No. That's just another piece of disinformation."

"So how did they communicate with it?"

"Badly. Like I said it was the 1940's. Their faces are mostly expressionless, their eyes are passive, so it's very difficult to read their emotional state. Most of it was done by pointing. We did manage to teach it some sign language, but we never got past the basics. We weren't sure if that was deliberate on the alien's part. One of the sci guys was a linguist. He didn't know. The marine biologist called in an expert on dolphin communications, but he had no luck either. Who knows, it might not have wanted to tell us anything, but they still learned.

"The alien was closer to a dolphin than a human. They changed its diet to seafood, and it gradually got better. Their language is sophisticated, even though we can't understand it. They have a poor sense of smell, excellent eyesight, and good hearing. Our scientists even speculate they can use echolocation. You know, generating sounds like sonar so you can see in the dark. The scientists were so proud of themselves. They started calling themselves 'The Order of the Dolphin'."

Chase paused for a moment to let all that information sink in and then continued. "This is where it gets interesting. They continued their studies on the alien for four years, and during that time a rash of sightings were reported, but only Majestic's people knew what was really going on. Its people came looking for it. Luckily, Majestic destroyed or hid all the evidence of the crash so quickly from the public that it also kept our subject hidden from its people. Majestic thought if they played it cool, basically ignoring the sightings, the aliens would give up and go away. It didn't happen. The number of sightings increased tremendously. We even had people claiming they were abducted.

"Nobody really believed it, but we thought it might be the aliens' way of sending us a message. We had their people, now they had ours. As the stories leaked, they felt pressure from the politicos. The populace was beginning to panic, and they didn't like telling their constituents that unknown objects were buzzing American skies and they didn't know what or who they were, and they couldn't do anything about it even if they did. Remember what happened when Orson Welles made that radio broadcast. The last thing they wanted was another incident of mass hysteria.

"Majestic decided the best course of action would be to give up the bodies of the three dead ones. They were of no use to them anymore since they already performed the autopsies. There was fear that the aliens might think we desecrated their dead, but for lack of a better idea, they brought the remains to a UFO hotspot, figuring that would satisfy them. The next night one showed up. They signaled to it, but it didn't respond. A white beam hit the bodies, they vanished, then the ship flew off. No one was even sure if they teleported the remains back to their ship or vaporized them. But no one cared. They all thought the mission was a success and celebrated. For the next few days, nothing was seen or caught on radar invading our skies. Majestic thought they pulled it off."

"And?"

"And they were idiots. You don't kidnap four kids and then release only three. Up until then, the aliens were unsure. Now they knew we had the other one, and they had no intention of leaving without 'em. Majestic treating them like morons just pissed them off. A few days later, July 1952, an armada of saucers swarmed over the Capitol. They let us know they were there too. Caught every one of them on radar at National Airport, Andrews Air Force Base, and Bollings Air Force Base. Even the commercial pilots noticed. Some of the saucers flew at speeds as low as a hundred miles per hour, others as fast as eight thousand. Andrews scrambled a fighter squadron to meet them. The aliens shot down two before we wisely broke off our attack. Then, mysteriously, Andrews Air

Force Base blacked out. They shut down an entire military installation without breaking a sweat. Scared the shit out of us. The following night, the alien was returned."

Gaines put on a skeptical frown. "I'm supposed to believe that?"

"Feel free to check it out. Even though we were busy with the Korean War, the Democratic convention and the summer Olympics, the sightings made the headlines in several newspapers. Since then, we just know they've been watching us. In '69 they watched our moon launch. Heck, it was because of them that we and the Russians pushed so hard to get there. It was because of them Reagan initiated the Star Wars defense program."

"So where do you fit in?"

"In 1953, after Majestic's complete mishandling of the situation almost ended in interplanetary war—one in which we stood no chance of survival—a procedure was written up in the event any spaceship ever crashed again—The Roswell Protocols. Simply put, any crashed spacecraft must be retrieved and hidden immediately. All physical evidence must be completely removed or destroyed. Peaceful contact must be established with any occupants. They must be rescued, receive medical attention, and be returned unharmed to their race when they come for them. It's our way of showing them that despite our past SNAFU, we are interested in a mutually beneficially relationship."

"In other words, don't piss them off."

"Exactly," Chase said.

"And we killed most of them," Gaines said, realizing the full magnitude of their error. This was why Chase was so angry at him. What consequences would they have to face?

"Now you understand what's at stake. It's not just the technology that's important. If any other country gets ahold of this stuff, they're not only going to use the technology against us, but they're going to make the same mistakes we did, and I don't think the aliens are going to react as kindly a second time."

"So, tell me, Colonel. How come you never shared this information with the other governments of the world to prevent such an incident?"

"Not my call. My guess is the reason back then was probably something under the guise of national security, and since then it has been put away and forgotten about."

"Great! Sooner or later aliens are going to come looking for their lost friends and when they do, they're going to find them butchered and bullet riddled. We're fucked. What do we do now?" Gaines asked.

"Do we have a deal?"

"Yeah," Gaines said. What other choice did he have?

"We get the ship and the occupants to a hidden underground base as quickly as possible. Last time their sensors didn't penetrate underground. Then call your Prime Minister and tell him that, sometime soon, he should be prepared for some pretty powerful visitors. And you'd better warn him, they ain't gonna be happy."

55

Prince Rupert, Canada

Stacy Michaels leaned back and took a long deep breath. The air tasted as aged as the décor. The recliner she sat in was worn and softer than it should have been. She was unsure what to expect and nervous over the prospect of reliving her nightmare in vivid detail in front of her therapist and the hypnotist, Dr. Peterson.

Jack Peterson was a pleasant man in his late fifties. His slightly round face was surrounded by receding salt-and-pepper hair and a neatly trimmed beard. He had a stocky build with a definite, though small paunch. "Would you like some water before we begin?" he asked.

"No... no, let's just get this over with," Stacy said nervously. She fidgeted a moment in the chair, settled in, and took another deep breath.

"Remember, it's important to relax," Peterson said. "If you fight me, the technique won't be effective. I can only do this with your complete cooperation."

Dr. Miller sat beside Stacy and held her hand. "It'll be fine, Stacy. I'm right here with you. Nothing bad is going to happen."

Stacy squeezed his hand tightly and took another steadying breath. Then another. Then one more. "Okay, I'm ready."

"Good." Peterson dimmed the lights and cued Miller to start the tape recorder. As Miller did so, Peterson spoke slow and calm. "You and I are going to take a journey.

We're going to go back in time... back into the hidden recesses of your mind."

Stacy snickered.

"I want you to relax completely and watch my left hand," Peterson said, raising his left hand up to eye level.

Stacy snickered again.

"Focus on my hand," he said, extending his palm out.

Stacy cackled. The sight of this portly, older man hypnotizing her, combined with her own anxiety, made her burst out wildly with laughter. Her eyes watered and tears streamed down her face. Then she stomped her foot twice and slapped the arm of the chair before catching herself. She held onto the arm of the chair tightly in a belated attempt to control herself and failed miserably.

Miller and Peterson tried to keep a mask of professionalism on their faces, but her laughter was contagious. Peterson chuckled and Miller started laughing.

It had been a long time since Stacy had laughed this hard. If nothing else, this was a pleasant and most unexpected change in her behavior.

"I think that's a little too relaxed," Peterson said.

Stacy wiped the tears from her cheeks. "I'm sorry, Doctor. I've just never been through this before."

"That's quite all right." Peterson removed his glasses and wiped a tear from his eye. "I haven't laughed like this with a patient in years," he added with a long sigh.

"It's just that..." Stacy stammered as the smile disappeared from her face. "With everything going on and the nightmares... I just can't take it anymore. I live in fear every day and I don't even know why." Her tears flowed down her blushing cheeks. She had done a 180-degree mood swing. What was funny to her a few moments ago was now terribly sad. She hiccupped and gasped for air, as the emotional strain of the last twelve hours took its toll.

"Just let it out, Stacy. You've probably been holding back for quite some time now," Peterson said. "I've treated many patients with problems similar to yours."

"I think I'll take that glass of water now," Stacy said, wiping her face with her sleeve. Her eyes were red, and her black mascara was running.

Dr. Peterson motioned for Miller to get the drink while he grabbed a package of Kleenex and handed it to Stacy. "I'm glad you're relaxed now. You should be very relaxed," he said in a soothing voice. He spoke to her as a friend, not a patient. "Take a deep breath and relax."

Without realizing it, Stacy complied.

"Let any remaining tension drain away. Just sit back. Completely clear your mind."

Stacy stared aimlessly.

Concentrate on the clock," Peterson said. "Watch the second hand slowly move... ever so slowly. Keep watching it. Your mind is clear." Miller came back in with the water and Peterson signaled him to stop and sit down. "Just keep focus on the second hand. It's okay to be tired. Just let yourself go but keep focusing on the second hand." His voice was soft and repetitive, entrancing her.

"Can you hear me?" Peterson asked softly.

"Emm," Stacy mumbled.

"Good. When I snap my fingers, I want you to go to sleep. The only voice you will listen to will be mine. I'm going to ask you some questions and you're going to search your mind for the answers. Do you understand?"

"Mmmm," she answered with a small nod.

"I need you to speak clearly. Can you do that?"

"Yes," she replied softly.

"Good." Peterson snapped his fingers crisply and Stacy went under. "The two of us are going to be together. There might be moments that will be very frightening to you, but I assure you, nothing bad will happen. You must be strong. You must look fear in the eye and not be swayed. Do you think you can do that?"

Stacy hesitated for a second. "Yes."

"Excellent. I want you to tell me about this bad dream you had last night. I want you to remember every detail vividly. I want you to become that person in the dream."

Stacy smiled and uncannily giggled like a little girl. Peterson raised his arm and held his palm outward, signaling Miller to stay still.

Stacy's giggling continued.

"How old are you?" Peterson asked.

"Five and three quarters," Stacy lisped in a little girl voice.

"What's happening?" Peterson asked.

"My daddy's tucking me in."

"Then what?"

"I wait for him to leave so I can have my tea party with Rufus and Mr. Cuddles." Her voice suddenly switched to an adult, a sign that on a subconscious level she was still resisting the hypnosis.

"Who are they?" Peterson asked.

"They're my stuffed animals, silly," she said childishly. Then her voice returned to normal. "That's when it happens. My room gets pitch dark except for the blue swirls. That's when the monsters come for me."

When she would reenact an event, she spoke like a child. When she played the observer, she talked as an adult.

"Tell me about the monsters. What do they look like?"

"Like sharks with hair." The adult voice was taking over. "Gray faces, round black eyes... powerful ugly creatures. The sharkmen from my children's books."

"How are they coming after you?" Peterson asked.

"They're chasing me." The child's voice came back as Stacy went fell deeper into a trance.

"Are you running?"

"Yes, but I can never get away. They reach out for me with their ugly webbed hands. They have small claws too. I try to scream, but nobody hears me. Then they cover my mouth with sticky stuff, and I can't scream anymore."

"Then what?"

"That's when I always wake up," her adult persona said.

"Always?"

"Yes... I'm not sure. I don't know."

"Stacy, I need you to listen to me. Forget the dreams. I want you to go back in time to when you were five-and-three-quarter years old. When I snap my fingers, I want you to go back to that exact moment in your life, when that dream really happened to you. I want you to become that little girl. Think back. Can you remember?"

Stacy paused for a few seconds. "Yes."

"At the count of five I'm going to snap my fingers. You are going to be that little girl. One... two... three... four... five." He snapped his fingers crisply.

Stacy giggled.

"Tell me what's happening, Stacy?"

"Wheeee, wheeehahaha. Thanks, Daddy." The child persona was back. "Good night, Daddy." Stacy beamed and her head tilted as if her father was truly there. "He's gone. We can play now." Stacy continued in real time. The tea party took longer this time than in the dream. She spoke and left silence for her stuffed animals to answer her. Suddenly Stacy's facial expression changed to fear. "Uh oh!"

"What's the matter?" Peterson asked softly.

"It's too dark. My flashlight won't work. It's so dark in here now," she whimpered. "Daddy. DADDY!" Now she was yelling, clearly terrified. She flailed her arms then brought them to her chest, as if she had just grabbed Rufus for protection. "Dad—"

She went strangely silent.

"What's happening Stacy?" Peterson asked.

She didn't say anything.

"I want you to be a brave little girl and tell me what's going on," Peterson said.

Her lips fluttered slowly. "The monsters are here. They're taking me. Go away. Leave me alone. GO AWAY!" she screamed, her tone fluctuating again between adult and child personas.

"I'm right here with you, Stacy," Peterson said. "There's no reason to be afraid. Where are they taking you?"

"Out of my room. They're taking me... somewhere else," her normal voice was speaking again but she was going with it. "I don't know where I am anymore."

"Try to remember," he added.

"I... I don't know. It's not home. No, it is home. I'm back in my bedroom again. I wasn't a moment ago, but now I'm back. They're still here. I'm in my bed and they're still here. They're surrounding me. Looking down at me. No, no, no, no. Get away from me. They're doing things to me I don't like. NOOOOOO!" she screamed in sheer terror.

"Wake her up now," Miller said.

"Who's doing things to you, Stacy?" Peterson asked.

"Go away. DADDY! DADDY! Make them stop," the little girl cried.

"What are they doing to you?"

"They're hurting me."

"Who's hurting you?"

"THE SHARKMEN. THE SHARKMEN ARE HURTING ME," her adult persona screamed. Then her voice became softer. "Daddy, make them go away, please," she pleaded like a child.

Then there was silence.

No more screams.

No more terrified expressions.

An anxious few moments passed before Dr. Peterson spoke again. "Are you okay, Stacy?"

"Yes, I'm okay." Surprisingly, it was the little girl's voice that answered.

"Where are you now?"

"I'm back in my bedroom," she said and then pouted.

"I thought you were already in your bedroom?" he asked.

"No. I'm back in my real bedroom."

"Who's with you, Stacy?" Peterson asked.

"Rufus, Mr. Cuddles, and Daddy, of course."

"Stacy, on the count of five I'm going to snap my fingers. When I do that, I want you to remember everything you saw, every detail of your experience, and I want you to come out of the trance. One... two... three... four... five." He snapped his fingers hard.

"Stacy, are you okay?" Miller asked.

"Yeah." She was groggy but her voice was normal.

"Do you remember what you just experienced?"

Stacy hesitated. "I'm not sure. I think. . . Was that real?"

Both doctors stared at each other. Despite everything they had just heard and seen, the truth was, they really didn't know.

56

Coast Mountains

Gaines sat in front of the computer monitor in the provisional canvas tent Carlson's team had put up. He was always impressed how quickly a dedicated group of professionals could set up a temporary base camp, even under the most difficult conditions. Doubly so that the technology within was such that he could communicate with Ottawa, via satellite relay, from the middle of a mountain range.

He had just sent in his field report along with a request for full cooperation with the Americans, including the sharing of documentation and facilities after the mission was complete. He knew his request would not be well received, but they would comply anyway given the extraordinary circumstances.

It would be a few minutes before he received a reply, along with instructions on how to proceed. To keep himself busy, he read the e-mailed intelligence estimate sent by the Admiral.

Early morning, 0535 Eastern Standard Time, only seconds before the UFO was caught on radar, the Anik E-1 commercial satellite, responsible for the transmission of credit card transactions, electronic paging requests, TV and radio broadcasts, faltered. Reason for failure

was a high intensity electromagnetic storm
triggered by a solar flare slamming into
the earth's magnetic field at supersonic
speeds. Cause was confirmed by two
observing satellites: the Fast Auroral
Snapshot Explorer and the Advanced
Composition Explorer. Intelligence
theorizes this event was also the cause of
the UFO crash. Our scientists at the
university support this hypothesis.

Interesting, but ultimately irrelevant, Gaines thought.

Rebecca entered the tent with two cups of hot coffee. She handed one to Gaines, who eagerly took it, enjoying the warmth on his hands. "The ultimate ration," he commented before taking a sip. The hot drink was just what he needed to keep him alert and warm. Even though he had caught a couple hours rest on the plane, it had been a long day, and he had a long way to go before it ended.

Rebecca briefly peered at the computer screen, then paced about. "Steele's been med-evac'd out. The doctors say he'll be fine."

Gaines nodded.

"Anything interesting?" she asked, referring to the E-mail.

"Not really. The think tank says an electromagnetic storm is responsible for the spaceship crashing. Imagine that. This whole affair started by bad weather in space."

"Hmmph. Interesting, but of no practical use."

Gaines grinned at her. "My sentiments exactly." He paused. "What are the three stooges doing?"

"Logan and Dr. Blaze are on board the ship. Logan's trying to decipher the writing. Blaze is... studying, for lack of a better word."

"Getting a head start, huh. Don't let them near anything until it's been swept, inventoried, and tagged. Have men assigned to them too. Let's keep a close eye on them."

"Already done."

"And Chase?" Gaines asked.

"He's in the other tent contacting his commanders. Everything he says is being monitored and documented to make sure it's on the up and up."

Gaines nodded thoughtfully then took another long sip, hoping the caffeine would soon have the desired effect.

"What are our orders?" she asked.

"I'll know in just a few minutes."

Gaines became lost in thought. He stared into her beautiful brown eyes, cherishing the pleasant shape of her face and her short but stylish hair. Ah, but that was only the surface. What he saw inside was even better. He admired the way she always carried herself. She was confident without arrogance. A pillar of strength that never wavered no matter what the circumstances.

He was in love.

He was tired.

Tired of waiting. Tired of living alone. Tired of succumbing to his subconscious fear of commitment. As soon as this mission was over, he would tell her how he felt.

"I didn't say it before but thanks for saving me," Gaines said.

Her expression warmed. "You're welcome."

He loved her smile. He quickly took another sip, as if there wasn't just a moment between them.

The quick change did not go unnoticed. "I'm sorry about Pierre," she said softly. "How are you holding up?"

Gaines sighed. His grief, too, would have to wait until this mission was over. "As well as I always do."

The computer beeped. Words scrolled across the screen.

"Here we go," he said. They both turned their attention to the screen as Gaines read the instructions aloud.

Losses regrettable. Proposal for cooperation with the Americans understood and accepted. Contact with government officials already established. Prime Minister has been alerted to possible crisis. Proceed on schedule. Transport all cargo to Yukon Base Five. Use all security measures you deem necessary.

"Possible crisis?" Rebecca said.

Gaines filled her in on his remarkable conversation with Colonel Chase from earlier in the day.

"You believe all that bullshit?" Rebecca asked.

"I'm expecting confirmation a little later, but yeah, I do."

"What are my instructions?"

"Tell Carlson I want everything ready for transport at 17:30. That should coincide with nightfall. Tell him I want everything completely concealed, covered, and camouflaged. We're going to take everything out by helicopter, then transfer the smaller stuff to trucks and go the rest of the way by ground. The ship is going to have to follow by air. We can't find a low hauler trailer big enough to transport it. I'm also requesting an aerial escort of four F-18 Hornets just in case. If more aliens do show up, I want to be prepared. I need you to clear the routes leading to Yukon Base Five. I want all traffic diverted. That includes air traffic, too. I don't want anybody within fifty miles of us in any direction."

***

At that moment, fifty miles above Earth on the outskirts of space, a pair of mechanical eyes were already watching. The data received was relayed via four other satellites and downloaded into the BADGE (Base Air Defence Ground Environment) computerized system for the Japanese Air Self Defence Force. The end result were real-time photos quickly appearing on a computer screen in the Tokyo office of General Sato Yamakazi.

Sato was extremely pleased with himself. His agents were trained well enough to recognize and purchase the most valuable piece of information he had ever seen—the exact location of the UFO. And they were loyal enough to bring it directly to him. He was certain, if they had given the information to anyone else in his government, his plans to retrieve the ship, his career, and most likely his life, would be at an end. He was just as certain that if any of those other miscreants were in charge, they would have let the most important finding of the new millennium slip away.

But he was a visionary. And as such, in his mind, he was the only one capable of pulling off the intelligence coup of the century. No one would stop him. Not his own countrymen and especially not the ignorant Westerners. They did not deserve the ship. They were nothing but a bunch of undisciplined cowboys who charged into every situation with guns blazing and lassos spinning, regardless of the consequences to their community. Society, duty, obligation, and honor meant nothing to them.

The truth—and he would never admit it—was that he was exactly the same.

57

Prince Rupert, Canada

Dr. Miller paced back and forth. He did not like what he had heard at all. Not from Stacy, and now not from Dr. Peterson. Stacy was freshening up in the bathroom and out of earshot.

"Listen," Miller said, "I know where you're going with all this, and you're wrong. I've known the man most of my life and he's not capable of that."

Peterson sat at the kitchen table, undeterred while drinking his Coke. "She's got all the classic symptoms. Weren't you listening to her? She was with her father. After her father left, the monsters came. She was taken from her bedroom to another similar bedroom, where somehow, she was violated. She was screaming Daddy the whole time. It is classic displacement and denial. The monster is her father. While it's happening, she displaces the event, so it takes place elsewhere—even though she as much as told us it's the same place. It's all symptomatic of a child who's been molested by her parent. I've seen it before."

Miller shook his head. "Look… everything you just said is true, but it's wrong. Don't you think I've investigated that years ago? That's not it. That poor girl is frightened to death of something, and we must find out what." He took a seat at the other end of the table and tried to settle down.

"I'm telling you," Peterson insisted, "she's frightened to learn the truth about her father."

"I was not molested by my father," Stacy said as she entered the room.

"I didn't—," Peterson stumbled, his face turning pink.

Stacy stopped him before he went any further. "It's okay. I'm not stupid. I know what you're thinking and why, but it's not true. I love my father. We have a great relationship. He would never have done anything like that. Whatever's causing my nightmares is from something else."

The room fell silent. No one knew what to say next.

Stacy rescued the moment. "You guys hungry? I haven't eaten anything all day."

"Sounds like a wonderful idea," Miller said.

"Fine," Peterson responded. As he rose from his chair, he reached down for Stacy's book, *Princess Zinthia vs. the Sharkmen*. He brought it with him, staring at the villains closely—so like the creatures she described.

It struck him. *What if it was real?*

What if…?

58

Alaska

Nikolai strode through the vast warehouse, passing large empty shipping crates that smelled unpleasantly of dead fish. Ignoring the nasty stink, he headed straight toward the back door and made his way onto the loading dock where he searched for two men whose faces he had only seen in photographs: Arkady Rusikov and Ivan Lisky, better known to their coworkers as Arnie Rayce and Stephen Lester.

Nikolai's eyes scanned the row of trucks, some of which were currently being unloaded. There were six men working. None of them matched the identity of the men he was looking for. He stared further and spotted Arkady on the west end of the loading dock, leaning against a wall, a cigarette protruding limply from his mouth. Nikolai removed a pack of smokes from his jacket pocket, knocked one into his hand then re-pocketed the pack before walking over to Arkady.

"Got a light?" Nikolai asked.

Arkady sized him up. He took another puff then expelled a long wispy cloud of smoke. "I don't smoke," he replied.

Nikolai fixed his intimidating gaze upon the man. Then he softened and he placed the cigarette on his ear. "Me neither. These things will kill you."

Arkady shook his head knowingly and took another puff. He turned to the men unloading the truck, then back towards the side yard where three men were cutting and sorting fish. "Hey, Steve!" he yelled out.

The largest of the three glanced over. Ivan Lisky stood six-five and was built like a tank. He was bald and his bushy eyebrows cast shadows over his unshapely face. He reminded Nikolai of some of the toughest men he had under his command. Arkady tilted his head sharply, signaling the man to come over. Ivan nodded, then grabbed a long gutting hook from the table and approached.

Nikolai focused on a scar that ran down the left side of Ivan's face. It wasn't present in the photograph from his files. The large man stared back at him.

"Looks fresh," Nikolai said.

"Come on," Arkady said. "What you need is this way."

The three men crossed the concrete dock, making their way to the opposite end.

"What happened?" Nikolai asked Ivan.

Arkady answered. "Bar fight. Our friend here took exception when some loudmouth started to berate Russian hockey. He figured his charm, and good looks would quiet the man. Instead, the guy unwisely smashed a bottle into his face."

Nikolai stared again at the scar and then at Ivan, who grinned back at him, proud that he defended his countrymen. Nikolai remembered what he read in his profile: cold-blooded, merciless, perfect for small-time jobs requiring muscles more than brains. "You didn't kill him, I hope."

"No," Arkady said, "even he isn't that stupid. Hurt 'em good, though. Luckily, the other patrons saw his actions as self-defense and the cops let him go." Arkady stopped at the truck parked in the last slot. "This one's yours."

Nikolai walked toward the front of the eighteen-wheeler, with Arkady and Ivan right behind him. He waited until he was out of the other worker's sight, then whirled swiftly and punched Ivan in the solar plexus, knocking the wind out of the big man. Ivan slumped back against the side of the vehicle gasping for air. Nikolai grabbed the gutting hook from his grasp and placed the sharp end against Ivan's throat. Suddenly, Ivan stopped gasping, and his eyes widened in fear like a deer caught in headlights.

"You are a stupid man, Ivan," Nikolai growled. "We spent years providing your cover and in a moment of national pride you seek to throw away all our hard work. Do you know what would have happened if you were arrested—if the police decided to delve into your background?" He leaned the blade into his neck, pushing the skin back but not hard enough to cut it. Then his eyes bored into Ivan's to gain his true measure. Lucky for Ivan, Nikolai saw remorse. "Your position may not seem like that big a deal to you, but it is very important to the rest of us. I hope you realize that now."

Ivan nodded as best he could.

"Good," Nikolai said, moving the hook away from his throat. "But if I ever hear about anything like this happening again, our next discussion will not be as pleasant." He momentarily played with the hook, testing its weight. Then with a flip of the wrist, he threw it. Its point imbedded into the ground only inches from Ivan's feet. He turned to Arkady. "Is the truck properly equipped?"

"There's a 9mm Beretta in the side panel of the door with plenty of ammo," Arkady replied. "Do you know about the rear?"

"Adjustable false panel in the back," Nikolai answered.

"Yeah, perfect for smuggling anything across the border."

"Keys."

Arkady reached into his pocket and tossed them to Nikolai. "When can I expect it back?"

"If all goes well, twelve hours." Nikolai took out the pack of cigarettes and replaced the one from behind his ear. He tossed the pack to Arkady. "I won't be needing these." Then he got in the truck, started it, and drove off.

Canada was at least two hours away.

59

Prince Rupert, Canada

Stacy reviewed the menu, undecided if she should choose the chef salad or the cheeseburger deluxe. She imagined taking a big bite out of a cheeseburger, the ketchup squirting out of the side of the bun, dripping onto her plate. *Or was it her blood dripping into a metal dish?* Startled by the unexpected image, she stopped daydreaming. *Was that a flashback or her imagination?* She didn't know. "So, am I certifiable?" she asked.

"Don't be too hard on yourself. I think we made a long step forward this afternoon," Miller said.

"How so?"

Peterson took the cue. "What if it was real?"

"Excuse me?"

"Let's say for a minute that everything you experienced while you were under was real."

Stacy was astonished. There was a fine line between her fears and the ridiculous. She had contemplated the possible causes of her nightmares since they began twenty years ago. Not once did she ever seriously consider the absurd notion they were real. The sharkmen were purely the stuff of fiction. She became annoyed. *This is what she wasted her afternoon on. This was progress.* "What's your story?" she asked abruptly.

"Come again," Peterson said.

Stacy's anger and frustration bubbled to the surface. "I find it hard to believe that in this small town there's a need for a regressive hypno-therapist—or whatever it is you call yourself. You're not going to tell me there are so many crazy people around here that you make a living doing this. What's your story?"

"I assure you, Stacy, Dr. Peterson is fully qualified for what he does," Miller interjected.

Peterson waved his hand. "My story's not important. What is important is your story. You're frightened to death from a recurring nightmare. An hour ago, we put you under and it was clear the nightmare is real to you. All I'm suggesting is that maybe it is real. Or maybe part of it is real—the essential part—and the rest is your imagination filling in the horrid details. Dr. Miller's been studying your case for years and he hasn't found a rational explanation for your phobia. Maybe it's time to look at the irrational."

Stacy calmed. "You think sharkmen really exist?"

"Maybe not literally, but figuratively. Let's go through everything you remembered. Did anybody hurt you when you were a kid? Could you give these sharkmen a different face?"

Stacy thought back, trying to remember every vivid detail. She recounted her story again but didn't remember anything differently. If it was real, it happened exactly the way she remembered. "I'm sorry. That's all I can recall."

"Forget about the sharkmen," Miller said. "You said before, when they arrived, you were in your bedroom. Then, when they came, they took you someplace different. Then, you were back in your bedroom... only it wasn't your bedroom."

"Yeah, that's right." Stacy searched her memories again. Perhaps she was concentrating on the wrong details. "All right, I'm positive I was in my bedroom. Then the lights went out and when they went back on, I was... elsewhere."

"What did it look like?" Miller asked.

"It was silver. Very cold too, and not just the temperature, if you know what I mean. But a few seconds later I'm in my bedroom again."

"Go back to the silver room," Miller said. "Is there anything you can remember about it?"

Peterson leaned forward. "Anything at all?

Stacy thought hard again. "No. It's just silver, cold, and sterile."

"Where are you?" Miller asked.

"I'm looking up. There's three sharkmen standing around me."

"Is anything happening?" Peterson asked.

"Nothing. Then... I'm in my bedroom again."

"But you said it's not your bedroom," Miller reminded her.

"Yes," Stacy said softly, a puzzled expression on her face.

"Why?"

"It looks like my bedroom, but somehow, I know it's not. The sharkmen are still there. I'm lying in bed. They're still surrounding me. There are more of them now."

"What are they doing?" Peterson asked.

"No. Forget that. Why isn't it your bedroom?" redirected Miller.

Stacy closed her eyes. She tried to visualize every detail of the room. "I don't know. It's colder but..."

"Keep thinking. Try to remember," Miller said.

Stacy squeezed her eyes shut, concentrating harder.

"Can I get you folks anything?" The waitress said, abruptly ruining the moment.

Miller slapped his palm on the table. "Damn."

The waitress started.

"I'm sorry, dear. We're ready to order," Peterson said. He looked at Stacy so she could order first. Her gaze was fixed on the waitress. "Stacy?" She didn't respond. Peterson noticed she was fixated on the waitress's nametag. He read it. "Perhaps we need a few more minutes to decide, Daisy," Peterson said.

The waitress placed her pad back into her shirt pocket and left with a sneer.

Stacy smiled. She was relieved and excited. "That's it. That's what's missing."

Miller sat on the edge of his seat. "What is it?"

"Now I know why it's not my bedroom. It didn't have Daisy."

"Come again," Peterson said.

"Daisy Duck. When I was a kid, I had a Daisy Duck night light. I was afraid of the dark and when the lights went out, I knew Daisy Duck would keep me safe. I wouldn't go to sleep without her."

"So?" Peterson still didn't get it.

"So, this room wasn't my bedroom because it didn't have Daisy. When the lights went back on, Daisy was gone, but when I woke up again, she was back. That's how I knew it wasn't really my bedroom."

"Are you sure?" Peterson asked.

"Yes... yes, I'm sure," Stacy said, with a sigh of relief.

"The sharkmen took you," Peterson said. "Brought you to a room that looked like your bedroom—but wasn't. They did things to you then returned you to your real bedroom."

"Yes. Yes." Stacy laughed.

The two doctors stared at each other.

"So, did we just make a breakthrough?" Stacy smiled as she posed the question.

"I think so," Miller answered. "I think so."

INVASIONS

60

Coast Mountains

The information officer entered the tent with a report at least fifty pages long. He handed it to Major Gaines, nodded to Rebecca, then stood at attention. "I believe this is what you've been waiting for from the Americans."

Gaines held the weighty manuscript in both hands. All this sent via satellite relay and downloaded through a secure channel into the computers temporarily set up in the next tent. Impressive, he thought.

He read the cover.

TOP SECRET / MAJIC EYES ONLY. NATIONAL SECURITY INFORMATION

BRIEFING DOCUMENT: OPERATION MAJESTIC PREPARED FOR PRESIDENT-ELECT DWIGHT D EISENHOWER: (EYES ONLY) 18 NOVEMBER, 1952

WARNING: This is a TOP SECRET - EYES ONLY document containing compartmentalized information essential to the national security of the United States. EYES ONLY ACCESS to the material herein is strictly limited to those possessing Majestic clearance level. Reproduction in any form or the taking of written or mechanically transcribed notes is strictly forbidden.

TOP SECRET EYES ONLY T52-EXEMPT (E)

"Thank you," Gaines said. The officer saluted and left the tent. Gaines turned the page and read. On each page the phrases "Top Secret" and "Eyes Only" were written or stamped at least three times.

SUBJECT: OPERATION MAJESTIC PRELIMINARY BRIEFING FOR PRESIDENT-ELECT EISENHOWER. BRIEFING OFFICER: ADM. ROSCOE H. HILLENKOETTER

NOTE: This document has been prepared as a preliminary briefing only. It should be regarded as introductory to full operations intended to follow.

Operation Majestic is a top-secret research and development / intelligence operation responsible directly and only to the President of the United States. Operations of the project are carried out under control...

Gaines was familiar with the formality of intelligence documents and rapidly scanned ahead. It was clear that this document was written after the events Chase described to brief the incoming president.

...by special classified executive order of President Truman on 24 September, 1947, upon recommendation by Adm. Theodore Chase.

Gaines pondered the name. *Was this Chase's father?* He filed the thought away and continued.

On 24 June, 1947, a civilian pilot flying over the Cascade Mountains in the State of Washington observed nine flying disc-shaped aircraft traveling in formation at a high rate of speed. Although this was not the first known sighting of such objects, it was the first to gain widespread attention in the public media. Hundreds of reports of sightings of similar objects followed. Many of these came from highly credible military and civilian sources. These reports resulted in independent efforts by several different elements of the military to ascertain the nature and purpose of these objects in the interest of national defense. A number of witnesses were interviewed and there were several unsuccessful attempts to utilize aircraft in efforts to pursue reported discs in flight. Public reaction bordered on near hysteria at times.

In spite of these efforts, little substance was learned about the objects until a local rancher reported that one had crashed in a remote region of New Mexico located approximately seventy-five miles northwest of Roswell Army Air Base (now Walker Field).

On 07 July, 1947, a secret operation was begun to ensure recovery of the wreckage of this object for scientific study. During the course of this operation, aerial reconnaissance discovered that four small human-like beings had apparently ejected from the craft...

Gaines continued reading. The report described how an effective cover story was established using a misguided weather research balloon. The rest described the covert actions of Operation Majestic, including the involvement of the Order of the Dolphin, the aliens' increasingly aggressive maneuvers, and the initiation of the Roswell Protocols, just like Chase had described. "This is fascinating stuff."

"Doesn't mean it's true," Rebecca said. "They could have had all this disinformation set up in advance for just such a contingency."

Gaines tossed the briefing report aside. On the remaining pages was the summary of the autopsy report. He showed Rebecca the anatomical diagram of the alien on the page. "Do you think they could've made this up in advance?" He held up the page so she could see it. It clearly displayed an image of the beings they had encountered.

Rebecca frowned. "That I can't argue with."

"I'll be busy for a while," Gaines said. "Do me a favor and check up on everything. I'd like to get a realistic estimate of our progress."

"Will do," Rebecca said. She left the tent. Gaines continued reading.

SUBJECT: OPERATION MAJESTIC - SUMMARY OF AUTOPSY REPORT OF EXTRATERRESTRIAL

BIOLOGICAL ENTITIES (EBE) FOR PRELIMINARY BRIEFING FOR PRESIDENT-ELECT EISENHOWER. DOCUMENT PREPARED 19 NOVEMBER, 1952 BRIEFING OFFICER: ADM. THEODORE CHASE

NOTE: This document has been prepared as a preliminary briefing only. It should be regarded as introductory to the anatomy / capabilities of the EBE's. A detailed autopsy report will follow.

The EBE's physical form is humanoid. This is important from an evolutionary standpoint for the humanoid form is generalized, having the ability to transverse and survive in many different environments. Their average height* is five foot three inches tall when standing erect (they hunch when they walk or run). Their average weight* is 122 pounds. Normal body temperature is 96.5 degrees indicating they habituate in a colder climate. Ages unknown.

A basic physical description* includes gray skin, large black eyes, inverted nose, small mouth (no lips, teeth), small ears, hair, slightly elongated arms, six fingers, four toes, webbing present between all digits, and short claws. Strong physical and biological evidence suggest that the EBE's evolved from an aquatic mammal on their home world and stayed close to these roots. Some of the characteristics that lead to this hypothesis are as follows:

* NOTE: Their physical description may not accurately represent their species due to the limited number of test subjects.

MUSCULAR/SKELETAL: The   specific alignment and formation of muscles suggests that the EBE's are equally adept underwater as they are on terrestrial surfaces. Pores between the fingers and toes secrete a biological substance that acts as a webbing between the digits, allowing the elongated forelimbs to be pressed against the body and used as flippers. Four ribs were found to be "floating", not attached to the sternum, enabling the rib cage to collapse under the pressure of a deep dive without being damaged. The skull is tilted slightly upward in line with the spinal column.

Musculature is denser than a human's, giving them strength disproportionate to their size, enabling them to survive under greater atmospheric pressures (i.e., underwater). We estimate that an average entity is strong enough to lift approximately 250 pounds although we have been unable to put this to a test. Entities are extremely flexible and would appear to possess above-average dexterity. We presume their lighter and stronger bodies can run and swim faster than the average man.

SKIN: Their skin is smooth and gray in color (other hues probable due to the varying amounts of melanin present in each subject). Underneath is a thin insulating layer of blubber. This oily tissue serves to conserve body heat and store fat, providing the entity with a reservoir of energy to sustain itself during periods when food is in short supply. Skin also acts as an osmotic membrane allowing water but not salt to enter its system and is continually sloughed off and replaced.

HEAD: Their faces are less expressive and their vocalizations are completely alien, making communication attempts extremely difficult (recommend an expert in kinesics, the study of body language, for any future encounters). Eyes are large, black, and shift accordingly with emotional state. They appear to function independently of each other giving them a wider range of peripheral vision. Pupils are present, though can only be seen upon close inspection.

They have no external nose, only two slits in the center of their faces that are used for olfactory sensing only. Because of this we believe their sense of smell to be very limited. Their mouths are small, lipless, and contain twenty-eight teeth. Ears are small and rounded. Frequency range of hearing unknown, though presumably excellent. All EBE's had long stringy hair.

Braincase begins at top of head and continues to the bottom of the back of head. Brain size is slightly larger than human, weighing over 4 lbs. Although brain size is not necessarily a measure of intelligence, the very fact that they were able to travel here across the vast distances of space indicates a superior intellect. Situated just below the braincase on the back of the neck are "blowholes," two external openings to the entity's nasal passages. The blowholes open and close by an involuntary reflex of the muscles. Both nasal passages join together into a single tube which fits over the end of the trachea, which then passes through the oesophagus. The fact that the trachea and the oesophagus are completely separate enables the entities to feed underwater without drowning.

Between the eyes and the braincase is an area of fatty tissue we call the melon. The significance of this finding is we believe the entities have the ability to echolocate (seeing with sound). Theoretically, the EBE's generate sound in the form of clicks within its nasal sacs situated behind the melon. The melon acts as a lens which focuses the projected sound into a narrow beam. When the beam strikes an object, some of the energy is reflected back, received and transmitted via the middle ear to the brain. The time lapse indicates the distance. Repeated tests have shown this ability to be present.

INTERNAL ORGANS: Most internal organs are remarkably similar in function and position to a normal human with some improvements. Their four chambered heart and circulatory system are impressive in several ways. The presence of retia mirabilia protect the vital organs from the effects of water pressure and trap any nitrogen bubbles which may form in the blood. Retia in the thorax and around the spine supply blood directly to the brain through arteries in the spinal canal. This arrangement ensures a constant supply of blood to the brain despite changes in pressure. Circulatory system is also designed to conserve heat using what is known as countercurrent heat exchange (See Appendix 1A) and has an increased capacity to store oxygen.

Lung capacity indicates they can hold their breath underwater for about six or seven minutes before requiring air. The lungs are powerful and replace 80% of their gases with each breath (the human exchange rate is 30%). The kidneys consist of many interconnected lobes called renculi to improve filtration when diving.

All subjects were male so one must draw the conclusion they also reproduce by mating with females of their species. Long retractable penises, with paired testes, are prehensile and fully emerge when erect.

Eisenhower must have loved that part, Gaines thought. Not only was the incoming President learning that extraterrestrials really existed and were a potential threat to the nation, but they had bigger and better penises too. He skipped forward to the next section.

61

On her way to the ship, Rebecca watched as Dupres released the magazine from his gun, allowed it to drop into his hand then, with a quick snap, popped it back into place, lifted the weapon butt against his shoulder, and aimed it on the back of Blaze's head as the American physicist entered the second tent.

"Getting antsy?" Rebecca asked.

Dupres peered out from behind the lens, cursing under his breath. He shot Rebecca a sharp glance, followed by a pained expression and a throaty grunt. "We should pop 'em. They illegally crossed our borders. They have no right bein' here. This ship should be ours, man—and ours alone. We died for it, not them. It ain't right."

Rebecca nodded. "I agree. Unfortunately, Major Gaines doesn't. So why don't you put the weapon away and find some way to be constructive."

Dupres angrily lowered the gun and reigned in his emotions.

"Where's Carlson?" Rebecca asked.

"Other side," Dupres answered.

Rebecca patted him on the shoulder, squeezing gently as she walked off, letting him know that she understood. She walked around the ship and spotted Carlson supervising three men who were removing a tree that had fallen on the ship. A rope was tied around the thick base, and they were strenuously pulling. Gradually the tree loosened, and its weighty bulk gave in to their demands.

She waited until the tree fell clear before approaching. "Gaines needs a progress report."

Carlson barked a final order, instructing a man to magnetically attach a steel clamp to the hull, before answering. "Going well. We'll have this thing dug up and clear for lift in a little over an hour," he replied. He removed his gloves and ground his hands together. "The copters are already on their way. So are the escorts. All alien articles, clothing, weapons, food, medical supplies, were fully inventoried and stored. The EB's are all bagged and tagged and ready to go as well. The only problem we're facing is with our deceased men. The weapons they used don't exactly leave a tidy corpse. It'll take days to recover all the body parts, but what's going to be nearly impossible is removing every trace of physical evidence. There's blood and guts everywhere. It's going to get dangerous too when the animals start sniffing around. I'm going to recommend to the Major that we scorch the area clean."

"He's not going to go for it," Rebecca said.

"That's the best way to guarantee a completely sterilized environment. What if these creatures brought a virus with them? We don't act accordingly we could jeopardize countless lives."

"The only living things within fifty miles of here are the forest animals and the Major's not going to let you burn down their home to save them," Rebecca said.

"How about national security reasons? What if someone sees what we're doing? What if the press gets a hold of this?"

"He'll tell you a forest fire will attract a lot more attention. Don't worry. This one's going in the books as a standard military search and rescue exercise. I don't think anyone's going to care."

"Then how did the Americans find us?" Carlson asked.

"Good point, but I've worked with the Major for five years. Feel free to ask him what you want. You can even put your opinions in a report to cover yourself. But no matter what you say, his answers are going to be just what I told you. He will, however, be glad to hear about your progress."

"Thanks... I think."

"Anyone still inside?"

"A few of my men are still searching around—and that Logan guy. He's been in there for hours trying to decipher the language. Don't think he's having too much luck though. And, yes, I'm having him watched closely," Carlson answered before she could ask.

"I'm going to check on him," Rebecca said, backpedaling away.

"Last report, he was on the second level."

"Thanks."

***

Logan squat down, intently studying a panel of alien writing. He slowly stood, tracing the symbols etched in the metal. Reading people was something that came natural to him. Decoding a written alien language was a whole 'nother ball game.

Around him at a casual distance, two soldiers watched his every move. Despite performing their duty, their body language told him they were bored.

He noticed Rebecca approaching from down the corridor. She was very comfortable in her own skin, truly confident. Under different circumstances, he would definitely be interested in her. But he'd seen the way her and the Major looked at each other. He watched their eyes closely when they were together in the ship. There was more there than just a superior / subordinate relationship. Logan was pretty sure they were involved.

When one soldier saw Rebecca approaching, Logan overheard him asking the other if he could go outside for some fresh air and a smoke. The other officer nodded, granting him permission to leave. The soldier turned his back to Rebecca as he sidled past her in the narrow corridor and went on his way. Logan noted Rebecca's body language and expression and immediately saw she considered the soldier's behavior rude but was too professional to linger on it.

"Men," Logan said to her.

"Excuse me?!" Rebecca said.

Logan rose to his feet. "Er... Never mind... I was just thinking it might be difficult being the only female officer."

"It's not," Rebecca replied. "What are you doing?"

"Trying to learn as much as I can about their language while I have the chance. I never got the opportunity I was brought here for, and I get the feeling that once this affair is over, Chase will have me shipped back home. If this is the only chance I'm going to get, I aim to make the most of it."

"What have you learned?"

"Just what I thought I would. Nothing. I'm wasting my time. Written language is secondary. The spoken language almost always comes first. Children can learn to speak quickly but reading and writing must be taught. To further complicate it, each written language has its own style, its own syntax. I can't even tell if these symbols are numbers, letters, pictures, or words, let alone what sounds or objects they represent. Without understanding their spoken language, we have almost no chance of understanding their writing. Even if these symbols are numbers, we don't even know if they use the decimal system. Their mathematics may be based on a binary system. It's impossible to know."

"What about the rooms you mentioned earlier?" Rebecca asked.

"Not much help. Those symbols might've indicated a bedroom, like I speculated, but I'm probably wrong. Their words are going to vary depending upon their perceptions and what's important to them personally. For example, the Eskimos have different words for snow. They have different words for falling snow, snow on the ground, wet snow, fluffy snow, and so on, because snow is important to them. Their language reflects that importance. To us, it's just snow. Conversely, Shona, a language in Zimbabwe, has only three words for colors. Can you imagine only one word representing blue, red, purple, and every shade in between? Not a chance. Color is very important to us. That's why we have thousands of color names in our language to represent all the different hues. We have no idea how these aliens think, so we can't possibly learn their language without spending time with them."

"You've got one hour. Keep going. You never know," Rebecca said.

One hour, Logan thought. It might as well be a year.

***

"Nice poker face," Chase said to Blaze, who was smiling so broadly he could hardly contain himself. "Care to fill me in?"

"I can do it," Blaze bragged.

"You sure?"

"Absolutely. The aliens did most of it—the hard stuff. Turns out they were almost finished before the Canadians rudely interrupted them. Now it's just a simple matter of completing what they started." His eyebrows rose.

"You have all the right tools?" Chase asked.

Blaze nodded affirmatively.

"How much time do you need?"

"Five minutes—but I need to be alone. They've always got eyes on me."

"Not much we can do about that. Sooner or later, though, we'll get a diversion. First opportunity you get, do it. Don't worry about me either. If I don't make it, I don't make it. Only important thing is the mission. Is that understood?"

"Crystal clear," Blaze replied. He understood perfectly.

62

Prince Rupert, Canada

Stacy and Dr. Peterson made their way to the small, dimly lit parking lot in the back of the building. The only illumination came from a lone spotlight attached to one of the many trees which encircled the concrete lot. They stopped at a navy pickup truck as Peterson fumbled to get the keys out of his pocket.

"This is what you drive?" Stacy said.

"2002 Dodge Ram, one hundred eighty horses—can hold up to two and a half tons in the rear," Peterson stated proudly.

"I'm not much of a truck aficionado."

"What do you drive?"

"Camry. I took a cab here though. Too frazzled to drive."

"Where do you live?"

"About ten minutes outside of town. I got a place that gives me a splendid view of the mountains."

"Well then, hop in. I'll give you a ride home and show you zero to sixty in six seconds," Peterson said with the enthusiasm of a man half his age.

"Six seconds?" Stacy squinted her left eye in a way that said she knew he was exaggerating.

"Maybe ten," Peterson said, with a wink. "Get in."

They did. Peterson used a small key to unlock the club security device attached to the steering wheel and placed it on the floor between the seats.

"I didn't think car theft was a big problem around here," Stacy said. She got comfortable in the seat, strapping the seat belt snugly across her body.

"I lived in L.A. for a few years. Old habits die hard." He started the truck, turning on the headlights before shifting the gear into reverse. He backed the car out of the lot onto the street and—

THUMP!

"What was that?" Stacy asked.

Peterson put the car in drive and started down the road. "I believe that was an old man accidentally driving over the curb."

"There was no curb. It sounded like something fell down in the back of the pickup," Stacy said, quickly glancing behind her.

"I probably just hit a pothole, and my toolbox bounced up and down. They haven't paved these roads in years," Peterson said, shrugging it off.

Stacy let it go. "So, tell me Doc—"

"Jack. My name's Jack."

"All right, Jack. What does a regressive hypno-therapist need with a pickup truck and toolboxes?"

"I own the plumbing supply store over on Elm," he replied.

Stacy's mouth opened wide, and she began to laugh. "I was right."

"About what?"

"There aren't enough crazy people in Prince Rupert for you to make a living."

"Not by a long shot." Jack chuckled as he made a left at the next corner into the heart of town. "Seriously, though, I am very qualified. I've been doing this for thirty years... down in Vancouver and in the States. Known

Brad Miller longer than that. We both grew up here. Brad decided to move his practice up here to be closer to his family. I came back to take over the family business. I guess I just got tired of listening to other people's problems and decided to go back to things that can be easily fixed—like plumbing. You wanted to know my story. Well, that's my story."

Stacy was so busy evaluating this tidbit of information she almost forgot where he was taking her. Almost. "Oh, sorry... Make a right here."

Jack turned onto a dark deserted highway that led towards the mountains.

"Thanks, Jack. I mean that," Stacy said. "With everything going on, somehow, I feel that today I finally took a step in the right direction. Kind of like I opened a door in my head that has never been opened before."

"I got some theories on that if you're willing to listen. I believe I know what happened to you, but I couldn't mention it in front of Brad. He would think I'm crazy just for bringing it up."

"This is not going to be about my dad again, is it?"

"No. Completely different. Have you ever heard of alien abductions?"

Stacy gaped at him as if he might still be joking.

Then a bluish-gray creature with large black eyes appeared in his rear-view mirror. Jack's eyes widened with fear. Stacy turned her head to see what stole his attention and, to her utter disbelief, a sharkman stood right behind her in the back of the pickup. Long thin black hair trimmed its fishlike face and rested on its black skintight body suit.

Stacy screamed as the alien smashed a toolbox into the rear window. Its face, seen through the distortion of the web-like cracked glass, frightened her more than ever before.

The alien hoisted the toolbox above its head, ready to strike again.

63

Coast Mountains

Logan shielded his eyes as the chopper hovered above the terrain, kicking up cyclical waves of snow and dirt. He wasn't sure if this was the fourth different helicopter sent or the same one on its fourth trip. Either way, it was irrelevant. The final pieces of extraterrestrial cargo were loaded on board, and he was next. He grabbed onto the hanging ladder and climbed up, rocking to and fro as he stepped higher onto each rung. Upon reaching the top, he gripped the soldier's outstretched hand and was pulled aboard.

Taking a seat, he glanced back at the twenty containers and two black body bags in the cargo bay. By the size and shape both bags contained dead aliens. What a waste, he thought. There was a lot of waste on this assignment. His talents went unused, except for an all too brief encounter that ended badly. His time on the ship, though interesting, proved worthless as he was unable to gain even a glimpse of insight into their language.

Nevertheless, he had a job to do—a job which kept him on the team. Chase needed him to chaperone this shipment. Rebecca, Blaze, and Dupres accompanied the first three and it was important to Chase that both countries participate equally, in every way, in the extraction and recovery of the ship. A petty demand from an untrusting egotistical man, Logan thought. A demand

that Major Gaines shrewdly gave into, for it pacified
Chase while giving him nothing of substance and granted
Gaines a favor which he could call upon later.

The irony struck him. For all the languages he knew,
both spoken and unspoken, and all the negotiating savvy
he possessed, it was only Chase's irrational paranoia that
allowed him to remain. Well... it was better than being
sent home, as he'd assumed he would be. At least doing
this, he still had an opportunity to learn. He was still in the
game. A game that Logan felt was being played poorly.

He had seen this before during heated contract
negotiations. Chase was playing win-lose, assuming
everything he wanted had to be taken from his opponent.
If he was to be the winner, then his opponent had to be
the loser. It was often the wrong way to think. A defeated
opponent distrusts you and his bruised ego will eventually
retaliate. All win-lose achieved in the long run was
creating an enemy from a potential friend. The best way
to negotiate, Logan knew, was to go for win-win, where
both parties mutually benefited from the agreement. This
way both sides prospered and cooperation was ensured.
But Chase's ego was too great, and his mind was too
small.

Logan gazed out the window, watching the spacecraft
get smaller and smaller with distance, as he resigned
himself to the situation. He knew Chase wouldn't listen to
him anyway, even though he had successfully negotiated
hundreds of business deals across the globe. *Unless*,
Logan wondered, *Chase wasn't*—

His thoughts were interrupted by the loud roar of an F-
18 Hornet passing the chopper on the left. He spotted the
silhouettes of the Sparrows mounted beneath its fuselage
and the four other missiles mounted beneath the wings,

unsure if that was reassuring or downright terrifying. He followed its path then saw four more helicopters hover above the spaceship.

64

Coast Mountains

The first stage in bringing the ultimate prize home was about to take place. The spaceship was free from any surrounding debris, save the white flakes and scree thrown about by the artificially generated winds of the helicopter rotors. Four, six-inch-thick steel cables with grappling hooks were dropped—one from each helicopter—and fastened to the magnetic clamps attached to the ship's hull. Two tugs on the cables told the pilots they were cleared for lift. Moments later, to the creaking sounds of strained metal, the ship was carefully hoisted about six feet into the air.

To prevent the spaceship from buckling under the pressure of its own weight, steel mesh netting was pulled underneath it and quickly attached to the four cables, forming a cradle. Black tarpaulin was then pulled over the spaceship to hide it from any casual, or not so casual, observers. When that was done, three tugs on one cable told the lead pilot they were ready. A ladder was pushed out the helicopter's open door, unraveling as it fell. The final rung bounced less than a foot away from where Gaines and Chase were standing. They climbed up, and when they were safely aboard, the remaining ground crew tugged each cable, telling the pilots to leave.

The four helicopters cautiously lifted off, rising gradually over the trees so as not to upset the invaluable cargo. Gaines glanced nervously around the surrounding skies, glad to spot one of the four F-18 fighter jets escorting them to base. They had full combat capabilities and orders to strike down anyone dumb enough to stand in their way. Hopefully that would prove unnecessary.

Gaines plotted out every detail of the transport in a methodical fashion. The flight to the rendezvous point with the eighteen-wheeler would take them ninety minutes. All the portable cargo would be transferred by then and the ground transportation crew would be ready to go. Every item, every alien entity, would be covered, preserved, and guarded for the six-hour-long drive through the mountains. Chase, himself, and the spaceship would continue on a shorter route through the air. If everything went according to schedule, by 2:00 a.m., Pacific Standard Time the mission would be over, with everything successfully hidden in the underground research facility code-named Yukon Base Five.

Gaines noticed Chase scanning the skies as well. Gaines hunched forward scanning the helicopter's radar screen. He saw seven blips, all of them friendly. The skies appeared clear and safe. Unless, he thought, there was something alien lurking from high above that they couldn't detect. That unsettling thought, he knew, would keep him on constant alert all the way to the base.

65

Prince Rupert, Canada

Jack Peterson was half paralyzed with fear. He believed in extraterrestrials. Enough so that he was certain they were the cause of Stacy's nightmares. But he was woefully unprepared for one showing up in the rear of his pickup to prove he was right. Especially one trying to smash in his rear windshield with a toolbox. It was more than his mind could grasp. Unable to cope, he slammed on the brakes bringing the vehicle to a screeching halt.

Stacy and Jack jerked forward. Their fastened seat belts held tight.

They were the lucky ones.

The alien's head crashed into the rear window, lengthening the cracks and staining the window crimson with blood. The toolbox flew forward, popped open, and rained an assortment of tools over the roof and down upon the hood. The metal toolbox, landing last, made the loudest bang as it careened off the windshield, bounced off the hood, and sprang onto the road below.

For a long moment Stacy stared at the gray-blue head through the crimson-stained broken glass—a real life sharkman. She found herself in a state of disbelief as she looked into its lifeless eyes, fervently hoping it was dead.

The alien immediately pushed its face away from the glass and rose.

"DRIVE, DRIVE, DRIVE!" Stacy screamed in a fit of panic, as if driving would somehow put distance between themselves and the alien. Not knowing what else to do, Jack pressed the gas pedal to the floor. The sudden acceleration threw the alien backwards, sending him sliding shoulder first into the back of the pickup.

"Oh shit, oh shit," Jack muttered.

"Oh God, oh God, oh God," Stacy echoed.

Jack glanced into the rearview mirror, watching as the alien got to its feet. It sprang forward again. He spotted a left turn ahead and he came up with an idea. "Hold on," he said, turning the wheel sharply, quickly taking the curve.

The alien stumbled to the right, catching the side panel of the truck to prevent itself from falling over. Jack swerved sharply in the other direction. Then he continually jolted the vehicle from side to side, hoping to keep the creature off stride.

Stacy stared, completely mesmerized as the alien labored to reach the rear window. For a moment it was as if she was in a zoo examining every detail of this inhuman beast trying to get to her. In front of her was her most popular fictional villain come to life. *No... It was more. It was the thing that haunted her dreams.* The moment abruptly passed as she realized the thin veil of glass would not separate her from the monster for much longer. She gasped as she spoke, hardly able to catch a breath. "It's not working. Try something else."

Jack saw a sharp right turn coming up. He waited until the last possible instant then rapidly cut the steering wheel clockwise. The right two wheels lifted off the ground, nearly tipping the truck over. As he hoped, the alien lost its grip, but the maneuver pitched the alien forward and to the left, directly behind him. Using the left side panel for leverage, it grabbed a wrench from the floor and thrust it hard into the glass, shattering it to pieces.

A shard slashed Stacy's cheek.

Jack fared worse. Even though he instinctively ducked when he heard the glass shatter, numerous fragments lacerated his head. Blood trickled down his neck and, no longer able to concentrate on the road, he tried to fend off the alien. As he turned to face it, the alien punched him in the face. His head snapped sideways into the steering wheel, knocking him unconscious. His foot slipped off the gas pedal. The vehicle eased off the road, slowing down as it rode over the thick underbrush.

Tears wet Stacy's face as the vehicle rolled to a halt. As bad as her nightmares were, all she had to do to escape them was wake up. This was infinitely worse. There was no place to run. Nowhere to hide. No way out. The alien's long webbed fingers reached inside the truck, gripping the rear frame where the window used to be.

In desperation, Stacy grabbed the club which lay on the floor between her and Jack. She fumbled for the latch and managed to unbuckle her safety belt. With all the strength she could muster, she swung the club at the alien.

The alien caught the metal bar in mid-swing and ripped it from her grasp. It glanced at Stacy, checked a watch-like device on its wrist and emitted sounds that she couldn't understand.

Stacy cowered helplessly in the front seat. A feeling of déjà vu overcame her. She had been in this situation before... a long, long time ago. At this moment, she realized that Jack was right. She had been abducted by aliens. She was a little girl when they first took her. They performed experiments on her so horrifying that the only way her mind could protect her was to block them out.

She remembered more. Two other incidents flashed through her mind. Abducting her at age five was only the first time. They came back for her again and again throughout her life. They stole her childhood, turning her into a frightened little girl. They were responsible for all of it. She would not let them take her again.

"YOU BASTARD!" she yelled in rage.

Releasing her anger, she slammed her palm into the alien's fingers. It lost its grip and tumbled backward. She quickly slid over to the driver's side, pushing Jack's limp body flush against the door, and in a fit of rage stepped hard on the gas. The truck jolted forward. The alien stumbled but managed to grab onto the seat. Stacy reached back and dug her nails into the creature's hand, feeling its blubbery skin ooze beneath her fingernails as she forced it to release its hold.

She gunned the truck over the lip separating the pavement from the dirt and the pickup truck leapt into the air and back onto the road. The acceleration tossed the alien to the back once again. When the tires touched down, they skidded on the concrete, and the vehicle sped off.

"Okay, okay," she muttered and took several deep breaths, though nothing could stop the racing of her heart. Now what? She looked over at Jack, who was still unconscious, then returned her attention to the road. She glanced in the rear-view mirror, adjusted it, and noted the alien was quickly recovering. Her panic returned.

The alien was now upright. She couldn't read its expression, but surely it was angry. As it approached, she intentionally drove the car off the road. The jarring from the unpaved ground jostled the alien to its knees. Now she could only see its odd-shaped head through the rearview mirror.

Her home was only five minutes away. There she could call for help. She quickly swerved back onto the road. She looked again into the rear-view mirror and saw nothing. "Oh my god, oh god, oh god." Frantically, she adjusted the mirror in all directions but couldn't see it. She whirled her head around to the right. She saw nothing. Then the driver's side window burst inward, and the aliens' slick hand reached through and grabbed the wheel. Stacy screamed again.

Jack stirred as more shards of glass lacerated his face, the sharp pain awakening him. The wind blew through the broken window stinging his open wounds, bringing him fully back to consciousness. He felt Stacy next to him struggling to keep control of the vehicle. Upon seeing the strange limb in front of him, he remembered the situation and pounded on the alien's arm repeatedly until it let go of the wheel. Then, just as suddenly, he blacked out from a blow to the back of his head.

"JACK!" Stacy yelled. She was only four minutes away from home, but she knew she would never make it. She veered the vehicle hard to the right and sped up again. She heard the alien grab hold of the frame, feeling its malevolent presence right behind her. She scanned the vehicle wildly, searching for anything that might be useful. Something triggered an idea and without thinking rationally, she acted upon it.

She slipped Jack's seatbelt over her head and under her right arm, securing herself as best she could. She turned the vehicle sharply to the left, driving it off the road once again. The alien grabbed her hair, yanking it hard as it stumbled to the right. The pain brought tears to her eyes.

It didn't matter. She just needed to keep the steering wheel steady a little longer as the truck bounced wildly over the rocky terrain. She took a deep breath and prayed. Her heart pounded. The alien reached in. There were scant seconds left when she chickened out and slammed on the brakes. But it was too late.

The truck smashed head-on into a tree. The air bag deployed immediately, cushioning Jack's and her impact. Moments passed before she regained her senses. Even with the safety device functioning properly, Stacy was in so much pain, she could barely move. But she had to make sure.

She pushed the white cushion away from her face and looked behind her. The rear of the truck was vacant. She looked ahead, scanning the dark array of trees through the thick white smoke which rose from the engine. A part of the wooded area was illuminated by the beam of the left headlight, which still functioned much to Stacy's surprise. About thirty yards ahead, she saw it. The alien was sprawled out on the ground like a limp doll discarded by a child. She watched it, making sure it didn't move. Breathing a sigh of relief, she removed her seatbelt and collapsed on the front seat.

66

Coast Mountains

The four CF-18A's—the F-18 Hornets of the Canadian RAF—soared through the darkening sky. Purchased from McDonnell Douglas in 2001, they were first used by squadrons based at CFB Cold Lake, Alberta, and soon became the favorite low-cost escort fighter / interdictor replacing the F-4's and the A-6E's. They carried up to six AMRAAM weapons, two fuselage mounted and two on each outboard wing store stations. Each was also equipped with an airborne self-protection jammer, reconnaissance equipment, a signal data processor interface to provide automatic adjustments, and all-weather night attack capabilities.

To pilot Virgil Ramses, code named Hound—the sole operator of the single-seat, multi-mission fighter—there wasn't a better place to be. "Lynx, you reading any activity?" he asked over the comm-link.

"Skies are clear," Lynx reported back.

"Sure is good to be back where we belong, buddy. In the Hornets, we are large and in charge."

"I know what you mean. Those whirlybirds just don't cut it."

"Bet you what we're guarding does," Moose said, the third pilot guarding the ship.

Grizzly, the pilot of the fourth F-18, interrupted them. "I recommend you can the comm chatter, Moose.

Otherwise, Gaines will have your head on the wall instead of that moosehead you gave him."

"You got that right," Gaines said. "I hear one more careless remark like that over the airwaves, it'll be your last."

"My apologies, Major," Moose said.

"Unaccepted. Don't do it again." Gaines paused. "We're one klick from rendezvous. Status report?"

"No activity," Hound said.

"All clear," Grizzly responded.

"Clear," Lynx reported.

"Same here, Commander," Moose said. "Looks like a cake walk."

"Don't treat it like one. Circle the perimeter. Anything even looks suspicious, I want to know about it."

***

Gaines' helicopter slowed down, as did the other three.

It was completely dark now. Below, he saw the lights of the ground transportation crew. From the frenzied activity it was apparent they had fallen behind schedule and were hurrying to catch up. He pulled out his new, personal two-way radio. "Rebecca, what's going on down there?"

Rebecca waved her blue flare so Gaines would know her position and then answered back. "Only two more minutes needed. The last helicopter preferred safety over speed and arrived a little late. Judgment call. I gave him the benefit of the doubt."

Gaines didn't like it, but he knew safe was better than sorry. He signaled his pilot to alert the others to hover until he personally saw the ground unit leave. "You got two minutes, no more." He put the radio away.

"What's the problem?" Chase asked.

"There is none. We leave in two," Gaines responded.

Chase disapprovingly shook his head. Gaines ignored him.

"We're going to have to kill him," Chase said.

Gaines quickly faced him with a puzzled expression.

"Let me rephrase. We're going to have to kill it," Chase said.

"It, what?"

"The alien that got away. It's the only way."

Gaines hadn't forgotten. He just didn't know what to do, so he filed it in the back of his mind until the immediate concerns were addressed. "What about the Roswell Protocols?"

"Don't much matter now. Even if the crash site is covered up, it won't make a hill of beans worth of difference if that alien makes its way home. Matter of fact, it'll look a hell of a lot worse. We have to find it and kill it."

"There's got to be a better solution," Gaines said. His guilty conscience wouldn't accept correcting one tragic mistake with another.

"If you think of one, let me know. Until then, I suggest we proceed with that course of action."

***

Hound banked his F-18 sharply to the left, reaching the area of the perimeter that was nearest to the coastline. A blip briefly flashed on his AN/APG-65 radar—then disappeared before he got a second look. The multimode digital air-to-air tracking radar could simultaneously track ten targets and display eight to the pilot. Hound quickly cycled through the modes. He stared at the display for a few seconds to see if the ghost image returned. It didn't. He engaged his night vision goggles but failed to see anything in the sky. "Lynx, you readin' anything?"

"Still clear, Hound. Have you got something?" Lynx asked.

"Don't know. Hound to Major Gaines. Got a brief flash on my radar, but it's gone now. No visual signs either—" Suddenly his radar beeped twice and continued pulsing as two small lights sped towards his position. "Holy shit!" He banked his jet left and climbed. The blips on his radar followed his maneuver and closed in quickly. "I got two on my tail. Can't shake 'em. Came outta—"

***

The explosion lit up the night sky. Gaines, Chase, and their pilots had to shield their eyes as the brightness of the blast shone through the chopper's windows. Their helicopter jerked down as the pilot of one of the other carrier choppers momentarily lost control.

The ground transportation crew treated it as a wakeup call. Their hurried movements halted for a moment—then every crew member moved with a newfound sense of urgency. They were now in the middle of a war.

***

"HOUND!" Lynx yelled desperately, refusing to accept his friend's death. He pulled back on the throttle hard, lifting his craft upward then turned west toward the direction of the blast.

Moose executed a similar maneuver. Whoever did this would pay. Except their radar screens were blank and they couldn't locate the assassin.

***

The confirmation Major Gaines was expecting came through on the radio. "Hound's gone. No idea why or how, but we're on it," Moose reported.

"Find out and take them out," Gaines commanded. He reached for his radio again. "Rebecca, get the hell out of here now."

"But—," Rebecca protested.

"No buts. Do it!" Gaines ordered.

"Sir?" the pilot asked looking for an order.

"Land. We're sitting ducks up here." Gaines turned to Chase. "Is it them?"

The skies brightened again before Chase could answer. This time the unfortunate victim was Grizzly.

***

The final portable items were loaded onto the truck and Rebecca had received her orders to go. Logan stood next to her. She handed him a gun. "Get in the front seat, I'll drive."

Logan did as she commanded. Rebecca ordered Carlson and Dupres to round up a company of jeeps to act as a convoy. Shortly thereafter, she had five jeeps escorting her: three armed with mounted machine guns, two with rocket launchers. By the time the spaceship, its carriers, and the Major and Colonel landed, they would be gone, leaving only Blaze and Carlson behind to meet them.

**

The pilot of the lead helicopter immediately ordered the others to land and they hastily began their descent.

"Ease up, Lieutenant. The spaceship mustn't be damaged," Gaines shouted.

"It's not them," Chase said. "Your fighters wouldn't have had any warning at all. Someone else found us and I want to—"

Gaines grabbed him by the collar. "The only ones who could have found us are you."

Chase grabbed Gaines' wrists, attempting to pull him off. "Now you're being stupid and paranoid," he said through gritted teeth.

Gaines turned sideways, threw Chase into a seat, and pulled out his gun to hold him at bay. "Cooper, radio Lynx. I want the enemy identified now." The copilot did as he was told.

"You're wasting time," Chase said. "Why would we take what we already have?"

Lynx reported in over the comm. "Major, I caught a glimpse in the flare. I think it was a Comanche, but it disappeared too quickly to get a good look and nothing's coming up on the scope. Can't rely on the night wear either—it's too risky."

"Comanches are yours," Gaines said to Chase.

"I'm telling you, they're not Comanches," Chase said.

Gaines wasn't sure what to believe. "Tell Lynx I want a positive ID, now!" he ordered the copilot. The helicopter rocked slightly with the weight shift as the spaceship touched down first. A few seconds later all four helicopters carrying the spaceship touched down as well. Gaines waved his gun, letting Chase know to stay put. "God help you if you're lying".

***

"Damn. How can I fight an enemy I can't find?" Moose muttered to himself in frustration. He banked his jet hard to the left, then hard back to the right, racing through the skies like a silver rocket out of control. He had to make himself as hard a target to hit as possible. "Lynx, we're going to have to take them down visibly. Forget the radar. Forget the night gear too. If they take down one of us, the blast might blind the other. Just keep your eyes to the sky and shoot at anything that moves."

***

"I read you, Moose," Lynx said. "Looks like we're up against stealth craft. Keep moving. We don't know how many of them there are."

Lynx pulled back on the throttle to gain altitude. It was time to scan the skies from above and see exactly what he was up against.

It was a move the enemy anticipated he would make.

67

Kenuchio Satsui and Ishiguro Kanuto were enjoying themselves immensely. As the pilot and gunner of Shadow, the first Ninja prototype, they were the deadliest warriors in the sky.

Like their namesake, they could not be heard. The Ninja's five blade rotor whispered only a 'whir' rather than the 'whop-whop-whop' of the standard four blade design. A special shroud encased the fantail, eliminating the noisy mixing of wakes from the tail and main rotors. At high speeds, their noise level blended in well with the background. At low speeds, they were completely silent.

They could not be seen. Shadow's black color provided perfect camouflage with the night sky, making visual ID difficult. They were undetectable by radar. The Ninja's shape was such that radio signals wouldn't bounce cleanly off it. The shrouds that covered the rotor blade roots were made with special radar absorbing material. The air-to-air missiles were carried inside on doors that swung up and out for firing and loading. The landing gear and six-barrel 30-millimeter gun also retracted into the body. They were even invisible to infrared detection. Its engine, hidden by V-shaped inlets, and its complex exhaust system built into its tail boom, suppressed its position-revealing heat.

They were smart and efficient. The virtual reality helmets they wore linked them almost telepathically to nose-mounted sensors. They were able to choose between a starlight view or an advanced infrared sensor that targeted even through smoke and haze. The onboard F-22 computers scanned the scene and helped them identify priority targets. Armed with a sophisticated autopilot, they were able to appear briefly from behind a mountain, survey the battlefield with one sweep of their sensor array, then return to cover while they planned an attack.

They were swift. The fly by wire controls helped them exploit the Ninja's top speed of 300 miles per hour. Their agility was such, that while hovering they could rotate 180 degrees in three seconds.

And most fearsome of all, their strokes were deadly. Their first target fell easily. After Whisper took out one F-18 with two anti-aircraft missiles (AAM's), they followed up quickly striking down a second F-18 with automatic gunfire. Then they disappeared, awaiting the enemy's next move. It was just as they anticipated.

Kenuchio thought these westerners were as simple-minded as they were predictable. He knew their invisibility would cause one to fly high for a visual survey. Riding high on his own self perceived superiority, he smiled as he moved in quietly for the kill. When he was within a mile, he ordered the shot. Ishiguro opened the swinging doors that carried the missiles, locked on, and fired.

68

The AAM appeared on Lynx's radar as soon as it touched the air. It was less than a mile away and closing fast.

"Got you," Lynx whispered.

The enemy took his bait. It was a risky gamble, but he knew from Hound's final words that the helicopters had to reveal themselves to launch a missile. He flew high for a visual survey, intentionally putting himself in harm's way, knowing the enemy would anticipate the move. But it was going to be a lot closer than he had calculated.

He throttled the aircraft sharply right, arcing in a semi-circle, hoping to dodge the weapon while simultaneously getting a fix on who fired it. Unfortunately, to do that meant having to avoid the rocket while heading towards it. He watched his radar as the AAM closed in. If he didn't move now, he wouldn't make it.

He sped up along the arc and dove. When the missile followed, he released chaffing to confuse its internal targeting sensors then banked away and ascended. The missile went straight for the countermeasure, leaving him a clear path to his target. He scanned the open skies for the enemy and spotted him a hundred feet below and to his left. Their pilot was smart. His escape route placed him between Lynx and the spaceship. Lynx couldn't fire back without the risk of endangering his own men. However, he did recognize his enemy before they disappeared in the distance.

"Major, this is Lynx. We're up against Ninjas. I recognize 'em from last month's intel briefing. Looks like they're everything they're supposed to be."

"I told you," Chase said.

"The Japanese?! How the hell did they get wind of this?" Gaines said. He grabbed the pilot's radio. "Lynx, are you positive?"

"Wouldn't have said so if I wasn't."

"Moose, did you read that?" Gaines asked.

"Loud and clear," Moose replied. "Soon as I spot one of those bastards, I'm going to blow them out of the sky. Copy and out."

***

"Rebecca, where are you?" she heard Gaines' voice over her radio.

"Moving as fast as we can," she replied.

She was driving the eighteen-wheeler over a hundred km/h (62mph) on the highway, its headlights the only guide along the dark road. Despite its appearance, the truck would have been inconspicuous if not for the fact it was surrounded by five jeeps loaded with military personnel. In truth, it wasn't. The entire truck was built with special armor plating beneath its ordinary exterior. The engine was housed within a solid steel casing to prevent external sabotage. The windshield and side glass windows were bulletproof. The tires were resistant to any puncture. Nothing short of a tank would be able to stop it.

"What do you know about the Japanese stealth helicopters called Ninja?" Gaines asked.

"Is that what's up there?" she asked.

"The Japanese?!" Logan said, with surprise in his voice.

"Affirmative," Gaines said.

Rebecca glimmered with anger. "One deadly beast, David. Designed and built for nighttime search and rescue in enemy territory. Silent, cool, quick, and lethal. By the time you spot them, you're already dead. I know they had an exercise scheduled for their first two prototypes this week. Britton was supposed to be looking into them."

"Looks like he wasn't paying close enough attention. Seems they've brought them straight to our front lines. Keep an eye out. You may be next."

"There are only two of them in existence. That means they're not able to steal the ship, which means they're here to destroy it," Rebecca said.

"By the same reasoning, you should be careful. They can still take home what you're carrying. Don't let them get it no matter what. Destroy it yourself if you have to."

"Understood." Rebecca placed the hand-held radio on the seat and kept an eye on the sky.

***

Gaines and Chase walked over to Lt. Carlson and Blaze and explained the entire situation. "Any ideas?" Gaines asked.

Blaze looked to Chase, who granted him an approving nod. "Yeah. You think your pilots can keep them busy for ten minutes?"

"They can do it." Gaines spoke with pride, even though half of the F-18 pilots had already been killed.

Blaze told them *half* of what he had in mind. Gaines relayed the plan to the fighter pilots.

***

"Ten minutes. Did you catch that, Moose?" Moose heard over his com.

"Lynx, in ten minutes this fight will be all over," Moose griped. "One way or the other."

"I prefer our way, Moose. Use maneuver eighteen."

A blip appeared on Moose's radar screen. *Behind him!* He quickly banked left avoiding an array of gunfire. The blip stayed on the screen. That was good, Moose thought. At least I can see him. He dove down, then up, then swerved right and left, avoiding the incoming bullets. Now, if he could just circle around and get behind him.

The chance never came. An instant later a second moving blip appeared replacing the first one. The Ninja had launched a missile and returned to stealth mode.

"Shit," Moose muttered.

"Moose," Lynx called through the radio.

"I'm still here, though maybe not for much longer. I got a missile coming in fast. Gonna see if I can lose it." He pushed the throttle forward and dove down at a forty-five-degree angle. The light on his radar told him the missile followed without skipping a beat. Moose swerved again. The light still followed him. It was going to be close. He pulled back on the throttle and arched up, like a horse stretching its neck to the sky.

The missile shot past him just underneath his tail fin. Moose righted himself quickly and turned the other way, causing the missile to lose lock. Five seconds later, the blip disappeared as the missile impacted with the ground.

"Whahooooo." Moose screamed, having cheated death by the narrowest of margins. "You're dead, motherfuckers. You guys are fucking dead." Moose spotted Lynx's transponder signal. He couldn't believe it. Lynx bet on his survival and had already initiated maneuver eighteen. That crazy, wonderful son of a bitch, he thought. I won't let you down.

Maneuver eighteen was simple and dangerous. When faced with an undetectable opponent, one pilot acted as bait, luring the enemy out, while the second pilot swooped in and took him out. However, the plan had one flaw. They were up against multiple targets and only one, if any of them, would be fooled. The other target was free to attack. It was a risk they had to take. Moose stayed low hoping to evade the Ninja's radar, maybe tricking its pilot into thinking he'd been killed. Staying in their predetermined flight patterns, they waited for the enemy to bite.

It didn't take long.

A flash appeared on the scope above and behind Lynx. From below, Moose spotted the Ninja, its side doors opening, a missile attached to a flap extending out. Moose climbed to attack. He acquired the target and locked on to it before it fired a single missile.

Lynx shouted into his radio, "Moose, abort. Get the hell out of there!"

The warning came too late. The Japanese had read the trap and reversed it. The second stealth helicopter was waiting for Moose and fired a barrage of machine gun fire through the side of his cockpit. Moose was hit so many times his body spasmed, forcing his hands to release the controls. His bullet-riddled body slumped forward onto the stick. The plane nose-dived to the ground, crashing ferociously into a mountain ridge like a bug splatting a windshield.

***

Lynx stared at the explosion. That was three friends he'd lost in as many minutes. He glared at his radar scope hellbent on revenge, but both Ninjas were gone. He was alone and his enemies were invisible and still out there. Lynx didn't dare panic. He didn't have the time. He needed to hold them off for seven more minutes.

He didn't think he'd last even one.

69

Blaze, despite the desperate situation, was enjoying himself. He ordered the pilots of the four helicopters to disconnect the steel cables and the clamps under the guise that they would be safer if his plan failed, though he had another reason in mind. Then, after cutting the ropes and removing the tarp, he had led a team into the spaceship's engine room where he issued instructions for them to repair the damage.

"This is crazy," Carlson said.

"It'll work," Blaze said.

For five hours this afternoon, Blaze had painstakingly traced every crystal strand he was able to. The technology, though incredibly complex and beyond his immediate comprehension, was designed for simplicity. The crystal strands were grouped together in sets. Each set formed a circuit between a function and the ships' power source—which Blaze believed was a compact nuclear fission reactor. Each circuit was also duplicated using alternative routes for backup. Except for three. The two sets that were disrupted by the damaged panel and a set behind a wall on the upper level—the bridge, as Blaze referred to it—that was intentionally cut.

All they had to do was reconnect the crystal strands using heat to fuse the replacement strands and that, theoretically, would restore the ship's function. What made it even easier was the aliens had already initiated and almost completed the repairs to the damaged panels.

Blaze saw how they patched the circuitry and knew he could repeat the process with the tools they had on hand.

He got Chase, Gaines, and Carlson started on repairs in the engine room, then headed to the bridge to repair the intentionally cut strands there on his own. Those required his personal attention because they were the important ones—the ones responsible for turning the ship's power on, to complete the circuit Blaze needed to spring his trap on the Japanese and save the spaceship. That's also why, he thought, they were the ones intentionally cut—to stop us from using this ship when the Canadian squad closed in.

The damaged circuitry in the engine room the others were working on was necessary only for the latter part of his plan—the part that would secure the ship solely for the United States. And the most ingenious thing of all, Blaze thought, was that he had the Canadians doing all the work that would ultimately cost them the grand prize.

He beamed, feeling like a grandmaster of chess, playing against two opponents at the same time. His strategy was so clever that he was about to call checkmate on both players, the Japanese and the Canadians, in one swift bold move. And his erstwhile opponents wouldn't even catch on until he was victorious.

If only they knew, he thought. He estimated it would be seven more minutes until they did.

***

To Lynx's own amazement, he was still alive. So far, he had anticipated where and when the Ninjas would appear and maneuvered himself safely away. He glanced at his digital timer. Only two minutes passed. Damn. He thought it felt longer.

His radar showed a bogey appearing behind him. Before he could react, a rocket was on his tail, so close he only had one chance.

He pushed the throttle stick forward and dove for the hard deck, heading almost straight down accelerating to over 1000 mph. The missile followed his path and closed on him. It was a race. It was that simple. If he won, he lived. If he lost, he died.

He waited until the last possible instant before pulling out of his nose-dive, narrowly missing the ground by only a hundred feet. The missile's internal guidance systems automatically compensated for his course change and made its own adjustments to cut off his angle of ascent. In a nanosecond the missile angled up and rapidly sped towards him.

It tore through Lynx's wake then smashed with powerful impact into the ground. Its warhead detonated, and what was once a peaceful harmony of green and brown was swallowed whole by a sea of destructive yellow. Instantly, the earth became a fiery pit spewing forth deadly flames. Its long-reaching waves of fire erupted skyward, drowning Lynx's aircraft in a deluge of heat.

Then, like a surfer riding out from the cone of a tidal wave, Lynx slipped free.

He was grateful to be alive. Unfortunately, he had to return to the skies and let the enemy know he was still here. Otherwise, they would go straight for the spaceship. He checked the time. Four more minutes to go.

***

Logan felt the truck rattle as a missile erupted behind them, taking out the rear of their convoy. The two remaining jeeps fired wildly into the air, hoping to hit the invisible target. One of the trucks in front of them launched a SAM. None of the missiles connected.

"Shit, they're on us already," Rebecca said.

The anger and determination on Rebecca's face was clear to Logan. He had negotiated with the Japanese many times. He spoke their language. He understood their culture. And even though he knew this was not their way, he also knew that to them, honor and duty were of the highest importance. If they failed, they lost face, causing them to lose their status in society. For them, that could be a fate worse than death.

The Japanese had a saying, Logan knew. Business is war. Up until now, Logan always believed that. Now he knew that no matter how heated things got in the world of business, war was much worse. In business he could negotiate. He could use their Japanese's strenuous peer pressure to his advantage, offering a way to save face in return for a favor. Here, he would never get the chance. There was no deal to be made. He knew they would be relentless even if they didn't personally believe in this battle. Because of their code, they would succeed or die trying. To do anything less would be dishonorable.

"They're not going to stop until they've destroyed us or taken what we're carrying," Logan said.

"Tell me something I'm not aware of," Rebecca shot back. She honked the horn twice and pushed the pedal to the floor. The two trucks in front of her took the hint and drove faster.

But no matter how fast they drove, they couldn't get away. The Ninja appeared from behind a hill and hovered directly in front of them, strafing the road with gunfire.

The driver of the lead vehicle didn't have time to react. Bullets tore through his windshield. The jeep swerved with unbalanced momentum and flipped over twice before bouncing off the road like a kicked rock.

The hail of bullets continued. The second jeep bore the brunt. Its tires popped, its engine fizzled and smoked, and it came to a screeching, unscheduled halt.

Rebecca slammed on the brakes, stopping their truck just inches behind it, however the sudden halt caused their truck to jackknife. The jeep behind her smashed into the back of the truck nudging the cargo hold even further out of line. Another trailing jeep slanted off the road to avoid hitting them.

Rebecca cursed and slammed her fist against the dashboard. Rapid-fire bounced off the front of her truck, ricocheting wildly in all directions. Two men in the front jeep fell forward as they were hit. The next concentration of bullets pounded their truck's bulletproof windshield. At first, the bullets bounced off, but under the continuous onslaught the windshield shuddered and creaked. The glass was going to live up to its bulletproof guarantee—but the frame would not.

"GET OUT!" Rebecca yelled. She opened the door, jumped out, and took cover behind it. Logan did the same on his side. An instant later, the entire bulletproof windshield crashed upon the steering wheel and front seat. If they had not gotten out in time, they would have been crushed.

Rebecca and Logan crouched behind their open doors as bullets continued pounding the steel. When they stopped, Rebecca leapt up and fired her gun at the Ninja. Six men from the second jeep did the same. Their ammunition was wasted. The bullets that didn't miss, "pinged" harmlessly off the helicopter's armored plating, and the Japanese responded with an even more brutal assault. Their gunner sprayed the area with hundreds of steel bullets. Two soldiers fell as shots cut them down. The rest of the soldiers ran for cover. Logan raced as fast as he could behind the truck for better protection. Rebecca, blocked by the jackknifed rear, ducked and rolled beneath it to avoid a hail of ricocheting gunfire, and met up with Logan at the rear doors.

"We need a better weapon," Logan said.

"No shit," she replied.

She reloaded a magazine and shot out the lock on the rear door. Then she grabbed hold of the door, pulled it back, and climbed inside the truck.

"What are you doing?"

"I'm going to get one."

***

Blaze had just completed repairing the circuit. All he had to do now was hit the button that would turn on the ship's power. That was the easy part. The difficulty would be the timing. How long would it take for the reactor to warm up? He grabbed his radio. "Are you done?"

"Almost," Gaines answered.

"I'm all set," Blaze said. "I'm estimating it will take about thirty seconds for the systems to become operational. Unfortunately, it's just a guess. There's a chance your pilot could get caught in our trap as well."

"Make sure that doesn't happen," Gaines said.

"I calculated the conductivity rate based on our own technology. It's the best I can do under the circumstances. It's going to have to do because everything must be timed exactly right. Tell me when he's 30 seconds out."

Taking down Lynx was not part of Blaze's plan, even though it would make 'Phase Two' easier. He had no problem taking down the Japanese fighters—after all they were trying to kill him—but Lynx was a different story. They were on the same team. At least for the next few minutes.

***

"Lynx, are you ready?" Gaines' voice came through the radio.

Lynx was in the middle of a barrel roll, busy evading a barrage of gunfire. "About time, Major."

"Begin flyby now. When you're thirty-five seconds out, signal back."

***

Rebecca grabbed one of the alien weapons. Its indicator was bright blue. She pointed it out the rear of the truck and pressed her finger into the curved indentation. Nothing happened. She threw it to the floor and grabbed another, getting the same result.

"They didn't work for us then. What makes you think they'll work for us now?" Logan asked.

Rebecca refused to give up. She tried three more, tossing each one to the ground in disgust as they failed.

"They're probably coded," Logan said.

"Do you always state the obvious?" she yelled. "Of course they're coded. If you had a weapon this powerful, would you allow it to be used against you?"

Logan crouched as the sounds of rapid gunfire bouncing off the roof suddenly echoed throughout the rear of the truck. Indents formed in the steel from multiple bullets impacting in the same spot. The reinforced plating wouldn't last long.

"Sooner or later they're going to tire of shooting at us and use a missile," Logan shouted, over the noise.

"Not right away. They want what we have in here as much as we do. For now, they're going to try to scare us into the open, make us panic. Once we're dead, they can land and take what they want."

"So how do we quickly decode them?" Logan asked.

Rebecca drew a knife from her belt. "Simple. We don't." She grabbed one of the black body-bags, unzipped it, and spilled an alien body onto the floor like a wet fish from a net. Without hesitation, she grabbed its hand and cut off the alien's elongated thumb with her knife. She grabbed some duct tape from a shelf and taped the lower half of the thumb onto her own, leaving the upper half exposed.

"That's disturbing," Logan said.

The steel rain ceased, the silence that followed broken by a commanding Japanese voice over a loudspeaker. "ATTENTION CANADIAN FORCES. IF YOU WISH TO LIVE, DROP YOUR WEAPONS AND COME OUT WITH YOUR HANDS UP. WE HAVE NO DESIRE TO INFLICT UPON YOU ANY FURTHER HARM. WE ARE INTERESTED ONLY IN THE CONTENTS OF THE TRUCK. IF YOU WANT TO LIVE, SURRENDER IMMEDIATELY. YOU HAVE TEN SECONDS TO COMPLY."

Rebecca cursed under her breath. "They're lying. They'll try to take us all down in one quick burst. If they succeed, they'll take the merchandise. If they fail, they'll blow it to bits and us along with it." She quickly swiped an alien weapon from the floor. "You ready?"

"Fingers crossed," Logan said.

They both climbed out of the truck. Around the corner of the truck six Canadian soldiers, all stood with their hands raised high above their heads. Dupres was among them. Logan raised his hands and walked slowly from behind the safety of the vehicle. Rebecca waited a few seconds then did the same.

The Ninja paused a few more moments. Then, as Rebecca had anticipated, it resumed fire. Two soldiers fell instantly in the first volley. Dupres and the others dove for cover.

Rebecca aimed the weapon at the Ninja, pressed the alien's thumb into the indentation—and it fired. A photon of blue light shot into the sky and sheared the rotor off the top of the stealth helicopter. It dropped like a stone.

On its way down, Rebecca fired again, an insurance shot that pummeled the Ninja as it fell. The blue light punched straight through the windshield and sliced through the pilot and the gunner before exploding out the tail of the ship. Two seconds later, the helicopter smashed into the ground.

The blue color in the weapon's display faded. With a shrug, she placed it in her pocket, took off the thumb, and walked towards the remaining soldiers, who were only now making their way out of the dense woods.

Dupres gave the downed chopper the finger, while shouting obscenities at it. As Rebecca approached them, the soldiers stopped for a second and gave her a huge round of applause.

"Whooooo," Dupres screamed as he clapped his hands. "Ma'am, if you don't mind me saying so, you kick some serious ass."

Rebecca took a bow and clapped back at them. "Thanks, fellas. Let's tend to the wounded. We still have a lot of work to do." She grabbed the two-way from its holster and radioed her success to Major Gaines.

70

Gaines was glad to hear Rebecca's update. Now it was their turn. He tensed, watching each second slowly tick off his watch. It was up to Lynx and Blaze to take down the second Ninja. Once Lynx gave the signal, Blaze would turn the power on, bringing back the interference field that jammed all electronics.

"NOW," Lynx shouted into the comm. "Inbound with the Ninja hot on my trail."

Gaines relayed the message to Blaze.

"Sprung," Blaze said, hitting the button.

For a moment nothing happened. Then the ship whirred and clanked to life. In the engine room, Gaines, Chase, and Carlson watched as a protective shield rose, completely enclosing the power sphere. It took ten seconds to lock into place. Ten seconds Blaze hadn't accounted for.

***

Bullets strafed across Lynx's right wing, one round hitting the fuel tank. Precious fuel sprayed into the air. Automatically, self-sealing foam quickly filled the bullet hole halting the leak and preventing any serious damage.

Lynx knew his straight line to the ship made him an easy target but that's what was needed to lure the enemy over the spaceship. It was their only hope for survival, even if it meant giving up his own.

***

The reactor finally began to glow. "It's starting," Chase told Blaze over the radio.

Blaze was busy at another control panel in the room, desperately trying to open the dome. He needed to see what was happening. It was more than just curiosity. It was essential to the second phase of his plan. He had traced the connection correctly but still didn't know exactly which switch on the panel was the right one. He grabbed his radio and responded to Chase. "Damn, it's taking longer than I thought. I overestimated the aliens' capabilities."

The trap was sprung but it was going to take too long to close—and they weren't going to get a second chance.

"Maybe we should get the hell off this ship," Carlson said. "The Ninja's going to fire at it as soon as he flies by, and we're standing in the middle of the bullseye."

"Sit tight," Gaines said. "We see this through. The only thing we're going to do now is wait and pray."

***

Blaze finally managed to get the dome open. Behind the retracting metal facade was a clear shield with a flawless view that magnified nearby objects of interest. Initially, it highlighted Lynx's F-18 as it zipped past. Then it highlighted and magnified a second object, a black helicopter that gave up its pursuit and slowed to a hover over the ship. After a menacing moment, it angled downward directly into Blaze's line of sight, as if it were staring directly at him.

The Ninja loomed in the darkness with terrifying presence. It reminded Blaze of a dragon. It dominated the sky, its hide looked impenetrable and strong, and those unfortunate enough to bear witness to it trembled. Then its wings spread, revealing the instruments of its fiery breath, missiles primed to launch that would obliterate them and the entire spaceship. For the first time, Blaze doubted his plan. 'Phase Two' became a distant thought as 'Phase One' seemed destined to fail.

Blaze was shaking. No, not just him. The entire ship was rumbling. An instant later the vibration changed to a comforting hum. It was working. The fission reactor had successfully generated sufficient electricity through the ship's outer conduits that an electromagnetic field surrounded the ship like a sheath and emitted an electromagnetic pulse. Every electronic device within a mile radius of the spaceship would be disrupted.

The Ninja was no exception.

***

Ishiguro's finger tensed. In one more second the wings would lock into place and the missiles would be ready.

An invisible pulse pierced the Ninja's thick hull, short-circuiting its onboard computers and its guidance systems. Sparks flew off the controls, momentarily burning whatever they touched before fizzling out. Ishiguro's virtual reality helmet crackled and caught fire. He hastily removed it, threw it to the floor, and stomped out the flames. The helicopter swayed wildly back and forth and spun. Ishiguro grabbed the stick with both hands, struggling fiercely to regain control.

To everyone's surprise, including his own, he managed to succeed.

***

"Oh, shit," muttered Blaze. He stared, bewildered from inside the ship. His eyes widened with fear as the Ninja did not fall. The trap sprung perfectly. The ship powered up and, just as planned, released an electromagnetic pulse against his enemy. Yet it didn't work. The dragon had been struck by the blade of science yet still soared. It had fallen back under the force of the blow but still lived.

Blaze had overestimated the effectiveness of the electromagnetic pulse. He thought it'd be strong enough to disable all their systems, and based on the helicopter's jarred movements, it damaged them, but something went wrong. Could their pilots have been that skilled that they kept the Ninja flying manually, even after that sudden burst? It didn't matter. Whatever the reason, the danger was still out there.

Think, Blaze, think. I bought us some time. There has to be something else here I can throw at it.

Then he looked up through the clear shielding and saw the helicopter slowly balance itself in the air. It shifted. Its tail rotor rose, its nose angled downward once again, and it spun back slowly in his direction.

Blaze knew time had just run out.

***

Kenuchio and Ishiguro put out the small fires. They no longer had their advanced technology. They no longer could acquire a lock on a target. The sputtering rotor let them know they probably wouldn't make it back home. But none of that mattered. They would still complete their mission.

Kenuchio switched all the controls from automatic to manual. Ishiguro got out of his seat, stumbled toward the wing, and armed the missile by hand. Once the Ninja was steady, they would fire the missile using manual controls—just as they did in the old days.

***

For the first time since this battle began, Lynx smiled. The Ninja had left its side panels open too long. Its shape, no longer invisible to I-band radio waves, appeared on Lynx's radar long enough for him to establish a target lock from a safe enough distance away that he was unaffected by the EM pulse. He also guessed by the way the Ninja moved that it was blind, its radar blown out by the pulse. The tables had been turned. He could see it. It couldn't see him.

When his targeting system locked onto the Ninja with a resounding long whine, Lynx fired one AIM-7 Sparrow from beneath his outer left wing store station and watched the trail of exhaust as it left in search of its prey. They wouldn't see death coming for them until it was too late. Only in the final second before their death would they see it and know nothing could stop it. They would experience that ultimate fear, the same way his friends had. Then they would share their fate.

***

Kenuchio was concentrating. It was difficult to precisely position his helicopter with the rotor threatening to stall out. Ishiguro waited patiently beside him for his signal.

Kenuchio was close. He thought they still might make it out of here alive. If, after they destroyed the ship, they could land safely, then they could hook up with the second Ninja and escape. He selfishly pondered the rewards that would be heaped upon them when they returned home. They would be well deserved.

That's when he saw death coming for him out of the corner of his eye. He screamed the command to fire, but before Ishiguro could do so, the Sparrow found its mark. The warhead detonated on impact, and in a violent fiery burst, the Ninja and its two-man crew were nothing more than a memory.

***

Blaze sighed in relief. It was the most beautiful display of fireworks he had ever seen. Phase One had worked, just not the way he had intended. Now it was on to Phase Two. He quickly resumed his work at a feverish pace, knowing the others might be here any minute.

He had yet to notice that right under his feet something phenomenal was taking place.

ENTITIES UNKNOWN

71

Prince Rupert, Canada

A white light shone down on Stacy's face, the minimal heat stirring her, the brightness piercing her closed eyelids. In a haze, she saw them. The aliens surrounded her, probing her with strange metal instruments that felt cold against her skin. Not again. She screamed, but no cry erupted from her throat.

"Ma'am," a strong voice called out to her. "Ma'am."

Stacy awoke with a gasp, quickly looking around in all directions. She was still lying in the front seat of the Dodge. Colored, concentric circles of light strobed across the inflated, white air bag. *Pain*. She brought a hand to her cheek, feeling the blood on her fingertips.

"Ma'am, are you all right?" The policeman leaned into the truck through the open passenger door.

"Huh," she mumbled.

The policeman's beam fell upon Jack. "We need a medic here immediately," he called out.

His partner, easily ten years his junior, opened the driver's side door and examined Jack's face, more than half of which was bruised purple and covered with drying blood. He felt for a pulse then waved over the Emergency Medical Technicians. He withdrew a pocketknife, deflated the air bag with a puncture, then unbuckled Jack's seatbelt and cautiously pulled him out of the truck onto the waiting stretcher.

It was the first time since the attack that Stacy got a good look at Jack. "How is he?"

"Don't quite know yet, ma'am," said an EMT. "He's got multiple lacerations and contusions. Looks like he's lost a lot of blood too. We won't know for sure until we get him to the hospital." Together, the four EMT's lifted the stretcher and carried Jack to the ambulance awaiting them on the road.

"How are you feeling, Ma'am?" the older police officer asked.

Stacy shook her head and stretched her neck, getting a kink out. "I'm all right, I think."

"This was some accident. What happened?"

"We were attacked by a sharkman... an alien. It appeared from out of nowhere and tried to kill us both."

Both officers stared at each other. "Excuse me, Ma'am. Did you say alien?" the younger officer asked.

"Yeah, he's right over there." Stacy turned to the front of the truck where the headlights still shone. The alien was no longer there. "No... no, no, no." She quickly exited the front seat and ran to the spot. The officers followed her. "I know I killed it. I know I did." She looked around in a panic. "There." She pointed to a rock stained with crimson fluids.

The officers stared at each other again. The older officer bent down for a closer examination of the blotch. He reached out for it.

"Don't," yelled the younger officer. "You could be disturbing a crime scene."

"Nah," said the senior officer. "It's probably just animal blood." He swept the red spot with a cloth, feeling the wetness. "It's fresh." He shined his flashlight about, until he picked up on a trail of blood that led deeper into the woods. He followed it for a few feet then scanned ahead. "You stay here. I'm going to see where this leads." He disappeared into the woods, his flashlight showing the way.

Stacy sat on the ground. "It's not dead."

"We'll find it, Ma'am," the young officer said. "Whatever it was that attacked you, we'll get it."

Stacy put her head in her hands and sobbed. "I can't believe it's not dead."

A twig snapped.

The sound of rustling leaves came from the dark.

Stacy jumped as the white flashlight beam once again crossed her eyes.

The older officer emerged from the thick trees. "Darnedest thing. The trail led up a tree, but there was nothing up there. I don't know about aliens, but something was definitely here."

"It's not dead," Stacy cried. "It's not dead."

"C'mon, we'll stay with you until they get you to the hospital, get a full statement."

Stacy nodded and they left.

72

Logan scanned the area from the front seat of the truck. Through the illumination of the moonlight and the burning fires he was able to survey the awful aftermath of the Japanese attack. He faced the lead jeep, fearful to look too closely at the riddled bodies which lay in clear sight. Instead, he focused his attention on the vehicle itself. It was destroyed—fit for the scrap yard. He turned his head towards the woods and the jeep that had flipped upside-down. The faces of the two soldiers scanning inside the vehicle with their flashlights, told Logan all he needed to know.

So much death. The lengths people went to for a chance to control new technology. But then again, he wasn't that surprised. He had seen the ruthless nature of some corporate moguls who felt the need to do whatever they had to, no matter how unscrupulous, to gain even the most minor competitive advantage. This was simply the next step up. Or was that step down?

Further ahead, his eyes glanced over the millions of shards of glass, shrapnel, and discarded empty bullet casings which littered the highway, to the flames consuming the downed Ninja, the cause of all this carnage. Its once proud hull was now reduced to nothing more than a smoldering metal carcass, another victim of someone's greedy relentless pursuit of power. The body of the pilot slumped forward in his chair, his safety harness still clinging to his corpse, perversely holding him in place. It was a fitting fate, yet still, he was glad he couldn't see the gaping chest wound that had ended his rampage.

Then he saw the worst of it—the tattered remains of soldiers being carried off the battlefield. The few who had survived did their best to tend to the wounded. Nothing brought home the real-life horror of the event more than that. It was an abhorrent scene—one he would carry with him for the rest of his life.

"On the count of three, lift," Dupres said.

Logan shook off the morbid thoughts so he could concentrate on the task at hand. Rebecca ordered him to assist Dupres in repairing the collapsed windshield, sparing him from the grislier tasks. With a quick heft, they lodged the windshield back into place. Then Dupres went to work reinforcing the frame.

The glass slid back into place and despite the relentless pounding it had taken, the truck was in respectable condition; a testament to what men could do when they set their minds to building instead of destroying. The windshield was the only thing on the truck that needed repair. The rest of the damage—the pock marks, the chipped paint, the dents—were superficial.

He took a moment to watch Rebecca. She had set up the portable satellite relay and was on the phone calling in assistance, microphone in one hand, receiver pressed against her ear in the other. Just like in the spaceship, she was professionally calm under pressure. Thanks to her, they were alive and everything was under control.

So, what was nagging at him? True, there were the countless lives of good men wasted, but there was more to it than that. Maybe he was worried about Blaze and the others. Maybe, it had something to do with the alien that had escaped. Whatever it was, he just couldn't put his finger on it.

"Dupres, you were one of the first men to make contact. What the hell happened that led to the fight with the aliens?"

"Grab that hammer for me," Dupres said. He hesitated a moment. "Fear of the unknown. Simple as that. We were afraid of them. They were afraid of us. Things just got out of hand."

Logan handed him the hammer. "What makes you think they were afraid?"

Dupres leaned back. "Because we made them afraid." He pounded the bent areas of the frame back into shape. "Friend of mine panicked. He saw one, got scared, and cut loose. That's how all this killin' started." He reflected a moment on those words. "They ain't killers, though. The aliens. If they were, I wouldn't be here. See this?" He used the hammer to point to the bandaged gash on his head. "One of them got me with that fancy weapon they got. There I am, lying helpless at their feet, and what'd they do? Just grabbed my radio and took it apart piece by piece so I couldn't alert anyone. The important thing was, once I was no longer a threat to them, they let me live."

"But you killed one yourself on the ship," Logan said.

"No, I shot high to scare it off. The asshole standing next to me killed it."

That reinforced Logan's belief that this whole sorry affair was due to ignorance, stupidity, and greed. He decided to change the topic before he got too angry. "What's that all about?" He motioned towards Rebecca, whose demeanor had changed. Where only a moment ago she was clearly having a conversation with someone, now she was obviously unsuccessful in her attempt to reach someone else.

"Doesn't look good, does it?" Dupres sighed. "Maybe things didn't go as well for the Major."

"I'll be right back." Logan left the front seat and walked over to Rebecca. "No one's answering?"

Rebecca lowered the receiver and began packing up the phone. "Smart boy. Is the truck ready yet?"

"Dupres will have it ready in a minute. What do you think happened to them?" Logan asked.

"We have to assume the worst."

"You're going to go on without them, aren't you?"

"I have to. I have a mission that needs to be completed."

"What about them?" Logan asked, referring to the wounded.

"I already called for assistance. They'll be here soon. That's the best I can do for them." Rebecca briskly made her way towards the truck.

Logan followed. "What if Gaines and the others didn't make it?"

"Then I'm going to make sure they didn't die for nothing. You ready?" she asked Dupres, who was putting the finishing touches on his repair job.

"Done. As long as nothing bigger than a bug hits it, it'll hold," Dupres said.

"Lock the back and get it started. I'll be right back."

While Rebecca told the remaining soldiers about the incoming emergency medical team on the way and issued some final instructions, Logan had a quick decision to make. He raced behind the truck, confirmed the fate of the jeep that was shielded behind it, and then raced back to the driver's side before Rebecca returned.

"Let's go," she ordered them.

"Just the two of you," Logan said. "I'm not going. The jeep behind us was well protected by the truck. It still runs. I'm going to take it back to the spaceship and check on the others."

"You aren't that concerned about the shipment, are you?" Rebecca asked.

Logan realized he was leaving the technology solely in Canadian hands—a move he knew Chase would disapprove of. One his professional side disapproved of as well. But their lives were more important to him. No matter his personal dislike for Chase, he had to go back to make sure they were all right. "I'm worried about something a lot more important."

"You're a good man, Logan Grey, but you'd make a terrible soldier," Rebecca said.

"So I'm learning."

"Good luck, mon ami," Dupres called out, sliding into the passenger's seat.

Rebecca climbed in, closed the door, and rolled down her window. "Call us when you find anything."

"Will do," Logan shouted as they got the truck running and drove off. He looked over to the other soldiers and felt bad leaving them behind, but there was nothing he could do for them anyway. He got into the jeep, reversed its direction, and drove back towards the ship.

73

Blaze browsed over the array of alien instrument panels. Undecipherable symbols flashed wildly. Touch-sensitive icons beyond immediate understanding lit up. Yet, not once did his confidence waver.

He knew he could do it. He knew he could complete Phase Two of his plan. He knew, by tomorrow, a new age of American scientific discovery would dawn, and he would be its pioneer.

His mind drifted back, recalling how he came to be here at just this moment. How at Groom Lake he had continually impressed his superiors until they revealed their ultimate secret, that a lot of the tech in the experimental craft he was working on originated from discoveries made from extraterrestrial technology recovered from Roswell. How they let him study the spacecraft, which led to his comprehension of the alien's designs, and his grasp of their use of physics—things previously considered theoretical—and led to him being appointed lead engineer of Project Starcross.

The foundation for the Project was built in 1947, a few days after the crashed spaceship was discovered. Unfortunately, just like the alien life-forms found there, only a fraction of the spaceship survived intact. Not enough that it could ever be salvaged, but enough so the design could be "decoded" and the pieces reverse engineered. The ship's fragments were brought back to Walker Field, where it was reassembled as best as possible. The Order of the Dolphin studied it extensively, but after exhausting every bit of knowledge that could be gleaned from it—from metallurgical to biological analyses—they transported it to a secret base and stored it away in a secure facility where it was forgotten about.

After the moon landing in 1969, proving manned space travel possible, interest in the Roswell spaceship was renewed. Once again funds became available. In 1971, Project Starcross was born. Its purpose was to discover how the alien spaceship worked, what principles it used, and to use that knowledge to develop advanced aircraft.

Now he was going to apply everything he had learned throughout his entire career, plus the hours he spent this afternoon, to bring home the real thing. No more speculation would be necessary. He would fly the spaceship straight back to the United States, stealing it right from under the Canadians' noses. And once it was airborne, there was no way anyone could stop him.

The gaping hole in the side of the ship didn't concern him. He knew the magnetic field which surrounded the ship like a sheath would, for all intents and purposes, act as a protective seal. The crystal strands in the engine room didn't concern him either. He knew Gaines, Chase, and Carlson were competent enough to have followed his instructions and had effectively repaired the circuitry. He also knew he had traced the flight controls to the correct instrument panel. His only worry was the human factor, or in this case, the alien factor. Blaze knew, for all his vast intellect, he was not a pilot. He wasn't sure if he'd be able to gain proper control over the ship so he wouldn't accidentally propel it way out into space.

He smirked, remembering how he conveniently forgot to mention that grim possibility when he suggested this strategy to Chase and his superiors this morning. When they discovered the general location of the ship, they knew the odds dictated it would be discovered in Canada. Use of military force was out of the question—it was simply not worth the risk of turning a close neighbor into an enemy—but somehow, they had to get their hands on it. To Blaze, this plan seemed like the perfect solution. Only a small team was needed, and it was the only peaceful way to smuggle the spaceship into U.S. territory.

The commanding officers denied him at first. Even Colonel Chase, who knew full well his abilities, doubted him. But then Chase decided the idea was so outrageous, so preposterous, so crazy, it might work. Besides, it was their only option. They had absolutely nothing to lose by trying. Or so they thought.

Blaze so eagerly anticipated the event, he brought along an atomic clock—a device so precise it measured time to a fraction of a second—so he could test Einstein's theory of relativity firsthand. According to Einstein, time slowed down the closer you traveled to the speed of light—and Blaze figured this would be the closest to the speed of light he'd ever come. Although even he wasn't completely sure why Chase asked him to magnetically attach it to the ship in plain view of the Canadians. He also didn't understand why its presence didn't give away his plan, although he did speculate when he saw people's reactions to it that Chase told them it was a bomb. He didn't care. He trusted Chase's instincts. As long as everything was in place so he could do what he had to, he wasn't about to look a gift horse in the mouth.

He got the ship running. Now he just had to figure out how to make it fly. He took a moment to check his watch then glanced at the timer on the atomic clock to make sure they were still synchronized. Back in his office at Groom Lake were a third and fourth timepiece which he knew were also in synch. When he arrived home, the difference between the clocks would give him an exact reading on Einstein's theory.

He cracked his knuckles, ready to glide his fingers gracefully over the console. Soon the ship would respond to his commands. Then he noticed something so unexpected, even he was taken off guard. The room was changing right before his eyes.

74

"Lynx, come in Lynx. Can you hear me?" Gaines shouted into the radio. But, as expected, the interference created by the EM field was too intense and static was his only reply.

"The ship's up and running, Major. The EM Pulse must've done the trick because we're all still alive." Chase said with a grin. "Good ol' Blaze. I knew he wouldn't let us down."

"Oh yeah, Colonel, then what the hell is that?" Carlson said. He pointed at a glowing film spreading outward from the floor by the reactor. As it glided towards them it altered everything it touched. The floor they were standing on was silver. The floor glossed over by the film was sparkling blue and had a pattern of weaving lines. "It might be some kind of internal security system."

"For the first time, Carlson, I agree with you," Chase said, as he trotted backwards away from the advancing film. "Let's get out of here." They fled the room, Chase leading them in the opposite direction of the bridge.

***

"Fantastic," Blaze whispered as he watched with childlike curiosity as the cloudy light swept towards him. He stood firm as it whisked past his shoes and continued on behind him. He turned around, watching intently as it seeped over the walls, altering their bland appearance.

Suddenly, three brown mesh structures appeared around the room. A larger structure with more presence appeared on the raised area in the center of the circular room.

When the light finally faded, the room was completely transformed. The floor had a charcoal tint with circles overlapping like a montage. The walls were grayish blue with intricate patterns entwined elegantly all around. Pictures of the alien life forms were proudly displayed on the walls, each one hovering around three feet apart. The control panels were now awash with holographic displays. Touch icons literally floated before him. Blaze gawked in sheer amazement. This ship was everything he had ever imagined and more—much more.

For all the years he had studied the alien technology, this was the one aspect his scientific mind hadn't considered. He was so wrapped up in propulsion systems, materials, and biological necessities, he never considered the amenities. Yet, from an aesthetic point of view, it made perfect sense. Each person was unique and therefore would want unique surroundings. This was the ideal solution. It was up to the crew to program in the environment they desired. This way, everyone enjoyed their long journey through space in maximum comfort. The entire spaceship was a template, and this was its final entry.

He couldn't wait to see how they lived, what their living quarters were like. But that would have to wait until later. Right now he had a job to do—and it just became a whole lot easier.

He saw a set of steps that weren't there before. They led up to the raised platform in the middle of the circular room. He placed one foot on the first step. It was solid. He climbed onto the platform and touched the structure he found there. It was a chair, soft and leathery, but a material he'd never felt before. Even better, it was the commander's chair. He glanced up at the clear protective dome and saw a holographic grid overlaid with unrecognizable symbols. He sat down and studied the grid and the holographic panel displayed on the side of the chair.

***

Chase led them toward the "exit" hole when he stopped. He remembered what Blaze had said about the magnetic field acting as a barrier. No one could leave the ship until he powered down. He changed directions, running down a circular corridor, trying to buy Blaze as much time as possible while still giving the impression he was trying to get to safety. He would need plausible deniability if Blaze failed.

Unfortunately, there was no place left to run. The glowing film was heading towards them from both directions of the hallway and there was no way to avoid it.

"I hope this isn't painful," Carlson whispered, as a bead of sweat dropped from his brow.

Chase and Gaines remained silent and stood firm. In seconds the light crossed over them with no ill effects. The hallway, however, was completely changed. The floor was navy blue. The walls were a mixture of dark green and black. The panels by the doorways glowed with colorful holographic imagery.

"Woah… incredible," Carlson said.

Chase walked to the nearest panel and watched the imagery literally float before him. He put an open hand through the light and stared as the images were now displayed on his palm. He pulled it away and the images returned to normal. The bland hallway now teemed with personality. Where once stood a soulless empty alien ship, now was a highly advanced technological and artistic masterpiece.

Gaines stared at the ship's updated appearance and his facial expression went dark. "Blaze," he muttered. Then he ran towards the bridge.

Chase and Carlson followed.

***

Blaze believed he knew which panels controlled the ship, as the buttons on this newly generated panel correlated to the buttons on the panels on the wall. The same way a remote control works a television set. All he had to do now was match symbols.

He noticed the wall panel and the holographic images that overlaid it then found its match on the panel next to him. Now, it was just trial and error with experience as his guide. His first guess was the large rectangular button marked with a ridged triangle inside of a circle. Nothing happened. Next, he touched a U-shaped button, and the ship shrieked.

He immediately recognized it as the alien's spoken language. He pushed it again and got the same sequence of high-pitched sound.

He tried another button. The ship generated another series of sounds, also in the alien's tongue. He tried another and got a new sequence of sounds. Every button pressed resulted in either a disappointing silence or a string of alien sound.

He fretted. If what he began to suspect was true, his plan was thwarted before it even began. His confidence only slightly shaken; he refused to give up. He got out of the chair and jogged quickly to the wall panel. He pushed the buttons there finding he got the same responses as he did from the "remote control" panel by the commander's chair. Now he knew for sure he was foiled.

He was sure he knew how it all worked, even if he didn't understand why. He knew how each crystal strand brought the energy from the power core to each machine. He knew how the ship glided effortlessly through space by magnetic levitation. Under different circumstances, he surely would have succeeded. But he also knew it would take months to find out if he was right. It would also take someone with a completely different set of skills than his own. He became lost in thought, commiserating over the missed opportunity.

That's when Gaines entered the room. He gazed through the clear shield at the nearby flames from the downed Ninja flickering across the night sky.

Blaze saw Gaines' eyes fixated on the fire. "It worked. Not exactly the way I planned but long enough for Lynx to finish the job."

"Thank God," Gaines said. Gaines took a deep breath and sighed with relief. "Good work, Blaze."

Chase and Carlson came running into the room.

"Why the hell did you take off like that?" Chase scowled.

"I just wanted to make sure Blaze was okay," Gaines said. "It's funny though, you didn't seem overly concerned about him."

Chase grumbled. "Ya know, Major, I think you still don't trust us." Chase walked over to Blaze and placed a reassuring hand on his shoulder.

"Yeah, I wonder why that is?" Gaines replied.

Blaze wandered about in a temporary fog then stared back up at the dome. The ship began to rumble slightly, and they all saw Lynx doing a flyby. That brought a smile to everyone's face. They were still alive. They had the ship—which was invaluable—and its cargo was safe with Rebecca.

"Blaze, I need you to power down this ship so I can radio my people," Gaines' said.

Blaze stopped obsessing. "Oh, sure. Not a problem."

Blaze's moment of glory was lost, but nobody had discovered his ploy, and he was sure he'd get his chance another day. The only important thing now was getting the ship to safety so that day would come. He saw the atomic clock he set up, realizing he wouldn't need it anymore. So, without thinking, he reached up and yanked it off the wall, completely forgetting that Chase had told everyone it was a bomb.

75

The jeep raced with an awkward jostle over the dark highway which was lit only by the dim pale moonlight and the jeep's flickering right headlamp. An odd whistling sound, created from the wind rushing through some damaged part of the cabin, filled Logan's ears. An odor that reeked of burning oil wafted alarmingly and lingered. Logan's previous quick positive diagnostic of the military vehicle proved premature.

A growing sense of apprehension swept over him as defeatist thoughts crept into the forefront of his mind. He was foolish to go off on his own to check on the others. He would never make it and end up stranded on this cold empty road until long after the mission was over. Logan pushed the thoughts away and gripped the steering wheel tighter as the vehicle pulled to the right. Then a worrisome 'thump-thump-thump' drowned out the whistle of the wind.

"Damn."

He cautiously halted the vehicle and got out to check the front passenger side tire. It was almost completely deflated. He squatted and listened carefully for the hiss. He waved his hand over the girded rubber until a rush of air pinpointed the exact spot of the leak. Then he crawled underneath for a closer look, spotting the cause as the moonlight reflected off a small piece of shrapnel which had imbedded itself between the treads.

He briefly wondered if his AAA membership serviced this area. *That's right Logan, make jokes so you can ignore the dire situation.*

He replaced the negativity with a wave of anger. It's just a flat tire—nothing that would hinder him under normal circumstances. He rushed to the rear and removed the sheath covering the spare tire. Despite his unfamiliarity with this vehicle, everything looked as it would on an ordinary car. He popped the hatch and searched within for a jack and a lug nut wrench, finding everything he needed.

Carrying it, he slid it beneath the frame and hoisted the right front-end of the vehicle into the air. Then he loosened the bolts one by one in a crossing pattern. This would only take a few minutes. Soon he'd be back on the road. Provided that the oil smell wasn't as serious as he thought.

Then why do I still feel apprehensive?

Something else bothered him. His instincts were crying out to him, telling him something was wrong. Not with the jeep, but with the mission. There was information he'd picked up that was staring him in the face, and yet he was blind to it.

He piled the lug nuts to his side, carefully so one wouldn't unexpectedly roll away. Then he removed the flat and let it drop with a wobble. He lifted the spare onto the screws and thrust the new tire firmly into place.

What am I missing?

He replaced the lug nuts then paused, needing a moment away from the mechanical smells. He wiped the soot from his gloves, stood erect, and inhaled a fresh breath of cold, crisp mountain air.

As he returned to work, spinning the wrench around each bolt with ease, his mind wandered. He played back the events that led him here, carefully analyzing the circumstances and assessing the threats. Nothing previously unknown came to the surface. Next, he went through the players, one by one, starting with Chase. He pictured him in his head and analyzed his body language. He looked for expressions, inflections, anything that should have registered with him but didn't. Then he moved on to the others.

He spun the wrench around the final bolt, then went back to the first one and tightened it. He continued through the next four as his thoughts turned to the Japanese. *They were a considerable threat. And an unexpected one? How did they find out about the spaceship? And if they knew, who else might know?* He brushed those thoughts away, filing them under things to worry about later.

He tightened up the last bolt then pressed his foot on the jack's release lever. The jeep returned to ground level with a hydraulic sigh—yet still he knew some detail was escaping his attention. He quickly reviewed the players in his head again, recalling the details of their personality, their posture, their gestures, their eyes, their demeanor, how they walked, how they spoke, searching for that one elusive tell. He found nothing.

He tossed the tools back into the hatch, then rolled the flat over to the rear and attached it to the mount. Still, even with the current crisis solved, the wave of apprehension hadn't lifted. The more he analyzed, the more it gnawed at him. He could feel it.

But it would have to wait.

He jogged to the driver's door, pausing as the reflected moonlight showed a trail of grease on the door handle. His gloves were blackened with grime and soot. He pulled them off and discarded them on the passenger side floor. His hands shone white and clean by contrast. He reached into his pocket for the keys and as he placed the key into the ignition, once again, he noticed his clean hands standing out in the dark interior.

His hands.

Their hands.

That was it. That's what was bothering him. He had recognized an instinctive reaction by someone involving their hands that betrayed their facade. He'd only seen it once before, yet it was unmistakable. He just didn't recognize it until now because it didn't fit neatly into the puzzle.

Or did it?

Perhaps the puzzle was just shaped differently than he thought. He replayed that person's every moment in his head. He recalled another gesture that at the time meant nothing but now was of the greatest significance. It all made sense to him. His stomach churned and his heart grew heavy. The threat was immediate. He had to act quickly or all would be lost. He turned the key, praying for the choke and chortle that would spark the jeep to life, praying that the oil smell was nothing serious.

The engine started without a glitch. Logan jammed the jeep into drive and raced toward the spaceship.

76

Nikolai stretched his broad muscles. His joints cracked and he yawned. The truck's seat was comfortable. *Too comfortable.* He sat up straight and took another sip from the cup of tea that rested on the dashboard. He had only caught a few hours of sleep on his flight to Alaska, which normally would be enough, but the waiting was wearing on him. An extra boost of caffeine was needed to insure he didn't doze off.

He had arrived at the designated location early, in perfect position to intercept the transport, but his contact was late. Something must have gone wrong. Flipping on the map light above the rear-view mirror, he set up his satellite transcontinental linkup and called Vaskev. It took two minutes to get him on the line.

"Poppa, the train has yet to arrive. Are you sure the schedule reads correctly?" Nikolai asked.

"Yes, son. There had been an unexpected delay. Fortunately, it appears to have been corrected. Remain at your station and it will be there in about fifteen minutes," Vaskev replied.

"Thank you, poppa, I was beginning to grow... concerned."

"Understood. See you soon. Godspeed." Vaskev's end of the line went silent.

Nikolai disconnected the link and folded the portable satellite dish back into the briefcase. Excellent, he thought. The operation was still proceeding as planned. Soon, the prize would belong to Russia.

77

Gaines eyes widened and he threw his hands out, instinctively bracing himself for an explosion. Nothing happened. A moment later he realized the "bomb" was nothing of the sort—instead a mechanical decoy used to manipulate him.

Chase cringed. In one swift absent-minded moment, Blaze jeopardized their recovery of the alien craft by removing his bluff. The "bomb", Chase's last remaining trump card, was flipped face-up on the table for everyone to see.

Blaze caught their glares. "Errr... um, it's just..." he stammered.

Gaines eyes spewed daggers. "We'll deal with that later. I need the power cut now so I can reach my squad."

"NO!" Chase hollered. "Not til you give me your word you'll still honor our agreement."

"You dumb arrogant sonuva bitch," Gaines spat. "I've been up front with you from the beginning, and all I got in return were lies and stupid games. Well, your last lie was just revealed. The game's over. You lost. Everything gets played my way now, and you're going to listen to everything I tell you to. You know why? Because if you make one more mistake, you piss me off one more time, I guarantee you'll never see this ship or any of its cargo again. But if you cooperate, like you should've from the start, I'll mention that to my superiors when we get to base and then maybe… just maybe… you'll still get what you want. Blaze, power down this ship. NOW!"

Chase scowled. He turned to Blaze angrily then sighed. "Do it," he said.

Blaze nodded and went to work. "Just give me a few seconds, Major. I want to make sure I can do it without losing the ship's new features." A few moments later, the low hum ceased, yet the ship's current programming remained. "Done."

"Carlson, get me in touch with headquarters." Gaines ordered, then got on his radio. "Lynx, can you read me?"

"Loud and clear, Major. Good to hear your voice again."

"Glad you made it. I'll get back to you in a minute with new instructions." Gaines changed the frequency. "Rebecca?"

"I was wondering when you'd call," Rebecca replied.

"Me, too. What's your status?"

"It's just me and Dupres, but we're back on track. I left the rest to watch the injured and called in an emergency medical crew. Logan's on his way back to you."

"We'll wait for him. Keep going. I'll meet you at home base."

***

Chase took a seat in one of the alien chairs and just stared through the dome. His thoughts were interrupted by a hand placed on his shoulder.

"Sorry, Colonel," Blaze whispered. "I didn't realize—"

"Not your fault. Was mine. I should've told you about it," Chase said.

"How come you didn't?" Blaze asked.

Chase got up out of the chair and walked. Blaze went with him as they circled to the other side of the bridge.

Chase stared around for a moment at the pictures of the extraterrestrials, figuring the largest image was that of the commanding officer. He looked up through the dome and briefly wondered what it would be like to command a ship like this. Then he stared at the floor filled with violet and bluish concentric circles, and all those thoughts vanished amid the odd hypnotic effect they created.

Next his eyes flowed to the instrument panels on the walls, amazed at their complexity. Chase fully understood how brilliant Blaze must be to be able to comprehend all this. He turned back to Blaze with a hint of compassion. "I knew you'd keep the atomic clock a secret... because that was your baby. But calling it a bomb—you'd never pull off a bluff like that."

"What makes you think that?" Blaze asked.

"You've got a terrible poker face. That's how I keep taking your money at the weekly poker games. You're God damn brilliant though. You really got this tub up and running."

"Yeah, but only halfway." Blaze lowered his voice a notch. "But get this. My grand plan... I had Gaines and Carlson making all the repairs that would've made it succeed. And they still haven't got a clue." His lips curled in a lopsided grin that made Chase chuckle.

"Your plan was bold. I'll grant you that," Chase said.

"I may be a shitty poker player, but I'm very good at chess."

"Then what the hell are we still doing here?"

"I had it," Blaze said. "I know I did. I was this close." He raised his fingers as if pinching the air.

"But?"

"The spaceship is voice activated. It's either a security lock out or just straight command functions. Either way, I don't speak the language." They looked back towards Carlson and Gaines. Both were busy on the radio doing what they had to do. "What now?" Blaze asked.

"We play it their way," Chase answered.

***

Having established contact with Yukon Base Five, Gaines explained the situation and waited for their response.

Finally, Smythe's voice came through the speaker. "Major, we checked with Britton. He confirmed your report. The Japanese have an aircraft carrier positioned in the North Pacific. Their government will be hearing from us shortly. You can count on that."

"Hold off on that, Commander. I have a better idea." Gaines relayed his thoughts over the phone.

Smythe agreed then continued to the next order of business. "We got something we think you'd be interested in. We got word that the Prince Rupert Police Department has a woman under watch. Seems to be a carjacking case but get this—she claims her assailant was an alien. Matches the description perfectly." He relayed all the specifics. "It happened about fifty miles from the crash site, Major. It can't be a coincidence. Should we alert the locals?"

"No. I want to keep this one close to the vest. We'll take care of it," Gaines replied.

"We're sending what you need. Good work so far. Don't let us down."

"I won't, sir. I'll check in again at 0100." Gaines turned to his left and watched with cautious eyes as Chase and Blaze made their way back from the other side of the circular bridge.

"What now?" Chase asked.

Gaines grinned. Chase appeared more resigned now, like someone who understood his untenable position. "Now we start taking care of business," Gaines said firmly. Gaines adjusted the frequency again. "Lynx, how much fuel you have left?"

"About half a tank, sir," Lynx's voice responded through the speaker.

"Missiles?"

"Five left. Two Sparrows. Three Sidewinders. My guns are fully loaded too." He was referring to the M61 20mm six-barrel gun with 570 rounds mounted in the nose.

"Good. I'm relieving you of your current detail. I got a better mission for you. You ready for a little payback?"

"Yes, sir," Lynx said.

"Here's your new target." Gaines gave him the coordinates of the Japanese aircraft carrier. "They won't be expecting you—but our men will. First strike's all yours."

"Yes, sir," Lynx's voice rang with determination.

"Enjoy yourself and be careful. Copy and out." Gaines put the radio away and addressed Carlson, Chase, and Logan. "Our alien was spotted in Prince Rupert. Carlson, see what transportation we still have outside that's working."

"Yes sir." Carlson snapped to attention, saluted, then left in haste.

"We're going to have to find that alien before anyone else does," Chase said.

"Yes," Gaines agreed. "But this time things are going to run my way. No more killing. Let's find a better solution."

"The ship?" Chase asked.

"That's our priority. Reinforcements are on the way. We'll just push our original timetable back an hour and everything's still in place."

"Good," Blaze said. "First the aliens, then the Japanese. I was wondering what'd come next?"

Logan charged into the room. He was puffing from the cold air and needed to catch his breath and looked disoriented from racing through corridors that were no longer familiar. "The Russians," Logan said. He paused another second to catch his breath. "But they're not next. They're already here. And they have the cargo."

"What the hell are you talking about?" Chase asked.

Gaines and Blaze stared, wanting to know the same thing.

In a slow calm voice Logan revealed what he figured out. "Rebecca. She's a Russian spy."

78

A thick eerie silence fell over the alien bridge. Logan's dramatic words hung in the air as each person processed them.

"LIKE HELL SHE IS!" Gaines shouted.

"God damn it, Gaines—she better not be," Chase said, with a hot head. "If the Russians get a hold of that technology the Cold War will look like a picnic."

"She's not!" Gaines yelled, pointing a finger at Logan. "If this is another one of your tricks—"

Logan stepped between the two of them. "Maybe I should have couched it better, but we don't have the time. If you'll listen to me for—"

Gaines got right in his face. "No. You listen to me. I don't know what kind of game you're playing but you just crossed way over the line. My tolerance for—"

"I don't play games and I'm not lying to you," Logan said. He changed his tone to sympathetic. "Look, I understand how close you two are but—"

Gaines grabbed him by his shirt and pushed him up against the wall. "Trust me. That's absolutely the last place you want to go."

"Hitting me won't change anything," Logan said. His resolve convinced Gaines to loosen his grip. "You have nothing to lose by hearing me out and everything to gain. Because if I'm right—and I am—then we still have time to get it back."

Gaines' eyes bore hard into Logan's who stared back. "I'm not him," Logan said, referring to Chase. "And don't forget who saved your life earlier today."

Gaines released him. "Talk fast."

"Yeah, this I gotta hear," Chase added.

"I was called up for this assignment because I'm an expert in kinesics—the science of body language. The theory being that if we encountered extraterrestrial intelligence, someone with my unique skill set would be best suited to communicate with it. I was chosen over anyone else—and Colonel, please feel free to correct me if I'm wrong—because I'm the best."

Chase didn't argue.

"That's the same reason you called upon Pierre Le Buc, and just like him, I don't normally work for the government. My regular occupation is acting as a consultant for major corporations to help them conduct business overseas. They need me because I can get them up to speed on another country's customs. They pay me the big bucks because I help them negotiate. Aside from being knowledgeable about foreign gestures and customs, I can tell better than anyone else what that man across the table is really thinking. I watch how they react to a proposal. I listen for the slightest inflection that'll reveal their true feelings. I read their body language to get beyond the façade—to find out who they really are and what they truly want.

"My success rate is near perfect. I only failed once to get everything I was asked to get and that was over five years ago. Since then, I've been perfect. That said, I'm telling you Rebecca reacts like a Russian."

"Don't you think we would've noticed that?" Gaines said.

"No, I don't. She was obviously very well trained. Her actions and mannerisms are perfectly Canadian. But I always look for reactions. No amount of preparation will conceal how a person will react in every single situation. When you live in a culture, wherever it is, you pick up on its habits and they become so ingrained on your psyche, they're there forever. When the Japanese ambushed us on the road, Rebecca and I got pinned down together behind the truck. You know how capable she is, how quickly she can think on her feet. She went into the truck, took one of the alien's weapons, and used it against the helicopter."

"She got a weapon to work?" Blaze said.

"Oh, that's just fuckin' great," Chase said.

"I'll explain that later. Anyway, she was trained to react to situations like that one. But after she single-handedly defeated the Ninja, Dupres and some of the other soldiers applauded, and her initial reaction was to applaud back to them."

"So?" Chase said.

"Russian ballerinas will often applaud back to an appreciative audience. It's their way of saying thank you. They're one of the few cultures that do that. Rebecca's extremely graceful on her feet. My guess is that she was a balletomane as a child and the habit became ingrained. When the unexpected situation presented itself, Rebecca reacted in a way that was natural to her. It's also not a behavior that a spy agency would think of reconditioning."

"That's pretty thin," Gaines said.

"Tells usually are, but there's more. That was just the tip-off that got me thinking. I saw the hatred in her eyes when you mentioned it was the Japanese that were responsible. It went deeper than the attack. More like an inborn bigotry. As I'm sure you're aware of, the Russians and Japanese are longtime enemies. That explained it.

"Also, something else struck me as strange. When she had the alien weapon in her possession, the Japanese asked for an unconditional surrender. We were outgunned, fighting a losing battle, and it sure as hell seemed like a generous alternative to me. Yet Rebecca knew it was a ruse. She knew that once they believed all of us were present and accounted for, they would kill us. So we played possum until Rebecca could get a clear shot. But when she had one, she hesitated. Only when they shot first, killing more of us, did Rebecca act.

"At first, I didn't think much of it. I was so grateful that her plan worked, I never even thought to question her timing. But it was calculated. She was waiting until more soldiers were killed, so she would have less to deal with later. Only when the gun turret pointed in her direction, jeopardizing her own life, did she fire."

"Are you trying to say she planned the Japanese invasion?" Blaze asked.

"No. What I'm saying is that she took a bad situation and turned it to her advantage. You would think after what just happened, she would want as many soldiers covering the cargo as possible. Instead, she let me take the only working jeep back here and left everyone else behind except Dupres."

Gaines' expression showed he wasn't convinced, but he said, "My department has experienced security leaks that benefitted the Russians for the last couple of years. But Rebecca… no way. I trust her with my life."

"You need more. Fine," Gaines said. "When I was in the spaceship studying the alien writing, she came to check up on me. When one of the soldiers walked past her in a relatively narrow corridor, he turned his back to her, and she became annoyed. She didn't vocalize it, but I noticed nonetheless. None of us would've thought anything of that, but in Russia, when two people pass each other in close quarters, like a movie theater, they always face each other. It's considered taboo to do otherwise."

"Is that all?" Gaines asked.

"Yes."

"It's not good enough."

"It had better be. Right now, she's riding away with a truckload of alien technology and you're the only one who can give the order to stop her."

Gaines shook his head. "See if you can understand this. I spent five years working side by side with this woman every day. She's shown nothing but loyalty and total devotion to her career. She's my best officer—bar none. Then you come along... and after spending a few hours with her, you've determined she's a spy. How do you expect me to believe you?"

Logan paused for a moment. He had hoped to avoid this as it might create further animosity. "There might be one more thing. It's personal. Can I talk to you alone?"

Gaines hesitated then nodded his agreement. Together they left the bridge and entered the hallway, stopping at the top of the ramp that led down to the level below, where no one was within earshot.

"With all due respect, and speaking to you as one guy to another, I think you're thinking with the wrong head."

Gaines was taken aback. "Hey!"

"I see the way you look at her. I know you're involved with her."

Gaines smirked. "What makes you say that?"

"It's obvious. It's written all over your face. You're in love with her."

"You're wrong. We're not involved."

"Really. Well, she's on the pill. She's involved with someone."

"Well, that's twice you're wrong. And I know for a fact she's not on the Pill."

"What makes you so sure?" Logan asked.

"That's none of your business."

"Okay," Logan said, respecting his privacy for the moment.

"What makes you so sure?" Gaines shot back.

"Her eyes blink twelve times more a minute than the average woman. It's a side effect of the Pill."

"That must come in handy in negotiations," Gaines said.

"I'm young, single, I travel a lot, and—just like you—I have needs. I meet a lot of women in a lot of different places and as crude as it might sound, speaking once again, just one guy to another, it lets me know just who might be a little more willing. I'm also not interested in finding out ten years from now that there's a little Logan running around who I didn't know about."

"Not much for safe sex, huh?" Gaines remarked.

"I'll tell you this. I can look a woman in the eyes, and I'll know every time if she's really on the Pill, or if she's lying to me. And I haven't been wrong yet. I watched Rebecca enough to know that's she's definitely on it. I might be wrong about your being involved with her. That was a logical assumption, although apparently incorrect. But I'm not wrong in that you want to be involved with her, and I'm not wrong about her being on the Pill."

Gaines mulled it over. "Rebecca can't have any children. That's why she chooses to focus on her career. That's why we're not involved. She knows one day I want kids, and she once told me it wouldn't be fair to me. But be that as it may, she has no reason to be on the Pill."

"Unless she's lying," Logan said. "But we're getting side-tracked. We can't afford to. You know, I met Le Buc years ago. He was a good man, taught me a lot. One of the most important lessons was, don't let your personal feelings get in the way of the facts. Everyone has a hidden side. Every person puts on a mask when they go out in public. The way to know your opponent is to see beneath the mask and your emotions only get in the way of doing that. If he were still alive, he'd tell you the same thing."

"Le Buc used to say that to me all the time." Gaines' eyes squinted. "On the plane… he said every once in a while, Rebecca lets slip a smile. Not a happy smile, just a slight rise in her upper lip, like she knows something that no one else does."

"A secret," Logan said. "Her secret."

"Son of a bitch." Gaines shook his head back and forth. "Son of a bitch."

Logan knew he had gotten through. "I'm sorry."

"Yeah. Me too."

Carlson appeared from the lower deck and trotted up the ramp.

"What's our transportation status?" Gaines asked him.

"All four of our helicopters are working fine, sir. One more is on its way."

"Just one. Shit." Gaines walked back into the bridge with the others following. "Okay, Carlson, I'm leaving you in charge of making sure this ship gets back to base."

"Yes, sir," Carlson responded.

"But you're going to have to wait until that chopper arrives. Blaze, you keep him company for the wait. You seem to know this ship inside and out. Make sure it doesn't do anything funny," Gaines said, a clear warning to Blaze. "Chase, you and Logan are going to take one of the transport choppers and fly to Prince Rupert. You weren't here then, Logan. We received a report that the escaped alien was spotted there by a local. Colonel Chase will fill you in on the details on the way. He knows these aliens from a past encounter. Make sure he fills you in on that as well. One thing. No killing. Logan, use that damn talent of yours to communicate with it. Together, you should be able to track it down and bring it in peacefully. Any problems with that?" Gaines asked Chase.

"All right," Chase said. "What are you going to do?"

"I'm taking the jeep. I'm going after Rebecca alone."

79

"How'd you do that, anyway?" Dupres asked as they rode along the highway.

"I cut off an alien's thumb and used it to trigger the weapon. Figured it was coded by either fingerprint or DNA," Rebecca answered.

"The beauty and savvy of the White Queen," muttered Dupres.

"Who?"

"Er... Never mind. What's our ETA?"

"If everything proceeds according to schedule, 0300."

They both squinted as a light shone through the windshield. A truck about a twentieth of a kilometer ahead of them was flashing its headlights. When they turned off, the road went dark and their eyes were less adjusted to the blackness than they were a moment before.

"What was that?" Dupres asked, his left hand still shielding his eyes as he tried to make out exactly what was ahead.

Rebecca applied pressure to the brake, slowing the truck, and grabbed the gun which lay next to her on the seat. "I don't know, but I don't like it."

"Me either," Dupres said, removing the weapon from his belt.

Rebecca reduced their speed considerably as they approached the origin of the light, a truck that waited on the side of the road by an off ramp. Standing next to its passenger side door stood a rather large man.

"Trouble," Dupres muttered. "Definitely trouble." Dupres gripped his weapon tighter and checked the magazine as Rebecca brought the vehicle to a complete halt. "Why are we stopping?" he asked, his eyes focused intently on the large man.

Rebecca pointed her gun at Dupres. "Because this is where I get off."

Without hesitation, she shot Dupres in the head, watching without emotion as his brains splattered the side window and his body slumped into the dashboard.

END GAME

80

A ship's radar is vital to its survival. As the ship's eyes it is essential to detect incoming anti-ship missiles and aircraft as early as possible to enable the proper countermeasures to be taken. The greatest problem, however, is that the range of a radar system is limited by the height the curved antenna can be mounted on the ship and the weight and size of the face as to ensure its accuracy.

An approaching aircraft posed a particular problem because at normal frequencies, in calm conditions, the aircraft's image can be reflected off the sea surface and confuse the radar, causing large errors in calculating speed and range. To overcome this, a much higher frequency in the millimetric waveband is used to provide accurate tracking. This method, integrated with an electro-optical or television sighting device, proves very reliable.

Aboard the Tsunami, the OPS-24 developed by Mitsubishi Electric Corporation handled the task. Equipped with D-band transmitter/receiver modules, consisting of silicon hybrid integrated circuit technology and discrete transistors which feed small groups of antenna elements, the radar can track at least 200 targets simultaneously with almost perfect accuracy while continuing to provide surveillance. Even flying close to the sea surface, there is nary a way to escape the OPS-24's mechanical eyes.

Lynx knew all of this from his many briefings as an officer in the Canadian Royal Air Force. Today, none of it mattered. He flew directly towards the Tsunami high and fast. He wanted them to see him coming.

***

Yakui sat in his small comfortable seat so perfectly straight his impeccably bright uniform showed nary a crease as he diligently watched the radar. When the blip appeared on the hazy green radar screen, moving rapidly towards the center, he swiftly checked the IFF transponder signal that identified it as foe. Without a trace of nervousness, he reported his sighting. "Commander, we have an unidentified intruder closing in on us."

Hirigashi, the Senior Watch Officer, stood up from his post and approached. "Is it from the Canadian ship that's been watching us?"

"Negative, this one is approaching from the mainland."

"What is the latest word from the Ninjas?"

"No word, sir. Our last radio contact with them was an hour ago." This was normal, as the Ninjas required radio silence to achieve maximum stealth potential. However, the aircraft approaching them not being identified as a Ninja was worrisome.

"I'll alert the captain at once."

***

Lynx wanted the men on the ship to know who it was who sent them to their graves. More importantly, he wanted to be close. As they'd be unsure of his intentions, they wouldn't dare fire first again.

Lynx planned to extend them the same courtesy the Ninjas showed him.

***

Captain Tanaku had just got word of the approaching F-18 over the comm-link. It was all he needed to hear to know his mission had failed. Inwardly, he was grateful. He believed all along that the attack against Canada was unwarranted and potentially disastrous for his country. He wished he'd been strong enough, independent enough, to refuse it. He should have, he thought, and taken his chances at a court martial trial. It would have been more honorable. But he did not, and now he would pay the price for his disgraceful actions.

But why did the Canadians only send one fighter?

He walked to the bridge to watch the radar screens. The other Canadian fighters from the aircraft carrier had not changed their positions and the Canadian jet heading towards them was closing fast. But it still hadn't done anything. Perhaps it was not attacking. Perhaps it was just sending a message. Tanaku ordered his men to standby. He wanted no more innocent blood on his hands.

***

When Lynx was within two miles, he armed his AIM-9 Sidewinder and locked it on target. "This one's for you, Hound," he said, as he pushed the red button firing the missile. Normally, he would use his advanced Hughes aircraft radar that allowed him launch-and-leave capability, designed so fighters could fire and get out of harm's way as quickly as possible. Instead, Lynx followed the missile directly to its target.

***

Captain Tanaku didn't want this fight and would have gladly accepted his own death to avoid it, but he could not let the men under his command be punished for his failings. That would be an even greater disgrace. He ordered his fighters, consisting solely of American aircraft F-15J's, F-4EJ's, and the new FS-X's, to take off. His men instantly scrambled to their planes.

Only one F-4EJ managed to takeoff before Lynx's missile hit the deck. The other fighter jets, filled to the rim with fuel, exploded violently. Many of the soldiers were propelled overboard as the shock wave lifted them off the deck with bone-shattering force. Metal shrapnel violently dispersed by the blast, pierced their uniforms and lacerated their bodies, killing them long before they impacted with the unforgiving icy cold sea. Any unfortunate soul still within the impact radius fell one second later to the searing flames that swept through the area.

Captain Tanaku watched helplessly from his view on the bridge. The glass shielding—far enough away from the blast—held under the diminishing force waves. He quickly returned his focus to the OPS-24 radar screen. The previously unthreatening Canadian fighter squad from the nearby aircraft carrier had taken off and were now headed his way. His eyes narrowed and his heavy heart sank as he watched two blips turn to four, four turn to eight, and eight become sixteen. His men didn't stand a chance.

***

Lynx saw the Japanese fighter take off as he flew in lower. He ignored it. His goal was an up-close look at the faces of the men who ordered his friend's death. Let the other fighter jets choose it out to see who would take down the lone jet. His target was right in front of him.

He pushed the throttle forward and closed in quickly avoiding the steady gunfire headed his way. He wasn't sure why, but he felt no fear. Maybe, with his friend's death, he just didn't care anymore. Or maybe, by defeating an unbeatable foe, the Ninja, he had stared death in the face and found it wanting. Either way, he felt invincible.

He buzzed the bridge of the aircraft carrier without being hit by a single round. Its weakened windows shattered under the assaulting sonic waves generated by his fly-by. Just before the lights went out from the earsplitting assault, Lynx saw the face of his enemy, Captain Tanaku, and the look of defeat in his eyes. He held the picture of it in his mind and savored it. He climbed higher and arched his F-18 around for another attack, knowing just where to aim his final shots.

***

Captain Tanaku hit the deck when the lights went out. His radar screen was gone, and he heard the screams of his men between the echoing sounds of battle. Instinctively, he knew he was next. Before he even saw the incoming missiles, he closed his eyes, accepted his fate, and prayed for forgiveness.

Moments later, Lynx's AIM-9 Sidewinders found their mark, obliterating the bridge upon impact. Two minutes later, under an unrelenting volley of air-to-ground missiles that turned night to day, the aircraft carrier was completely destroyed. Even the lone Japanese pilot to make it to the air was shot down.

The Tsunami was sunk, and its entire crew was gone.

81

Gaines drove as fast as the road allowed so he could reach Rebecca as quickly as possible. Not solely to stop her. He had to know the absolute truth.

He relived every moment he had spent with her, concentrating on the happier times that he would never have again. *Logan had to be wrong. He had to.* Even if she was Russian, he couldn't be right about everything. Rebecca would never have hesitated so the Japanese could murder more of his men. She was strong, professional, and very capable, but she wasn't cold like everyone thought. He had seen her softer side. The connection they shared couldn't have been fabricated.

That must've been why she didn't allow herself to get close, he thought. If she truly didn't care, she would have slept with him. She would have used him in every conceivable way, playing on his emotions like a violin. But she didn't. Because she knew some day her betrayal would be revealed, and the pain would be too great. *In her own way, she must've been protecting me.*

He knew it was a rationalization, but he didn't care. He had to reach her in time. If she didn't do anything foolish, he could make things right. He would change her mind, make her see how much he loved her, and she would stay. He would protect her from a vindictive investigation and in time everything would work out fine. It had to.

He came upon the scene of the battle and slowed down. He drove around a destroyed jeep, doing his best to avoid the fragments of glass and shrapnel that were strewn all about. The first thing that caught his attention were the fires burning brightly around him, but they seemed to be small and under control. Then the death toll of Carlson's men became immediately obvious. EM personnel were either treating the wounded or carrying away the dead. One injured man was being airlifted away, the pilot of the helicopter being careful to avoid spreading the flames with the winds generated by his rotors. *Could Rebecca really have contributed to this carnage?* No, he couldn't believe that.

He spotted the remains of the Ninja in the woods. Eight men with hoses were wetting it down to cool its heated surface. Before him, the dead Japanese pilot was still in the cockpit, as if on display for his crimes like they did in the Old West. He was the monster, Gaines thought, not Rebecca.

He opened the jeep's window and called over to the man in charge. After being assured everything was under control, he continued on. There was nothing more he could do for them anyway. He had more important matters to attend to. When he passed the lead vehicle, the road was clear, and he accelerated.

Soon he was back driving at excessive speeds. Sensing he was closing in on her, he became more determined. He could do it. He could save Rebecca from herself. He could prevent any more mistakes and stop this insanity right in its tracks before it went any further. He could restore order back to both their lives. He would not give up on her.

He pressed the pedal to the floor and the speedometer crossed one-forty kph.

82

Prince Rupert

Dirt and pebbles bounced beneath the rotor wash as the helicopter Logan and Chase rode upon landed in the recently vacated parking lot. Awaiting their arrival, the Chief of the Prince Rupert Police Department jacked up the collar of his overcoat as the artificially generated gusts blew toward him.

"Welcome to Prince Rupert," Braxton shouted, as they walked toward him.

En route, both Chase and Logan had changed into standard Canadian military fatigues. It was all that was available, and they looked impressive enough so they could pass themselves off as government officials,

"Thank you, Officer," Chase replied.

"Jerry Braxton. Jerry's fine." When they were fully clear of the rotors and the background noise faded a bit, Braxton continued. "So, what's this all about anyways? Some woman bumps her head in a car accident, claims aliens attacked her, and suddenly I've got military intelligence in my jurisdiction."

Chase and Logan continued walking. "Far more down to earth, Jerry," Logan said. "She's a possible victim of an international drug smuggling operation."

"Where is she?" Chase asked.

"Down the first corridor... then make a right and two lefts. Room 104," Braxton said.

Chase nodded his head and walked away from Braxton. The Chief started to follow, but then Logan stopped and gave him a stern glance and a head shake that halted him in his tracks. With Braxton cowed, Logan turned and continued behind Colonel Chase, thinking to himself how with the proper credentials and the right body language he could probably get away with anything.

A quick jaunt later they entered the room of patient Stacy Michaels. She was fully dressed, sitting on an examining table with her legs hanging over the edge. She had a bruise on her forehead and her hands and cheek were bandaged, but no apparent serious injuries.

Stacy glanced their way. "Does this mean someone finally believed me?"

"Yes, ma'am," Chase said. "We received a report and were sent to investigate."

"We're from Canadian intelligence. This is Colonel John Chase. I'm, uh… Special Agent Logan Grey." Logan extended his hand.

She hesitated then shook it. "Stacy Michaels," she said, following up by shaking Chase's hand as well. "So, what can I tell you gentlemen that I haven't already told them twenty times?" She gave an eyeroll to the policemen standing in the doorway.

Chase signaled the policemen politely with a nod so he would give them some privacy. Then he walked over and closed the door. "We'll need you to go over it again."

She looked annoyed, showing the toll of her grueling experience.

"We apologize for the inconvenience. It's just that when one hears a story like yours second and third hand... well, we'd just appreciate it if we could hear it straight from the source. Then we'll check in on your friend and see about getting you safely home," Logan said.

Stacy started her story with the ride in Jack's pickup truck, recalling every detail she could remember. "Next thing I remembered, the medics found me and the alien was gone. His blood was found where I last saw it, but it was gone."

"What color was the blood?" Chase asked.

"Red. Just like ours. But I told them a hundred times, it wasn't human."

"Describe its hands?" Chase asked.

"The hands?"

"Yes. You said it reached in to get you. What did its hands look like?"

"Like ours, but totally different. Gray skin and webbed. You know, like a duck. Might have had sharp nails. I couldn't tell. It was too dark."

"The head?" Chase asked.

Stacy rubbed her eyes with both palms.

"Colonel." Logan motioned him to the side before she could answer so they could talk privately. "She's for real. I've been watching her for tells. If she lied, I couldn't detect it, and I doubt she's that good."

"I'm not doubting you. I need to know if everything she's telling us is accurate," Chase said.

"We need to find out why," Logan said. "She's obviously had a traumatic experience. Getting her to tell the same story over and over again isn't going to help."

Chase looked at Stacy. She briefly glanced back and then dropped her head into her hands before running them hard through her hair.

"Yeah," Chase acknowledged.

"I think if we tell her what we know, it'll be helpful. Kind of a quid-pro-quo sort of thing."

"Do it," Chase said. "Just keep it basic. Nothing more than necessary."

Logan walked back over to her. "You okay?"

"Yeah," Stacy replied.

"We believe you," Logan said. "What I'm about to tell you is highly classified. Under law you are not allowed to share this information with anyone—not even your own mother. Do you understand what I'm telling you?"

Chase added to it. "Ma'am, what we're about to tell you is classified under the strictest regulations of national security. Under Article 18, subsection 2.1, any person knowingly revealing information protected as a matter of national security can and will be tried under the penalty of treason, whereupon the strictest sentence shall become mandatory upon conviction. Is that understood?"

"Yeah, I guess," she said with a shrug.

"No guessing," Chase said. "Not with this."

"Okay. Yes, I understand."

Logan took it from there. "Late last night a spaceship crash-landed in the mountains less than sixty miles from here. Its point of origin is unknown, but it was clearly not from Earth. We know that one of the aliens got away, and you're the only person we've met that has had contact with it."

Stacy stared away from them. "It's true," she muttered under her breath. "But why me?"

"That's what we need to find out," Chase said.

"Why me?"

"Is there something that you didn't tell us?" Logan asked.

Stacy seemed totally lost in her thoughts. After a long moment, she leapt off the table. "Can we see Jack Peterson, now?"

"Did you hear what I just told you?" Logan asked.

"Mmm hmmm, yeah. Everything's fine," she said, though clearly it wasn't.

Chase nodded to Logan, and they took her to see Jack. She walked into the recovery room. Jack looked terrible. His head was wrapped in gauze, and dark blue and purple bruises spotted his face below the edge of his bandages. He was unconscious.

Logan and Chase watched from the doorway.

"I say we stay with her. Her story, while I believe it, just doesn't make sense," Logan said.

"The police say the physical evidence backs up her story to a tee," Chase said. "There was blood—we'll have to confiscate that sample by the way—and they found that guy's toolbox and windshield fragments from his pickup scattered over a mile away from where she crashed—along with skid marks confirming the sudden stop that sent them flying."

"Yeah, but why would an alien attack them? There's got to be more she's not telling us."

"I know. As long as I've studied them, attacking people at random while they're driving has not been their standard M.O."

Stacy approached them, still feeling dazed. "Can I go home now?"

"Sure, Ma'am. We'll take you," Chase said.

83

Inside the Spaceship

The long corridor curved to the right, somehow feeling much larger than it was before, which Blaze knew was just an illusion. It made him appreciate their technology all the more. The ceiling glowed with the incandescence of the deep sea, but still provided sufficient light, like when you look up from underwater on a bright sunny day, though without the refraction of light that made everything wavy. The sea blue floor was softer on his feet than the cold silvery metal that was previously there. The walls came alive with purple-hued lights that formed holographic images real enough to fool the eye and solid enough to touch.

He stopped to study one that caught his fancy—an object shaped like a sideways S, doused in a pool of green and purple light. It was wormlike, but its movements indicated some unknown purpose.

He reached for it, his hand passing clean through the projection. Upon further study, the light seemed to bleed out from a small panel lodged into the wall. Yet he knew the panel was also a holographic creation since it wasn't there before, only the panel was solid. Blaze's eyes shifted about, noting many other images lining the corridor. He smiled—a thousand mysteries to unlock, each a clue to a new technology that would change the course of mankind. The ultimate puzzle that, when solved, led to the ultimate prize.

A pulsating concave blob on the ceiling caught his attention. He glanced up, listening to its barely audible rhythmic beat that reacted to his presence. He stepped toward it and its pulse quickened. He stepped back and its beat eased. Then, in a moment of unquenchable curiosity, he grabbed it, feeling the soft light vibrate in his hand with such increasing frequency it tickled his palm to the point where he had to let go. A small laugh escaped him as he heard Carlson gasp and then relax as the pulsating returned to its original slower beat.

Like an anthropologist on a dig, Blaze indulged himself in each area, drowning himself in the tiniest of details. He walked on a few feet further, Carlson beside him, and gazed down the alien hallway. "All GBIV, very little ROY," Blaze said. "Probably due to their aquatic ancestry. Their physiology must have evolved to allow them to survive in an aquatic environment as well as on land, therefore giving them a higher ocular range with which to view the electromagnetic spectrum."

"In English?" Carlson asked.

"Notice how most of the colors are blues and greens. There are very few reds, yellows, or oranges. They perceive things differently. They can see into what we call the ultraviolet spectrum, but they shy away from the warmer shades—probably because their ancestors were aquatic."

"Hmmm," Carlson mumbled. "We've been at this for almost an hour. Maybe we could explore a living quarter."

"Sorry, Lieutenant. I tend to move slow when I analyze," Blaze said, stopping at the nearest door.

"No need to apologize. I'm just a little eager to see how these things live." Carlson cautiously touched the panel next to a door.

The doors slid open, revealing a room approximately twenty-by-twenty that was reasonably square in shape, except for the rounded far wall, presumably the location of the outer hull of the ship. To their left floated a black structure with rounded corners that looked like a table with no legs, except for its unusual curves. A few feet behind it was what appeared to be another moving 3-D image. A diagonally striped cabinet was located on the back wall. Adjacent to that was a low smooth platform elevated a few feet above the moving, blue floor. *Moving!*

"You first," Carlson said.

Blaze crouched down and touched the floor. His hand went through the blue light and straight to the soft floor underneath. He pulled his hand back, stared at it for a second, and then repeated his actions. "Remarkable. Simply remarkable."

Blaze walked into the room as if nothing was unusual and went straight to the hovering curved "table" that had sparked his interest. It felt solid. He looked beneath it then ran his arms underneath, like a magician waving a hoop over a levitating girl. There was nothing holding it up. "I love this ship," Blaze muttered.

Carlson stepped into the room—and then jumped back as if he had just accidentally stepped in a puddle.

Blaze laughed. "Come on in. The water's fine."

Carlson checked his boots. They hadn't even a hint of dampness on them. "I could've sworn I just stepped into a puddle." He put his foot in again, toe first, then pulled it back out. There wasn't any moisture on his boot. He shrugged and walked in towards the 3-D picture.

"Incredible," Blaze said. "Looks like a liquid, feels like a liquid, but in actuality it's just a sophisticated effect. They manipulate their environment with exact precision and then coordinate it with realistic holographic imagery. In this case, they must have controlled the temperature and humidity of the area inches above the floor then combined it with a fancy light show to simulate the feel of water."

Blaze waved his arm above the table again, stopping when a violet glow appeared on his sleeve. "Ah, see that. Just like I said." He moved his arm around, trying to locate the source of the ultraviolet light. "There's probably some ultraviolet image here that we're unable to perceive."

Carlson eyed a continually changing, three-dimensional holographic image. It began with two smaller aliens standing side by side. They were fully clothed in colorful form-fitting outfits, knee-deep in a swamp-like body of water. The sky was bright with a reddish tinge.

The aliens separated and headed towards different odd-looking trees. What followed was a coordinated ballet of motion as they leapt from branch to branch, one alien seemingly chasing the other. One dove into the water, temporarily disappearing before resurfacing behind some vegetation. Then it made an acrobatic dash through water, land, and tree branches, before gracefully landing next to the other. The other one moved quickly and splashed him with water, until both stopped and grinned. The image recycled and both aliens were again standing side by side, and the action replayed itself. "What do you make of this?"

Blaze looked for a minute, smiling at the two playful aliens. "Home movies. These must be the kids. And our first glance at an alien world."

Both paused for a minute, fully taking in the magnitude of that moment.

"Wow," Carlson said.

"We'll get a better look later." Blaze resumed studying the room. He walked to the back and triggered an image of two pilots smoking cigarettes, shooting the breeze, just outside of the ship. It was the Canadians, yet Blaze wasn't seeing through a window but instead an image of what was directly outside that area of the ship as if a window had been there. He pushed his hand through the image and felt the cold metal wall behind it, the image appearing briefly on his hand before he pulled it away. "Everything is incredible. Every facet of this ship represents a monumental advance to every existing area of science." It was his dream come true. "I'll bet the reason this ship is intact, and most of the aliens survived, is that this computer generated a stasis field to cushion the impact. A holographic airbag, if you will, that appeared instantly throughout the entire ship holding everything in place. That would explain why nothing was thrown about."

Carlson walked over to the platform and sat down. Then he laid down. "Not bad. Think it sleeps one or two?"

"Too small. Definitely one," Blaze answered. Suddenly he realized something. Something that no one had thought of asking. Something important that they needed to know. "Shit. I'll be right back."

Blaze bolted from the room.

84

Gaines spotted their cargo truck a few hundred feet ahead. It was parked on the edge of the road, its rear doors spread wide open. He pulled up behind it, headlights on, grabbed a flashlight, drew his weapon, and got out slowly. The truck looked abandoned, but he wasn't taking any chances.

He shone the flashlight's beam into the hold, confirming his suspicions that the precious alien cargo was gone. Then he studied the ground, seeing two sets of footprints in the snow. The smaller ones, making a shorter indentation with an imprint of a standard issue Canadian boot, had to be Rebecca's. The larger ones weren't Dupres' because the imprint was different.

But who else could they have been? And where was Dupres?

Gaines cautiously made his way to the front. He stepped forward quickly and aimed his gun and flashlight into the front seat by the driver's side. There was no one there. Raising the beam slightly, he noticed the bloodstained passenger side seat and instantly his second question was answered. There was no mistaking it now. Rebecca was exactly what Logan said she was, but maybe she wasn't the one who killed Dupres.

When he went around to the passenger's side for a closer look, he saw the second set of tire tracks. The transfer of so much cargo would have taken some time. He felt the hood of the truck. Still warm. He knelt feeling the snow surrounding the second set of tire tracks. It was soft, meaning they left recently. He could still catch them.

Luckily, he was familiar with the area. He got back in the jeep, drove about a mile ahead and then pulled over to an elevated section of the highway. The surrounding terrain was relatively flat, affording him an excellent view of the road. In the distance he saw the lone, red brake lights of a truck driving west. He got back in the jeep and followed.

85

Carlson ran through the corridors, growing more disoriented with each rapid turn through the strange alien environment. The longer it took to find Blaze, the more harrowed he became. Not only would Major Gaines give him hell for letting Blaze out of his sight, but also because being alone on this spaceship unnerved him more than he cared to admit.

What was Blaze doing? Where had he run off to?

Carlson took a deep breath, regained his composure, and decided to go back up to level three where Blaze had first eluded him. Sure enough, there Blaze was, hunched over by the door to the room they had explored together, his breathing labored, his face was pale with concern.

Carlson approached him with rapid strides. "You mind telling me where you went and what the heck you were doing?"

Blaze stood erect, trying desperately to catch his breath. He failed, hunched over again, and held his hand out waiting for his breathing to ease. "How many bodies did you load aboard the truck?" he asked Carlson between gasps for air.

"What are you talking about?" Carlson said.

"How many aliens did you load aboard the truck?" Blaze asked again.

"Thirteen. Why?"

"Thirteen, plus one that got away. Shit," Blaze said.

"What's wrong?"

"I just did a bed check."

"So?"

"We got thirteen aliens. I counted seventeen beds. There isn't just one alien loose on this planet. There are four."

86

Headlights approached behind them, their glare reflecting off the truck's side view mirrors. Whoever it was, they were moving fast. Nikolai turned to Rebecca who also saw them from the right side-view mirror.

"Are you expecting anyone?" Nikolai asked.

"No," she answered. "Slow down. Let's get a better look. If it's nothing, let them pass."

Nikolai eased off the gas, watching as the vehicle closed in. Through the brightness he saw the silhouette of the jeep. "It's military," he said.

The headlights flashed, requesting them to pull over.

"It's one of mine. Stop the truck," she said.

"That's foolish. They can't stop us."

"If we don't stop, they'll radio ahead and then we'll be facing greater numbers. Pull over. I'll take care of it," Rebecca pulled the alien weapon out of her pocket and reattached the alien's thumb to her own with a small strip of duct tape.

Nikolai pulled off the road and stopped. He reached into the side panel and grabbed his gun.

The jeep stopped a safe distance behind them.

Rebecca stepped out of the cab, keeping her right hand and the weapon concealed in her coat pocket. She hoped to talk her way out of it, and if need be, use her credentials. But if all else failed, she was ready to do the worst. That's when she noticed the man standing at the rear of the truck, illuminated by the jeep's headlights, was

Gaines, a scowl on his face, his gun pointed directly at her.

"David?!" she said, truly surprised to see him. *What was he doing here? Did he know?*

"Just tell me why?" Gaines said. He moved closer, keeping his gun aimed squarely at her chest. "Why?"

"Why what? And for god's sake, put down the gun," she said.

"I don't think so, Rebecca," Gaines walked slowly to his left, peering around the driver's side to see if anyone else was there. He saw no one. Or is that even your real name? What is it? Natasha? Olga?"

Rebecca's face changed. His comments left no room for doubt. He knew. *But how?* It didn't matter. She had to get away. Slowly, she eased her hand into her pocket.

"That's right. I know everything. Take your hand out of your pocket—NOW!"

She did as he ordered. "David," she said gently, as she took a step towards him.

"No! Don't say a word and don't come any closer." Gaines tensed up looking at her hand. "Take that thing off your thumb."

Logan must've warned him. Or one of the other soldiers. She hesitated then began unraveling the duct tape with her other hand.

"Toss it over to me now," Gaines said.

She threw the alien thumb a few feet in front of him. Keeping his eyes on her, Gaines stepped forward and squashed the thumb under his boot.

"Were you going to use that on me, like you did on the Japanese? Were you going to kill me like you did Dupres?"

"I would never hurt you, David. You must believe that."

"A non-denial. So, you did kill him. Who's in the truck?" Gaines demanded.

"No one."

"Bullshit." Gaines waved the gun, motioning her to walk with him to the driver's side. "Tell them to come out, now." When she didn't move, Gaines fired a shot, just to the side of her head, shooting out the driver's side window. "I'm done being fucked with. Tell them to come out now."

Rebecca approached him in a seductive manner. "We both know you're not going to shoot me, David. We both mean too much to each other."

"So come back. Turn this asshole over to me. Let me bring you in peacefully, and I'll make sure they go easy on you."

She smiled softly. "You would do that for me?"

"Yes."

He kept his eye on the driver's side, approaching it while maintaining a safe distance from her. He waved his gun again, motioning her to back off. She did. Then Gaines pressed his back to the side of the truck and slid toward the door. With one quick motion, he jumped in front of the driver side window and fired two shots blindly into the cab. He reached the gun in and fired lower, just in case the driver had ducked to the floor.

Nikolai jumped down from the roof. His left foot smashed Gaines' right arm, driving it against the window frame and jarring the gun from his grip. The gun clanked off the frame and fell inside the truck, out of his reach. Nikolai's other leg cracked into Gaines' forehead, knocking him down.

Gaines fell hard. Nikolai landed crouched, like a big cat—then sprung into an offensive stance.

Gaines swiftly got up, stumbling backwards to create some space between him and his attacker. Another punch came in quickly. Gaines leaned back and rolled with the blow, lessening the impact, only to be on the receiving end of a right hook that jostled his teeth. His instincts kicked in. He thrust his right arm up, blocking the incoming left, then jabbed Nikolai in the gut with his right.

Nikolai's abs were so solid, and Gaines' punch so sloppy, the blow hurt his hand more than it did Nikolai. Still, it created a moment that allowed him to back away and study his adversary.

Nikolai was six inches taller, easily fifty pounds heavier, and his look suggested all that extra weight was muscle. He glanced at Rebecca as he lifted his arms up into a fighting stance. "Who's your new friend?"

She didn't answer.

Nikolai advanced, leading with a right hook that Gaines blocked, then followed with a left jab that connected. Gaines' eye would be black tomorrow, but he remained on his feet.

He feigned a right that distracted Gaines then threw a left that Gaines blocked. Gaines countered with a hook but missed. Then he followed it with a front kick that Nikolai sidestepped. Nikolai pushed his leg to the left, slipped behind him, and grabbed him from behind in a choke hold.

Gaines' training kicked in. Using his heel, he kicked Nikolai in the shin. Then he repeatedly pounded Nikolai's cold hands with his knuckles until his grip loosened. With his neck free, he tilted his head forward, then snapped it back fast, head-butting Nikolai in the mouth. With momentum on his side, he spun around quickly and delivered a follow-up right hook.

Gaines' fist smacked into Nikolai's palm like a fast ball in a catcher mitt—and Nikolai squeezed. Nikolai stared at Gaines as blood trickled into his mouth. Then Nikolai threw a right hook of his own. Gaines caught Nikolai's wrist before the powerful blow hit. The two men were locked in a test of strength and Nikolai was clearly the stronger man.

Nikolai shifted his weight and used his momentum to toss Gaines into the hard steel of the truck. He followed with a devastating right that split Gaines' lip.

Gaines' mouth filled with blood. As the next powerful punch flew toward him, Gaines ducked. The powerful impact of Nikolai's fist colliding with the truck resounded. Gaines counterattacked lower. A jab to the groin that folded Nikolai, quickly followed with an uppercut that crunched his jaw and straightened him out.

Nikolai fell.

Gaines stepped forward and kicked at Nikolai's head, but Nikolai caught his boot. Then Nikolai turned his wrists, twisting Gaines' ankle in a direction it wasn't meant to go and threw Gaines aside. Nikolai shook off the nausea of the low blow, and charged Gaines, who was attempting to get to his feet. His shoulder thrust into Gaines's gut, his arms wrapped around Gaines' waist, and the two men tumbled over with limbs flailing wildly.

Gaines tried to get up. He used the momentum of the roll and got on top. Then he coiled his arm ready to strike another blow. But Nikolai's knee shot up, thrusting deep into Gaines' ribs. The impact sent him flying off before he could land the blow.

Both men quickly got up.

Gaines favored his right side. Blood dripped from his nose and mouth coating the left side of his face. He spat red into the snow. "You ready to give up yet, you big dumb son of a bitch."

Nikolai remained silent.

Gaines feigned a jab then threw a right cross.

Nikolai deflected the punch and latched hold of Gaines' arm. Then he sidestepped, placed his free hand on Gaines' elbow, twisted his torso, and spun Gaines into the truck. Nikolai held Gaines in the arm-lock and thrust a bone-crunching side kick into his exposed rib cage.

A short involuntary yelp escaped Gaines' throat. He winced from the pain.

Nikolai shoved his forearm powerfully into Gaines' arm, snapping the bone in two.

Gaines collapsed to his knees, his right side paralyzed from pain, his breathing labored from broken ribs scraping against his innards. The battle was over. Gaines was not getting up.

Nikolai stepped away as Rebecca approached. "It is over," he boasted.

"Very nice," Rebecca said. She twirled the gun in her hand like a cowboy. "We sparred together in training all the time, and I rarely beat him." She shook her head and focused on Gaines. Oh well, she thought. She aimed her weapon at Gaines' head.

Gaines gazed up, too injured to do anything. His eyes stared at hers pathetically, like a lost puppy.

Rebecca chuckled. "Just for the record David, my real name is Valeri Ignosovitch, and I never truly cared for you a day in my life." She tensed her finger to pull the trigger.

"Nyet!" Nikolai shouted, grabbing her hand. "We have done what we came here to do. We are agents of the Soviet Republic." He showed her his gun which he kept unused within his jacket. "We may kill, but we are not murderers." He let her go.

"Look at that, David. It's your lucky day." She laughed out loud. She stepped closer, grabbed his hair, and stared into his bloody face. She puckered her lips, as if about to kiss him. Then she smashed him in the face with her gun. As he fell unconscious at her feet, she turned to Nikolai. "I'm sick of this country. Let's go home."

87

Prince Rupert – Stacy's House

Logan admired the white vaulted ceiling that led up to the skylight. He felt like he was in a ski chalet. The living room was spacious. An L-shaped couch framed two sides of a white tiger rug. The third side had a recliner. The open side faced a large brick fireplace with a rack that held all the standard tools—tongs, a shovel, a corn broom, a poker, a blower, and a wooden holder for the logs.

To the right, a big-screen television sat on a contemporary black stand, which contained a DVD player and an assortment of movies. Against the far wall was a hi-fi stereo component system with mounted speakers. On the same wall, paintings were mounted to balance the contrast. Logan glanced at the Monet, briefly, before his attention was captured by a bookcase. Interested in Stacy's taste in reading material, he wandered over to peruse.

Logan noted that Chase eyed the place with a different agenda in mind, noting the exits, a habit often picked up by men in the military. There were sliding glass doors that led outside to a deck that might or might not have stairs that led to ground level. The other doors led to a bathroom, a kitchen, and a dining area. Against the east wall stairs led down to the front door, a laundry room, and a one-car garage. Another staircase went up to a gallery walk that led to two rooms and the master bathroom.

Stacy returned from the kitchen, holding three steaming coffee mugs in her hands. She handed one to Chase and put the other two on an end table. "Anything with it?"

"Black's fine," Logan said.

"Cream, two sugars," Chase replied.

"I'll be right back," Stacy said, returning to the kitchen.

Logan pulled one of Stacy's books from the shelves and thumbed through it. He placed it back, noting the book next to it was written by Stacy herself. He grabbed the thin book and scanned the title — "Princess Zinthia and the Sharkmen of Azador's Revenge". That was telling, he thought. He opened to the middle and saw her illustration. Stacy was Princess Zinthia. Immediately, he turned back to the inside front cover to check the copyright date. The book was printed in 2006. "Colonel, take a look at this." He brought it over and showed Chase.

They were both staring at it when Stacy came back, cream holder in one hand, a cup of sugar packets in the other. Their expressions spoke volumes.

"Care to explain this?" Logan asked.

She placed the milk and sweeteners beside the coffees, a thoughtful look in her eye. "Everything you have told me is true, isn't it?"

"Yeah," Logan answered.

She put her finger in her mouth and began chewing on her knuckle. Then she paced. "I think... no, I *am* an abductee," she said.

"Come again?!" Chase said.

"I get it. Hearing myself say that for the first time sounds so bizarre. But apparently, it's true. I should have mentioned it back at the hospital, but... you know... how exactly does somebody bring that up?"

She sat down. Chase took a seat in the recliner. Logan sat next to her.

"I just found out myself this afternoon. I didn't believe it. Heck, I still didn't believe it until that thing attacked us."

"I don't understand," Chase said.

"You think I do?" She reached for the coffee but decided to leave it where it was. "Since I was a little girl, I've had nightmares. Not just ordinary bad dreams, but the same terrifying nightmare over and over again. See those sharkmen I drew? They were the images that continually haunted me. My parents took me to therapist after therapist, but they all said the same thing, 'Don't worry, Mrs. Michaels, she'll grow out of it.' What a joke."

She snorted and slid to the other end of the couch, suddenly too uncomfortable to sit close to them.

"Funny part is they were right. Over time, the dream faded and eventually I forgot about it. But then, years later, for reasons no one could explain, they returned worse than before. I saw a therapist during that period, too. She suggested I write about the experience to help me understand it. I'm not sure if it helped or not, but it made me realize I liked writing. When they finally faded once again, I decided to pursue writing full time.

"You're holding my third book. Pretty funny, huh? Well, they say write what you know. Anyway, when I got on my feet, I decided to start over, so I moved here. That was six years ago. One year later, the nightmares started again. This time more vividly than before. That's when I started seeing Dr. Miller. He was the best. The one I found easiest to talk to. He was more like my friend than my doctor, if you know what I mean. He taught me how to live with it and once again the nightmares gradually faded." Stacy got up and walked over to the sliding glass door and peered out over the mountains.

"Until last night. I was out here when I heard a noise as loud as thunder."

"That must have been the sonic boom the ship made before it crashed," Logan told her.

"Yeah, well..." Stacy went on. She described the nightmare she had that night. How it was more vivid than ever before. How it sent shivers down her spine and frightened her more than anything else. She told them about the emergency visit to Dr. Miller, and the subsequent hypnosis session involving Dr. Peterson.

Chase reached for his coffee and took a sip. "The police report says Dr. Peterson owns the plumbing supply depot on Elm."

"Yeah. Apparently regressive hypnotherapy doesn't pay the bills," Stacy said, with a half-smile.

Logan stood up. He cupped his hand around his chin. "That still doesn't explain why they tried to kill you. Do you have any idea why they were after you?" Logan asked.

Stacy's eyelids rose and she shrugged.

"Sorry. I had to ask," Logan said, grabbing his coffee.

Chase's cellular phone rang. He flipped it open. "Yeah."

"It's me, Colonel." The voice that rang out from the phone belonged to Blaze.

"Give me a minute," Chase said, then walked out of earshot.

A moment later he flipped his phone closed and waved Logan over to him so they could speak privately.

Logan gave Stacy a reassuring smile and walked over. "What?" Logan asked.

"Blaze says there are four aliens loose." Chase recounted everything that Blaze told him.

"Are you sure? Maybe they had guest rooms or something," Logan said.

"According to Blaze, the ship's completely programmable. If they needed another bed, they could've created one in a minute."

"Four… Jesus," Logan muttered.

"Oh, he's got nothing to do with this," Chase said.

"What now?" Logan asked.

"We'll wait here until we hear another report of a sighting. Going out looking for them is a waste of time," Chase said. "And who knows... maybe the alien that tried to kill her will come back."

Chase had no idea how right he was. For in the skylight looking down on them with vacant hollow eyes was the alien. Its eyes fixed on Stacy. It slowly withdrew from the glass and disappeared into the night.

88

Rebecca felt no remorse. More than an hour had passed since they left Gaines' unconscious battered body on the side of the road, and already she had forgotten him as if he had never existed. Her only thoughts were about returning home. She took a swig of Vodka from the bottle Nikolai had given her, a small taste of things to come.

"I thought you would appreciate that," Nikolai said. "My way of saying congratulations on a job well done. But let's not indulge too much."

"Spaseeba," Rebecca replied, wiping the alcohol from her lips. "How much further?"

"Another hour," Nikolai answered.

Rebecca took another swig then placed the cap back on and put it away. After all, it wouldn't truly be time to celebrate until they got home. In this business it was important to keep your wits about you. "How are we getting this stuff out?"

"We have comrades stationed at—"

Rebecca interrupted with a laugh. "I haven't heard that word in a long time. Too long. It will be very good to get back. How is life in Moscow?"

"In some places worse, others better," Nikolai said. "You need not worry though. After this assignment, I'm sure General Vaskev will see to it that your accommodations rank among the best."

"Good." Rebecca smiled. She couldn't wait to return. Her superiors would treat her as if she was a hero—and she was, she thought to herself. She remained undetected in enemy camp for five years. During that time, she smuggled out an untold number of secrets that would have made any KGB agent proud. Her idea for a pipeline worked flawlessly. Nobody suspected that each time she visited her gynecologist she was actually dropping off information.

She told Gaines she couldn't have a child because of certain "female difficulties". It was the perfect lie. Not only did it allow her unlimited visits to her doctor, who no one suspected was also a spy, but also it played on his sympathetic nature. She learned that any time she needed to get closer to him, she just had to reveal more of her vulnerable side. He fell for it every time.

"So, how are we going to get this stuff out?" she asked again.

"We have a contact in Alaska. He runs a fish market. We are going to off-load everything into crates and then leave by freighter. Within one week's time, everything we acquired will be in Russia."

"And with that fool out of the way there is no one to stop us."

As if on cue, headlights glared at them from further up the road. A huge truck, its cab facing toward them, its rear sideways, blocked the two-lane highway.

"Is that part of the plan?" Rebecca asked.

"No." Nikolai kept his speed steady in spite of the impromptu roadblock.

"I'll take care of it." Rebecca reached into her pocket and withdrew the alien weapon. Then she remembered Gaines squished the thumb. There was no time to go into the rear and get another. "Damn it. I can't use this." She looked toward the truck, which loomed larger as they approached. She remembered her weak moment when she stopped to avoid a jeep, and it almost resulted in her losing the alien cargo to the Japanese. She didn't want Nikolai repeating her mistake. "Ram it. Don't stop. Just drive straight through it."

They were getting close.

Nikolai slammed on the brakes, halting the eighteen-wheeler.

"Damn it," Rebecca shouted, pounding her fist against the dashboard.

"This is not the armored truck you were driving before. If we hit that truck at this speed, we'll both be killed," Nikolai said.

They stopped about twenty yards short of the truck. In between, a lone figure stood firm, holding a gun in one hand aimed directly at their windshield. The other hand, still to the side, held an Uzi. The figure stood about five and a half feet tall and was clothed in heavy winter garb. A hooded, black, down jacket pulled tightly around the individual's face concealed it in darkness. One thing was clear. Whoever the mysterious figure was, they knew exactly what they were transporting.

Their windshield cracked suddenly as a bullet drilled through the glass, lodging itself in the metal wall behind them. The figure darkened as two more shots took out their headlights. Now only Rebecca and Nikolai were bathed in bright light, like criminals held for interrogation at a police station.

A voice screamed at them. "Put your hands where I can see them and step slowly out of the truck."

Nikolai already had his gun handy. So did Rebecca.

The glass cracked again. Another bullet pinged between them and ricocheted through the roof.

The figure dropped the gun and held up the Uzi. "I know you can see this, Nikolai. Next time, I use it. You have two seconds to make your decision."

A female voice. And whoever it was knew him. That changed the equation.

Nikolai raised both his hands, showed his pistol, and left it on the dashboard.

"Your turn." The figure aimed the Uzi at Rebecca. She quickly did the same, following Nikolai's lead. They both opened their doors and stepped slowly out of the vehicle. "Walk in front of the truck and get on your knees."

Nikolai's eyes betrayed his recognition. He knew her, too.

"Do it. If I was going to execute you, I would've done it already," the woman said. "Get down on your knees and you'll live."

They eased to the front of the truck and dropped to their knees on the cold concrete road as their captor commanded.

The figure approached; face still hidden beneath the hood. Nikolai squinted in the bright headlights.

"Nikolai, I didn't think trapping you would be so easy," the voice taunted him. Then the hood turned to face Rebecca. "You must be Valeri, or should I say Rebecca?" Holding the Uzi firm in one hand, the figure brought the other hand up and removed the hood.

Nikolai's mouth gaped wide. "What are you doing here?"

Nikolai's wife Katrina smiled at him. She paused, and then in a dead serious tone answered. "I'm here to inform you, my dear husband, that as of this moment, your life as a spy is over."

89

Prince Rupert – Stacy's House

The TV was tuned in to the local news; the incident with Stacy went unreported. Logan turned it off, preferring to concentrate on the aliens to discover whatever it was that would explain their contradictory behavior. He mulled over his encounter this morning—which at this point felt like it happened a week ago--and recalled everything Gaines and Dupres told him, coming to the same conclusion. Their actions were defensive in nature.

So why were they suddenly aggressive? And why Stacy? What was the connection?

He believed she was abducted, but there had to be more to it than that. Studying her was quite different than stalking her. The only difference was they were in control when they took her in the past. Now they weren't. Now their situation was more desperate.

Which didn't offer an answer.

Stacy approached quietly, startling him with her voice. "At least they kept me off the air," she said. "The last thing I need is publicity like that."

"Unless the alien makes a more public appearance, no one else will hear about it. Your government will see to that," Chase said, apparently forgetting that Stacy considered them to be the government.

"Are you cold?" Logan asked, hoping to distract Stacy from the slip up. "I'm cold."

Stacy nodded. "That's because this room is directly above the garage. I kind of like it, though. It gives me an excuse to start a fire and wrap myself up in a blanket."

"Can I get one started now?" Logan asked. The idea of a fire appealed to him. It had been a while since he had sat in front of a fireplace, and the memory was a good one.

"Sure. That'd be nice." Stacy smiled at him.

Logan walked over to the fireplace. He opened the glass door and reached underneath to pull the lever that opened the flue, learning it was already open. He looked toward the holder. Only two logs remained from the cord. Choosing the healthier of the two, he squatted and placed it in the ash-ridden fireplace. "I see you use this often."

"Every night. Almost. When I was a kid, my father used to sit with me and read me stories. When I sit here, it reminds me of that... helps me write better too."

Logan adjusted the log, reached over to get a match, and turned to her again. "Last time I made a fire, I was on a ski trip with my dad."

Stacy's expression became a shroud of uncontrollable fear. She stopped breathing, paralyzed for a moment. Then she screamed.

Before Logan could even stand, the sound of a log falling off its holder caught his ear. He swiftly spun his head around to see why. There, crouched inside the fireplace, was an alien, its eyes cold, its mouth rigid, its body lithe and strong. A small amount of soot marred its light gray face and dirtied its long stringy hair.

An instant later, it pounced, like a tiger on its prey, landing on top of Logan and forcing him to the ground.

Chase spit out his coffee when he saw what Stacy was screaming at. He dropped the cup, ignoring the ceramic as it shattered on the floor, and withdrew his gun, unable to get off a clean shot because Logan was flailing wildly, trying to get the alien off him.

Its webbed hand cupped Logan's face and drove his head to the floor. Chase leapt over the couch and ran forward. From this range he couldn't miss. The alien leapt away and skittered back up the chimney before Chase could fire the shot. Chase cursed, ran forward, closed the flue, and shut the glass doors to the fireplace.

Stacy rushed over to Logan. "Are you all right?"

Logan sat up. His lip trickled blood. "Yeah, fine."

Chase repeatedly scanned every entrance, pointing his gun repeatedly at each one. "What the fuck was that?"

Logan wiped the blood from his mouth and stood up. "I think it was trying to take me out to get to Stacy."

Something thumped on the roof.

"You still want to talk to them?" Chase asked.

Logan didn't answer.

"I didn't think so. Let's get out of here."

Logan and Chase glanced out the window. Below was the police car they borrowed to get here. On top of the car's roof, an alien prowled. It leapt to the ground by the rear tires. Logan saw the blade protruding from its wrist and noticed the front tires were flat. Chase aimed his gun at the alien, ready to fire through the glass window that separated them.

"Gaines said no killing," Logan reminded him.

"Not when it's them or us," Chase said. He cocked his gun.

The window shattered—but glass shards flew in not out. Fragments slashed Chase's forehead. Beads of blood formed and trickled down like sweat. A gray hand reached in like a blur and snatched the weapon from

Chase's grasp. Another gray hand latched onto Chase's forearm, yanking him forward to pull him out of the house.

Logan quickly wrapped his arms around Chase and pulled him back.

Stacy ran to the fireplace and grabbed the poker. She raced back to the window screaming and whacked the alien's arm twice until it finally let go. All three quickly moved to the center of the room, away from any windows.

"Shit," Chase cursed, rubbing the blood from his eyes.

"Do you have another gun?" Stacy asked.

"We can't kill them," Logan said.

"Oh yes we can," Stacy insisted.

Chase pulled a .22 caliber pistol from an ankle holster. "Looks like you're outnumbered, Logan."

"Gaines gave us strict orders," Logan said.

"Gaines figured we would be up against one. There's at least two out there, probably all four."

"Doesn't matter. It's still wrong," Logan said.

"WRONG?! These things are trying to kill us!" Stacy yelled then took a breath. "The hell with Gaines, whoever that is. You guys weren't tortured by those things your entire life. They're pure evil, and death is what they deserve." She looked over at Chase. "You got an extra gun for me?"

"Sorry, ma'am. Two's my limit." Chase surveyed everywhere at once. "Do you have a car?"

"It's in the garage."

"That's—"

The skylight fell in beside them. Glass rained down on the living room, showering the floor only a few feet from where they stood. An alien jumped down. Even before it landed, Chase fired at it twice. He missed both times, and before he could fire again, the alien touched down and sprang into the kitchen.

"Shit, they're fast," Chase mumbled.

More glass shattered. Shards sprayed everywhere. A lounge chair sped towards them from the now broken sliding glass doors that led to the deck.

Chase instinctively turned and fired once. A spark flew from the metal arm of the chair as it bounced off the floor. In the shadows, an alien darted through the opening and took cover behind the couch.

"Down the stairs. It's our only chance," Chase shouted.

Logan ran first with Stacy right behind him. Chase backpedaled, covering the rear. The alien in the kitchen stuck its head out. Chase fired once. The bullet ricocheted off the door frame as the alien ducked. For good measure, he fired an additional shot then hurried down the stairs.

Logan waited for him at the bottom, holding the door open leading to the garage. When Chase ran in, Logan slammed the door behind him. He tried to lock it but realized that the door could only be locked from inside the house.

"Forget it," Chase yelled. "Get in the car." Chase got into the blue Camry's driver's seat, forcing Stacy to move over to the passenger's side. Logan dove in the back. "Give me the keys," Chase ordered.

Stacy reached above the steering wheel and pulled down the visor. The ignition key dropped into her other hand. She gave it to Chase, who gave her an incredulous look. "It's a safe neighborhood," she replied.

"Yeah, safe," Chase replied. "Open the door."

Stacy hit the electronic garage door opener and the door slowly rose.

Chase started the car and held his right hand on the gear shift. "C'mon. C'mon." The door was halfway open when they saw an alien standing in their path, aiming one of their energy weapons directly at them. "Oh shit."

Stacy panicked. "We're gonna die. We're gonna die. No, no."

The alien didn't fire.

Logan watched it curiously, as if suddenly he was emotionally detached and not about to become its victim. The alien was staring at Stacy. "It's because of you, Stacy. He won't fire because of you."

"His mistake." Chase shifted into drive and pushed the gas pedal to the floor. The rear tires screeched on the concrete garage floor and the car lurched forward. Chase fully intended on running the alien down. At the last instant, it jumped up and over the car. "What the fuck?" Chase said, following its graceful motion.

"LOOK OUT," Stacy screamed.

Chase was going too fast. He turned the wheel sharply to his left but couldn't avoid the police car parked in the driveway. With a loud smash, Stacy's car came to a sudden unexpected halt. Chase threw it into reverse. The tires spun out as he saw the front end was jammed into the police cruiser. "SHIT!" Chase slammed the wheel.

One alien landed on the windshield and stared in. Chase fumbled for his pistol and aimed it where the alien was, but it was gone before he could get off a shot. To be safe, he pumped two rounds through the roof then checked on Stacy and Logan. Stacy was fine. Logan pushed himself up from the narrow floor.

"I'm fine," Logan said.

Chase pulled the latch and kicked open the car door. Logan exited as well. Two outdoor lights illuminated the driveway. They were surrounded by trees on three sides and the house on the other. But where did the aliens go? Logan reached in and helped Stacy out of the car.

"What the hell do they want? Why are they doing this to me?" Stacy said. Her fist tightened around the metal poker she still held in her hand.

"Stay calm," Chase said. "It's not over yet."

Logan saw a black shape leap between the branches from the corner of his eye. One thing was clear to him. They didn't want to kill Stacy, but they definitely wanted her. The question was why. He looked at her. She had fire in her eyes, even though she was clearly terrified by the events. *What's so special about her? What does she have that they want?*

"Let's get to the road," Chase ordered.

"No," Logan said.

"We're sitting ducks for their energy weapons. If we stay here, they'll blow us to kingdom come."

"No," Logan said. "They won't risk harming Stacy. They want us to move. Once we're a safe distance from her, they will kill us. If we cluster together, they won't use their long-range attack."

The situation reminded him of what Dupres told him. Instead of the alien killing him, they took apart his radio, cutting off his communication line. They left him because he was no longer a threat. *Did that mean they were a threat? Would the aliens leave them alone if they were helpless?*

Wait, that logic was flawed. Dupres had also mentioned that the ship's power had interfered with the radio transmission. They couldn't communicate with each other because the ship's power was on. So that couldn't have been the reason why the aliens took apart Dupres' radio. They had to know that. Gaines mentioned they dissected his radio, too.

A rock hit the car. Chase turned toward the sound, and an alien pounced from the trees in the opposite direction, bouncing off the hood and tackling Chase before he could fire a shot. It was the oldest trick in the book and Chase fell for it. Its webbed, dark gray hand knocked Chase's arm and sent the gun flying.

Logan ran to help him, but another alien dropped down between them, a sharp metal blade protruding from its wrist.

Chase was on his own, locked arm-to-arm in a struggle for control. He overpowered the alien and got on top of it. The alien tapped a button on his wristband. A blade shot out of the housing slicing Chase's hand. Then, it positioned its foot under Chase's stomach, rolled backwards, and used its powerful legs to flip him.

Stacy charged into the fray. With the poker outstretched, she barreled toward the alien to skewer it through its back. The alien blocking Logan leapt at her and knocked her to the ground, the poker dropping beside them.

Logan's only chance—as distasteful as it was—was to go for Chase's gun. But he couldn't risk being drawn too far from Stacy or one of the aliens still lurking in the trees would strike him down from a distance. A desperate plan formed in his head. If he couldn't use Stacy for protection, he would use one of them. He screamed at the alien who just threw Chase, taunting it, daring it to attack him. When the alien took his bait, Logan dashed for the weapon. But it moved much faster than Logan anticipated.

The alien that held Stacy had a gash across its forehead. It was the same one that had attacked her in the truck. She lashed out at it, kicking and screaming. But the alien pinned her legs and began dragging her away.

She reached out for the poker, snatching it with her right hand. Then rocks pelted the alien from behind. It stopped and turned. Stacy pulled her legs in, leaned forward, and struck the alien in the head while it was distracted. She kicked her legs free, stumbled to her feet, and ran towards Chase.

"Two can play at that game," Chase muttered, dropping the remaining pebbles from his hand.

Logan felt the alien's presence closing on him. He dove forward for the gun. In one move, he scooped it up, rolled over, and turned to face the alien. He lifted the gun up to shoot.

The alien pounced.

Logan couldn't pull the trigger. He couldn't kill. It wasn't his nature.

The alien barreled him over, landed on top of him and popped the blade from its wristband. The thrust jabbed deep into Logan's left shoulder. He screamed in pain and instinctively reacted by cracking the gun against the side of the alien's head.

In a fit of panic, he smacked it again and again, until the alien stopped moving. Logan tilted its head to make sure its blowholes still were. A blue flash splashed the ground to his left, raising a cloud of dirt and leaving a small crater.

Logan saw Chase wrap his arm around Stacy. He spotted Logan squatting over the fallen alien about twenty yards away, just beyond the blue flash. "Come on," he yelled out. Then, with Stacy beside him, Chase ran for cover in the garage.

Logan was in trouble. If he fled, a blue beam would strike him down. Unless... he grabbed the alien around its neck and dragged it with him, using its body as a shield. The alien Stacy had knocked down rose to its feet, shook its head vigorously, and then walked towards him. A black-skinned one dropped from the trees and surrounded him. If he let go of the body, he was dead.

Logan dragged the alien back with him into the garage, next to Chase and Stacy only to see the fourth alien waiting for them by the inside door, cutting off their escape back into the house. Its energy weapon was pointed at them. The other two aliens closed in, blocking the exit back to the driveway. They were trapped, their backs literally against the wall.

"Talk to them," Chase ordered, with the dangerous eyes of a cornered animal. "Tell them you're going to kill their friend if they don't back off."

Logan sighed. "No. There's only one way to end this. I finally understand what they want."

90

Nikolai lifted off one knee.

"Don't even think it," Katrina said, with a wave of her gun. "We need to settle some things first, dear Nikolai."

"You know this woman?" Rebecca said.

"She's my wife."

"Looks like you weren't a very good husband," Rebecca remarked.

"Shut up, Valeri," Katrina snapped. "I know all about you, and I know exactly what you are capable of. One more word from you and I will not hesitate."

"How?" Nikolai asked.

"I read your mission file while you were preparing to leave," Katrina replied. "I knew where you were going, and I knew the coded frequency Valeri was using to communicate with you. I followed you every step of the way and I knew you would eventually end up here."

"Why?" Nikolai asked.

"Because I am tired, Nikolai. I'm tired of living with a man who gives more to his country than he gives to me. I'm tired of being lonely. Do you even realize I raised our son, Mikhail, practically alone? He's twelve years old and hardly knows his father. You always promised me it would end one day. That once again you would be the man I married, but when was that going to happen? When? When I am old and gray. When I am so broken and desolate there is nothing left of me to love."

"But Katya, what I do, I do for our country. For the future of all our people."

"And what about the future of your family?" Katrina asked, sharply. "No more Nikolai. It ends today. One way or another you are going to make a choice."

Nikolai rose slowly, arms still raised, his wife's anguish too important to him to ignore. "We can talk about it when we get home, Katya. I promise."

"No. It's too late. I can't go home any longer," Katrina cried.

"What are you talking about?"

"I sold your secrets, Nikolai. I contacted the Japanese through some very illegal channels and informed them where the spaceship was. When our government learns what I have done, I will be branded a traitor. I can never go back. I used the money to get our son safely out of the country and to follow you here. If you go home, you will be alone when you get there. Or you can defect to Canada and stay with Mikhail and me. I'm sure the Canadian government will welcome you, considering the invaluable bargaining chip you hold—and they will protect us. Isn't that right, Rebecca?"

"You did not do this," Nikolai barked. "You betray our country… then ask me to do the same."

Katrina shook her head, disgusted. "Why do you love it so? You fought your whole life for them. What did they ever give you in return? You watched friends die in battle. For what? So some corrupt politician could take credit for your actions and attain even more undeserved power to abuse. Don't you see how they've used you? They took an honest, courageous, good, strong man, the best I've ever known, and turned him into a mindless puppet to do their bidding."

"You can't judge Russia by the actions of a few bad men."

"Why do you still defend them? Haven't you seen enough corruption to last ten lifetimes?"

"It could still work," Nikolai insisted.

"Most people aren't like you, Nikolai. They use the power given to them for their own selfish needs. That is why it does not work. In your heart, you know this to be true. Yes, there was a time our country needed you, but that time is long past. That war is over, and your family needs you more."

"I won't betray my country, Katrina. You know that."

"AND HOW WILL YOU BE BETRAYING THEM?" she screamed in frustration. "By failing to steal alien technology which will be used by our government to restart the Cold War? Think what would happen if one of the rebel factions got a hold of this. Do you think you can prevent that?"

Nikolai hesitated. "Vaskev is a good man. He will not let that happen."

"No, he wouldn't. But do you really believe that there won't be at least one corrupt power broker who would sell these to the highest bidder, making billions, while the good people of our country die in a horrible bloody war? What would be so bad if the Canadians kept it? Sure, they will use it to build weapons, but they won't be aggressive with them, and they won't use them against us. The only way you will truly be betraying our country is if you bring these weapons of death to them."

"Don't listen to her," Rebecca spat out.

Katrina ignored her. "Stay with me, Nikolai. I need you. Our son needs his father. We can start over anywhere we want—live like we've always dreamt of. I have millions of dollars stashed away. We can own a farm. We can buy that ranch you've always wanted."

"All fairytales," Rebecca shouted. "I know these people. These westerners are warmongers. I lived with them for five years, bathed in their filth and greed. I know. They'll use this technology to slowly destroy us, like they did before. Whereas back home, glory awaits us."

"Shut up," Katrina yelled.

Rebecca continued. "They'll build better weapons in the name of democracy and try to infect us with their western beliefs."

Katrina raised the butt of her Uzi, ready to silence her with a hard rap to the head. Rebecca sprung up, blocked Katrina's thrust with her left hand, and grabbed the gun with her right. With practiced ease, Rebecca twisted the weapon in and up and stole it from Katrina's grasp. A split second later, her finger on the trigger, Rebecca pointed the weapon at Katrina.

"Don't," yelled Nikolai.

"I killed a man, Nikolai. For me there's no going back," Rebecca said.

Nikolai stepped forward. Rebecca spun the weapon and fired at Nikolai. Only one bullet sprang from the chamber. It hit Nikolai in the shoulder, driving him back and down to the ground.

Katrina reacted swiftly. Before Rebecca figured out the selector switch was set to single fire, she knocked the weapon from her hand with a front crescent kick to her wrist.

Rebecca responded with a wild left hook. Katrina blocked it and hit Rebecca with a sharp jab to the ribs. Then Katrina grabbed her wrist, twisted it inward and up, and turned it counterclockwise, flipping her over hard.

Rebecca slapped the ground with her free arm, spreading the impact evenly over her body to cushion her fall. Katrina threw a finishing blow, but Rebecca deflected it then kicked up into her face with enough impact to make her release her hold. Then Rebecca sprung to her feet and charged.

Rebecca slammed Katrina into the front grill of the truck. Katrina locked Rebecca's arms, rotated her torso, and threw her around. Rebecca did the same, but this time they fell as the grill wasn't there to stop their violent dance. Together they tumbled off the road and onto the snow-coated grass.

Rebecca rolled on top. She clawed at Katrina's face, digging her nails into her skin, drawing blood before Katrina could grab her hand. Her other hand still free, she slid her thumb into Katrina's mouth and grabbed onto her cheek, stretching it violently and forcing Katrina's face into the cold wet snow.

"You dumb bitch," Rebecca said. "I'm going to take these weapons back to Moscow with your husband. Then I'm going to make him fall in love with me the way you couldn't."

Katrina struggled to push her off, swiping at Rebecca's face.

Rebecca leaned back, avoiding the slap. "Look at you. You are weak and pathetic. No wonder he never came home—"

Katrina jabbed her thumb into Rebecca's neck, cutting the words off at her throat. With Rebecca stunned, and the pressure reduced on her cheek, she turned her face toward Rebecca's thumb and bit down hard.

Rebecca screamed.

"QUIET," Katrina yelled, as she punched her in the throat again, killing the scream. Then, using her legs, she threw Rebecca off her. She sprang up and kicked

Rebecca in the gut, feeling her ribs buckle. She followed with a right to the jaw. Then another that cost Rebecca a tooth. "Maybe on your next assignment, your contact will be a dentist," Katrina said.

Rebecca stumbled back. Blood ran down her chin. She quickly moved into a defensive stance, hoping to fend Katrina off. When the next punch came, she ducked underneath but only had the strength to respond weakly with a side kick.

Katrina blocked it, moved in, and swept her other leg out from under her, sending her sprawling to the ground. She stood over her, her long fingers balled into a fist. "I'm not done with you yet. Get up."

Rebecca hesitated. She spit. A mix of blood and saliva dripped from her mouth and drooled on her chin. She wiped it with her left hand, while her right hand stealthily reached behind and grabbed a handful of snow, dirt, and rocks. Rising slowly, feigning surrender, she waited until she was on her knees. Then she lashed out, throwing the handful of dirt she gathered into Katrina's face. The scree spread wide and flew into her eyes and Rebecca charged furiously, tackling her onto the edge of the road.

When they hit the pavement, Rebecca swiftly punched her in the face. Then she reached back for more dirt and rubbed it in her eyes again.

"How does it feel to be blind?" Rebecca taunted her, the words so hoarse they barely escaped her throat.

Katrina groped wildly and grabbed a handful of hair. She yanked Rebecca's head hard to the side, bringing her face closer to hers. Then she reached up with her opposite hand and pressed her thumb into Rebecca's right eye socket. "You tell me," she shouted.

Rebecca pulled away before Katrina fully gouged her eye. But her backward momentum was enough that Katrina managed to roll her over onto her stomach and get on top, still maintaining a hold of her hair.

Unfortunately, her vision hadn't cleared yet and Katrina was fighting on touch alone. Rebecca's squirmed beneath her. Katrina held on as best she could, but something didn't feel right. Rebecca wasn't trying to get up. She was trying to scramble sideways. As if she was reaching for something. A rock? Something else to smash her head with. Katrina went for her right arm, to pin it down. It was fully outstretched. She heard the faint sound of fingernails scraping concrete. Distracted she lost her grip on Rebecca's hair. The sound of metal scraping concrete caught her attention. Not a knife. Heavier. Her Uzi. Rebecca had managed to grab her fallen Uzi.

Quickly, she slipped down and grabbed Rebecca in a choke hold. Metal tapped concrete. Rebecca had lifted the gun. She tightened her grip while also managing to rub her eyes with her sleeves, partially clearing her vision.

Rebecca had her weapon, clutched in her hand, adjusting it, tilting the barrel toward Katrina by balancing the butt of the gun against the road for support. Rebecca almost had her lined up.

With her free hand Katrina grabbed Rebecca's chin and yanked it up and to the side. She heard Rebecca's neck snap, a dying gasp, followed by metal clanking down on the road. She released Rebecca, slowly stood up, and wiped the dirt from her eyes.

Her vision hazy, but clearing, she looked down at Rebecca's lifeless body. The gun was still in Rebecca's grasp, her finger firmly around the trigger. She kicked it away, then saw Nikolai lying on the ground next to the truck. She ran over to him and held him in her arms.

Nikolai stirred and groaned in pain. "Please, don't squeeze too hard."

"Are you okay?" she asked.

He looked at his blood-soaked shirt and touched the wound to his shoulder, wincing at the sharp pain. "I've been better, but I've also been a lot worse," he grunted.

She kissed him long and passionately. Nikolai reached around her with his good arm and held her tight. After a long emotional minute, she pulled away. "What is your decision, my beloved? Do you want to be with me or your country?"

Nikolai stared at her, all the memories and moments they shared in his eyes. His choice was clear.

91

While still holding the gun to the alien's head, Logan shrieked as loud as he could in his best imitation of their unusual speech pattern. He failed miserably, but he got his point across. The aliens halted their advance and lowered their weapons. Slowly, he moved the gun away from the alien's head, held it out in front of him in a non-threatening manner, and placed it sideways on the floor. He let the alien go free. It was time for the negotiating to begin.

"What the hell are you doing?" Chase said, in an angry whisper.

Logan kicked his gun aside. "Win-win. I know what they want and we're going to give it to them. And everybody lives."

"They'll make it back home to their race and tell them what happened today," Chase said.

"That's exactly what I'm hoping for," Logan replied.

Logan opened his arms wide to show them he wasn't concealing any weapons, showing them how he had willingly made himself vulnerable and placed the aliens in control. An alien thrust forward to attack, but the bulky one Logan sized up as the leader stopped him. Logan had read them right, and if he continued to do so, they were all going to live. That is, if Stacy didn't kill him for what he was planning to do.

The bulky, black-skinned alien with the dark hair approached. Logan stood his ground, consciously trying to keep himself from shaking. If he could remain calm, everything would be all right. The alien reached out and touched his cheek, a cold, slippery caress, but a caress nonetheless. He stayed still as long fingers slid down to his chin, leaving behind a wet, secreted film that made his skin crawl, as if a slug was oozing across his face. Dark eyes, he once thought vacant, filled with intent as they bored into his. Then it spoke, a rapid torrent of short, high-pitched sounds that made his body tingle and itch.

Don't you dare move, Logan. The slightest movement might be misinterpreted and ruin everything. But what wouldn't? Logan's mind raced, searching for the one sign that would see him through—the one gesture that would bring this "conversation" to the next step. He thought about an up and down nod, but then nixed it knowing in certain parts of Eastern Europe it meant no instead of yes. He had no idea what a nod might mean to these aliens. He needed something universal, something not ingrained in any culture. He needed something that would translate inherently to all species.

He remembered the simplest one. He smiled, a simple sincere gesture of respect and friendship. The alien paused and jerked its head back. Then it smiled too, showing its crooked yellow teeth as its nose slits wiggled humorously.

Logan spoke softly, without turning his head or moving in any way. "Stacy, I need you to come towards me. Don't be afraid. I need you to trust me," he said, wondering just how badly he was betraying her.

Stacy didn't budge. "I don't trust them. These bastards ruined my life."

The aliens recoiled at her tone.

Logan kept his smile. "I can end that pain once and for all, if you just trust me. If you want all your nightmares to end, you must confront them and get past the fear."

Stacy approached slowly, growing more fearful with each step.

The lead alien gazed at Logan—and Logan took it as a hard questioning stare. Its smile disappeared, a serious expression across its mouth. Logan waved his arm towards Stacy, palm open, as if he were offering her to them.

And he was.

The lead alien turned quickly to Stacy and a high-pitched whine erupted from its throat. This was the darker side of their ability to echolocate, a high frequency burst that threw off Stacy's equilibrium and cut off all electrical impulses to her brain, effectively paralyzing her. She collapsed, but worse, her conscious mind still registered the activity, and her eyes exploded with terror. It was an effect Logan hadn't anticipated.

"You bastard!" Chase said as he lunged toward her.

An alien, agitated by Chase's unexpected advance, bolted forward.

Logan stepped between them both, his back to the alien, his face to Chase. He placed his hand on Chase's solid chest, backing him off. "Let this play out. You have to trust me."

Two aliens circled Stacy. One turned her head to the side. The leader tore off its thin chest pouch, unfolded it, and pulled out two items. One was square and shone bright purple. The other was a small cutting tool, one edge sharp, the other serrated.

"Goddamn you, Logan," Chase swore. "If you're wrong, I'm going to kill you myself."

Logan didn't respond. He wasn't a hundred percent sure, but every instinct told him he was doing the right thing.

The alien shone the flickering purple ray on Stacy's eyes placing her in a trance. It took the knife, which emitted a blue pulsing ray upon her skin, and made a tiny C-shaped incision behind her left ear. It pulled a thin cylindrical tool from its pouch and sprayed a substance on the knife, cleaning it, then put both away and pulled out a small silvery semicircle. It placed the semicircle over the incision. Four miniature prongs descended from the bottom and went into her neck. A few seconds later, the prongs extracted a small sphere the size of a ball bearing that was etched with remarkable detail. The alien folded Stacy's skin flap back in place then ran the purple light over it. It adjusted the top of the tool and the light turned aqua. Before their eyes, Stacy's skin healed itself, barely leaving a scar when they were done.

The alien took the small sphere and placed it in the pouch with the other tools. The leader looked at Logan. It spoke a series of incomprehensible clicks that lasted around thirty seconds.

Logan just listened, fairly certain the alien meant well. It placed its webbed hand on Logan's forehead, leaving a line of damp, odd smelling secretion. Then, in unison, the four aliens turned, scampered out of the garage, leapt gracefully into the trees, and vanished into the night. As quickly as they had first appeared, they were gone.

Stacy stirred.

Logan lifted her in his arms, carried her up the stairs, and laid her gently on the couch. "Can you get her a glass of water? I'd like to be the first person she sees when she wakes up."

"Yeah," Chase said.

As Chase left, Stacy blinked, then her eyes opened slowly. "What happened?"

"It's all over. They took—"

Her eyes widened with remembrance and filled with tears. Her face reddened. She slapped Logan hard in the face. "You bastard! I trusted you and you gave me to them—like I was a bargaining chip."

Logan's guilt pained him more than the slap. "It's not what you think."

She swung at him again. This time he caught her hand. "You lied to me. You bastard. You lied." She yanked her hand free and inched away on the sofa.

"Please, just let me explain," Logan pleaded.

Chase came in with the glass of water. "Here, drink this. It'll make you feel better."

Stacy took the glass and drank. She wiped the tears from her face and drank some more.

When she finally calmed down, Chase took the glass and placed it on the end table. "I'd like to hear your explanation too," he said.

Logan stood up and faced Stacy. "The aliens never wanted to kill you. They just wanted to get home, and you had the piece of equipment that could get them there." He turned his attention to Chase, searching for the words to explain better. "When they first found the ship, there was an interference zone. We later learned that it was caused by the ship's electromagnetic field when its power was turned on. So, I figured the reason they were taking everyone's radios apart was not to knock out our lines of communication, but because they were looking for a proper transmitter to send a signal back home.

Unfortunately, the radios we use aren't nearly as advanced as theirs, so they were useless to them."

"Wait a minute. You're telling me in that incredible ship they had, they didn't have one transmitter capable of signaling home. Not even one emergency beacon," Chase said.

"Yes. Well... not these four anyway," Logan said. "Remember, when we got to their ship, it was essentially dead. They probably had sent a signal when they first crashed, before Gaines' team arrived. But then, with the threat of them being overrun, they had to cut their power. Probably to keep us from learning their secrets, but that also cut off any signal they were using. Or even if that signal was still transmitting, they weren't going to be on the ship any longer, so they needed a portable beacon. I'll bet when we thoroughly examine the cargo, we'll find all their portable emergency transmitters with the dead aliens. But these four that escaped didn't have one, so they had no way to get home and no way of contacting home either.

"Which is where you came in. They've been abducting you and studying you since you were a child. They even found you again when you moved to Prince Rupert. To do that, they had to have planted a device on you capable of transmitting a signal back to them, so they would know where you were at all times. That's exactly the device they would need to get back home. Since you were only sixty miles from the crash site—probably their closest abductee—you became their primary target. It was much easier for them to come after you than to go back and try to get a transmitter from their ship. They weren't trying to kill you. They just wanted your implant."

"How did you know they wouldn't kill me to get it?" Stacy asked.

"It's not their way. They could have killed me and some other people today, but whenever a choice presented itself, they did otherwise. I let them have you because it was win-win. They get to go home. We get to live."

Stacy slapped him again. Then she punched him and kept punching him. "You used me. Just like they did. You're no different from them," she said, still crying.

Logan caught her hands. "In a way, and I'm truly sorry for that. But you don't understand. I never give in on a negotiation unless everyone wins. That includes you. Your nightmares are over. They took away your implant. That means they'll never be able to find you again. It's over."

She stopped struggling. "You mean it's really over?" She fell against him and wept.

Logan held her tightly. "Yeah, it's all over."

92

Major Gaines had no idea how long he had been unconscious. He just wished he still was as agony coursed through his entire body. Slowly, and painfully, he got up. He wiped the dirty blood-stained snow from his face with his left arm. He had tried using his right, but it was completely useless.

He searched for his cell phone, but as he suspected, it was gone. His eyes scanned up and down the dark highway. His jeep had four flat tires and was driven into a ditch off the side of the road. He had no way to contact anyone, and no one knew where he was. He was alone, stuck in the middle of nowhere, the brisk wind biting at his skin, stinging his wounds. He cursed himself for going after Rebecca alone.

Figuring the nearest town was about a five-mile hike, he started walking. He made it around half a mile when headlights blared from the distance behind him, filling him with hope. The rumble of the approaching vehicle was music to his ears, like a glass of water to a dying man in the desert.

He moved to the center of the road, waving wildly, and flagged it down, clearly relieved when the truck slowed down and stopped in front of him.

Nikolai shifted the gear to park, pulled up on the emergency brake, and stepped out of the rig. Katrina opened the door on the passenger side and did the same.

Gaines' first reaction was defensive. He turned towards them defiantly and raised his fists, prepared to go down fighting.

Nikolai respected that.

Gaines noticed the woman beside him was not Rebecca. He dropped his hands in confusion.

"Major, I would like you to meet my wife. She's, how do you say... a very persuasive woman. I believe you two should talk," Nikolai said.

Katrina walked over to Major Gaines. He didn't know what was going on, but whatever it was, it had to be an improvement.

"A pleasure to meet you, Major," Katrina said, as she extended her arm outward to shake his hand.

Though her face showed signs of battle, Gaines found her smile irresistible. He cautiously and wearily shook her hand with his left. He looked at her, then Nikolai, then back at her. He was completely bewildered. "I'm charmed," he responded, for a complete lack of anything better to say.

Katrina's smile grew brighter. "Yes. Yes, you are."

93

The Following Morning – Yukon Base Five

Nikolai drove the truck up to the first guarded security gate. Gaines sat beside him in the middle, and Katrina was next to him, pushed up against the passenger door. He stopped the truck at the guard booth and rolled down the window.

"My name is Nikolai Rasputin. We have special delivery for Admiral Brock."

The rookie MP immediately drew his firearm.

Major Gaines reached over and showed him his credentials. "It's fine, soldier. You can stand down. They're with me." He wondered what the rookie must have been thinking. A major, whose face looked like pulp, coming into a top-secret base with two Russians who didn't look much better. *Heck,* he thought, *the guard probably won't even be able to identify me by picture ID.*

"I'll have to check with the Admiral. It's the first time we've ever had a Russian come to visit us."

Nikolai turned to the guard. "No. It is not." He looked at Gaines, and for the first time in a long time, Nikolai smiled.

Gaines hoped he was kidding, but deep down he knew he wasn't.

"You're all cleared, Major," the guard said, with a salute.

"Thank you," Gaines replied.

The gate opened. They drove down the road in silence, stopping five miles later at the end. Lights flashed and the ground shuddered. "Don't be alarmed," Gaines said. "This is the entrance."

Nikolai looked at him and smiled again. "I know."

"You're enjoying yourself, aren't you?" Gaines said.

The ground in front of them began to rise as they descended into the base. When they reached the bottom, they drove to an underground loading bay. A man directed them into a parking space and Nikolai pulled in.

Gaines was glad to see Carlson, Blaze, Logan and Chase waiting for him. They seemed glad to see him too, which meant the ship was safely secured. He was also glad to see Commander Smythe at their side. Katrina and Nikolai exited the cab. Gaines limped out after them.

"Jesus Christ. Let's get a medic team up here—now!" Smythe ordered.

Gaines nodded.

"You look like shit," Chase said.

Gaines chuckled. "You should see the other guy." He pointed at Nikolai.

"Pleased to meet you," Nikolai said with a smile, a hand clutched over his bullet wound. "This is my wife, Katrina," he added. "I think we have much to discuss."

EPILOGUES

94

The Following Afternoon
Tokyo, Japan

Twenty heavily armed soldiers stormed the offices of Japan's defense ministry. Everyone knew why they were there, even before they reached General Sato Yamakazi's door.

News of the Tsunami's destruction traveled fast. The Prime Minister of Japan had received a call from Canadian's Prime Minister just minutes after he found out about it. Upon hearing the explanation and the offer of proof, Japan's government sprang into action. Within two hours, the party responsible for this tragedy was found and his arrest order issued.

But Sato had friends who warned him. He barricaded the door and sat on his knees in front of his desk. In his hand, he held the short sword which he formerly displayed proudly in his office. He pondered a moment as he heard the stampede of footsteps run through the halls.

He couldn't fathom how his plan had failed. It must have been the incompetence of the men beneath him, he thought. He had done nothing wrong. He was Japan's greatest hero, but now he was going to pay the price for the failings of others. In his mind he cursed his fellow government officials, branding them cowards. He would not allow himself to be disgraced by the likes of them.

As the door burst open, he thrust the sword into his belly and cut sharply across, leaving his entrails for the armored soldiers as they aggressively charged into the room. The final thought that raced through his mind was that he would die as he lived—a courageous and honorable man.

When the newspapers printed the story the following day, the citizens of Japan would learn the truth.

95

The light from the crescent moon reflected brightly off the dark blue surface of the Pacific Ocean. It was cold, the winds were relatively light, and the seas were calm. Among the small, white-crested waves, four aliens swam gracefully about, playing with their newfound friends, two bottlenose dolphins who flitted beside them throughout their journey. They had spent the entire day traversing the icy waters, bringing them as far away from land as they could possibly get. There a signal was activated.

As they expected, a swirling royal blue light appeared from above, dimming the magnificence of the stars. The ocean stirred under unseen forces. A spaceship, undetected by any earthbound radar, dropped silently from the heavens. The aliens and the dolphins rubbed past each other and an alien spoke. The dolphins emitted similar sounds in return. One alien hugged a bottlenose and patted its head lovingly before a beam of white light appeared to whisk the aliens away. The spaceship hovered a few seconds longer, as if contemplating its next move, then without warning, sped away into the darkness of space.

96

November 12th, 2009
Ottawa, Canada

Major Gaines had endured a long morning and had a longer afternoon still ahead of him. He had called all the families of the men who died to personally express his condolences and to let them know they did not die in vain. He couldn't reveal the specifics, but he assured each of them that their sacrifices would result in the betterment of all Canadians, and eventually all mankind. He also told them how proud he was to have served with each and every one of them.

This afternoon he had a more difficult task. He would visit the Le Buc family, who he'd gotten to know quite well over the years and express his sympathy in person. He rubbed the cast on his arm as his skin underneath it began to itch.

Smythe walked into his office. "How did it go?"

"About as well as you could expect." Gaines frowned. "The worst part of the job. I can't believe I was the only one who made it. It's wrong."

"Don't beat yourself up over it. These things happen. I know it's tough, but each one of those men knew the risks going in—just as you and I did."

"It doesn't make it any easier," Gaines said.

"I know. That's why I came personally to give you this." Smythe placed a gold star on his desk. "You've just been promoted."

Gaines left it there. "I don't deserve it."

"Of course you do," Smythe replied.

"Didn't you read my report? Everybody under my command died. I involved the Americans. Rebecca played me for a fool. Heck, if it wasn't for Nikolai's wife showing up at the last minute, I would've lost it all."

"You always were too hard on yourself," Smythe said.

"That's what happened."

"That's the way you see it."

"I see it that way because that's the way it was."

Smythe shook his head. "Let me put it for you another way. Your mission was to recover the alien spaceship. You completed that successfully, but you also accomplished a hell of a lot more. You uncovered the leak we've been experiencing for years. You turned an invaluable Russian agent over to our side. You managed to get us a prototype of Japan's newest stealth helicopter. And you recruited the top scientist in the world, Dr. Blaze, to lead our research effort, aside from getting the Americans to share with us all their knowledge. You earned that star, David. It's just a matter of changing your perspective."

Gaines thought about that for a minute. This was why he was never any good at politics. He didn't see things quite as gray as everyone else did. He got up, leaving the star on the desk. "I've got a funeral to attend."

"I understand," Smythe said. He left the room, closing the door behind him.

Gaines sat back down. He picked up the star and stared at it for a moment. A tear rolled down his cheek. It was all he had left.

97

November 24th, 2009
Yukon Base Five

Blaze entered the main staging area. In front of him on the huge warehouse floor was the spaceship in all its glory. He grinned, ear to ear. He never imagined getting a better assignment than the one he had, but after being named project coordinator responsible for researching the spaceship, he was proven wrong. This was his dream come true.

Another man entered the staging area behind him. "Good to finally meet you, Dr. Blaze," said the man, whose face beamed just as brightly.

Blaze didn't recognize the face. The voice, however, was familiar. "Do I know you?" Blaze asked.

The man shook his hand. "Yes. Claude Devereaux. Perhaps you know me better as Lynx."

Blaze nodded. It was a pleasure to meet the man who saved his life. "Nice to finally see you face to face." He tightened his handshake and cupped his other hand on Lynx's shoulder.

"You'll be seeing a lot more of me, Dr. Blaze," Claude said, his smile growing broader. "I'm your test pilot."

Claude too had his dream come true.

98

January 18th, 2010

The UFO returned, once again evading any radar detection. It hovered silently over the house at thirty-five thousand feet. They had lost Stacy Michaels as a test subject, so they needed another to take her place. An invisible beam hit the house below. In the bedroom of the man sleeping within, it turned blue.

Five aliens appeared out of nowhere. The man woke, startled by them briefly, before all of them disappeared into nothingness. Two hours later he awoke again. He was back in his bedroom, unable to remember anything that had just happened. He glared at the digital clock— 4:23 a.m.—and growled. Exhausted, he decided to go back to sleep. An hour later he awoke, sweating from a horrible nightmare. Once again, the exact details slipped his mind, just a vague recollection of being helpless. A scary, yet familiar face, flashed into his consciousness.

He got out of bed, deciding to get an early start. He showered, got dressed, and then walked to his door, embarrassed by just how much the aliens he encountered two months ago came into his dreams and frightened him to the core. He shook his head and pushed their image from his mind. Then Colonel John Chase grabbed his cap off the stand, closed his door, and went to work.

99

April 3rd, 2010
Palo Alto, California

Ring… ringggg...

"Goddamn it! Who the hell is calling at this hour?" Logan Grey mumbled to himself.

"Shut it off," said a tired female voice.

Ring… ringggg...

Logan quickly grabbed for the phone. "Yeah."

"Is Fox there?" a voice said.

"Fox?" Logan said, puzzled.

"Yes. This is Dana," the voice said. "You won't believe what I discovered?"

"I think you have the wrong number." Logan hung up the phone.

"Who was that?"

"Wrong number." Logan looked over at the woman in his bed. She was beautiful, yet completely unlike anyone else he had ever met. She was sweet, down-to-earth, and uncomplicated. He could definitely get used to having her around. He watched her for another minute and then decided he wasn't letting her off that easy. He leaned over and nibbled her ear.

She moaned lightly, enjoying the sensation. She gave Logan a deep long kiss. Then she pushed him down, pinned his arms over his head, and nibbled on his neck.

Yes, he could get used to having her around, and the thought of that didn't even frighten him. He was totally falling in love with her. "Hi sweetheart. How'd you sleep?"

"Great." She loved being in his arms.

"Any nightmares?" he asked.

"Haven't had one in months," Stacy answered. "But I've been having very naughty dreams." She smiled brightly and adjusted her hips just so, to get a positive reaction. She kissed him deeply again. Then Logan overpowered her and got on top. She smiled coyly, "I think Princess Zinthia finally found her Sir Right."

The End... for now

Word from the author:

First off, I'll just say I believe in life elsewhere in the universe. Werner Von Braun said it best, "Our sun is one of 100 billion stars in our galaxy. Our galaxy is one of billions of galaxies populating the universe. It would be the height of presumption to think that we are the only living things in that enormous immensity." Now whether they have made it to Earth or not is another matter entirely. Personally, I believe they have on many occasions and, if you have picked up this book, my guess is you believe the same.

When I wrote this book my ultimate goal was to write the most fun, action-packed, and thrillingly fast-paced novel I could, but I also wanted to make it as realistic as possible. The lecture about the possibility of extraterrestrial life and their technology that Dr. Blaze gives to Logan Grey on the plane is all based on real science. The explanation of events Colonel Chase gives to Major David Gaines is mostly based on actual UFO mythology, with some minor elements tweaked to fit the story. For the military buffs out there, I researched our weapon systems and aircraft capabilities as best I could and I hope I accurately detailed all of our human technology as well.

I hope you enjoyed the book. As an added bonus to you, here's a cartoon I drew decades ago.

CLOSE ENCOUNTERS OF THE FOURTH KIND

Be well. Have fun. Enjoy life to the fullest. And hopefully I'll see you all for another story.

Best Regards,

Allan Burd

Acknowledgements:

To all my friends who pre-read the manuscript and gave me their feedback and support, and in some cases, valuable research material.

To my kids who love to read my work.

To my awesome wife who supports me in every way and is my best friend.

To my mom and dad for having me.

Thank you. I love you all.

About the Author:

<u>Allan Burd</u> is a science fiction, supernatural thriller author hailing from Long Island, NY.

In addition to this, his first novel, he has written many other books, numerous short stories, and children's books (both picture and chapter), and has screenplays, teleplays, short scripts, comic strips and more in the pipeline. His specialty is creating high concept thrillers that keep you white-knuckled until the very end. If you're into aliens, monsters, or action-oriented supernatural suspense, Allan Burd is an author to follow.

For more information visit www.allanburd.com